PRAISE FOR *THE FIFTY-FIRST STATE*

"*The Fifty-First State* is a place of tenderness and terror, with beautiful vistas of generosity of heart. I read this novel in one sitting, moved by its deeply imagined coming-of-age story, grateful for a writer whose compassion is matched by her talent."

—REBECCA NEWBERGER GOLDSTEIN,
author of *36 Arguments for the Existence of God: A Work of Fiction*

"Lisa Borders is a writer of fine emotional intelligence and boundless compassion for her characters. In *The Fifty-First State,* a story of finding family after devastating loss, estranged siblings Hallie and Josh face problems so credible and realized that I worried for them as if they were friends of mine, and they surprised me in the way friends do."

—SHERI JOSEPH, author of *Where You Can Find Me, Stray,*
and *Bear Me Safely Over*

"*The Fifty-First State* is an embrace of a novel—warm, intimate, enveloping—and, like all the best embraces, it starts with a thrill and ends before you are entirely ready to let go. I read it in one sitting and would have found a way to do the same even if it were twice as long."

—YAEL GOLDSTEIN LOVE, author of *The Passion of Tasha Darsky*

"A big-hearted novel about the surprises—big and small, tragic and gloriously sweet—that turn the tables on seemingly quotidian lives. *The Fifty-First State* is a place where good news and fluke disasters live side by side, whether in the lurking menace of a sorry neighbor or the shifting nuances of developing love. That is to say, a delightfully realistic world readers will enthusiastically recognize as their own."

—DAPHNE KALOTAY, author of *Sight Reading*

ALSO BY LISA BORDERS

Cloud Cuckoo Land

THE FIFTY-FIRST STATE

Lisa Borders

Engine Books
PO Box 44167
Indianapolis, IN 46244
enginebooks.org

Printed in the United States of America

10   9   8   7   6   5   4   3   2   1

ISBN: 978-1-938126-20-8

Library of Congress Control Number: 2013935828

For three extraordinary women: my mother, Ruth Creter Borders;
my aunt, Helen Delaney (1917–2006);
and my cousin, Cathay Delaney Knipscher (1946–2008).

Life changes in the instant.

—Joan Didion, *The Year of Magical Thinking*

Maybe everything that dies someday comes back.

—Bruce Springsteen, "Atlantic City"

THE ACCIDENT

At the same time a white Dodge Ram pickup truck driven by Donald Corson, sixty-six, of Oyster Shell, New Jersey drifted across three lanes of traffic on Route 42 in Bellmawr and grazed the side of a green Ford Taurus, Corson's seventeen-year-old son, Josh, stood on line in his high school cafeteria in Floyd, New Jersey, pondering one bad offering after another—Sloppy Joe meat that looked like dog food, Chow Mein that looked like vomit—and opting for an apple and a carton of milk as his lunch. While Corson's second wife, Brenda, in the passenger's seat of the pickup truck, was trying frantically to pull the steering wheel to the right, out of the way of the fast-moving traffic, even as she wondered at her husband's sudden slump, the distant look in his eyes, their son stood in a corner of the cafeteria near a girl named Missy Dalton, a girl he'd been in love with since ninth grade, a girl who Josh knew was out of his league but he couldn't help himself—she was just so, *so*. While Missy was smiling, not unsweetly, and walking to her table of friends and Josh was internally berating himself for always saying the most incredibly lame things in the universe to Missy Dalton, Brenda Corson lost control of the steering wheel and the truck skidded in a few dizzy arcs. While the truck was still spinning, Donald Corson's daughter from his first marriage—a girl he and his wife had named Holly, but who had lived in New York for nearly twenty years and reinvented herself as Hallie—had just finished a photo shoot in the Lower East Side for a music magazine called *Lush Life*, a magazine that, as far as Hallie could tell, was highly regarded in New York and unheard of anywhere else in the country. As Hallie was packing up her camera, lenses, light meter, shoving the flash and cord into her bag, cars piled up on Route 42 as a result of the Corsons' skidding truck. A red Toyota Tercel driven by a nineteen-year-old Rowan College sophomore with a heavy foot on the gas pedal who also happened to be text messaging her boyfriend while the Corsons' truck went out of control in front of her and who, when she looked up and saw the skidding truck, hit her brakes far too hard and far too late, slammed into the Corsons' pickup just as Hallie was getting into a taxi which would take her to Soho, where she was having lunch with a photo editor at *Interview*. As Hallie was fretting in the cab that, at thirty-seven, she was too old to get work at a magazine like *Interview*—the photo editor would clearly see how she had squandered her youthful promise, would see that she was just Holly Corson, a nobody from a crappy little town on the Delaware Bay—a minister from an A.M.E. church in Philadelphia's Germantown section hit the side of the Tercel with his baby blue Honda Prelude after he tried, unsuccessfully, to steer around the wreck. The moment Hallie pulled her cell phone out to let the editor know she might be late, that her taxi was stalled in traffic on Bowery Street, was the same moment the minister saw a tractor-trailer fast approaching in his rearview mirror with a horror that Donald and Brenda Corson and the college student—all three of them dead—were spared.

As the tractor-trailer plowed into the three vehicles twisted together on Route 42—white, red, and blue, a macabre abstract Americana sculpture—and ignited a small fire, a brown-and-white dog, curled on the floor in an upstairs front bedroom of the Corsons' comfortably run-down house—a neighbor's long-suffering pet which Josh had snuck in the night before—kicked its leg four times in its sleep, growled slightly, then was still.

PART I

CHAPTER 1

Josh Corson took his seat among the other nine kids who'd made it all the way to French IV, and waited for their teacher to hand out the tests. He'd tried to read over his notes during lunch, but he'd been distracted by the sweater Missy Dalton was wearing, the way it rode up and flashed her belly button as she adjusted the elastic in her long, dark hair. This test was a lost cause, but still Josh opened his notebook for a quick cram.

"Hey, how do you conjugate *s'éteindre* again?" Nicki Kepler asked. She sat next to Josh in both French and English, and they sometimes ate lunch together, but they weren't really friends.

Josh pointed to the page in his notebook. "I'm screwed," he whispered to Nicki. "I didn't study at all."

Before Mr. Murdock could hand out the tests, Josh heard a knock on the door; it was Miss Piper, the principal's secretary. She was twenty-five years old and, by popular decree of the boys in Floyd High School, was "hot." (Josh didn't disagree.) Mr. Murdock spoke with Miss Piper for a minute out in the hallway, then approached Josh's desk, put his hand on Josh's shoulder.

"You're wanted in Mr. Cicirello's office, Josh," Mr. Murdock said in a tone Josh couldn't quite read. Josh felt his teacher's eyes on him as he left the room.

Whatever the reason for his being called to the office, the timing, Josh thought, could not have been better. He'd have to do a makeup test, for which he'd now have another chance to study. But it was strange that Miss Piper came for him. Usually they just called people out of class over the loudspeaker.

Miss Piper wore heels and a brown skirt short enough that Josh couldn't help but notice her legs. They were nice, those legs. Her stockings sparkled. "Did I do something wrong?" he asked.

"You didn't do anything wrong, Josh." Miss Piper placed her hand on his forearm. "Mr. Cicirello just needs to talk to you."

Then Josh had a sinking thought: it was about the dog.

The previous night, after giving up on studying, Josh had walked the half-mile to Nancy Ackerman's place. She had been their closest neighbor for as long as Josh could remember and he considered Nancy his friend, even though he knew most kids would think that was weird; she was old enough to be his grandmother. But Nancy's house was dark when he'd arrived, and her car was gone.

As he turned away he saw the dog, the skinny, floppy-eared brown-and-white dog that for the past two years had lived tied to a tree outside the rusted-out trailer across from Nancy's place. Josh knew the sight of the dog bothered Nancy as much as it bothered him, and that she snuck the dog food when she could. She was afraid to do more. The dog's owner, Cal Stutts, was known for his temper. Nancy had told Josh that once, after she called the police for a fight she'd overheard at the Stutts' home—everyone in town knew that Cal used to beat his wife, that that was the reason she'd left him—Cal had walked over and threatened to slit the throats of both of Nancy's horses if she called the police on him again. After that, Nancy had chosen to avert her eyes from anything that went on across the street.

But Josh, looking at the doe-eyed dog curled in the grass, the moon shining on its bony back, found that the impulse he'd had for years would not go away. His friend Ram had once told him, "We must be the change we wish to see." It was a quote from Gandhi, and had been Ram's response when Josh first asked him what the point was of giving up meat—as Ram had long before—when hardly anyone else was vegetarian. Josh's desire to save this animal—to "be the change"—was greater than his fear of Cal Stutts. He hopped the sagging fence to the Stutts' property, eying Cal's truck in the driveway and a light on in the trailer, untied the rope, scooped the bewildered animal in his arms, jumped the fence again, and ran home. His parents already in bed, he'd quietly settled the dog in his room, cut off the grimy nylon collar with a pair of scissors—the buckle was rusted shut—and fed her some chicken he'd found in the refrigerator. His parents had left for Philly to sell the last of the field tomatoes before Josh and the dog were even awake that morning. He hoped he'd get home before they did.

But Cal had to know by now that his dog was missing, Josh thought, slowing his pace slightly to match Miss Piper's. What if Cal blamed Nancy? What if he'd done something to Nancy's horses?

"Is it…about the dog?" Josh asked Miss Piper as they turned down the school's main hallway.

"The dog?" Miss Piper asked. Josh felt an overwhelming relief. He noticed a tone in her voice—a niceness, that was always there, but something more, something Josh couldn't quite identify.

All the boys in Floyd High School had crushes on Miss Piper, and Josh was sure she knew it. She spoke to boys and looked at boys in much the way Missy Dalton spoke to, looked at, boys—like a girl who was used to getting the attention of boys, who knew she could have her pick of whatever boy she wanted.

As they continued down the hallway, the faint sweet smell of Miss Piper floating by him, Josh imagined that she wasn't taking him to the principal's office at all; she was taking him to the janitor's closet, which was full of mops and brooms and trash barrels and was always locked. But maybe it wasn't full of brooms and trash barrels; maybe Miss Piper had turned it into a secret sex lair. Maybe there was a bed in there, and a secret fireplace, one in which Miss Piper could start a roaring fire with the push of a button. Maybe that was where she took the boys she wanted to seduce, the ones she wanted to turn into men. Josh felt the stirrings of a hard-on and tried desperately to stop it before Miss Piper might see. He thought of innocuous things, random images: the rows and rows of tomato plants at his parents' farm; the Statue of Liberty, which he'd seen once on a trip to New York; his room, the clutter of books and CDs and Miss Piper stretched out on his bed and—Stop it! He wondered if he was the only person in the world who yelled at himself in his head.

Through the window of the principal's office, Josh could see Miss Piper's empty desk; beyond that, through the open door to Mr. Cicirello's office, he saw Nancy, at his school, talking to his principal, and Josh's first thought was: It *is* about the dog. But if Cal had done something to Nancy's horses, she'd be talking to the police, not getting Josh out of school. He saw how pale Nancy's face looked, and how her gray hair was loose, not pulled up or back the way it often was. Her hands, which usually gestured wildly, were knotted in her lap. Something about the way she held her hands told him that this had nothing to do with the dog, Cal, or the horses—that it was worse, worse even than that. Josh didn't want to try to imagine something worse than Nancy's horses being killed; and yet he knew deep down that whatever had happened would be so bad it was something he could not imagine, something it would never even occur to him to imagine.

He had an absurd thought, an echo from childhood: *I want Mommy*. He even thought it like that, Mommy, not Mom. He hoped his parents were on their way back from Philly already, that they'd come and pick him up and talk to him about whatever this horrible thing was that had happened. As his mind tried to reconcile the two scenes—his parents, pulling into the parking lot of Floyd High School in his father's battered white pickup, empty bushel baskets stacked like lampshades in the flatbed, a stray green tomato or two rolling around amidst some loose soil; and Nancy, sitting in his principal's office, her arthritic hands rubbing over and over themselves in her lap—Miss Piper seemed to snap out of some kind of fog. She knocked on the glass, glanced at Josh, and opened the door. She started in ahead of him, stopped for a second, turned to him.

"Josh," she said, and put her hand on his arm.

Mr. Cicirello motioned him inside, then got up himself and closed the door. Josh could see that Nancy had been crying. The milk he'd drunk at lunch started churning into something moldy and acrid.

Nancy started to talk, but he only heard what she said in fragments: an accident on Route 42, a pile-up with his father's truck, some other cars, a tractor-trailer. He missed the details of how and why, who was at fault; he wasn't even sure if Nancy said that part or not. The truck caught fire, Nancy said—Josh heard that part clearly. But when he tried to picture it—his mother and father trapped in the cab, the radio on the country station that his father liked but his mother didn't, smoke pouring through the windows rolled halfway down in the Indian summer heat, flames licking the sides of the truck—he found it easier to imagine the back of the pickup, the empty bushel baskets, the stray two-by-fours and scraps of wood that were always in the flatbed, all of it burning orange and yellow, the flames languid as those in a fireplace or a bonfire. They burned with a kind of symmetrical beauty, Josh imagined, those neat stacks of wooden baskets. It was like they'd been meant to burn, like they'd never held tomatoes; it was like the truck itself had never contained anything but the baskets. It was like he'd never had any parents at all.

CHAPTER 2

Hallie Corson sat in a corner of her boss Joy's Soho studio, staring at the display on her cell phone. It was 3:08 p.m., and she'd received two calls from Oyster Shell, her father's house. She knew both messages would be from Brenda; Hallie and her father barely spoke in person, and he never called. Brenda would get it in her head—usually around some holiday—that Hallie should come home, and she'd badger her until she either gave in and made the three-hour trip, or fabricated a convenient out-of-town photo shoot.

Joy shrugged off her robe and sat nude on the tattered antique loveseat they'd set up in a far corner of the studio. She wriggled her shoulders and stretched her neck, then fussed with her pink-streaked hair—the color was too young for her, but Hallie wasn't about to say so. As her boss got into position Hallie took a light reading, then nodded. Joy rearranged the strands of hair falling at her shoulders and struck her pose.

Hallie walked to the far end of the studio, glancing up at the dozens of exotic birds sitting obediently on their perches. By the time they were done, she would be covered in bird shit and feathers; Hallie couldn't believe she was stuck in this role again after all these years. She had once been Joy's assistant, but she ran the business now. It was up to the steady stream of eager young photography students to do the scut work: taking light readings, turning the cassette in the vintage Deardorff field camera, getting shat upon by the birds as well as, occasionally, by Joy. But one assistant had given his notice three weeks ago, the other had called in sick, and that left Hallie, who began a fast trot in Joy's direction with her arms raised high.

The birds began flapping their wings, a few of them squawking, and soon scores of Senegal parrots, umbrella and sulfur-crested cockatoos, peach-faced lovebirds, cockatiels, a toucan and an African gray parrot coasted past, gliding just below the studio's ceiling. When the birds were close to the loveseat, Joy began pressing the cable release, and continued shooting as the African gray—Albert, Joy's favorite—perched on her right shoulder. The rest of the birds hovered above Joy for a few crucial seconds, feathers and droppings and the occasional seed husk drizzling down upon her. Hallie tried not to think about the globs she'd felt drop onto her own hair. Soon, the birds would light on the loveseat, the tall lamp next to it, or the filing cabinet, and Hallie would return them to their ceiling perches and start the process again.

There was a time when Hallie had felt lucky to be working with Joy Dennison. *The* Joy Dennison, first seen in a *Life* magazine spread as one of the regulars at Andy Warhol's factory parties, dressed in Mary Quant and blowing smoke in a delicate ring through her pink-frosted lips. Joy was a twenty-one-year-old art student when the once-famous photo was taken; Hallie was not yet born, but she'd seen the shot in a stack of magazines she'd found in her attic when she was twelve, the year after her mother died. As Hallie had sat in the dusty attic poring over the magazines— snowed in that harsh February, her father downstairs grumbling about how much it would cost to plow the farm—she'd looked at the date of the photo, June 1969, and imagined her mother, eight months pregnant, gazing at the images from Warhol's parties, secretly wishing she were there. Hallie had ripped the photo out of the magazine and, for a time, it was taped above her bed next to a Rick Springfield poster.

Years later, when Joy's name came up in a college photography class, Hallie remembered not Joy's own work but that early photo of her. And when Hallie, in her last semester, stumbled upon a notice in the fine arts building that Joy Dennison was looking for an assistant, it felt like fate.

"*Encore, une fois,*" Joy said, a slight edge of irritation in her voice. The French was an affectation since Joy had dated a Parisian businessman the previous year.

"Sorry," Hallie said, looking up at the ceiling. Half of the birds had returned to their perches on their own, and she quickly carried the others back herself.

"Leave Albert," Joy said. "He's posing so nicely."

"Leave Albert," the African gray squawked.

Hallie's best friend Lawrence had said more than once he felt Joy had ripped her off, considering how lucrative her boss's work with the birds had become, and how many of the ideas had been Hallie's. Was she being exploited? Joy had promoted her to business manager, paid her very well, let Hallie use her fancy darkroom from time to time. Back when Hallie's artistic career had promise—those heady days when Hallie's shots of dismembered mannequins had landed her a mention as an "up-and-coming young artist" in a 1995 issue of *Photo District News*, and a spot in a group show whose crowded opening was speckled with a few genuine celebrities—Joy would allow her, albeit begrudgingly, to work her hours around her own shoots. It was less of an issue, now, with her freelance shoots only sporadic and her artistic career nonexistent.

Hallie put her arms up to rouse the birds from their perches and ran a second time, the birds flapping and gliding past her, straight to Joy. Hallie could see that her boss would get some great shots this time. Several feathers of different hues were caught in Joy's hair; and Maya, the peach-faced lovebird who was Albert's main rival for Joy's affection, released a murky white stream down her mistress's left breast. This was exactly what Joy wanted: to look something like a decrepit statue in a mausoleum, once beautiful but now aged, scarred, shat upon. She was calling this series "Time Flies."

Hallie repeated her "running with the birds" four more times before her boss was satisfied.

"I think you got some great shots," Hallie said when they were done. "Maya shit right down your boob."

Joy laughed. "I felt it," she said, accepting Albert from Hallie's outstretched index finger.

Hallie saw that she now had three voice messages, all from her father's house. She resented Brenda's lack of patience; Hallie would call her back when she was good and ready. She had just enough time to shower off the feathers and bird shit and catch the N Train to West 4th to meet her friend Alison for dinner.

HALLIE'S FIRST STOP after she emerged from the subway was for coffee; she needed to wake up a bit before she obliterated herself with margaritas. As she headed down MacDougal her phone rang. It was Lawrence.

"Hey," she said. "I'm meeting Alison for Mexican in ten. You and Kenneth want to join us?"

"Kenneth's almost finished making dinner," Lawrence said, and cleared his throat. "I wanted to hear how your meeting went with that editor at *Interview*. I can't believe you didn't call me after."

Hallie sighed. "That editor was twenty-five years old. At most." She knew she should elaborate, but didn't feel up to it.

Lawrence was silent for a few seconds. "What went wrong?" he asked, in the exasperated tone that sometimes infuriated her.

"Did I say anything went wrong?"

"You wouldn't be telling me how old he was," Lawrence said, "if it had gone well."

Hallie took a sip of coffee, slowing her pace. "Nothing happened. He just didn't seem impressed."

Lawrence was quiet for a few seconds. "His boss is on the board of the Bloom Foundation with me. I'll talk to him and see if I can find anything out."

She wanted to tell him not to bother, but she'd missed Lawrence in the two years he'd been with Kenneth, felt like she saw him less and less, and was grateful that he was still meddling in her life.

"Thanks," Hallie said. "I don't think I made any major gaffes, I just think I didn't wow him."

"We'll see about that." Lawrence operated under the assumption that he could bend people to his will; in his adult life, this was often true, though Hallie had no trouble remembering him at eighteen: skinny, acne-riddled, closeted.

Hallie's phone beeped, and she glanced briefly at the screen.

"Lawrence, I have to go. Brenda filled my voicemail with messages I haven't listened to, and she's on the line now."

"Maybe Oyster Shell got a new stoplight," he said. "Maybe they've decided to pave the streets with—snails!" It was an old joke, and Hallie laughed for Lawrence's benefit, but now she just wanted to talk to Brenda and get it over with.

But when she clicked over to the incoming call, the voice she heard wasn't Brenda's; it was male, and it took Hallie a minute to recognize her brother, Josh. She'd talked to him infrequently enough since his voice had changed that it still startled her, how much like a man he sounded. By the time she understood who it was and could attempt to make sense of what he was saying—something about trying to reach her, something incoherent about Mom and Dad—he was gone, his voice replaced by that of Nancy Ackerman, her father's longtime neighbor. Hallie turned the corner onto Bleecker as Nancy started talking, but when she began to realize what Nancy was getting at, that her father and his second wife were both dead, Hallie stopped walking and whirled around, looking for a place to sit. When she didn't find one, she stood still for a second, the cell phone in one hand, the coffee in the other; to a casual observer, the cup slipping from her hand might have looked like simple clumsiness, even as it hit the ground and splattered milky-brown liquid on her shoes and she made no move away from it, no attempt to step from the puddle forming at her feet. She might simply have been engrossed in an important but routine conversation; her face betrayed nothing. But what had happened was simple overload. It had been too much to ask of her body: to take in this information and, at the same time, to walk, hold the phone to her ear, keep a grip on the paper cup.

CHAPTER 3

Josh stood on the front porch while Nancy talked on the phone with Hallie. He kicked at the railing, trying to erase the memory of the look of pity Nancy had just given him as he'd handed her the phone. He was a senior in high school, almost an adult. He needed to act more grown-up.

But Josh felt fairly certain that no matter how hard he'd tried, he wouldn't have been able to tell Hallie about Mom and Dad. He didn't fully believe it himself; he kept imagining that it was all some sort of mistake, that someone else's parents were killed in the accident, that his own mom and dad were injured but alive. It didn't matter how badly they were hurt—he wouldn't mind pushing his mom around in a wheelchair, or helping his dad more at the farm if he couldn't do the work himself—so long as they were alive.

If Josh had said it aloud, that his parents were dead, he was afraid the saying of it might actually make it so.

He heard a car coming and looked down the long driveway, hoping it was Ram. Nancy had left him messages, but Josh knew that when Ram was collecting data in Mollusk Creek he didn't check his phone until he was finished, around sundown. A month ago, Josh would have been in the creek with Ram, gathering and tagging frogs, but his summer job had ended when school started.

The green sedan with the Pearl Township logo on the side pulled into view; Todd Schwegel, the township sheriff, was back from the hospital in Camden where he'd gone that afternoon to identify Josh's parents. Josh gave Todd a weak wave as he got out of the car.

"Hey, Josh," Todd said in a soft voice. He was dressed casually, in jeans and a red Phillies cap, not in uniform.

"Hi." Josh cast about desperately for something to say so that Todd wouldn't tell him he'd seen his parents' bodies, and that they were truly dead. "I thought you might be Ram," he finally blurted. He didn't think Todd would mind his saying that, since Todd and Ram were friends. They had gone to high school together, with Hallie.

"You haven't talked to him yet?"

Josh shook his head. "Nancy left messages. I'm sure he's been in the creek all day."

"I could ride out there and get him for you." Todd swatted at a mosquito. "Let me just go in and talk to Nancy a minute."

"Oh yeah—sure." Josh opened the door, and Todd walked past him.

Josh heard Nancy finish the call, heard Todd start to talk to her about the hospital, but he couldn't bear to really listen. At the same time, he couldn't not listen. He stood on the stairs where he could hear what they were saying without having to actually be in the room.

"It's a good thing you and Josh didn't go," Todd said.

"But you're sure it was them?" Nancy asked. "I keep thinking that with all those cars involved in the accident, there could have been a mistake."

Josh shifted his position, leaning into the banister.

"It's no mistake, Nancy." Todd's voice cracked a little.

Josh didn't hear the next few things they said. He tried shifting the image in his head—his father's burning truck—to one he found comforting: Miss Piper's legs in those sparkly stockings, Missy Dalton's long, shiny brown hair. He was working so hard at not thinking about his dead parents and not crying that when he looked up and saw Nancy and Todd standing at the bottom of the stairs, he was surprised.

"Todd's going to drive out to the creek and get Ram," Nancy said.

"Can I come?" Josh blurted, immediately flooded with a need to see and talk to Ram. Josh considered Ram his best friend, even though Ram was a lot older.

"Sure," Todd said. He looked at Nancy. "What time is Holly getting here?"

"Late," Nancy said. "She's coming from New York."

"We'll be back in a bit," Todd said, and he opened the front door, motioned Josh to follow him.

•

MOLLUSK CREEK WAS only a few miles away, but the ride felt like it would never end. After a minute or two of silence, Todd cleared his throat.

"You been following the Phillies?" he asked.

"Not really," Josh said. He wished Todd had asked him about books or music, something he could answer.

"No? I thought you were a Phillies fan."

"Dad is." Josh's Mom sometimes joked that only the Phillies had the power to take her husband's mind off his tomatoes.

Todd gave Josh a quick sideways glance with a smile that looked like a wince, and then it hit Josh: Dad *was* a Phillies fan. That didn't sound right. Josh didn't want it to sound right.

They passed his dad's farm, the greenhouses and tractor and rows of tomato plants, now bare of fruit. *Who will run the farm?* Josh wondered. He felt sick to his stomach and knew he needed to somehow turn off his brain. He closed his eyes and tried to conjure Miss Piper or Missy Dalton, but all he could see was his parents' burning truck. He hoped he wouldn't throw up.

Finally they reached the creek access road. Before they could turn onto it, Josh saw a fast-moving pickup truck heading toward them. He knew immediately it wasn't Ram; he never drove that fast. Ram had told Josh he always wanted to be able to stop if a turtle or rabbit or possum was in his path, and Josh, who'd just gotten his license a few months before, had taken this to heart—he'd driven his father's truck so slowly one Saturday that Dad had said he had to be the only teenage boy in the world who drove like an old lady. As the pickup sped toward him Josh noticed the rusted spots, recognized the junkyard passenger's door whose faded red stood out against the blue of the rest of the truck. It was Cal Stutts. Josh slipped down in his seat. The sound of crushed shells spitting and popping beneath Cal's tires got louder, then faded.

"I've got half a mind to pull him over for speeding," Todd muttered.

"Let's just go see Ram," Josh said, slumped as low as his long legs would allow.

Todd was quiet for a moment. "Okay," he said, and turned onto the road. Josh sat back up in his seat and rolled down his window. He could smell the cedar from the stands of trees they were passing; it was dark enough that the tree frogs had started their chirping. Before Ram moved to Oyster Shell, Josh hadn't put much thought into the variety of wildlife in Pearl Township; he hadn't even realized that there were so many different species of frogs. And all Josh had known about the Southern lion frog—*Rana leoninus*—was what he'd observed himself.

Josh was twelve, swimming in the creek on a hot July day with his mom and Nancy nearby, when he discovered the deformed frogs. At the edge of the water, Josh had registered strange motion from the corner of his eye: a frog writhing in the wet sand. He'd squatted to look more closely and seen a withered extra leg flailing on the animal's left side. Then he saw another frog missing its right hind leg. Josh had crawled around on the wet bank of the creek for a few minutes; he'd stopped counting at fifteen, and then called his mom and Nancy over. They'd quickly packed everything up and left the creek.

It was three weeks later that Josh first met Ram, after Nancy had made a bunch of calls to the state's Environmental Affairs Department. Ram was the field agent assigned to the case.

"Ramesh Rao," the man had introduced himself, shaking Nancy's and Josh's hands where they stood at the edge of the creek. "You can call me Ram."

"Rao," Nancy repeated. "You're not related to the doctors named Rao who used to practice in Floyd, are you?"

He nodded. "They're my parents."

Nancy had smiled then, and Josh could see her visibly relax. All the adults he knew, especially his dad, felt that the state government catered to North Jersey; long before Josh was born his dad had been part of a small movement to make South Jersey the fifty-first state, though he'd told Josh he knew from the get-go that it would never amount to anything. If this Ramesh Rao was from South Jersey, then he might actually care about Mollusk Creek.

"Your mother used to be my doctor," Nancy said, "before they retired and moved back to India. I think I met you once, when you were about ten."

While Ram and Nancy were talking, Josh had watched Ram's eyes surveying the creek. It had looked as it looked every summer, an explosion of color: red cardinal flowers, purple pickerelweed and yellow tickseed mixed among the green salt grasses at the water's edge. Then, Josh hadn't known the plants' names; he'd just known that the creek was pretty. And he'd become afraid, as Nancy and Ram chatted, that the creek looked *too* pretty.

"You have to kind of squat down to see the frogs," Josh had blurted, sounding more impatient than he'd meant to.

Ram had shot Josh a look, but he then stepped closer to the water's edge. Josh followed him. There were hundreds of frogs in and out of the creek, all normal enough at first glance. For a brief second, Josh had wondered if he and his mom and Nancy had imagined the whole thing. Then he saw a frog attempt to jump, but fail; one withered back leg trailed behind it, weighing it down. Another frog crawled along as an extra limb flailed on its side. Ram picked up a frog and ran his fingers over the smooth green skin of its forehead. When he put the creature down, Josh saw that it had no eyes. The gentle way Ram had stroked the blind creature's head, and the care with which he put it back exactly in the spot where he'd found it, made Josh like him. Ram sat down where the bank was dry, his head in his hands. Josh squatted next to him.

"It's really bad, isn't it?" Josh asked.

"To be honest, I've never seen anything like this," Ram said. "But I've read about it."

"You have?"

"There have been sightings like this around the country, and in Canada. A few in the Midwest. This is the first one I know of in New Jersey."

"What do you think it is?" Josh asked. "I mean, what caused it?"

Ram had explained some of the theories he'd read, about parasites and contaminants and UV radiation. And he'd told Josh, too, about the arsenic and other chemicals that had leached into the Maurice River decades ago; the old Superfund site was in Vineland, less than thirty miles upriver.

Josh never could have guessed then how close he and Ram would become, after Ram lost a battle within the state environmental agency for further study of the creek, quit his job, moved to Oyster Shell and formed the Mollusk Creek Trust to study the problem full-time.

"Josh, do you want me to walk over there and get him?" Todd asked. The way Todd was looking at him made Josh think it wasn't the first time he'd asked the question. They were parked now, where the banks were dry, and Josh could see Ram close to the creek, sitting at the edge of his truck's bed, releasing a frog into the water.

"Maybe we should just stay here until he's done," Josh said. He didn't think he could bear to tell Ram what had happened.

"I'll go get him," Todd said, and he was out of the car before Josh could protest.

Josh watched as Todd approached Ram. He slid over to the driver's side of Todd's car and rolled the window down so he could hear.

"Hey there," Ram said, laying the wet mesh collection bag flat out in the bed of his truck. "I was going to call you after I got back to the office. Cal Stutts is on a tear about somebody stealing his dog."

"Josh is in the car," Todd said, gesturing with his head. "He's been trying to call you."

"I haven't listened to my messages," Ram said.

Todd removed his Phillies cap and fingered it nervously. "There was a bad accident today. Up in Bellmawr, just over the bridge."

Josh couldn't hear what Ram said after that, and he couldn't hear Todd's response. But he saw Todd look down at the ground, holding his fist to his mouth. As Ram moved toward Todd's car, toward Josh, he caught his gaze, and something about it, the intensity of it, made Josh wish he'd never come out to the creek, that Ram still didn't know. As close as Josh felt to Ram, he also knew that he wanted no part of this, the look Ram was giving him, the feelings that were threatening to explode. He scrambled out of the car and ran away from him, away from the creek, into the woods.

"Josh," Ram called.

As Josh heard Ram's feet on the path behind him, he wished he'd just stayed in the car—then, maybe, he could have pretended he was okay. This was stupid; he couldn't run forever. But it seemed to Josh that as long as he ran, he was keeping his parents alive, just as not telling anyone they were dead had kept them from dying. He moved as quickly as he could will his legs to work, over tree roots, pushing aside leafy branches, but Ram was gaining on him. The moment that Josh stopped running, the moment Ram caught up with him, would be the moment his parents died. That moment came more quickly than Josh expected, and though it was as terrible as he'd imagined, it also felt something like relief.

Chapter 4

Hallie's apartment was spacious by New York standards, a large studio with a separate sleeping area. She'd lived there for a decade, since Lawrence had come into the fortune his boyfriend Jonathan left him and inherited the building. Hallie arrived home to find Lawrence packing her suitcase, her bed covered with dresses, a black skirt and sweater, jeans, long-sleeved crew necks.

"Sweetie," he said, and gave her a hug. Her legs buckled and he steadied her, sitting them both on the bed.

"I called a car for you," he said. "It's the best service in Manhattan."

"Service?" she said after his words reached her; she seemed to be operating on some sort of delay. "I figured we'd rent a car."

"Rent a car? Hallie, you haven't driven in years. Do you even still have a license?"

She looked at him then, trying to comprehend what he was saying. Large parts of her brain were still back on Bleecker Street, listening to Nancy, but the substance of Lawrence's message got through: he was not going with her. She was on her own.

She watched as he got up and folded the slacks, put them in the suitcase. They'd been best friends for nearly twenty years. Was it unreasonable for her to expect him to go with her?

"I guess I thought you would drive me," she said.

Lawrence stopped packing and looked up for a moment. "Sweetie, I wish I could. Kenneth and I will drive down tomorrow. But my *New Yorker* piece is due in the morning, and if I miss that deadline...well, you know. It's my one shot." He'd been talking about the article for months, an excerpt from a memoir-in-progress about his relationship with Jonathan.

Hallie put her head in her hands. How could she face Oyster Shell, Josh, all of it—by herself?

Lawrence sat down next to her again. "I'll be there tomorrow. Kenneth will probably have to come home for work on Monday, but I can stay longer if you need me. We'll ride the bus back, like the old days."

She knew the reference to the old days was supposed to make her smile, and she tried to conjure those post-college years when she and Lawrence were broke in Queens, when he would come along on her rare visits home because she couldn't face her father and Brenda by herself.

"I should check my e-mail," she said, though she wasn't sure why she was saying it.

"Why don't you do that," Lawrence said, "and I'll pack your clothes."

By the time she'd written a global e-mail to everyone she could think of who'd be expecting to see her in the next week, and packed up her laptop, Lawrence was loading her suitcase into the trunk of a Lincoln Town Car.

HALLIE HADN'T EXPECTED the driver to know how to get to Oyster Shell, but he must have been an old hand at navigating South Jersey's minor highways; he took the back roads Hallie's father had always favored. They were on Route 206 now, heading towards Hammonton, driving through cranberry country. Her father had taught her what crops were grown in every region of the Garden State.

"Dandelions," he would say as they passed through Vineland. "Cranberries," as they made their way through Hammonton.

"What about tomatoes?" Hallie had asked once, and her father laughed.

"Tomatoes," he said, "grow all over New Jersey. They like the soil here."

"I'm glad something likes it here," Hallie's mother said, and even at that age—Hallie must have been about eight—she'd recognized her mother's unhappiness. But who could be happy, Hallie wondered, with a man like her father? The answer came immediately: Brenda. Brenda had seemed happy with Hallie's father in a way that Hallie's own mother never had.

An image flickered in Hallie's mind, a brief flash of the details Nancy had given her on the phone—her father and Brenda, trapped in a burning truck—but she banished that picture as quickly as it came. She closed it off in a corner of her mind, the place where she put all the terrible things that happened. That was where her mother's death resided, where her estrangement from her father dwelled, where her ex-boyfriend, Damien, fell out of love with her. The accident could live there too.

As the driver closed in on what Lawrence called "Deep South" Jersey, it occurred to Hallie how odd it would be to drive through the unpaved streets of Oyster Shell like this, in a Town Car. It was the kind of thing she might have enjoyed if her father were still alive, knowing how he'd have disapproved of the spectacle of it, and the waste of money. But now, with him gone, it seemed perverse, disrespectful.

"Could you drop me off in Floyd instead of Oyster Shell?" she asked the driver, leaning forward.

"Whatever you want," the driver said.

Hallie called Nancy, who answered on the second ring.

"Do you think you could pick me up in Floyd?" Hallie asked. "The driver can't take me any further." She saw the driver glance at her in the rearview mirror, but he kept silent.

"Hold on a second," Nancy said. Hallie could hear muffled voices before Nancy came back on.

"Ram and Josh will pick you up. Call when you're a half hour away."

"Ram?" Hallie asked.

"Ram—Ramesh Rao. Didn't you know him in high school?"

It was such an Oyster Shell thing, Hallie thought, to assume that she'd immediately identify someone she hadn't seen in twenty years—by nickname alone! Brenda was always dropping names into conversations like that, people Hallie barely remembered.

"I did," Hallie said. "Sorry. My brain's not working very well."

"I have the same problem," Nancy said. "We'll see you later."

"MISS, WE'RE ALMOST there," the driver was saying. Hallie was on her side, her face pressed into the delicate sweater Lawrence had brought her back from his last trip to Paris. She had dozed off.

"What time is it?" she asked.

"Almost midnight. Where in Floyd do you want me to drop you?"

Hallie hadn't given Ram and Josh the half-hour head start. Where should she have them meet her? She closed her eyes and pictured the center of Floyd and what passed for a bus stop—a weather-beaten bench with a small New Jersey Transit sign next to it.

"Just take me to the bus stop on Main Street," she said. It was the same stop where her father had found her when she'd tried to run away at seventeen, shortly before his marriage to Brenda.

Hallie called her parents' house again, told Nancy she'd be at the bus stop in Floyd soon, was assured that a ride was on its way. Her phone rang as soon as she finished the call with Nancy. It was Lawrence. Hallie watched his name flash on the display and considered it, then switched the phone to silent.

The driver made a few turns, and soon they were passing the main entrance to the Huxley Glass Works, the biggest employer in Floyd. Hallie remembered the stir her sophomore year of high school when the youngest Huxley son—a senior at a private school—and several of his trust-fund pals crashed a Floyd High School dance. Hallie and her friend Christie had danced with two of the boys, but they'd known better than to go home with them.

As they reached Main Street, Hallie was surprised to see how the storefronts had been redone. For as long as she could remember, the town had looked frozen in the fifties, with signs in nuclear-era fonts. But apparently there had been some sort of revitalization project. The old Trask Theatre, which had gone out of business when Hallie was about six and been vacant the entire time she was growing up, now housed an art gallery. An art gallery, in Floyd! If only Mom had lived to see this, she thought.

"Where do you want me to leave you?" the driver asked. They were at the intersection of Main and Front streets, by the bus stop; there was no shelter, just the bench and the small sign.

"Here is fine," Hallie said.

"Here?" the driver asked, looking out at the deserted road, brightened by only a few streetlights, the storefronts darkened.

"Here." She thought it might be good to sit alone for a few minutes before Ram and Josh got there. She had no idea how she'd summon the energy to talk to Josh.

The driver pulled over and put the car in park, turned and looked at Hallie. "Miss, I can't leave you alone in the middle of nowhere, when you're upset like this."

Hallie wondered if she looked upset, then realized that Lawrence might have filled the driver in. Was he right? She was used to wandering around New York by herself at night, but no street she walked in New York was ever this deserted.

"Maybe we should just wait until they get here," Hallie said.

"Of course," the driver said, "but really, I can take you anywhere. Your friend paid for the whole night."

Hallie nodded, but didn't respond. Twenty minutes later, a blue pickup truck appeared across the street. As Hallie squinted in the dark, the passenger door opened, and a young man got out. It had to be Josh, Hallie thought, but he looked so different. Could boys change that much from fifteen to seventeen? He was tall now, like their father, probably a little over six feet. As he crossed the street, though, Hallie saw that Josh was built differently from their dad. He was very thin, and, despite his height, gave the appearance of fragility; it looked like a good wind could blow him away. Their father had been solid, muscular, but perhaps that was from working on the farm. Perhaps as a teenager he'd been skinny like Josh.

Hallie got out of the car just as Josh reached the curb; he was under a streetlight, and she could get a better look at him. He was wearing jeans, Timberland boots, a Death Cab for Cutie t-shirt. Josh's hair was brown, darker than hers, and wavy, cut short in a style that was not quite flattering but not altogether unhip, either. All in all, he looked much more like the teenagers Hallie passed on the street in Soho and much less like a farm boy than she would have expected. They were a few feet away from each other; Hallie felt Josh sizing her up as well.

"I know this will make me sound like every other stupid adult you haven't seen in a couple of years, but man, you're tall," Hallie said.

Josh regarded her for a second. "You look the same." His expression was blank.

"Are you okay?" she asked, and that was all it took: he started crying, quietly, an understated but steady flow of tears. She put her arms out and he lurched a few steps forward and fell into her; his body was surprisingly light for its size. Hallie saw the pickup truck do a u-turn, pull in behind the Town Car. Her driver got out and popped the trunk. Hallie steered Josh over to the bench and sat him down.

"I need a Kleenex," he said, and it struck Hallie that her father had always called them that too, Kleenex, as if there were only one brand. Hallie retrieved her bag from the backseat of the car, opened it to find that Lawrence had packed a giant wad of tissues. She handed Josh several.

"Sorry," he said, after using all the tissues and pocketing them.

"For what?"

"I don't know…losing it, I guess." Hallie still had one arm around him; she saw a wild look in his eyes, fear, anguish and exhilaration all mixed together. She remembered that feeling from when her mother died, the odd edge of excitement that had tinged her grief; her life was changed forever, and there were moments when Hallie had felt she was on the steepest, scariest roller coaster ever imagined. For a second or two, the ride felt exciting. The problem was, there was no way to get off.

"I think if anyone has a good excuse to lose it, you do," Hallie said.

"I guess." He pulled one of the used tissues from his pocket and wiped his nose.

"I didn't know you liked Death Cab for Cutie," Hallie said.

"Huh?" Josh looked confused for a moment. "Oh, the shirt. I bought it to impress a girl."

Hallie tried to smile, but it felt more like a grimace. "Did it work?"

"No," he said. "Not that I know of."

She saw a man—Ram—get out of the pickup truck, take the bags from the driver and put them in the truck's bed. She *had* known him in high school, and he'd been one of the smart kids; what on earth was he doing here? He looked good, though. In high school, his face had been a bit too boyish, too open and eager; now, with a few years etched on it, he looked handsome, and more guarded.

"I didn't know Ram was living back here," Hallie said to Josh.

"He's been in Oyster Shell for a few years," Josh said. "He told me he knew you."

"Well, in high school," Hallie said.

"He told me about the time you guys went to see the Ramones in Philly."

Hallie had forgotten about that trip. She and her friends had kind of used Ram, who'd been the first one in their group to turn seventeen and get his license. He was in their social circle, but he wasn't someone they usually hung out with, wasn't someone they would have considered dating.

"We got lost on the way back," Hallie said. "I remember hoping Dad would be sorry if anything happened to me."

"Sorry for what?" Josh asked. "Did you guys have a fight that night?"

Sorry for telling her that he and Brenda would be getting married, Hallie thought, but she wasn't going to let Josh know how much she'd resented his mother. "Yeah, we fought," Hallie said, "but I can't remember what about. We fought a lot when I was a teenager."

Josh nodded.

"Did you?" Hallie asked. "It's normal, you know, if you did."

Josh shook his head. "Not really. Dad and I get along okay. We just don't talk much. He's kind of hard to talk to."

Hallie nodded. She saw Josh's eyes moisten again, and handed him another tissue.

"I said…I meant, he *was* hard to talk to." He blew his nose quietly.

"I knew what you meant." She didn't know this boy, not really, but something about his use of the present tense and his awareness of it, his attempt to correct himself, cut through her.

"Hey," she heard a man's voice, and looked up to see Ram standing in front of them both. "I don't want to rush you guys, but I was thinking you might be more comfortable back at the house."

Hallie looked past Ram and saw that her driver had already gone; if he'd said anything to her, she hadn't noticed. She never even tipped him.

"Let's go," Josh said, rising from the bench. "I want to go home."

The three of them piled silently into the cab of the pickup truck. Hallie let Josh get in the middle and she took the passenger's side. As they turned off Main Street she saw that the rest of Floyd hadn't changed at all. They passed the police station, the Floyd Public Library, and then the Wawa where Hallie, in tenth grade, had bought a pack of cigarettes on a dare. Ram turned left at the Wawa and soon they were on the rural highway whose rutted twenty miles connected Floyd to Pearl Township. Hallie studied a stretch of modest homes and wished that she could bail out at one of them, that some kindly stranger might take her in. But she knew she was trapped, and that soon, she'd be back in that big, drafty house she'd worked so hard to escape.

CHAPTER 5

Sandwiched in the truck between Ram and Hallie, Josh thought the ride from Floyd to Oyster Shell was maybe the longest ride of his life, so much longer than the terrible drive out to the creek with Todd. The awful silence was typical of Hallie's rare visits. Both she and their father would become so quiet in each other's presence—it was a loud silence, the kind of silence that screamed with all the things not being said.

"You okay?" Ram asked about halfway through the ride, and then Hallie looked at him, too, and Josh felt so self-conscious that he just nodded and stared down at his shoes.

When they got back to the house, Nancy's car was still in the driveway. Before Ram had even turned his truck's motor off, Nancy stepped outside, onto the porch. Hallie opened her door and ran up the steps, and Josh watched as the two of them hugged.

"My mom told me they used to be really close." Josh was glad to have said something, anything.

"Nancy and Holly?" Ram quickly corrected himself: "Hallie, I mean."

"I forget sometimes that her name used to be Holly."

"What did your parents call her?"

"Mom called her Hallie," Josh said. "Dad...you know, I can't remember him even saying her name. I think he would say 'your sister.' Weird, huh?"

"Not really. They didn't get along so well."

Josh's mom had always said that his sister's remoteness, the large gaps of time between her visits, had more to do with his father than it did with him or his mom.

"She's never gotten over her mother's death," Josh's mom would say after Hallie begged off a visit, or was short on the phone. "It's hard for her to see her father with a new family."

But Josh had always suspected there was more to it than that; he'd learned from a young age that his mother tended to analyze things in simple terms, while his father didn't seem to analyze at all. Josh had often wondered where he came from, for he looked at the world in the most complicated terms possible: what was right and what was wrong was never obvious, or easy to define, and it seemed to Josh that the world was a minefield of choices and unforeseen consequences.

"I'll get her suitcase," Ram said. Josh walked up to the porch, where Nancy and Hallie were saying good night.

"I forgot to tell you," Nancy said to Josh. "Father Dobrinich stopped by earlier, when you and Todd were out at the creek."

Josh was relieved that he'd missed Father Dobrinich. For the past few months, he had become increasingly convinced that there was no God, no heaven or hell, but he'd continued going to St. Francis of Assisi Church because he didn't want to hurt his mother's feelings. And every Sunday he'd taken Communion even though he felt like he was not partaking of the body of Christ at all, but of a flat piece of tasteless bread that was made in a bakery somewhere.

He'd mentioned it to his father, just last month. Josh was helping him nail the porch railing, which tended to come loose every so often. All his life, Josh had gone to church with his mother and his father had stayed home; Dad had always said it was because of the farm, but Josh knew other farmers who went to church on Sunday. He wasn't in the habit of talking to his father about anything of substance—he was much closer to his mother—but just then, with all his doubts swirling around, he had to know.

"Dad," Josh said, "why don't you go to church with me and Mom?"

His father stopped for a moment, wiped sweat from his face with his t-shirt. "Well, your mother is more into all that than I am." He took a long swig of the iced tea Josh's mom had left on the porch.

"Are you Catholic?" Josh asked, and it seemed so odd to him as he asked it, that all this time, he'd never even known what religion his father was.

"I was raised Methodist," his dad said after a pause. He kicked at a small spike of wood sticking up from one of the porch steps. "I'm gonna have to sand that down."

"So why don't you go to a Methodist church?" Josh asked.

His father finished off the glass of tea and set it back on the porch, ice clinking. He looked at Josh for a minute before he answered.

"I'm not a religious man," he said. "Your mother is. That's all there is to it."

"Are you an atheist?" Josh asked, feeling excited by the possibility. He'd been thinking for months that he was, maybe, and if his father was too—well, it would be the first real thing Josh knew of that they had in common.

"Oh, I wouldn't go that far. Let's just say I have my doubts, is all." He picked up a hammer and a nail and turned back to the railing, but looked over his shoulder at Josh for a second before swinging. "And let's keep this conversation between us men, okay?" He winked, and Josh felt a small flicker of delight; he and his father had a secret! This was uncharted territory for them both.

"We could stop by your church tomorrow, if you want," Hallie said. He stared at her for a second, remembering where he was. That conversation with his dad happened a month ago. Dad was dead now. So was Mom. Josh had never in his life felt so weird in his own skin, so uncertain of the basic facts of reality.

Josh nodded, but hoped he'd find a way to get out of it. He didn't want to hear Father Dobrinich tell him that his parents were at peace, in heaven. They had died in an accident and a fire, and nothing would erase that truth. If there was a God, he wouldn't kill people's parents; especially not Josh's mother, who'd believed all her life.

Just then the dog—Cal Stutts's dog—let out a howl from Josh's bedroom.

"I didn't know you had a dog," Hallie said.

"Neither did I," Ram said.

"Yeah—I just—I found her yesterday," Josh said. "I should let her out."

"I already did," Nancy said. "And I left some cans of dog food in the kitchen."

Josh stood rooted in his spot, waiting for Nancy to tell him that he had to give the dog back to Cal, but she just hugged him. "I'll be back tomorrow morning with some breakfast," she said, and headed out to her car. Was it possible that she hadn't recognized the dog?

Inside, Josh saw the four big cans of pet food lined up next to the stove. He opened one, then rummaged in the cabinet for a bowl.

"What kind of dog is it?" Ram asked.

"A mutt," Josh said, spooning the dog food into one of his mother's small mixing bowls. After two scoops, he imagined his mother calling out sharply: "Not my mixing bowl, Josh!" The thought stopped him for a second, until he realized that she wasn't there, would never be there again. He could feed the dog from the good china if he wanted.

"Can I see her?"

Josh looked at Ram and wondered, for a second, if he was on to him.

"You know," Josh said, "I'm kind of tired. Maybe tomorrow?"

"Sure," Ram said, glancing at Hallie. "You must want to spend some time alone with your sister."

That wasn't what Josh had meant; he'd just wanted Ram to stop asking questions about the dog. But now he couldn't figure a way to tell Ram he'd like him to stay.

"Will you come by tomorrow?" Josh asked.

"Sure, if you want me to."

Josh nodded, feeling like he could cry any second if he let himself. He didn't want Ram to leave at all; he wasn't even sure what to say to Hallie. He barely knew her. He considered just telling Ram the truth, that he'd stolen Cal Stutts's dog and he actually really wanted Ram to stay. But he was certain Ram would make him give the dog back, if only out of concern over what Cal might do in retaliation. And he felt at that moment like saving the dog was the most important thing in the world. He hadn't been able to save his parents—while they were dying, he was either still at lunch or in his English class, listening to Mrs. Wyckoff lecture about the Romantic poets and writing a poem in his head about the way Missy Dalton's breasts looked in that sweater she was wearing. His parents were burning, maybe still alive and burning to death, and he had been thinking of Missy Dalton's breasts. Josh thought there was something wrong with him that his parents could be dying and he could not somehow feel it.

But he could save this dog. He'd known for years what was happening to her and had finally done something to stop it. He wanted to believe that if he saved the dog, some sort of cosmic balance would be restored, that he would be forgiven for not knowing his parents were dying, that nothing else bad would happen. But he didn't really believe there was anyone out there to forgive him. What he was sure of was that saving the dog was a good thing, a thing he could do.

And then Ram had his arms around him and was clapping him on the back, and Josh realized that he was crying. His father had told him many times over the years that men weren't supposed to cry, though his mother disagreed.

"Don, he's ten years old," Josh remembered his mother saying. They'd been watching a movie on TV about chimps that were kept in labs, having terrible things done to them.

"Well, he's a boy," Josh's father had shot back. "He shouldn't be crying like a girl over some damn monkeys!"

"They weren't monkeys," Josh remembered choking out at his father through his tears. "They were *chimpanzees*."

His father glared at him for a moment before he spoke. "Whatever kind of animal it is," he said, his voice a low, simmering boil, "a boy who wants to grow up to be a man shouldn't be crying over it."

Since then, Josh had become aware that he was better read and better educated than his parents, both of them high school dropouts. And realizing that had made him feel bad that he'd spent a good chunk of his early adolescence throwing facts back in his father's face, and it had made him feel okay on the occasions that his father would try to belittle him when Josh talked about the things he'd learned in school, about Hester Prynne, for example, suffering with the Puritans, or Cathy and Heathcliffe, suffering for love. Josh's mother was more open to the things he was learning. She'd read some of the books for his English classes with him, just so they could discuss them. Her favorite was Jane Austen's *Emma*.

"Why don't you sit down," Ram was saying, steering him to the couch, "and I'll go upstairs and feed the dog." How long had he been standing there crying? Josh didn't know. Time was moving strangely, slowing way down and then speeding up abruptly.

"No," Josh said, "I'll feed her."

But Hallie already had the bowl of dog food in her hands. "*I'll* feed her," she said, and disappeared up the stairs.

"I'm okay now," Josh said to Ram, sniffing his tears back up into his head.

Ram studied his face like he was trying to crack some sort of code. "You don't have to pretend, you know."

"I know," Josh said. "I'll be okay tonight. Come over in the morning?"

"First thing." Ram moved toward the front door. "But you can call me tonight if you change your mind, okay? Even if it's like three in the morning."

"Okay." Josh was pretty sure he wouldn't sleep at all that night, and he liked the idea that he could call Ram at any hour, even though he probably wouldn't.

Ram called goodbye to Hallie up the stairs, and left, and Josh was alone. With Hallie, but alone. Josh wondered how long she would stay, and for the first time it hit him: what would happen to him? Hallie wasn't going to stay in Oyster Shell, and he had no other close relatives, except a couple of uncles on his mother's side—a family of drunks and crooks, Josh had heard his mother tell Nancy once when she didn't know Josh could hear. The last time he'd seen any of them was when he was twelve.

He heard what must have been Hallie's cell phone ring—it played an old song that he knew but couldn't immediately identify—and he heard her talking, quietly enough that he couldn't make out the words. Josh climbed the stairs and went into his bedroom, where the dog was licking the now-empty dish for any flecks of food she'd missed. "The End of The World As We Know It"—that was the song on Hallie's cell phone. Last year in English, Mr. Fenton had asked Josh for an example of irony, and he couldn't think of one. Nicki Kepler, the most political girl in school, the girl who stuffed flyers about Guantanamo and the Patriot Act and the genocide in Darfur in everyone's lockers between classes, had raised her hand and answered, "George W. Bush." A few of the kids had laughed, a few had glared at her, and the rest had simply looked puzzled. Josh hadn't quite gotten it—maybe Bush was a bad guy, maybe he wasn't, but how was he ironic?—but now, he had a real example and felt he finally understood the concept. That song, playing in a cheesy-cheery cell phone version on a night when it really was the end of the world—*that* was irony.

He sat on the floor and put his arms around the dog; she was as starved for love as she was for food, and she abandoned the empty dish for Josh, licked his arms while he petted her. He put his head down in her sour-smelling fur and thought about what he'd call her. He wanted to name her Brenda, for his mother, but he was afraid people would think that was sad, or weird. He had to name her for his mother in a secret way that nobody else would get. He stood and scanned the spines of the books on his shelves while the dog resettled herself at his feet, and then he saw it: *Emma*. He would call the dog Emma. Josh said the name aloud, and the dog looked up at him with eyes that said he could call her anything he wanted.

JOSH FELT THE dog moving around on the bed, and he rolled over, glanced at the clock. 6:07 a.m. The last time he'd looked, it was just after four, so he'd slept for about two hours. Or maybe he'd just been lying there, half-awake. Josh sat up and turned on the light, the dog snuggling by his side.

It was still dark outside, and very quiet. Josh looked around his room, at the big bookshelf his father had built for him—Josh's goal since the age of thirteen had been to fill it, and he was close—and at the CDs strewn about the floor, in and out of cases, his school books tossed in a corner, *Calculus* and *English Romantic Poetry: An Anthology* peeking out from under the clothes he'd worn yesterday. It looked like his room, and yet it felt different now—or perhaps he was different, and what felt odd was that the room hadn't changed.

Josh pulled from his nightstand a book he'd found in the attic a few months ago: *Howl*. He knew it had belonged to Hallie's mother because her name, Jenny Barton, was written in a girlish script inside the slim volume's front cover. It must have belonged to her before she married Dad, which meant she was young, about Josh's age; he'd overheard enough to know that Hallie's mother was a teenager when she had her, and it was obvious from the photos he sometimes came across. Jenny was beautiful, like Missy Dalton or Miss Piper. There was one picture where she looked so pretty and so Josh's age that he'd found himself fantasizing about her, and then halfway through became totally creeped out: she was his sister's dead mother! It had freaked him out so much that he didn't touch himself for a week afterward as penance.

Jenny had written notes in the margins of the book, and was

particularly intrigued by references to sex or madness. She was a fascinating mystery, so unlike both of Josh's parents. Her death was even mysterious; Josh had no idea how she'd died, whether she'd been sick or if it was completely unexpected. Dad had always looked so pained on the rare occasions Jenny's name was mentioned that Josh had never worked up the nerve to ask. He opened the drawer in his nightstand and took out his box of index cards, and a pen. *What happened to Jenny?* he scribbled on a blank card.

Josh stroked Emma's back and wondered what would happen that day. He assumed he wasn't going to school. Hallie wasn't going to make him go, and neither were Ram or Nancy. And who would help Nancy with the horses today? He usually cleaned stalls for her on Friday and Saturday mornings, the days her other barn help was off. Josh glanced again at the clock—it was close to 6:30 now—and he picked up the phone and dialed Ram's number.

"Hey," Ram said. "I'm glad you called."

"Did I wake you up?" Josh asked.

"Not really. My alarm was about to go off, and I was lying here staring at it." Ram coughed a little. "Did you get any sleep?"

"Not much."

"You should have called me earlier."

"I guess." Josh had thought about it, but he hadn't known what to say.

"Is Hallie up?"

"I don't know. I haven't gone downstairs yet."

"Do you want me to come over?"

"Yes, but could you go to Nancy's first and help her with the horses? I just don't…" Josh didn't know what to say. Don't want to? Don't feel right about it?

"No problem," Ram said. "I'll throw some clothes on and head over there. I'll come see you after."

"Thanks, Ram. See you later."

He hung up and looked down at Emma, knowing that once Nancy and Ram talked, the subject of the dog would probably come up. But he was going to fight for Emma. He would do anything else he was asked to do, but he wasn't giving her back. Cal Stutts could come and beat him up; he could burn the house down, though Josh didn't think he'd do that.

Josh's dad had been nice to Cal, had given him work on the farm and other things, too, vegetables and sometimes spare parts for his truck or old clothes. Now there was a whole closet full of clothes that Cal could use, but Josh didn't want to think about that. He opened the book instead.

Josh read *Howl* until it got light out without making much progress. He would read a few lines, realize he had no idea what it had said, then read it again. Finally the dog sat up, looked at him and barked a little. She had a weird bark, low-pitched with a hint of a yelp, and she looked at Josh like she was trying to tell him something. He rubbed behind her floppy ears, looked into her brown eyes.

"You need to go out, girl?" he asked her. Emma's tail thumped on the bed.

Josh got up, pulled on yesterday's jeans and a clean t-shirt. All of his favorite t-shirts were dirty; this was an old one, for Some Dark Angel, a goth band he'd been way into his sophomore year of high school. It was a little snug, the shirt, and kind of short, and Josh hoped his mom would do some laundry today so he wouldn't have to scrape the bottom of his t-shirt drawer tomorrow. He was about to gather the dirty laundry from his floor and throw it into the hamper in the hallway when he remembered that his mother wasn't there to do the wash. Who would do the wash? Josh sat on the edge of his bed and struggled against the tears he felt forming, lost the fight and gave in for a few minutes. Emma pressed her nose into his lap; he leaned down and buried his head in her fur. She smelled ripe and very dog-like—he would have to give her a bath, soon—but she was also warm and soft. Josh pulled his gray hoodie off the floor and wiped his face with the hem, then slipped it on. He opened the bedroom door and motioned for Emma to follow him down the stairs.

HALLIE WAS ON her cell phone, stretched on the family room couch with a pillow and blanket like she'd slept there, an old movie playing softly on the TV. She held the phone away from her face, looked at Josh.

"I hope I didn't wake you," she said, and then, into the phone: "Lawrence, I have to go."

Josh shook his head and walked out back with Emma. When they returned Hallie was in the kitchen, the blanket wrapped around her.

"What's the dog's name?" she asked as she spooned dog food into a bowl.

"Emma," Josh said. The dog ran into the kitchen and wiggled by Hallie's side as she placed the bowl on the floor.

"Emma needs a collar and leash."

"Yeah, I know." Josh watched as the dog seemed to inhale the food without chewing.

"Hmm," Hallie said. She was quiet for a moment. "There might be a leash and collar in my old room. When my mom's dog died, I kept a few things of hers in the back of my closet. But that was so long ago, Dad or your mom might have cleaned all that stuff out by now."

Josh knew Hallie's room hadn't been touched, except when his mother vacuumed and dusted every Saturday.

"I bet it's still there," Josh said. "In the closet?"

"I think so," Hallie said. "In a shoebox."

Josh ran back upstairs, Emma at his heels. He liked the way she followed him everywhere.

Hallie's room was Josh's favorite place in the house when he was younger; he used to slip in there and lie on the bed, studying the posters on the walls. The guys all looked like girls in the 80s, and Josh would sometimes stare at Boy George or the redheaded guy from Duran Duran, wondering what they looked like without makeup. Josh was just discovering rock music at the time, was into the Foo Fighters and Pearl Jam, and only understood rock stars who looked like real people, real guys—this was before he got into Some Dark Angel, and the band's lead singer, Damien, and all the bands Damien told interviewers he liked: Bowie, the Cure, My Bloody Valentine. When Josh was thirteen or fourteen he'd once spent an entire weekend listening to all the vinyl records in Hallie's room, and took the two good ones—a Clash, an Elvis Costello—from the midst of dozens of sugary-sweet 80s synth pop confections.

Josh opened Hallie's closet door and pushed aside the old dresses and shirts still hanging there. Several dusty shoeboxes sat on the floor in the back; he found the leash and collar with a bowl on which someone had painted the word "Candy" in multi-colored letters. He put the collar around Emma's neck, grabbed the leash and ran back down, Emma by his side.

"So your mom's dog was named Candy?" he asked Hallie as he fastened the leash to the collar, Emma's excited wiggling causing him to miss on his first try.

"Yeah," Hallie said. She opened the back door and Josh walked Emma out to the sandy stretch of backyard where the wild grasses were sparse, the bay not far beyond. Josh was surprised when Hallie walked out with them. She was still wearing the clothes she'd worn yesterday.

"They had her before I was born," Hallie said. "My mom and Dad, I mean. I think he gave her Candy as a puppy." She glanced at Emma, who was rooting around in the grass. "We'll have to get her more dog food today. After I figure out everything else that needs to be done."

"Yeah," Josh said. "I guess you have to talk to, like, lawyers and stuff?" He was so glad Hallie was there. He had no idea how to talk to people like that.

Hallie smiled a little. "Yeah, lawyers and stuff. I'm not really sure myself."

They walked closer to the water, and Josh saw the delight in Emma's eyes as she lunged at the shorebirds. "I think there's a will somewhere," he said. He knew his mother had mentioned it to him; but where had she said it was?

"Somewhere in the house, or with a lawyer?" Hallie asked.

Josh thought for a second. Why couldn't he remember? He had that feeling of wanting to cry again.

"It's okay," Hallie said, her hand on his back. "I think we should go in and have some coffee, and watch something really dumb on TV, and wait for people to start bringing casseroles over, and worry about wills and lawyers later."

Josh liked the way that sounded—almost normal, but not so normal that it would be an affront to his parents' being dead. He nodded yes, and didn't tell Hallie that he'd never had coffee before. He wasn't sure if he would like it, but he could pretend.

•

THE COFFEE TASTED terrible on its own—strong and bitter. Hallie had put out milk and sugar, and Josh thought if he added enough, maybe he could drink it. He put a couple of spoons of sugar in, tasted it, and tried a few spoons more.

Hallie was watching him. "Did I make it too strong?"

Josh took another sip. Now it was sickening sweet but still had that awful taste. "No," he said. "I guess I just don't like coffee."

"Why didn't you say so? You don't have to drink it if you don't like it."

"Okay," he said. He got up, dumped the coffee in the sink, and poured himself a glass of orange juice. Hallie was giving him an intense look.

"I was trying to be cool," he said.

Hallie smiled, but she looked like she felt sorry for him. It was awful. "Is drinking coffee cool?"

"I guess so," Josh said. "There are all these shows where cool people sit around and drink coffee." For a long time, Josh had pictured Hallie's life in New York that way: like an episode of *Friends*, pretty people with pretty problems that got resolved in a half-hour.

"Not that I watch that much TV," he added. "I read a lot."

"I saw all the books in your room," she said. "Pretty impressive."

Josh shrugged, but he was glad she'd noticed. He wanted her to stay for as long as possible, and she wasn't going to stay in Oyster Shell if she thought he was ordinary.

"Do you know where you want to go to college?" she asked.

"Not really," he said. "I was going to just apply to some local schools, but Mom and my guidance counselor freaked out after I took the SAT."

"Freaked out?" Hallie poured herself more coffee.

"I scored really high in Critical Reading." He wanted to say the part he'd overheard his mom telling his dad: that he'd gotten the highest reading score of anyone in Floyd High School that year, higher even than the kids who had 4.0 averages, the ones who were battling it out for valedictorian.

Hallie looked at him. "How high?"

Josh shrugged. "High. I don't remember the actual number." It was a lie; he knew the number, 790, just one notch below a perfect score.

"Maybe you should talk to the guidance counselor again."

"Maybe," Josh said. "But she's kinda lame."

Hallie laughed a little. "That's in the job description."

Josh attempted a smile. He was sweating a bit, so he unzipped the hoodie and shrugged it off his shoulders, letting it fall onto the linoleum. Don't just leave it on the floor, Josh! his mother would have said. He left it there for a minute, testing the powers of the cosmos, then decided to pick it up. Hallie was eying him.

"I picked it up," he said, exactly the way he might have said it to his mom.

Hallie shook her head. "Your t-shirt," she said.

"Oh, it's a band. I used to really like them when I was younger."

She still had a weird look on her face, faraway and startled. "You know about me and Damien, right?"

Josh shook his head.

"Yeah, I guess you wouldn't," she said. "I never brought him here."

"You know Damien Dark?" Even in Josh's most glamorous fantasies of Hallie's life in New York, he'd never thought that she hung out with rock stars.

Hallie smiled. "Damien *Maslowski*. He was my boyfriend a really long time ago."

Josh had read enough about Some Dark Angel to know the lead singer's real last name. "That's so cool."

"He wasn't famous then. He had this other band that played around New York."

"Tattered Halo," Josh said. "I have their EP."

"Wow, you must have been a huge fan. I wish I had known."

While Josh tried to decide whether he should tell Hallie he was still enough of a fan that he continued to post on a Some Dark Angel internet message board, Emma let out one of her weird barks, and a few seconds later there was a knock on the door. Hallie got up from the table and answered it.

"Can I help you?" Josh heard her say, and he went to the door to see who it was, stopped in his tracks at the first glimpse. Cal Stutts! Shit!

"Hallie," Josh whispered, trying to stay out of Cal's eyesight, trying to get her attention. "Hallie."

But she didn't seem to hear him, just kept talking, and Josh went into the kitchen, where Emma was hunched in a corner, growling low. She knew who was there.

"Don't worry, girl," Josh whispered to Emma. "You're not going back." He pushed her into the laundry room and shut the door, then went out to face Hallie and Cal Stutts, to make his stand.

CHAPTER 6

"Can I help you?" Hallie asked the man at the door. Everything about him was filthy, from the stringy blond hair hanging below the grease-stained John Deere cap to the worn-out jeans and dingy white t-shirt. She figured he was either homeless or lived in one of the shacks on Shellpile Drive. Most of the people who lived there were descended from the oyster shuckers, employed by three generations of Corsons before the blight that destroyed the family business when her father was a teenager.

The man smiled, his lips tightly closed. Hallie heard Josh whispering behind her, but before she could turn to him, the stranger startled her by saying her name—her old name.

"Hey, Holly. Don't know if you remember me. We went to school together."

Hallie stared at him. He must have been a classmate from Pearl Township Elementary.

"Cal Stutts."

Sixth grade, the year her mother died. Cal was one of the few kids from her class who'd gone to the funeral. He'd shown up in dress pants that clearly didn't fit him, his greasy hair slicked back in a way that he must have thought made him look more formal, more grown-up. She remembered, too, how in the procession to the cemetery, she'd seen Cal walking away from Barker's Funeral Home, down Port Norris's main street back towards Oyster Shell. From the funeral home to his house it must have been five miles. It was a cold January day, and his jacket was thin.

"Dad, we have to give him a ride," Hallie had said, pointing out the window, but her father shook his head.

"We can't. We got a whole line of cars here." But he had looked out the window, too, and both of them watched as their car approached the boy, then passed him.

"It's been a while," Cal said to Hallie, reaching down and rubbing his left shin through his grubby jeans.

"It has," Hallie said. "It's really nice of you to stop by. You worked for my father on the farm, didn't you?" She was certain she'd heard her father mention this some time in the past few years.

Cal scratched his cheek and was quiet for a moment. "Yeah, I stopped by today to see if he needs any more help."

Hallie puzzled over his response for a second, and then put it together. "You don't know."

"Know what?"

She closed the door and walked out to the porch, motioning Cal to sit down on the bench. She wondered how many times she'd have to repeat this story.

"Cal, I have some bad news. My dad and Brenda were in an accident yesterday."

"An accident?"

"Coming back from Philly. They both died."

Cal immediately took off his cap. "Oh, my," he said, and was quiet for a moment.

"I know it's a shock," Hallie said.

Cal nodded. "Must be—hard for you." She could see he was fumbling for words.

"I'm more worried about Josh."

Cal looked at the ground. "Yeah," he said. "Tough break."

"I can't imagine what he's going through," Hallie said. "I had such a hard time when my mom died, but at least I still had my dad."

"I remember when your mom died," Cal said, and a look passed between them that told Hallie he remembered that funeral, too.

Just then Josh opened the front door and called out, "Hallie, I really need to talk to you now!"

Hallie threw a sharp glance at Josh as he closed the door. "Excuse me for a second, okay?"

On the other side of the front door, Josh was pacing furiously, his face bright red.

"What is up with you?" Hallie asked. She immediately regretted the sharpness of her tone. *His parents just died*, she reminded herself.

"It's Cal," Josh said. He motioned her into the kitchen. "I stole his dog."

"Emma is his dog?"

"Yes, but she can't go back there. She was tied to a tree for, like, *two years*, and he never really fed her, and no one wanted to do anything because he said he'd kill Nancy's horses. I don't want Nancy's horses to die, but I don't want Emma to die, either. She's not going back there!"

"He said he'd kill Nancy's horses?"

"Yeah. After Nancy called the police on him for beating up his wife."

Hallie was startled by the picture of Cal that was emerging. Had he gone so awry in the past twenty years, or did Josh and possibly Nancy have a distorted view of him? "He can't be that bad," Hallie said. "He worked for Dad."

"Dad felt sorry for him," Josh said. "Also, he could pay him way less than anyone else would work for. Cal is really, really bad, Hallie. And I'm not letting Emma go back there." There was a stubborn set to his jaw that reminded Hallie of their father.

Now Hallie wondered if Cal really had come over for work, or if part of his mission had been to retrieve the dog. She weighed it in her mind. However exaggerated her brother's portrait of Cal might be, the dog was certainly better off with Josh; Cal looked like he didn't have enough money to feed himself, let alone a pet. And the boy seemed so attached to Emma. Perhaps she could talk Cal into letting Josh keep the dog. She went into the kitchen and retrieved two coffee mugs, poured two cups.

"What are you doing?" Josh asked.

"Stay here," she said, and headed back out front with the coffee. Hallie sat down next to Cal on the bench again, handed him a mug.

"I wasn't sure how you take it," she said. "I guessed black."

"You guessed right," Cal said. He took a long sip.

She decided to launch right into it. "Josh just told me that he took your dog."

"I was wondering what happened to it," Cal said. "Noticed it was missing yesterday." Was his nonchalance calculated?

"I'm really sorry," she said.

Cal nodded and took another sip from his mug.

"I have a big favor to ask," she said. "Is there any way you could let Josh keep the dog? He seems so attached to her, and with all that's just happened..." Hallie stopped for a second, took a sip of coffee, considered how to phrase the rest of it. "I know it's a lot to ask, Cal, and if there's any way I can make it up to you, just name it. If you could let him keep the dog, I'd be grateful."

She watched a series of complicated expressions play across Cal's face. For a flicker of a second, his eyes flashed anger, but then his features softened.

"Yeah, what the hey," Cal said. "It was my ex-wife's dog, anyway."

Hallie smiled at him. "Thank you so much. I don't know why Josh has gotten so attached to your dog, but she seems to be making all this a little easier on him."

Cal touched her forearm. "No problem," he said. "Maybe we could—" Hallie's stomach sank with dread at the thought that Cal was about to ask her out, but he stopped mid-sentence, took another sip of coffee, took his hand off her arm.

"Maybe you can use me if you need any help around the farm, or any odd jobs or anything," he finally said.

Hallie shifted on the bench, relaxing her back as relief washed over her. "Absolutely," she said. "I'm sure we'll need some work done. I have no idea what we're doing with the farm at this point."

"The hothouse plants'll need tending," Cal said, after taking another gulp of coffee.

"Do you know what needs to be done?"

"Sure."

Hallie hadn't even thought about the plants in her father's greenhouses, the herbs and tomatoes, all of them waiting to be watered and God knows what else. "Tell you what," she said. "Why don't I give you a call tomorrow morning and we can go through the farm together, see what needs to be done?"

Cal smiled broadly at her then. He was missing several front teeth, and two of the remaining ones were blackened, rotten. "Sure thing," he said. "But I don't have a phone. I'll just stop on by." Cal finished off what was left of the coffee, handed Hallie the empty mug.

"I haven't made the funeral arrangements yet," she said, "but I guess

I'll call Barker's. You know the place."

Cal nodded. "I'll check back with you on that." He rose, tipped his hat to her in a way that was almost courtly as he put it back on, and walked away. Hallie noticed a pronounced limp as he headed out to the main road.

Josh opened the front door as soon as Cal was gone.

"Thanks," he said, sitting next to her on the bench.

"You're welcome." Hallie took a sip of her coffee.

"You shouldn't let Cal work the farm by himself, though. Dad always said he didn't know what he was doing. He had to watch him and give him, like, really specific tasks."

Hallie looked at Josh. "Do you know what needs to be done out there?"

Josh looked down at the ground, shook his head. "I hated working on the farm. Dad only gave me really specific tasks, too." He looked back up at her and smiled slightly.

"So how about if the three of us go over there tomorrow and see if we can figure it out? We should at least keep alive whatever plants are growing, shouldn't we?"

"Yeah," Josh said, but Hallie could tell from the look on his face that he didn't want to go to there.

"You don't have to go if you don't want to," she said. She reached out to squeeze his hand, but he shifted away before she could touch him.

"No, I will." He was quiet for a moment. "Do you think you're going to, like, sell the farm?"

"I think," Hallie said, "we have to find that will before we can make any decisions. But I'm not going to decide anything without you." In truth, Hallie suspected it had all been left to Josh, the farm, the house, Brenda's battered little Geo sitting in the driveway. And if, as she suspected, Nancy was named Josh's guardian, Hallie would have no real say in anything. Part of her hoped that was the case, and another part resented her diminished role.

Josh nodded. "I think it's at the lawyer's office," he said. "The will, I mean."

•

LATER THAT AFTERNOON, after the church and the funeral home, Hallie sat in the attorney's office in Floyd, the will in her hands, trying to absorb its contents. She'd been surprised to find that her father's estate was divided equally between her and Josh. But that wasn't the biggest surprise.

"Are you sure it says I'm Josh's guardian?" Hallie asked.

"It's right here," he said, leaning across his desk and pointing out the relevant passage.

Hallie silently reread the paragraph, grateful that Josh had gotten overwhelmed after the funeral home and asked her if he could wait in the car.

"You seem surprised," the lawyer said. "Your stepmother said she'd discussed this with you."

Hallie started to protest, to say that of course Brenda had never discussed it with her, when a snippet of remembered conversation floated across her mind. It must have been five years ago, or six. Brenda was going on and on, like she sometimes did; Hallie was standing over her kitchen counter, leafing through some photos she'd just developed, and only half listening. But Brenda had said something, Hallie thought now, about doing their wills, and about Josh. Hallie imagined she'd murmured noncommittally.

"I think Brenda misunderstood me," Hallie said.

The lawyer watched her, didn't say anything.

"It's just that I live in New York."

The lawyer nodded.

She should have seen this coming. On the phone that morning, Lawrence had even tried to warn her about it.

"I'm sure my parents made Nancy Josh's guardian," Hallie had said to Lawrence. It seemed natural; Nancy was close to Josh, and Hallie knew her father had once named Nancy *her* guardian if anything happened to him, after her mother died. Of course, that was before Brenda.

"Just be wary," Lawrence had said. "They'll work that small town guilt on you."

But Hallie knew, as she read the passage in the will for a third time, that it wasn't small town guilt that would make it hard to walk away. It was Josh himself. Hallie had always thought that her own best qualities— her intellect, her sense of artistry, a certain tenacity that had served her well, living in New York—she'd gotten from her mother. And so it had been easy to dismiss Josh, to think of him as someone unrelated to her. Easier still when she hardly ever saw him. But from her first glimpse of those books in Josh's room—a collection like Lawrence's, full of classics, quite a few that Hallie had never read—she'd been forced to rethink Josh.

"What would happen if I couldn't take care of him?" Hallie asked the lawyer. She knew how awful it sounded, but she had to find out.

The lawyer was quiet for a moment. "I guess we'd have to look for another relative to take him. Is there anyone you can think of?"

Hallie shook her head. "There's really no one on my father's side," she said. "Maybe on Brenda's." She knew that Brenda had several brothers; she'd met two of them once. They'd looked like the kind of guys who get busted on *Cops*. "Actually, there's no one in the family," Hallie added. "What about a family friend?"

"Nancy, you mean," the lawyer said. *How does he even know about Nancy?* This was what Hallie hated about South Jersey, this insularity.

"Honestly, I think Josh would be better off with Nancy than with me."

"Well, you're certainly free to ask her," the lawyer said.

Hallie thought it over for a minute. Nancy *would* say yes, wouldn't she? "What would happen if she couldn't do it?"

The lawyer scratched his chin. "Well, if you couldn't do it and Nancy couldn't and no other family members stepped forward, I guess he'd go into foster care."

"That's not an option."

"I'm glad to hear that," the lawyer said.

JOSH WAS PARKED half a block away. Hallie could see him sitting there in the driver's seat of Brenda's little car, staring blankly out at Main Street. On top of everything else, the poor kid had had to drive her into Floyd because she hadn't been behind the wheel in so long. She should have told him to stay home.

Hallie knew this might be her only chance to talk to Lawrence alone, at least until he and Kenneth arrived later that night, so she ducked back inside the building and pulled out her cell.

Kenneth answered Lawrence's phone. "Hallie," he said, "I never got to talk to you yesterday. I'm so sorry."

"Thanks," she said.

"We're sitting in the most awful traffic. For an hour. We're not even out of the city yet. Here, I'll put Lawrence on."

She heard the phone being transferred, then Lawrence's voice: "We should have left earlier," he said. "I'm sorry. Three o'clock on a Friday—what was I thinking?"

"It's okay," Hallie said. "I wanted to tell you something quick, while Josh isn't around. I just read the will."

"And?"

"They named me Josh's guardian." She was surprised by the rush of emotions she felt as she said it. There was the expected fear and panic, but something else, too—a weird sort of pride, that her father and Brenda had thought her capable of raising Josh.

"I knew it! We've got to get you out of there."

"I think I'm stuck here for a while," she said. "At least until I can talk Nancy into being Josh's guardian."

Just then she saw Josh, pulling the car up closer to the lawyer's office. Had he seen her duck out, and then go back in?

"Lawrence, I have to go," she added. "We can talk about this after you get here. I'll see you later."

Hallie slipped the phone in her bag and got into the car. "Door to door service," she said to Josh. "I'm a lucky woman."

He tried to smile, but only accomplished a thin stretch of his mouth.

"You hanging in there?" she asked him.

"Not really."

She'd thought he would want to help decide the funeral arrangements, that he deserved to; they were his parents, and Josh was far closer to them both than Hallie was. But now, she saw, he was too young for all this, and a feeling gnawed at her that she'd already failed him. Nancy would be better at this, she thought. Nancy would have known to have him stay home.

"When those people in the funeral home were talking about caskets and stuff," Josh said, "all I could think was that Dad would want to be buried in a tomato. Like, a giant red casket that looked like a tomato."

Hallie laughed. "Or maybe under a giant tomato plant."

"Yeah." Josh was quiet for a minute. "And Mom would go along with it if it was what Dad wanted."

So that was why her dad and Brenda got along so well; because most of the time Brenda just went along with him. Hallie's own mother had been a fighter, the screaming and the breaking of glass more frequent than she liked to remember.

"We're doing what your mom would have wanted with the service, aren't we?" she asked.

Josh looked out the window. "I guess," he said. He tapped his index finger silently on the steering wheel, then looked at Hallie. "I don't really know. I don't know what she wanted." He had that look again, like he was about to cry, but Hallie had learned that if she reached out to comfort him, he shrank away.

"Well, she'd want the service to be Catholic, right?" Hallie asked. "I mean, your priest seemed to think so."

Now Josh was crying a little, and Hallie didn't know what to do. She squeezed his hand, then pulled away before he could start looking any more uncomfortable.

"When my mom died," Hallie said, "Dad decided everything, and it pissed me off."

Josh pulled a tissue from his pocket and blew his nose. "It did?"

"Yeah. I mean, he had her buried in Haleyville, and I knew she wouldn't want to be there. I always thought she should have been buried somewhere she loved."

"Like where?"

"New York. She always wanted to live there, to be an artist there." Hallie was certain her mother had felt trapped in Oyster Shell. She'd never said so, not in so many words, but Hallie believed her mom would have traded all the bay landscapes she'd painted, the displays at the Floyd Public Library and the ribbons she'd won at the 4-H art fair, for a single painting in a New York gallery, or an evening with the kind of people Hallie took for granted.

"I didn't know that," Josh said.

"Yeah. I used to go to her grave and tell her I was sorry she was stuck there." Hallie felt her stomach roil.

"That's so sad," Josh said, and he wiped at his eyes with the tissue, then started laughing a bit at the same time. "Thanks for cheering me up!"

Hallie laughed a little too, but she couldn't get rid of the nagging feeling that she was wretched at this, that she wasn't cut out for motherhood. She'd convinced herself in the past year or two that it was a choice she was making, that she didn't want to be saddled with someone else's wants and needs. But now she was faced with the stark reality: she couldn't have kids because she would be a terrible mother.

"What I was trying to say was that I let you make all these decisions because Dad didn't let me, but I don't think you really wanted to. I'm not doing anything right."

Hallie saw something flash in his eyes, some kind of fear or panic.

"If there's something else you want to talk about, you can," she added. But she feared what he might say. He had to be thinking about what was going to happen to him, and Hallie didn't know what to tell him.

"I'm just glad you're here," he said. "That's all."

"Me too." It was inane—they both knew she hated coming home—and he gave her a skeptical, very teenage look.

"I mean, I'm glad I can be here for you," she said, and she meant it. While there were people who depended on her—Joy needed Hallie to run the studio, and she felt certain that despite his occasional aloofness, Lawrence relied on her emotionally—Hallie had never felt this deeply needed by anyone. Certainly not by any of the men she'd dated, or even Damien, her only long-term boyfriend, the only man she'd ever lived with; he'd managed, every day of the three-and-a-half years they were together, to make her feel like he had one foot out the door.

Perhaps Nancy could take care of Josh during the week and Hallie could come down to Oyster Shell on the weekends. She could spend that much time with Josh. She should.

Josh looked at her for a few long seconds, like he was trying to puzzle something out. Then he shifted the car into drive.

"Let's go home," he said, and pulled away from the curb. As they turned off Main Street, Hallie's phone rang. It was Lawrence again.

"We just heard on the radio that the tunnel is backed up for two *hours*," Lawrence said. "I feel terrible."

"It's my friend Lawrence," Hallie said to Josh, and then to Lawrence: "Maybe you guys should just give up and come tomorrow morning."

"No, we're coming tonight," Lawrence said, "but we might try to get out of this traffic and go have dinner somewhere first."

"Take your time." She noticed they were about to pass the China Palace, the best Chinese food in Floyd—which wasn't much by New York standards, but still.

"Josh, do you want to get some Chinese food?" she asked. He nodded, and pulled into the restaurant's parking lot.

"Chinese?" Lawrence repeated, and Hallie only realized he wasn't talking to her when she heard Kenneth answer, "How about Thai?"

"I'm going to go," Hallie said. "I'll see you later tonight."

"Tell him to drive carefully," Josh said. She repeated his words to Lawrence.

"Oh," Lawrence said. "That breaks my heart."

"Mine too."

INSIDE THE RESTAURANT, Josh studied the takeout menu as if he might be tested on it.

"Let's just order a bunch of stuff and we'll see what tastes good when we get home," Hallie said.

Josh nodded, but then he pointed to a dish on the menu. "Buddhist's Delight," he said. "That's what I usually get."

She read the description: an assortment of vegetables and tofu. "Don't you want any meat or chicken or anything?" she asked.

Josh shook his head. "I'm a vegetarian."

"How long have you been a vegetarian?"

"Two years," Josh said. "It drove Dad crazy."

Hallie smiled. "Two Buddhist's Delights," she told the woman behind the counter.

They were silent as they waited for the food. Josh's sadness was palpable, and Hallie couldn't help but wonder what might have happened if her father had left a little earlier, or later, or hadn't gone to Philly at all. It would be so much easier if she could just obliterate her thoughts with vodka martinis, if she were back in New York drinking herself into a stupor while Lawrence and Kenneth and Alison flanked her at the bar. It would be easier, of course, if there were no Josh. Yet she couldn't help feeling that, on some level, she was glad to be with him, less alone than she might have been in New York. That Josh's existence was the only thing that helped any of this make any kind of sense.

CHAPTER 7

Josh stood stiffly in front of his bedroom mirror, in the new suit Hallie had insisted they go all the way to the Hamilton Mall to buy. Why she thought he couldn't buy a suit at the Cumberland Mall, he didn't know; but he'd gone along with it, remembering that his mother had always liked shopping at Hamilton, too. It was one of those women things that Josh didn't understand.

He was trying to tie the necktie, a satiny gray thing. Emma let out a loud yawn and seemed to smile at him. Could dogs smile? Josh wondered. Could they love? Because Emma looked at Josh like she loved him, and she'd only been his dog for four days. He checked back in the mirror and made one more futile stab at the necktie, then gave up.

Downstairs, there were more people standing around than Josh would have liked, and they all looked happier than he thought they should. His Uncle John, the brother Josh's mother especially could not stand, was telling two of Dad's cousins a story punctuated by his own loud laughter. Josh was pretty sure Uncle John owed his dad money, and he fought a sudden urge to walk over and demand it, if for no other reason than to stop the awful laughter.

Hallie's friends from New York were there, too. The photographer Hallie worked with had arrived two hours earlier with a gray parrot in a cage; Josh worried that Emma might attack the bird if it got out. He never used to worry about bad things happening, and he'd never understood why his father was such a worrier. Once Josh's dad had completely freaked out when his mom, who was in the shower, didn't answer the phone. Josh had thought his dad was crazy, to get so worried over nothing. But now he felt the same way.

Lawrence was there with Kenneth, his—boyfriend? Was there a different word for it, if it was two guys? Or was Kenneth—Lawrence's husband? Josh knew that in New Jersey—in North Jersey, where all the decisions were made—the court was considering some kind of gay marriage or civil unions. Nicki Kepler had stuck a flyer about it in his locker last week.

Josh went into the kitchen looking for Ram. Kenneth was the first person he ran into.

"Do you need some help with that?" Kenneth asked, motioning toward the tie, and Josh nodded.

Kenneth put down his wine glass and tied Josh's necktie. Josh wondered at first if he'd feel weird, having a gay guy tie his tie; but he didn't. He'd never really spent much time with anybody who was gay before, but it seemed to him that maybe it wasn't such a big deal.

"How are you doing?" Kenneth asked.

"I don't know," Josh said. It was the truth; he had no idea.

Kenneth nodded. "I can't even imagine what this is like for you," he said, and Josh appreciated it, that he didn't say some stupid cliché that was supposed to be comforting but wasn't.

"Are you ready?" Hallie asked, eying him with that worried look he was starting to get used to.

"I guess," Josh said. He still had no idea what was going to happen to him, whether Hallie would stay in Oyster Shell for a while or, if not, who he was going to live with. He figured his chances that Hallie would stay were greater, the less of a pain in the ass he could be. "I mean, sure, let's go."

Out of the corner of his eye he saw his uncle studying a porcelain doll that sat in a glass jar, on a table in a corner of the family room. It was something his great-grandmother had brought from Poland and eventually given to her only granddaughter, a possession his mother had prized.

"He's going to take that doll," Josh blurted, and Hallie looked confused for a second, then followed his line of vision. "It's from Poland. It's really old."

"I'll get Lawrence to keep an eye on him. He's good at that sort of thing."

•

AT THE FUNERAL home, Josh and Hallie stood in front of the closed caskets. A line of people filed past the framed family pictures that Hallie and her friends had picked out for the display; they'd invited Josh to help, but he'd known he would lose it completely if he did. There was a picture of Josh's dad, looking happy and young, holding Hallie when she was a baby; Josh imagined her mother must have taken it. In a similar shot when Josh was the baby, Dad looked older, and his eyes held the sadness that Josh had come to know. Josh's favorite picture was one he'd taken that summer, his mom and dad sitting on the front porch. Hallie had it enlarged and framed, put it on an easel so it loomed behind the caskets.

The line of people just kept coming. Had they really all known his parents? Some of them Josh didn't even recognize. Hallie seemed to be doing a good job of talking to everyone. He was grateful she could do it because whenever he tried to open his mouth, nothing came out that made sense. Sometimes he could understand the things people said to him, but his brain couldn't formulate a response; other times, it sounded like they were speaking a foreign language, not a familiar one like French or Spanish but one he'd never heard, some tribal language, maybe, or something made-up like Klingon. People always compared times like this to nightmares, but the truth was he'd never had a nightmare this bad. He'd never been the kind of kid who had scary dreams or feared monsters in the dark. But nothing truly scary had happened to him until now.

During a brief visit before the wake, Nancy had told Josh to be brave. In his favorite books, the heroes and heroines often had awful childhoods, terrible things happening to them, things so much worse than Josh's life, even now. Oliver Twist was brave. So were Anne Frank and Joan of Arc, and they were real people. At least he wasn't doing hard labor for a bowl of gruel, or hiding in an attic from the Nazis, or hearing voices that told him he had to save France. He thought maybe he *could* be brave. But Josh hadn't known how to explain any of that to Nancy, so he'd said nothing.

Josh's teacher, Mrs. Wyckoff, had just left with her husband; Josh knew he must have talked to them, but he had no memory of it. Mr. Murdock and Mr. Cicirello and their wives were just a few people away from Josh and Hallie in the line. Josh was trying to figure out if there was a group of coherent words he could put together to say to them when he realized he had something much larger to worry about: Missy Dalton and her father had just walked in and joined the back of the line.

All of Josh's teachers and even Miss Piper had come, but up until then, few students. Malik Turner and Ray Watson, Josh's two best friends from grammar school, had been there earlier; it was nice of them to come, Josh thought, when they hadn't really hung out much since sixth grade. But Missy Dalton—this was different. Was it possible that she liked him? He'd never thought so before, but now, he had to wonder. Surely not as much as he liked her, but maybe just a little—he'd take any fraction she had to offer. Josh imagined leaving the viewing with Missy, finding an empty room in the funeral home, maybe, or taking her to the car. He could even take her to his home; no one was there to object except Emma the dog, and that parrot Josh hoped was still alive.

And then he remembered: his parents were dead, their bodies burned so badly that no one had even discussed the caskets being open, and here he was, thinking about making out with Missy Dalton. It was even worse than how he'd fantasized about Miss Piper on his way to the principal's office. At least then, he hadn't known what had happened; now he did, and there was a corner of his brain that could still imagine sex. There was something deeply, weirdly wrong with him that he could even think this.

Mr. Murdock and Mr. Cicirello clapped Josh on the back and said something to him; Josh had no idea if he replied or not, for he was working hard to formulate something he could say to Missy, preferably in English, preferably words that made sense together. As Missy and her father got closer in line, Josh caught Missy's eyes. She gave him a sad little smile—just the right kind of smile, not a happy smile but a smile that said, hi, I'm here, and I'm sorry this thing happened to you, and she was wearing a navy blue dress with little ties at the sleeves and her hair was long and brown and shiny and she looked so beautiful and so perfect that a soft "Oh" escaped Josh's lips. It wasn't loud, but Hallie heard him.

She touched his arm. "What?" she asked, but Josh couldn't quite speak. He saw Hallie follow his line of vision to Missy, and then she did one of those weird, psychic things that women sometimes did. His mother had done things like this, and Nancy, too. Hallie looked from him to Missy and back and he could tell she knew everything about it— his longing, and the miracle that Missy had actually come. He wondered if it was just a female thing, this sort of telepathy. He knew his father had never had it—his father didn't even register things you directly told him—and Ram didn't seem to be very psychic, either.

Hallie turned her back so that Missy couldn't see what she was doing, and she straightened Josh's tie, then reached up and pressed his cowlick down. She pried open his hand and took a wad of crumpled tissues out of it, placed them in the pocket of the skirt she was wearing.

"I'm glad we got you a nice suit," she whispered in his ear, and Josh realized in amazement: she doesn't think it's awful, that I'm thinking about Missy.

Now Dr. Dalton and Missy were in front of Hallie, Dr. Dalton introducing himself, telling Hallie that Missy goes to school with Josh. And then Missy was standing in front of him, looking somehow smaller than she looked in school, surrounded by her friends.

"Hi," she said to him.

"Hi," Josh said. They looked at each other for a second. Josh had no idea of what to say to her, and he was pretty sure that Missy had no idea what to say either. Then, unexpectedly, Missy stepped forward and put her arms around him. She was almost a foot shorter than he was, her head only coming up to his chest; he tried his best to slouch into her embrace. It was a short hug but a fierce one, that clean smell she had nearly making him dizzy, the feel of her thin arms around his body almost more than he could bear. When she stepped away from him, she said, "Your mom and dad were really nice. This just sucks."

It was the absolute best thing she could have said. She wasn't saying she was sorry, like everyone else did, which Josh thought was stupid; it wasn't like they were responsible. She wasn't trying to turn it into some kind of fairy tale where his parents would be floating on white clouds, playing harps or some such bullshit. She was just calling it as it was: that they'd been nice, they hadn't deserved to die, and it sucked, which it absolutely did.

Josh hoped Missy could read all this on his face when he said, "It does suck." He wished there was a way he could tell her that what she'd said was perfect, that everything about her was perfect. But he could only hope that Missy was a little psychic, that she could somehow know all the things he couldn't say to her.

"I made you something," she said, and pulled a CD case out of her purse. "It's just—well, it's a bunch of songs I thought you might like."

Josh took the disc from her, touching her fingers as her hand moved away. He looked at the front: "Death Cab For Cutie rarities," it said, written in purple and silver with the kind of glittery ink he associated with girls. Missy had also drawn an elaborate flower, a flower that somehow managed to look sad, and at the bottom she had written, "For Josh." She had spent actual time on this, Josh realized, put time into picking the songs and burning the disc and drawing the cover art. It might have taken her, like, an hour, a whole hour that she was thinking of him.

"I hope—" Missy said, and she looked uncertain for a second, even insecure, which she almost never seemed to be—"I know you like them, the band I mean, so I tried to pick out songs I thought you might not have. Like, live ones, and demos and stuff."

So she *had* noticed his t-shirt. "Thanks," he said.

"I wasn't sure if it was, I don't know, weird or something to make you a disc instead of giving you a card, but these songs make me feel better when I'm sad."

"It's way better than a card," Josh said, and Missy looked relieved. He wanted to say that it wasn't just better, that it was amazing; that he now had something to look forward to, going home and listening to songs Missy had picked out for him and staring at the flower she'd drawn and imagining her drawing it for him. It seemed so much better than the thought of going home, to a home without his parents, had seemed before. But he couldn't figure out how to say any of this to her, and the next thing he knew Missy's father was clapping him on the back like all the other men had, saying goodbye, and Missy was looking at him as her father led her away from Josh, out of his life for now, and not, Josh hoped, forever.

Other people came by after Missy left, people Josh knew, but he forgot them as soon as they were gone. Finally the line thinned out and Josh was hoping they could go home—he felt exhausted, he wanted to sleep—when he saw Cal Stutts in the back of the room.

Cal was wearing a suit that didn't fit him, the pants swallowing his legs and dragging on the floor. Josh wondered if he'd borrowed it—did Cal even have any friends?—or if he'd gone to the Salvation Army or something. Cal took a seat in the back and hung his head down, his eyes closed. His lips were moving. Was Cal praying? Josh looked at Ram, and

Ram nodded; he saw it, too.

Josh had hated Cal for years—because he'd threatened Nancy and hurt his own wife, because he often looked at Josh like he wanted to beat him up, and because of what he'd done to Emma. Josh's dad had always claimed that Cal wasn't as bad as everyone made him out to be, that he'd had a harder life than Josh could imagine, but Josh hadn't cared for excuses. All he'd had to do in the past for proof that Cal was evil was to look at the skinny dog tied next to his trailer. But Cal looked different now. He looked smaller in that big suit, less threatening; he looked like what he maybe actually was, a guy who was really poor, and who just didn't know how to treat people, or even dogs. It didn't excuse anything Cal had done, but Josh saw, for the first time, a bad person rather than a monster.

Hallie said "Excuse me a minute" to the people she was talking to, went and sat next to Cal. He opened his eyes and looked at her and they talked, both their heads down. There was no line anymore, just people scattered around, talking in little groups. Ram walked over and stood next to Josh, but neither of them said anything; they both just watched Hallie and Cal. Josh had no idea what he was doing as he left Ram's side and drifted to the back of the room, where he took the empty seat on the other side of Cal. Cal looked at him, his eyes narrowed, like he didn't know what to expect.

"Thanks for letting me keep the dog," Josh said. "And thanks for coming."

It might have been the first thing Josh said all night that made any kind of sense. Cal nodded to Josh, and looked down at the floor. But when Josh caught Hallie's eyes, she was looking at him in a new way, an expression on her face that he hadn't seen from her before, her eyes half-shut yet really taking him in. It was a way Josh's mother had looked at him many times—when he'd volunteered several of his Saturdays for the church's coat drive last winter, or when she found out how well he did on the SAT. Josh wondered if what he'd just said to Cal counted as the bravery Nancy had asked of him, though it felt less like courage and more like just figuring something out.

CHAPTER 8

It's like the Mad Hatter's tea party or some twist on the Village People, Hallie thought as she looked around the kitchen table in her childhood home: a famous pink-haired photographer, a soon-to-be-famous writer, an investment banker, a radical environmentalist, and an absurdly well-read high school senior. Rounding out the sextet was Hallie herself, the photographer without a career, the farmer's daughter formerly known as Holly. Even here in Oyster Shell Hallie felt, as she often did in New York, that she was the least interesting person at the table. She'd spent so much of her life wishing she were more—more beautiful, more talented, more like her mother. But self-pity seemed juvenile to her now, with Josh, a seventeen-year-old orphan, sitting across the table.

Hallie scooped a little more macaroni and cheese onto her plate, grateful that the casseroles and fruit baskets had finally started to arrive. She also put some on Josh's plate; she hoped this wasn't too motherly, but he hadn't been eating much, and he was so thin already. Josh didn't seem to notice the food. He'd changed into a sweatshirt and jeans after the funeral, and now had Albert perched on his arm. Emma was closed in Josh's bedroom with her dinner.

"This is cool," Josh said to Joy. "I've never held a parrot before."

"Pet him," Joy said. "Pet his head and tell him he's a pretty boy."

"Pretty boy," Albert repeated. Josh smiled and stroked Albert's head lightly with his index finger.

"He's an African gray, right?" Ram asked Joy, and she nodded.

"How did you get him?" Hallie saw Josh shoot Ram a look.

"Hatched from the egg," Joy said. "From a breeder."

Ram was silent, but his shoulders were rigid, his eyes steely.

"There's a whole room at Joy's place that she turned into an aviary," Hallie said, hoping to break the tension. "They have a pretty cushy life."

"But they're not wild," Ram said. Josh shot him another look, and Ram's face softened a little. "I'm sorry," he said. "It's none of my business."

"I understand where you're coming from," Joy said. "When I first got Albert and a few of the others, I didn't think much about it. Now the only new birds I get are rescues."

"Rescues?" Josh asked. The boy had a way with animals, Hallie could see. Not only did Emma look at him like a moony-eyed teenager, Albert appeared to have fallen asleep in the crook of Josh's elbow. She'd worked with him for years, but Albert had never relaxed that much with Hallie.

"It's a lot of work to take care of birds. People buy them on a whim, and when it gets to be too much, they don't want them anymore." Joy looked at Hallie. "Remember what Maya looked like when I first got her?"

Hallie nodded. "Her feathers were like ratty fringe."

"And now, she's the Heidi Klum of my aviary!"

"Could I come and watch you guys work sometime?" Josh asked, but as soon as the words left his mouth, he hunched his shoulders and squirmed in his seat. "I mean, I don't know when you're going back to work, Hallie, just sometime, whenever." He focused his eyes on Albert, stroking the bird's head again.

Hallie felt an anxious flutter in her gut. She was losing any hope she'd had of Nancy helping out with Josh; Nancy was seventy-four years old, and taking the deaths hard—she'd skipped the wake, and Ram had driven her home right after the funeral. If Hallie couldn't get back to work in New York soon, she had no way to support herself and Josh. Her father had died with barely enough in the bank to cover the funerals, and she'd already had a disturbing conversation with his insurance agent about possible lawsuits from the accident. She could easily lose the house and the farm and be left with nothing but a huge bill for Josh's college tuition. Hallie rubbed her temples as she felt the beginnings of a headache.

"Anyone who Albert likes this much," Joy said to Josh, "is welcome in my studio anytime."

There was a knock on the front door, and Joy got up. "That must be my driver," she said. "Josh, would you help me get Albert back in his cage?"

Josh got the bird into his cage without effort, and Joy picked up her overnight bag. Hallie walked with the two of them to the door.

"Call me when you have an idea of when you'll be back," Joy

whispered to Hallie on her way out the door. To Josh, she said, "I'll see you in Soho."

After the car drove away, Josh ran up the stairs. Seconds later, he reappeared with Emma on her leash.

"I'll take a walk with you," Ram said, following Josh and Emma out back.

Once they were gone, Lawrence looked at Hallie. "We're *dying*," he said. "What's the deal with the hottie?" He nodded his head toward the back door.

"Ram? I told you. I went to high school with him."

"You went to high school with a lot of people," Lawrence said, "and none of them are hanging out at your house every day." He took a sip of coffee. "And I'll best most of them aren't as sexy."

Hallie shook her head and laughed a little. "He moved back here a couple of years ago to start some environmental group. He's friends with Josh."

"Ram told me he's completely vegan," Kenneth said. "He doesn't even wear leather shoes."

"Isn't there a vegetarian shoe store in Soho somewhere? You should take him there after the two of you start fucking," Lawrence said.

Hallie rolled her eyes. "I don't think he's really my type. Did you see the way he looked at the Queen of Sheepa when I put it on last night?" Lawrence had bought the butter-soft sheepskin jacket for her in Italy the previous fall.

"He looked at it like he saw little murdered lambs," Lawrence said. "Who cares? Just take him to bed and don't wear the jacket around him." They all watched through the window as Josh and Ram walked under the floodlight behind the house.

"*Ram*. It's like a porn star name," Lawrence added.

Kenneth shook his head. "You're terrible," he said, but his eyes smiled.

Hallie knew that Lawrence was trying to take her mind off things, but she couldn't play along. "That's not where my head is right now," she said. "I need to talk to you."

"I know," Lawrence said as the back door opened. He dropped his voice to a whisper. "Don't worry, we'll figure it all out."

•

HOURS LATER, RAM gone home, Josh in bed for long enough that Hallie thought he had to be asleep, she carried a bottle of Jim Beam—her father's—and a cup of coffee into the family room. Hallie stretched out on the couch while Lawrence, his own cup of coffee in hand, eased into her father's ratty brown tweed recliner.

"I've always thought these chairs were hideous," Lawrence said, "but I have to admit, this is really comfortable."

"Is it? I don't think I've ever sat in it."

"Why not?" Lawrence sipped from his cup, then placed it on an end table.

Hallie poured a generous dose of whiskey into her coffee, passed the bottle over to Lawrence. "It's Dad's chair. Nobody else ever sat in it."

"Interesting." He added a shot to his cup.

Hallie drank a large gulp, grabbed the bottle, and poured more liquor in. "So," she said, lowering her voice. "What the hell am I going to do?"

Lawrence nodded. "I've been thinking about it."

"And?"

"Boarding school. I could help with the tuition."

Hallie sighed. Boarding school would be an easy out for her. She took a long sip of coffee; it tasted like straight whiskey. "His parents just died. I can't ship him off."

Lawrence sat up a little in the lounge chair. "Well, that was my big solution," he said. "What are you thinking?"

"Maybe I can bring him to New York."

Lawrence snorted. "You're joking, right?"

"I know there would be a lot to figure out," Hallie said, "but no, I'm not."

"And what are you going to do? Enroll him in P.S. I've Got a Gun in My Locker?"

"Well, you were willing to spring for private school a minute ago," she said. But she had trouble picturing Josh in high school in New York, even if she did have the money for a school that wouldn't be dangerous.

Lawrence was quiet for a moment. "Look, I'll help you out if that's what you really want to do. But I don't see him being any happier at, say, Dalton, than he'd be at a boarding school." He took another sip of his coffee. "And where would he even sleep? Your apartment's not big enough for two."

"I know. I'd have to find a bigger place."

"You *do* know how much a two-bedroom would cost? At market value?"

Hallie sighed. "I do, yes," she said. Her rent was half what Lawrence could get from a stranger for the same apartment.

"It's a huge responsibility," he said. "Raising a kid."

The headache that had been threatening her all day with short pulses at the sides of her skull now began to really pound. "You think I don't know that?" Her voice sounded louder, more angry than she'd intended. "I'm already stuck with it. I'm responsible whether I want to be or not."

"Don't get mad at me. I'm trying to help."

"I know," she said. "I'm sorry." But what really bothered Hallie was his lack of confidence. He didn't think she was capable of raising Josh; he didn't think she was capable of anything, really. Ever since her father had cut her off in college, Lawrence had treated her like Poor Hallie, the girl her father no longer wanted. She was tired of being Poor Hallie. And she would not allow Josh to become Poor Josh, the boy his sister refused to take care of.

"What about Nancy?" Lawrence asked. "Is she ill?"

Hallie shrugged, and took another sip of the whiskey-laden coffee. "She's old, Lawrence. I'm afraid she might be too old."

Hallie heard a yip from Emma, and the front door slammed shut. Josh? She looked at Lawrence, and they both got up. Through the front window she saw her brother, walking down the road with Emma on her leash.

Hallie followed. "Josh, wait," she called out. Emma looked back and wagged her tail, but Josh quickened his pace.

"Slow down," Hallie called. He continued walking, but not as quickly. She caught up as he took a right, towards the lower bay.

"Come back home," Hallie said. There was a chill in the air, and she shivered in the thin cotton crew neck she'd changed into after the funeral.

"I'm not running away, if that's what you think," he said, still moving deliberately down the road. "I'm going for a walk." She caught a glimpse of his face in the moonlight, but couldn't read his expression. "I do this all the time."

"Go for walks in the middle of the night?"

"Yeah. Sometimes when I can't sleep, or just have to get out of the house. Mom and Dad sleep like rocks. They never know." Hallie waited for him to correct the tense, but he didn't, this time.

"Where do you go?"

"You'll see. Unless you want to go back. I don't care either way."

The moon was nearly full, and bright. Josh looked older than he had just four nights ago, the night she'd arrived. More complicated. When his skin clears up, when his face matures a little, he's going to break hearts, Hallie thought—she could see, in the moonlight, the man he would turn into.

They walked for ten minutes or so without saying anything, Hallie rubbing her hands on her upper arms, wishing she'd thrown the Queen of Sheepa over her shoulders. Josh glanced at her a few times, then unzipped his sweatshirt. Underneath it he was wearing a t-shirt with a cartoon drawing of William Shakespeare.

"Here," he grumbled, tossing the sweatshirt at her.

"Thanks." They arrived at a structure Hallie had never seen before, a simple boardwalk stretching out over the marshes. It looked endless in the dim moonlight.

"Don't thank me. I hate you. I used to think you were so cool, but you're not."

"Tell me what you heard that makes you hate me," she said. "Because I really think you didn't hear everything."

Emma stalled at the first wooden plank and made a whimpering sound. "Come on, girl," Josh said, running a little, and the dog obeyed. Hallie trotted to keep up with them. She could smell the briny bay and hear the water lapping.

"I never knew this was here," Hallie said, grasping the railing. "When was it built?"

Josh didn't answer.

Finally they came to a wider stretch of boardwalk; Hallie made out a concrete slab of bench in the dim light. She sat down, hoping Josh would do the same.

"You're probably sitting in bird shit," he said. She looked down and squinted in the darkness, bringing into focus the white streaks all over the bench.

"Too late."

Josh stared in the distance for a minute, then sat on the bench himself, as far away from her as he could get. Emma scrambled up and flopped between them.

They just sat there for a few minutes, looking out at the bay, and then Hallie turned her face up toward the sky. Her mother had known all the constellations, had a book they would take outside on nights like this one. Hallie had forgotten it since moving to New York. She'd forgotten there were stars at all.

"Do you know any of the constellations?" she asked Josh, and he nodded.

"I used to look at them with my mom," she added.

Josh rubbed his hand absently over Emma's back. "I have a book of your mom's," he said. "*Howl*. The Allen Ginsburg poem?" He fiddled with the dog's collar. "She wrote stuff in the margins."

"Really?"

"Yeah. I found it in the attic. I'll give it to you when I'm done."

"Okay."

"I'll mail it to you."

"You'll mail it to me?"

"From my boarding school." His voice dripped with sarcasm, which she knew was teenage for pain.

"I guess you didn't stick around for the part where I said I wouldn't do that. Send you to boarding school."

He looked at her, the expression in his eyes a tangle of questions and pleas. "So…what's going to happen?"

"Well, I guess I'm going to stay here for a while." *For a few weeks until I figure out a better solution.* But even as she thought it she felt her life in New York slipping away from her like a cast-off skin, something the gulls might fight over as it floated on the surface of the bay.

"For how long?" he asked, his voice cracking. "I just really need to know. Are you going to stay here until I graduate? Am I moving in with Nancy or Ram? Am I moving to New York?" He pulled a tissue from his jeans pocket, wiped his nose with it. "I think I have a right to know."

The sadness that swept through her just then was so sudden and unexpected that she felt hot tears form in her eyes before she had time to stop them. She realized, with some surprise, that she wasn't crying for herself; she was crying for Josh. She had let this poor kid go for four days with no idea what his future was. He deserved better.

"I don't have any tissues left that I haven't used," he said.

"That's okay." Hallie wiped her face with the sleeve of his sweatshirt. She looked at Josh and realized what she needed to know, the question she should have asked days ago.

"What do you want?" she asked. "I mean, of all the possibilities you mentioned. If you could pick, which one would you want?"

Josh looked away from her, back out at the bay. His arm was around Emma's neck, his fingers rubbing inside the dog's collar.

"I want you to stay," he said quietly, still looking out at the water.

Hallie looked up at the sky. She saw the Big Dipper clearly, always the easiest find. What else should be up there at this time of year? Pegasus? Orion? She had forgotten so much about Oyster Shell. She had even forgotten the things she'd wanted to remember.

"I'll stay," she said, but her voice lacked conviction.

"Until you find someone else to do it," he said. "Then you're gonna take off." He didn't even sound angry, really, just resigned. That was the part that did her in.

She got up and stood in front of him, then crouched so they were eye-to-eye. She didn't know how she would support him, exactly, but everything in New York—running Joy's studio, her own stalled work, the three-martini nights with Alison, the galleries and fancy fundraisers with Lawrence and Kenneth—felt remote and ill-defined, as if it were all an elaborate dream she'd once had. She wanted to believe it would all be there in a year, but she didn't think it would be. That life was already gone.

"I'm staying," she said, and she looked him hard in the eyes, so he'd know she meant it. "Until you graduate."

Josh walked over to the railing, pulled a penny from his jeans pocket and tossed it into the water. She stood next to him.

"It's not so bad here," he said.

Hallie had spent most of her life hating Oyster Shell, taking her first opportunity to escape it and then, later, doing everything she could to dodge its pull. But just then, surrounded by water, the sky full of stars, her brother by her side, it didn't seem like the worst place in the world, even if it had swallowed her old life whole. Tomorrow morning, a week or a month from now, she might go back to hating Oyster Shell, but just then, she didn't.

"It's not," she said. She slipped her arm around Josh. He didn't pull away.

PART II

CHAPTER 9

When he heard the car, Josh was sitting up in bed, flipping through his index cards. He hadn't scribbled down a thought since that morning after his parents died, and, shuffling through the cards now, they seemed meaningless, these sentences and phrases he'd once felt were worthy of saving.

Emma barked twice. Josh figured it was Ram outside, dropping Hallie off; he was glad he hadn't had to drive her around today. Josh felt nervous around Hallie, afraid she'd change her mind and leave. He had an image in his head of the perfect stoic orphan he could be, if only he were less emotional, and he'd been trying to act the part.

He got up and looked out the window; in his driveway, standing next to a car he didn't recognize, was Nicki Kepler. She had blue streaks in her messy-looking black hair and a stack of books and notebooks in her arms. Nicki disappeared from his view, and a few seconds later he heard the knock on the door.

It had been eight days since that afternoon he'd found out his parents were dead, and Josh didn't know what to say to Nicki Kepler. He didn't want to talk to anyone from school, not even Missy Dalton. Nicki knocked again. He glanced in the mirror above his bureau—the sweatpants and C.Y.O. t-shirt he was wearing looked okay, at least not too grimy—and he went downstairs, the dog trailing behind.

Nicki smiled when he opened the door. She looked prettier when she smiled, Josh thought—she usually looked so serious.

"Hi," he said.

"Hey," Nicki said. "I called earlier, but no one answered, so I figured I'd just come. I hope that's okay. A few of us got all your assignments and everything together." She shifted the weight of the books in her arms.

"Um, sure," he said, taking the stack from her. "I mean, thanks.

Come on in."

"Cool house," Nicki said as she followed him into the kitchen, where he set the books and papers on the table. "Is it really old?"

"Yeah," Josh said. "It was built in, like, 1880 or something." Josh knew the house had been built by a Corson in 1882. There was a historical society plaque somewhere that his dad had refused to display.

"I've never really been out here before," she said. "To the bay, I mean. It's pretty."

"Yeah," Josh said. He didn't know what else to say. It felt weird to have Nicki Kepler in his house.

Nicki had moved to Floyd at the beginning of their sophomore year—with her mom, from Brooklyn, after her parents' divorce—and she'd never fit in at their high school. Josh didn't either, but the way he didn't fit was different from the way Nicki didn't fit. He'd never really found a group to hang out with, but a lot of people said hi to him in the halls, and he operated under the mean kids' radar. Nicki was the kind of girl who drew attention to herself, with crazy colors in her hair and the political t-shirts and flyers and her accent, a New York accent like you'd hear in a Scorcese movie.

"Do you want a soda or something?" Josh asked.

"Sure."

He pulled a bottle of Sprite from the fridge, grabbed a couple of glasses from the cabinet. Nicki sat down at the kitchen table as he poured.

"Not everything I brought is school work," she said. "There's other stuff."

"Like what?" The stack of books looked daunting to Josh. On top of everything else, he was supposed to make up the work he'd missed because his parents died? Part of him wished he could drop out, finish high school next year. But Hallie would never stay in Oyster Shell if he weren't in school.

"Well, there's a big card a lot of kids signed." Nicki pulled it from the stack. It was handmade, as big as a magazine. There was a drawing on the front in charcoal, of the bay, with shorebirds and clouds in the sky.

"Missy Dalton made it," Nicki said, "and passed it around in a bunch of your classes. Some of the jocks even signed it."

Josh opened the card and looked at all the signatures. It was weird, that all these popular kids had signed their names. It was like his parents' deaths had made him some kind of celebrity.

"I copied all my French and English notes for you," Nicki added. She took a sip of her soda. "There's a book in there from me, too. Just something to read."

Josh sorted through the stack. "*The Autobiography of Malcolm X*?" It was very Nicki.

"Yeah," she said. "I read it this summer. It's really empowering."

"Thanks." He paged through the book and a sheet of paper fell out. It was one of Ram's flyers for the Mollusk Creek Trust.

"Where did you get this?" he asked, holding up the flyer.

"There was a stack of them at the Floyd Library. I was thinking of checking out the next meeting, and since it's in your town I thought you might be interested." She took another sip of soda. "It's awful, about those frogs."

"I belong to this group," Josh said.

"Really?"

"Yeah, the guy who runs it is a friend of mine. I think you'd like him."

"Cool. I'll definitely check it out." Nicki ran two fingers along the rim of her glass. She was quiet for a minute, then looked at him intensely. "Josh," she said, "I just…I wanted to tell you I'm sorry I didn't go to the funeral."

Josh was surprised she felt she had to apologize for it. "I didn't expect you to."

"I know. I mean, we don't really hang out together that much, just a little in school, but…" She looked like she was about to say something and stopped herself. "I wanted to go, but I wasn't sure if you'd want kids from school there. I finally decided I shouldn't go. But then I heard Missy went, and I felt stupid."

"You shouldn't feel stupid."

"It's not that I didn't care. I just didn't know what to do."

"Sure, whatever," Josh said. It was starting, that feeling like he wanted to throw up and then go to his room and cry. He had to get them on another topic of conversation. "So what's going on in school?"

Nicki was quiet for a moment. "We have a foreign exchange student," she said. "Her name's Monika. With a 'k.' She's German."

"That's cool."

"I feel bad for her. Poor girl comes all the way from Germany and ends up in *Floyd*." She said it like Floyd was one of Dante's circles of hell.

"It's not such a bad place," Josh said.

Nicki was quiet for a moment. "I go to my dad's in Brooklyn every other weekend, and every other Sunday night on the ride back, I try to tell myself that."

Just then Josh heard the front door open, and he relaxed in his seat. Finally, Hallie was home.

"You should have seen me," Hallie said to Josh as she entered the kitchen, two takeout bags in her hands. "After we came back from Floyd, I talked Ram into letting me drive his truck out to the creek. And I didn't hit anything!" Where had she brought dinner from this time? Josh wondered if Hallie was ever going to actually cook.

"Hi," she said to Nicki as she put the bags on the counter. "I'm Hallie."

"Nicki. I just came over to bring Josh some stuff from school."

"Is that a New York accent? I live in the West Village." Hallie quickly corrected herself: "Lived."

"Brooklyn," Nicki said. "And we lived in Queens when I was little."

"I lived in Queens for years," Hallie said. "After college." She took off her jacket and flung it over a chair. Josh tried not to picture the sheep that had died. "How did you end up here?"

"Divorce. My mom thought moving to the middle of nowhere would be good for her midlife crisis."

"Yikes," Hallie said.

Nicki looked from Hallie to Josh. "So did you move back here?" she asked Hallie.

"Yes," Hallie said. "For the next year." She said it with certainty. So why did Josh still feel the plan was tentative, that it could change if he said or did the wrong thing?

"I got you some Buddhist's Delight again," Hallie said to Josh. "But I can make something if you don't feel like it." She said the last part without much confidence, and Josh realized: maybe she doesn't know *how* to cook.

"No, Chinese sounds good," Josh said, though he doubted he could eat anything.

But then Hallie looked at Nicki. "Do you want to stay for dinner with us?" she asked. "I have a ton of food here."

Josh threw Hallie a sharp look. Not only had he run out of things to say to Nicki, but his life was so weird now. They didn't eat normal meals. They didn't even eat at the kitchen table; a few nights ago they'd decided to rent all seven seasons of *Buffy the Vampire Slayer*, and they'd taken to watching it during dinner, and after. Two or three episodes a night. Josh found it weirdly comforting, watching a pretty girl save the world over and over again, yet he couldn't possibly explain any of this to Nicki.

Nicki glanced at Josh, then at Hallie. "I should probably go."

Josh was afraid she had seen the look on his face. "You can stay, if you want."

"Nah, my mom's expecting me home soon. But maybe another time?"

"Sure." Josh followed her as she headed to the door.

"Do you know when you're coming back to school?" Nicki asked when they were on the front porch.

"I'm not sure. Probably some time next week." He wished the answer was never.

She nodded. "Well, I guess I'll see you then." Her head was down and she shuffled her feet as she headed to the car. Josh could see he'd hurt her feelings.

"Nicki," he said.

"Yeah?" She was at the car door now.

"It was really nice of you to drive all the way out here. I'm sorry if I acted, I don't know, weird. I'm just still kinda freaked out."

She looked at him for a moment, and then she ran over to him and hugged him. The way she lunged, he thought she might knock him over. She hugged him hard. Nicki wasn't fat, exactly, but she wasn't tiny like Missy. She had big breasts and he could feel them as she hugged him. Nicki didn't have that nice smell Missy had, and her hair wasn't as shiny. She hung onto him for long enough that it started to feel weird, but Josh didn't know how to get her to stop without hurting her feelings again, so he just stood there. Finally she pulled away.

"Okay, I have to go," she said, her eyes bleary and wild-looking. "I'll see you next week." She almost ran to the car, and was inside it before he could answer.

Josh watched her car until it disappeared down the road, and then he went back in the house. Hallie was waiting in the front hallway.

"I'm sorry!" she said. "I shouldn't have just invited her like that."

"It's okay."

"Is she someone you can't stand?" Hallie walked with him to the kitchen.

"No, Nicki's alright. I just didn't feel like having to talk to her for a long time."

Hallie nodded. "You didn't know she was coming over?"

"No, she just stopped by."

Hallie pulled two dinner plates out of the cabinet. "She lives in Floyd?"

"Yeah." Josh got a bowl out so he could feed Emma.

"Hmmm." Hallie spooned some rice on both plates.

"What?" He tried to hold his breath as he scooped the dog food from the can.

"Well, I don't think she would drive all this way for just *any* guy."

Josh put the bowl down on the floor, and Emma ran over, inhaling its contents.

"What do you mean?" he asked.

"I mean, I think she likes you."

"*Likes* me, likes me?" It had never before occurred to Josh that Nicki might like him.

Hallie smiled. "Yeah."

"I don't think so," Josh said.

Hallie didn't say anything; she spooned some of the Buddhist's Delight—too much, Josh thought—over both plates of rice.

"You really think she likes me?" Josh leaned against the counter. "Oh man. I feel sick."

Hallie touched his arm. "Don't feel sick. It's nice to have someone like you."

"But I don't like her. I mean, she's nice, but I don't like her that way."

Josh took his plate into the family room, set it on the coffee table, and put in the Buffy disc. Hallie brought her food in and they both sat on the couch, avoiding Dad's recliner. Josh imagined Hallie felt as weird about sitting in it as he did.

•

"Is THAT ALL you're eating?" Hallie asked about halfway through the first episode. Josh looked down and realized he'd hardly touched his food.

"I feel kinda sick."

"Should I take you to the doctor tomorrow?"

"No." He was hoping to drop it there, but she gave him one of those super-concerned looks. "I feel sick when I'm nervous."

"What are you nervous about?" she asked. "I mean, besides the obvious."

Josh thought a minute. Should he say it? "I'm freaked about going back to school."

Hallie looked at him. "You don't have to go back right away."

"No?"

She shook her head. "I mean, eventually, but if you want to spend another week at home, that's fine by me."

"Really?" Josh felt a little bit better, for the first time all day.

"Sure. I'll call your principal."

Josh was so grateful that he was afraid he was going to cry. He felt the tears starting, and headed off to the bathroom. Hallie started to follow him.

"Don't," he said, but it came out meaner than he'd intended, and she looked at him like she was a little hurt, kind of the way Nicki had. "I just need a couple of minutes. Please?" Hallie nodded like she got it, and Josh ran to the bathroom, where he blasted the water full force.

EMMA WAS WAITING outside the bathroom door when he was finished, with the same worried look on her face that Hallie sometimes got. It had never before occurred to Josh that a dog could worry, but then he thought of everything Emma had been through. Of course she could worry. She probably worried all the time about going back to Cal. Josh sat on the floor and hugged her; she smelled better since the bath he and Ram had given her.

Hallie was at the kitchen table, with a legal pad and a calculator and his dad's ledger books from the farm.

"What are you doing?" Josh asked.

"Oh, just trying to figure some stuff out." She turned the calculator off and closed the ledger book.

"Are we, like, really poor?" Josh had no idea how much money the farm made, but he knew it couldn't have been doing so well—his mother had taken a job in the cafeteria at Pearl Township Elementary School last year.

"No." She said it like she wanted him to stop asking questions, but he felt like he should know. If they had no money, he should know. Josh sat down at the table.

"Tell me," he said, and he was surprised by how grown-up his voice sounded.

Hallie searched his face. "The money that was in the bank only covered the funerals," she finally said. "I'm trying to figure out if I should make a deal with Cal to run the farm, or if I should sell it." She rubbed her forehead. "He's been going there every day and watering the plants. I haven't even been to the farm since that day last week we all went down. I need to get on top of this."

Josh thought it over for a moment. "There's a lot more that needs to be done besides watering," he said. "I don't think Cal has any idea of all the stuff Dad used to do." It was true, but it wasn't the only reason Josh thought having Cal involved was a bad idea.

"I know. I want to give him a chance, though. Cal has never had too many breaks."

"Dad used to say stuff like that, too."

"Really? That could be the first thing we ever agreed on." Hallie got up and poured herself a glass of wine. "I could work for Joy on the weekends sometimes, but that won't be enough money, even if Cal can turn a profit at the farm. I'm going to have to get a job here."

Josh nodded. First she needed to relearn how to drive. All the stuff he'd been worrying about—going back to school and facing the kids, and Missy and Nicki—seemed stupid now.

"You want to watch Buffy?" he asked, not knowing what else to say, and Hallie nodded, and they went back into the family room. As Buffy was kicking yet another vampire's ass, Josh remembered something his mother had once told him.

"The attic," he said, and bounded up the staircase to the second floor, down the hall to the attic stairs, Hallie and Emma following. "Mom said Dad used to hide money up here," he called over his shoulder as he climbed the narrow staircase.

Josh groped around in the dark until he felt the switch cord, and pulled it. The room was bathed in soft yellow light. He looked around at all the boxes, the broken chairs and lamps, and wondered where to begin.

"This might be an antique," Hallie said, motioning toward a low wooden table. "We should go through all this stuff sometime."

Josh knew the table was very old, but he had no idea if it was an antique or not. "If you were Dad, where would you hide money up here?"

Hallie shrugged, tapped at the keys of an old electric typewriter. "I wrote all my high school papers on this."

Josh looked at the typewriter. "You didn't have a computer?"

"Nobody had computers yet," she said. "At least, nobody at Floyd High." She glanced around the attic. "Where did you find that book of my mom's, anyway?"

"Oh," Josh said, and he walked over to a battered chest of drawers, partially collapsed against one wall of the attic.

"My mom had this in her studio," Hallie said. "She kept painting supplies in it."

"Where was her studio?"

"Your room, actually."

There was something kind of thrilling about knowing that he slept in the same room where the beautiful Jenny used to paint. "The bottom two drawers are full of paint and brushes and stuff. But the top drawer is where I found the book." Josh carefully pulled it open, afraid the drawer would fall apart in his hands, and stepped aside so Hallie could see. There were books on painting—Van Gogh, Vuillard—and two novels, *The Awakening* and *Madame Bovary*. Josh had already read *Madame Bovary*; he was planning to start *The Awakening* next. Hallie pushed the books aside and uncovered two sketch pads, a bulging manila folder beneath them; under that, a portfolio made of laminated paper.

She opened the manila folder. On top was Holly Corson's fall report card from sixth grade at Pearl Township Elementary. December, 1980. All As.

"The last one she saw," Hallie said. She set the folder on the floor and opened the portfolio. Josh looked around for the small metal box he'd once seen his dad hide money in, though now that he was up in the attic, he was feeling less certain about the whole thing.

He opened drawers in other banged-up pieces of furniture, looked in cobwebby corners, but no metal box turned up. Josh even looked in the big cardboard box where Dad kept his porn—the box was marked "farm equipment," like that would keep Josh out—the magazines underneath a piece of plywood topped off with some old sprockets and gears, all of which Josh had always carefully replaced each time he looked at the pictures. Now Josh dug underneath the old copies of *Playboy* and *Hustler*, but there was nothing else in there. He glanced over at Hallie; she was still sorting through whatever was in the portfolio. Josh put the box back together, walked over and looked at what was in her hands. Photos. There were hundreds of them: sunsets by the bay, bowls of fruit, Hallie when she was about five, a boxer dog that he assumed was Candy.

"Mom used to take photos first and then work from them," Hallie said. "I have a lot of the paintings that came from these."

"You have her paintings?" Josh asked.

"Sure. Most of them are hanging in my apartment. Nancy has a few, too."

"She does?"

"That painting in her living room, of the horse? Mom did that. It's Zeus, the first horse Nancy had."

"Wow." Josh had looked at the painting a million times, but it never occurred to him that Jenny was the artist.

"They used to hang all over this house, but Dad took them down after she died."

Josh sat down next to Hallie and reached into the portfolio, came up with an envelope that said "Spring/Summer, 1980." He opened it, expecting to see the kind of pictures Hallie was sorting through, but he saw something else entirely. These photos were of the dead: dead flowers in a vase, rotted fruit in a bowl, a dead sparrow lying in a bush, a possum by the side of the road. She'd taken many shots of the possum, apparently over time; it was more decomposed in each photo. Josh was so repulsed that he dropped the pictures.

"What?" Hallie asked, and she leaned over and picked up a few of the photos. "Wow, Mom was changing direction."

Josh didn't know how to respond—he was still horrified by the images of the rotting possum—and Hallie looked at him. "She didn't kill it, Josh. She just took a picture of a dead animal by the side of the road."

"I know," Josh said, but he was thinking: how does a person go from painting sunsets on the bay to roadkill?

"This must have been the last thing she was working on," Hallie said.

Josh was very glad that Jenny hadn't done paintings of the things in the photos.

"You look upset," she added.

"No, it just surprised me," he said, but in truth, he *was* repulsed. He'd always thought he had an idea of who Jenny was—a little kooky, maybe, a little adventurous, but very sweet and kind. She'd looked kind in pictures, nicer than girls that pretty usually were, Missy Dalton-nice. But these photos made him think he didn't know Jenny at all.

"In my art classes in college, I saw people try much more disturbing things than this. There was a guy who did a self-portrait using only his own shit, pee and blood."

Josh narrowed his eyes at her. "Please tell me you're kidding."

"I wish. That painting stunk up the whole art department."

Josh smiled a little, but he was thinking: painting with your own shit is stupid, but it's not nearly as creepy as studying a decomposing body.

"Really. Artists try all kinds of things. I'm sure she was just experimenting." Hallie reached out and chucked him in the arm. "She would never have killed an animal for a painting, if that's what's worrying you. She loved animals."

What bothered him was the darkness that must have been in Jenny, some powerful compulsion to know and understand the reality of death. Had Jenny known she was dying? He still had no idea what had happened to her. "Was your mom…did she have cancer or something? Nobody ever told me how she died."

Hallie shook her head. "It was an accident. In the garage."

"The garage?"

"The tool shed." Hallie drew her legs up closer to her body. "Dad stopped putting cars in there after she died."

"Oh." Josh hoped she would go on so he wouldn't have to ask. But she had that faraway look, so he posed the question in a soft voice: "What happened?"

"She was heating her car up and the garage door slammed shut and jammed. She was overcome by the fumes before she could get it back open." Her voice was weirdly detached, like she was reciting something she'd memorized.

Josh tried to imagine it. Heating the car up, the door slamming shut. He pictured the tool shed. There was a small window on the back wall, behind a metal shelving unit. All Jenny had to do was turn the car off or open that window. It couldn't have been an accident.

"How old were you?" he asked.

"Eleven." Hallie hugged her knees.

Does she know? Josh wondered. He could imagine believing that story at eleven, but how could she believe it now? "Do you—"

"I'm gonna take all this stuff downstairs so it doesn't get ruined," Hallie said. Josh picked up the dead possum photos that were still on the floor, glanced at the top one, then slid them all into an envelope. Jenny *was* dying, he realized. Before his parents' accident Josh had never understood how people could commit suicide, why they'd want to die; but after saying good night to his mom and dad nine nights ago and then never seeing them again, he had less trouble imagining that kind of despair. There were times he wished he had been in the truck, times he wished he'd died with his parents.

There was something childlike about the way Hallie gathered her mother's things and held them in her arms, and it cut through Josh. His parents hadn't chosen to leave him. Her mother had. For the first time ever, Josh felt sorry for Hallie.

"I don't think there's any money up here," he said.

Hallie got up and headed down the attic stairs, one arm curled around the folders and portfolio and envelopes. She could not take care of him, Josh realized; from this point on he would have to take care of himself. He might even have to take care of her. And suddenly the last eight days seemed almost like a vacation, the way he'd wallowed in his own orphanhood, the sadness and loss and fear all blunted by shock. Of this he was certain: the days ahead would be much worse than the ones he'd been through so far.

CHAPTER 10

Hallie walked past the rows of basil plants, their aroma overpowering the scent of the cup of coffee in her hand. The plants didn't appear to be doing badly; perhaps they weren't as perky as the last time she'd seen them, but they smelled as good as the fresh herbs at the Union Square Greenmarket. She touched the soil in several of the pots, as her father used to. But she couldn't remember if the herbs were supposed to be kept moist, or on the dry side.

"Do you think these are too dry?" she asked Cal, catching up with him near the cilantro.

"I'm doing it just how your Daddy did it," Cal said.

She wanted to believe that Cal could run the farm. The herbs looked just about ready to sell, and the other hothouse was full of tomato plants, the fruit still tiny and green. At least she could get some money for this crop, she thought, and buy herself some time to figure out what to do.

Hallie left the greenhouse, motioning Cal to follow her to her father's small office. They both sat down at the battered wooden desk, piled with seed and fertilizer invoices, a Rolodex bulging with the phone numbers of restaurants and farm markets and the state agricultural extension service, a Jersey Fresh coffee mug with a thin film of mold atop a quarter-inch of liquid. Was it the last cup he had? She started to picture her father at his desk, sipping coffee in the pitch dark of the early morning, then stopped herself.

"So I think those herbs are all ready to be sold," Hallie said. "Don't you?"

"Sure," Cal said.

"Do you know where Dad usually sold them?"

Cal was quiet for a moment. "A truck come here a lot. Your dad said it was some shi-shi place up north. Wellington Farms, I think."

Hallie flipped through the Rolodex. "Wellingford Farms?"

"That's the place." Cal coughed a little and shifted in his seat.

Hallie sat back for a moment, wondering how exactly to work this. "Cal, I'll tell you what. I'll call these people and schedule a pickup. If you can get all the herbs packed up and ready to go, I'll split with you whatever we make. How does that sound?" She had no idea if it was a fair wage for Cal, or, for that matter, fair to her. But it was simple, and right now, simple was all she could handle.

Cal's face brightened. "Sure thing. You just tell me when they're a coming."

Before Hallie could respond, her phone rang. It was Nancy.

"I'll come find you after I've scheduled that pickup," Hallie said to Cal as she answered. "Hi, Nancy."

Cal hesitated for a moment, then left the office.

"Who was that?" Nancy asked.

"Cal. He's here at the farm with me. We're trying to sort everything out."

"Don't let him get too involved," Nancy said.

Hallie didn't answer. Everyone in Oyster Shell seemed adamant that she not allow Cal to work the farm, and they all felt free to offer up their opinions; even Todd Schwegel had stopped at the farm that morning to "check up on things." She supposed they all meant well, yet none of them would go so far as to help Hallie with the farm themselves. They just wanted to tell her what not to do.

"So what's up?" Hallie asked. She pulled a pad from her purse and jotted a note to herself: *Look up growing conditions herbs.*

"I have a lead on a photography job for you."

"Really?" Hallie put down her pen. "What kind of job?"

"At a newspaper."

Nancy's career as a reporter had seemed glamorous to Hallie when she was a child. There was a photo, somewhere, of her eight-year-old self proudly holding up the front page of the *Floyd Daily News*; she'd crossed out Nancy's byline and written, "By Holly Corson." As a photographer, Hallie had discovered that she didn't particularly care for journalism. But she certainly needed a job. "The *Daily News*?"

"No. Orren Huxley's paper."

"Is he one of the Glass Works Huxleys?"

"He's *the* Glass Works Huxley, now," Nancy said. "The old man died a few years ago."

"And he started a newspaper?"

"Yeah. It's a weekly." Nancy paused. "Orren's a bit eccentric," she added. "For years, he's been going on at city council meetings about how the *Floyd Daily News* only publishes bad news. He always said he would start a newspaper one day, and it would only print good news."

"You're kidding."

"Last year, he launched *Good News*. It's a silly rag, but Orren pays as well as the *Daily News* does. You should send him your resumé."

"*Good News*," Hallie said. "Thanks. I'll check it out."

TWO WEEKS LATER, Hallie pulled into the parking lot of a modest brick building on the grounds of the Huxley Glass Works. It was her first solo trip to Floyd from Oyster Shell, and she felt proud to have pulled the drive off without incident. There were two small cars in the parking lot, and a brand-new-looking red SUV with a bumper sticker: *South Jersey— The Fifty-First State*, in red-and-blue lettering.

Inside, there was no receptionist, just a bank of eight cubicles equipped with computers and bottom-of-the-line office chairs. Two of the cubicles appeared to be unused; the others were heaped with note pads and Post-Its and soda cans.

An incredibly handsome man was typing furiously in the nearest cubicle. His skin was both very dark and very soft-looking; his head was shaved bald, the baldness somehow suiting him. Hallie only realized she was staring when he looked up at her and smiled. He introduced himself: Marcus Washington, editor-in-chief.

Hallie shook his hand. Before she could say anything, a paunchy man with an oily combover hustled from the back of the room. "You must be Miss Corson!" He appeared to be in his late forties; too old to be the Huxley who had crashed that dance at her high school, but possibly his older brother.

"Mr. Huxley," she said, taking his lead. So formal, she thought, especially for Floyd.

"Come back to my office," he said, and she shrugged the Queen of Sheepa off her shoulders as she followed him to a large corner room. He'd appointed it with expensive-looking furniture—a mahogany desk, chairs upholstered in dark red velvet.

"Your resumé is very impressive," he said, motioning for her to take a seat.

"I have my slideshow here." She pulled out her laptop and clicked on the program. Her mannequin shots from ten years earlier were synched to a Bjork song; as Bjork gave way to Blondie, Hallie's more recent shots of bands were displayed.

Unlike the photo editor at *Interview*, Orren seemed impressed. "All this *New York* experience. What brings you to Floyd?"

Hallie explained what had happened.

Orren leaned in closer. "And you're staying here with your brother?"

"Yes," Hallie said. She knew it sounded noble, that it impressed strangers, her giving up her life to take care of Josh.

"Well, that tells me a lot about the kind of person you are."

No it doesn't, she thought. Every day she dreamed of escape. But she smiled in a way she hoped looked humble.

"Let me show you what we're doing here." Orren handed Hallie a copy of the paper.

The lead story was the pumpkin festival at the Cumberland County Fairgrounds. There was also a ribbon-cutting on a new senior citizens' center, a pet hamster saved from a house fire—the photo showed a firefighter in full gear, the hamster barely visible in his gloved hand— and a student-of-the-week feature, the teenage girl's face poorly lit and slightly out of focus.

"It's very—positive," Hallie said, fumbling for words.

Orren beamed like a proud father. "Isn't it?"

After they'd discussed salary—a reasonable per-photo fee, given that this was Floyd—Orren told her she had the job, and to come to the paper's staff meeting next week for her first assignments.

As Hallie and Orren shook hands at the building's exit, an old-model car barreled up. It was painted a bright metallic raspberry, the sides decorated with black fringe; the roof was covered with what appeared to be leopard-print contact paper. The car came to a sudden stop a few yards from Hallie and Orren, straddling two parking spaces. The driver's door opened, and a young woman emerged. She looked to be in her early twenties, with platinum blond hair that she wore in dozens of miniature ponytails, clipped with light blue plastic children's barrettes. Her eyes were also blue, dramatically made up. She was slim, and wore a form-fitting, bright blue dress, a finely-knit wraparound sweater in a paler blue over the top. The young woman headed toward them on platform shoes so high, Hallie was impressed that she could walk.

"That's Cecile O'Neill, our graphic artist," Orren said to Hallie. "She's from Philly," he added, as if her appearance needed further explanation. To Cecile, he said, "That was a very long lunch, Miss O'Neill."

"Sorry!" the woman called out to him, though she didn't sound sorry at all.

"See you next week," Orren said to Hallie, and then to Cecile: "Follow me, please."

BACK IN BRENDA'S car, Hallie texted the new cell phone she'd just bought Josh to see if he wanted a ride home from school.

C u outside, Josh texted her back. Hallie drove to the pickup area at Floyd High School, and waited. It didn't look much different from when she had gone to school there. A row of yellow buses was lined up at the opposite curb.

She had more time than she wanted to think about what she'd just done. Taking the job at *Good News* meant she was truly committed to staying in Oyster Shell, at least for now. It also meant she'd have a shot at paying the electric bill, and for Josh's new phone. Hallie sighed and opened the copy of *The Awakening* that she'd found in the attic. But she kept rereading the opening paragraph, unable to concentrate, and finally she leaned back and shut her eyes. She'd never been one to nap, but since the accident, she found herself dozing off most afternoons. At night, she barely slept at all.

Hallie was half-asleep when the bell rang; she opened her eyes in time to see the doors fly open, the sidewalk flood with teenagers. When Josh finally emerged from the crowd, he was walking with a blond girl— not Missy or Nicki, the two Hallie had met. The girl was smiling at Josh.

Hallie watched as Josh stood and talked to her for a few minutes; then they were joined by a group of four other girls, whose clothes and attitudes suggested popularity. Missy Dalton was among them. Missy and Josh and the blonde talked for a minute while the other three broke into their own group, then all five girls walked away together. Josh walked over to Hallie and opened the passenger's door.

"Hey," he said. "Thanks for picking me up."

"You could have gone with your friends, if you wanted."

"My friends?"

"Well, Missy, and that girl you were talking to."

"Oh." Josh tossed his backpack onto the floor, and settled into the passenger's seat. With his long legs he looked like a giant in Brenda's little car, the scale all wrong. "That was Monika, the exchange student from Germany. She lives with the Daltons."

"She looked like she wanted to keep talking to you."

Josh shook his head. "You think any girl who talks to me likes me."

"No," she said. "I only think it about the ones who actually do."

Josh rolled his eyes. "Missy invited me to a Halloween party at her house. She's never invited me to one of her parties before. Usually just the popular kids go." He looked at Hallie through a stray lock of wavy hair. "I hope it's not because she feels sorry for me."

Hallie thought about it. Missy was clearly fond of Josh, but she wasn't going to date him, not now. In ten or fifteen years, Hallie imagined Missy would look back on high school and remember Josh as the guy she *should* have dated.

"I think you should go. It sounds like more fun than watching *Buffy the Vampire Slayer* with your spinster sister." Hallie pulled into the line of cars waiting to exit the parking lot. "I can help you with a costume."

"A costume?"

"It's a Halloween party. Don't you need a costume?"

"No, it's just a regular party. And I'm not even sure I'm going."

"You can always leave early if it's no fun." She crept the car up to the changing light.

"Maybe," Josh said. He turned the radio on to WMMR, one of the few stations that came in on the crappy car radio. The lead singer of Green Day was asking to be awakened when September ends.

"Can we go to Pete's and get a milkshake?" Josh asked. "I really want a milkshake."

"Sure," Hallie said, a bit surprised that her old after-school hangout was still in business. They waited through another change of the light, the traffic moved, and Hallie headed for Pete's Luncheonette.

THEY WERE IN a booth poring over menus when Hallie saw Father Dobrinich walk in.

"Josh, your priest is here," she whispered.

She hadn't thought much about Josh's disinterest in going to church those past few weeks, since she'd never gone herself; to Hallie, Sundays meant the *New York Times* and brunch with Lawrence. But everyone from Nancy to the guidance counselor at Floyd High School thought Hallie should put Josh in therapy, or at least make him talk to his priest. When Hallie had asked Josh about it, he'd made it clear that he particularly did not want to talk to Father Dobrinich. She hadn't pressed him for a reason.

Before Josh could answer, the priest had spotted them.

"Josh!" Father Dobrinich said as he approached their booth. Josh stood up, but the priest motioned him to sit back down. "How have you been?"

Josh tossed a panicked glance at Hallie. "Okay." He clammed up, the way he did when he was nervous or shy. Hallie wished she'd known this about him years ago, that the inarticulate Josh wasn't who he really was.

"We've missed you at St. Francis," Father Dobrinich said.

Josh nodded.

"I'm afraid it's my fault that he hasn't been to church," Hallie said. "We've had a lot to do, as you might imagine." She gave Father Dobrinich a smile she'd perfected in New York: the back-off smile.

"Of course. But I hope, Josh, that you'll come talk to me sometime soon."

"Sure," Josh said, like it was the last thing on earth he wanted to do.

The priest stood quietly for a moment, as if calculating whether to press harder. But he simply said goodbye to them both, and left the restaurant.

After they'd ordered, Hallie said, "Do you mind if I ask why you don't want to go to church?"

Josh shrugged. It was one of those moments when Hallie wished she had some sort of maternal instinct, but she had none. She could only forge ahead blindly.

"It doesn't make a difference to me if you go or not," she added. "I just wondered."

The waitress put two glasses of water on the table. Josh took a sip of his and then looked at Hallie. "I haven't believed in it in a really long time. I just went to humor Mom. Not that I think anything's wrong with religion," he added quickly, as if afraid of offending her. "It's just not for me."

Hallie sighed. "I go back and forth on it myself. I'd like to think there's some kind of afterlife."

Josh looked out the window, and Hallie followed his gaze. It was a quiet, clear fall day outside, the sun beginning to wane. She watched a squirrel scurry along the edge of the parking lot, then disappear up a tree.

"I really think we're just animals, like any other animals," Josh said. "Sometimes we live to be eighty or ninety, and sometimes we have bad luck and we don't."

Hallie considered it for a moment. The bad luck of being on the wrong highway at the wrong time, a brief flicker of a mistake, metal crashing into metal, sparking a fire. The bad luck of that garage, the fumes, her mother. The bad luck of being the son and daughter of bad luck. If she were superstitious, she'd believe her family was cursed. But she didn't want Josh thinking that way.

"Maybe," she said. "But I also think we've had our lifetime share of bad luck."

"I guess," he said, but there was a look in his eyes she couldn't make out, something that was at once inscrutable and worrisome.

CHAPTER 11

For the entire drive from Oyster Shell to Floyd, Josh had been battling his nerves, but now, as he pulled up in front of Missy Dalton's house, he thought he might actually have a heart attack. His chest pounding, he looked at himself in the rearview mirror and saw the pimples dotting his forehead and cheeks, the wavy hair that looked thick and shaggy around his face. He'd made a decision not to cut it as a sort of mourning rite, and it was a weird length now. Josh hated everything about the way he looked, except for his eyes. They were his mom's brown eyes.

He was wearing a sweater and jeans that Hallie had picked out, an outfit she'd taken him shopping for earlier that week. He had thought it looked cool at the time, but maybe he was relying on her too much. He walked the path to Missy's house, looking down nervously at his clothes.

Missy's house was big and new-looking, in the wealthy part of Floyd near Union Lake. The kids who lived here were called Lakers; the other kids said it like it was an insult, but Josh doubted the kids from the Lake cared what other people called them.

He reached the front door, took a deep breath and rang the bell. It felt like forever before the door opened. He'd expected Missy, but it was Dr. Dalton who greeted him.

"Josh! I'm so glad you could make it." Dr. Dalton clapped him on the back like he was a long-lost friend. "Let me show you to the basement. It's the adult-free zone."

"Thanks," Josh said. They walked down a long hallway with pictures on the walls. Josh spotted one of Missy at age three or four, wearing a pink bathing suit, playing in a sprinkler. Josh would have given anything to be able to take that picture home with him. Dr. Dalton opened a door at the back of the hall and motioned Josh down the stairs.

"You won't see much of me unless it gets loud, or my wife gets worried." He smiled at Josh. "Have fun."

The stairs were dimly lit. He heard some sort of canned maniacal laughter, and felt something tickling his head and neck as he walked down. When he reached the bottom of the stairs, it was all blackness, except for a tiny spotlight on a sign: *This way*, it said, with an arrow, the sign painted red like blood. The party was somewhere on the other side of a wall; he could hear it. He moved his hand along the wall and felt a doorknob, opened it, and stepped into a crowd.

The first thing he noticed: the costumes. Matt Harding, a football player, and his girlfriend were dressed as the Tin Man and Dorothy; Caitlin Carey, captain of the cheerleaders, was a mermaid; Marilyn Manson and Marilyn Monroe walked arm-in-arm; the rest were ghosts and witches, kids he probably knew but couldn't make out in the dim light. Missy hadn't said anything about costumes; he was sure of it. He carried in his mind something like a tape recording of everything she'd ever said to him, and he replayed the conversation now. All she'd told him was "Halloween party." As he tried to figure out what to do, the crowd parted, and Missy was in front of him. She was Tinkerbell, with a pixie hat and a little wand, a green leotard and tights. Her legs were like the shapeliest flower stems.

"Josh, you made it!" she said, and threw her arms around him. She sounded a little...drunk? How could that be, with her father just upstairs?

"Great costume," he said, and smiled at her.

"Do you know who I am?"

"Tinkerbell."

Missy hugged him tightly. Her gestures seemed exaggerated. "Thank you! Everyone keeps saying I'm an elf. I knew *you* would get it."

She knew *he* would get it?

"So where's your costume?" she asked, and then pulled her arms from around his neck. Her eyes got wide. "Did I forget to tell you it was a costume party?" She giggled a little, then looked serious. "I'm sorry!"

"It's okay," Josh said. "I should have figured."

"No, it's my fault," Missy said. Monika joined them. She was dressed like an old-time movie actress, with an evening gown and a blond wig, dark eyebrows and red lips.

"*Gute nacht*," she said in a voice that Josh guessed was supposed to sound sexy.

"Do you know who Monika is?" Missy asked.

"Are you a movie actress?" he asked.

Monika nodded. She had false eyelashes on and blinked at him a lot.

"She's a famous German actress," Missy said. "From a long time ago."

Josh's mind spun in a slight panic. The only famous German he could even think of was Hitler. "I'm sorry," he said. "I don't know."

"Marlene Dietrich!" Missy said, lightly punching his arm. Josh tried not to get aroused by Missy's touch. He stole a glance at her green-sheathed legs.

"Of course," Josh said. "Duh."

"It's okay," Monika said. "No one has got it." Her accent sounded a little thicker than it usually did in school. She looked at Josh for a moment. "You have no costume?"

Josh glanced down at his clothing. "I came as an American teenager," he said. Monika laughed longer and harder than the joke deserved. Missy smiled at him.

"I'll be right back," Missy said, and disappeared into the throng of people.

"Do you want some punch?" Monika asked. "I warn you, one of the boys poured vodka in there."

Josh smiled. So Missy *was* a little drunk. "Is there just soda or something?" Josh had never tried alcohol, and he wasn't going to start now. He didn't want to risk making a fool of himself.

Monika nodded. "Come with me," she said, and led him through the crowd. The room seemed vast, and he nodded to a few kids he knew by sight, but had never talked to much. People seemed friendly enough—no one looked at him like, oh my God, what is Josh Corson doing at a Lake party?—but still, he felt completely out of place. He was the *only* person not in a costume, he could see now. What an idiot.

Monika plucked two cans of 7-Up from a long table, and handed him one. "Would you like to sit in the backyard?"

He looked around for Missy, but she was nowhere to be seen. "Sure," he said, and followed Monika out a door.

There were lawn chairs scattered around, and Halloween lights strung atop a wooden fence. The Daltons' swimming pool was covered for the winter. Couples sat on the lawn chairs, or stood and talked. A few were kissing. It was chilly out but not really cold.

Monika smiled at him. Josh knew he was supposed to say something, but he had no idea what, so he just smiled back and then looked around for Missy. Where was Missy?

"Where will you go next year? For university, I mean." Monika took a sip of 7-Up.

"I haven't thought about it much," Josh said.

Monika nodded and did that weird batting thing with the false eyelashes. "I hope to go to university in *Munchen*—Munich," she said.

"That's cool," Josh said, but he was thinking how he didn't care what Monika planned to do with her life. He just wanted to talk to Missy.

Then he saw Missy out of the corner of his eye. Josh turned his head; she was standing with a guy who was dressed like Captain Hook. Josh had never seen the guy before. Why were their costumes coordinated? Missy and the guy walked over.

"Josh! You've never met my boyfriend Cole, have you?"

Josh wanted to rip the fake hook off the guy's hand and impale himself with it. Her *boyfriend?* The guy was about Josh's height, but looked bigger, like he worked out.

"Cole Huxley," the guy said, putting his non-hook hand out for Josh to shake.

"Josh," he said, and paused for a few seconds before adding, "Corson." He shook hands with the guy. It killed him.

"Cole goes to Deerborn," Missy said. It was a prep school up near Philly.

"I wondered why I never saw you in school before," Josh mumbled.

"My father went to Deerborn and he thinks all the Huxleys have to go there," Cole said. "It's ridiculous. I'd be much happier at Floyd High with sweet Melissa." The two of them exchanged a look that made Josh sick to his stomach.

"You could always get expelled," Missy said, and laughed. Her laugh sounded like bells, each peal a microscopic splinter of glass, slicing Josh into little pieces.

He felt like he might throw up again, everything from the past month swirling around his mind and settling in a sour hole in his gut.

"Can you tell me where your bathroom is?" Josh asked Missy.

"I have to go too. I'll take you." She exchanged a look with Monika and whispered something in her ear before taking Josh's arm and steering him back inside.

"There's a bathroom down here in the basement," she said. "It's kind of rustic."

"That's okay," Josh said. He knew he would only have a short time alone with her, and he wished he could come up with something to say that would be so amazing, she'd ditch Cole and leave the party with him. But he knew that was stupid. She'd never leave her own party.

"I didn't know you had a boyfriend," Josh said. But he should have known. No girl like Missy would not have a boyfriend.

"You didn't?" Missy stood in front of him, by the bathroom door. "Yeah, I guess I don't talk about him that much at school. I don't want to be one of those girls who only talks about their boyfriends, you know? It's boring."

Josh nodded, but he wished she was one of those girls. Then he'd already have known. Then maybe he'd never have fallen in love with her.

There was a cup of punch on the table next to them and Missy picked it up, shrugged and took a sip. Josh could smell the alcohol in it. "I'm not supposed to say anything, but someone here has a crush on you," she said.

At first, Josh misheard Missy, thought she was saying she knew Josh had a crush on her. He stood rooted in his spot, mortified.

"You know, don't you? Monika?"

Now Josh took a step backward. "Monika has a crush on me?"

"Oh my god, you didn't know!" Missy laughed. "And here I thought she was being so obvious."

Josh was still trying to absorb the information. "Monika has a crush on me?" he repeated.

Now Missy was eying him, her brow furrowed. "She's really nice," Missy said, "and doesn't she look great in that costume?" She sounded like she was trying to sell him something. "And she's really smart, too."

The only reason he'd been invited to the party was because a girl from Germany happened to be staying at the Daltons' house, and happened to like him. Josh felt like he was going to melt into the floor. His stomach was roiling.

"I don't feel so good," he said. "Excuse me."

JOSH KNEW HE'D been in the bathroom for a long time. People occasionally pounded on the door, some of them yelling drunken-sounding threats. What Missy had told him sent him to that place again, that place where he felt like there was no ground beneath him, he was falling, and landed only after throwing up whatever he'd eaten. Tonight's was pizza from earlier and a few sips of 7-Up. He was just about to clean up the toilet and splash water on his face when he heard another knock on the door.

"Josh, it's Missy's dad. Are you okay? Can I come in?"

Not only did everyone know he'd been in the bathroom all this time, Missy had gone and gotten her *dad*. Josh had made a complete fool of himself. Maybe he *should* let Hallie send him to a boarding school; he could never show his face at Floyd High again.

"I'm fine, Dr. Dalton," Josh said in a voice he hoped sounded fine. "I'll be out in a minute."

"Let me in, son," Dr. Dalton said. "Unlock the door." He said it in the kind of voice Josh's dad would have used, a firm voice that it was hard not to obey.

Josh unlocked the door and stood as far away from it as he could, hoping no one would see him when Dr. Dalton entered. He came in quickly and closed the door behind him.

"Are you sick?" Dr. Dalton asked.

Josh had flushed the toilet but hadn't wiped the seat up, so it was obvious that he had been sick. "I just throw up easily," he said. "It's no big deal."

Dr. Dalton nodded. He wiped the toilet seat and closed the lid, then sat on it.

"I'm sorry about the mess," Josh said. "I was going to clean it up."

Dr. Dalton held his hands out. "It doesn't matter. I'm more concerned with you."

"I'm fine," Josh said, way too quickly to sound convincing.

Dr. Dalton was quiet for a minute. "You're going through something that a lot of adults wouldn't be able to handle."

Josh looked at Missy's dad, his face creased with concern. *He thinks it's all about my parents being dead*, Josh realized with a twinge of relief.

"I shouldn't have come," Josh said. "It was too soon." He was an awful liar! Would Dr. Dalton see through him? He didn't appear to.

"It's good that you tried, though," Dr. Dalton said. "Maybe by the time Missy has her Christmas party, you'll feel more up to it."

Like I'm going to be invited to that, Josh thought. "Is there any way for me to get out of here without anyone seeing me?" he asked. "I really just want to go home."

Dr. Dalton nodded. "I have an idea." He stepped out of the bathroom for a minute, then stepped back in. "Help is on the way."

There was an awkward silence while they waited.

"Do you like sports?" Dr. Dalton asked. "The Eagles?"

Josh shook his head. "I hardly know anything about sports." Josh's dad was never really into football, only baseball. He used to try to get Josh to watch Phillies games with him when Josh was little. But it had always seemed boring to Josh, the games moving so slowly. Now he wished he would have sat down, at least once, and watched baseball with his dad.

Dr. Dalton nodded, and he and Josh both looked at the floor until Missy came in.

"Are you okay, Josh?" she asked. He hated what she could do to him, how she could make him feel. Even knowing she had a boyfriend, he still loved her.

"Yeah, just totally embarrassed."

Missy had brought a white sheet with eye holes cut out of it—a makeshift ghost costume. "If you wear this, no one will know it's you," she said. "You can just leave if you want."

Josh took the sheet from her.

"Or you could stay," she said. "No one will give you a hard time. I promise."

"Thanks, but I really just want to go," he said, pulling the sheet over his head.

"Are you feeling alright to drive home?" Dr. Dalton asked.

"Oh yeah," Josh said. "I'm fine now." It was a lie, but they accepted it.

Missy smiled a little. "You make a good ghost," she said. "I'll walk you out."

Josh was terrified that kids would be lined up outside the bathroom waiting to mock him, but no one was. Monika wasn't there either, to his relief. As Josh and Missy headed up the stairs, Dr. Dalton called out, "Is this punch spiked? I smell booze."

"Shit," Missy said, hurrying Josh through the house. "I'm in trouble now."

"Big trouble?" Josh asked as they headed out the front door.

"Medium trouble." She walked with him across the lawn. "Mom and Dad don't care if I have a glass of wine when I'm home, but they're always lecturing me about other kids drinking here, how much trouble everyone could get in." She glanced back at the house, her mouth a tight line. "It's Cole's stupid friends from Deerborn. They always spike the punch."

You didn't seem to mind drinking it, Josh thought, but he didn't say so. They reached the street, and Josh's Mom's car.

"Maybe when you're feeling better, you and Monika could go out with me and Cole sometime," Missy said. "We could go to a movie or something."

"Maybe," Josh said, wondering how he'd get out of that. It sounded like the worst torture he could possibly imagine.

"You sure you're okay now?"

"Yeah." No one else was around, so he pulled the sheet off and handed it back to Missy. He was quiet for a moment, struggling for something to say. He longed to be in the car, driving away. "Missy, I'm really sorry about everything. I feel so stupid."

She shook her head. "You don't have to apologize. I just wish there was something I could say. It's so…" She glanced back at the house for a moment. "I mean, I'm going to go back there and get in trouble from my dad, and it's like, I'm lucky he's there to yell at me. You know? I think about what happened to you and I can't imagine what I'd do." She looked at the ground. "I think about it a lot, what happened to you. Is that weird?"

"No," he said. Missy got it. She was the only person his age who seemed to really get the enormity of it. And knowing she was capable of getting it just made it worse; having Missy as a girlfriend might save him, might get him through these endless awful days, but it was never going to happen. She had a boyfriend, and Josh couldn't compete with that guy.

"Your dad seems nice," Josh added. "Tell him I said thanks." He allowed himself one final glance at her legs, walked quickly around to the driver's side and got in the car. He left Missy standing there on the lawn in her Tinkerbell costume as he pulled away.

JOSH DROVE IN circles for more than an hour. He drove around Floyd, past the lake, past the high school, past the Huxley Glass Works. He drove past the Union Lake Dam and into Millville. Finally he ended up in Vineland. He was crying hard by then, so he pulled into the parking lot of the Cumberland Mall. He parked the car near JCPenney's and wondered how long he could sit there. He couldn't bear the idea of telling Hallie what had happened.

Josh leaned back in his seat and closed his eyes, but he opened them immediately when he pictured his parents in the burning truck. He should have been in that truck, should have died with Mom and Dad. A part of him whispered in his ear how easy it would be. Razor blades, a few cuts on the wrists, just like the kid in *Ordinary People*. You were supposed to cut vertically, Josh had read, not horizontally, if you really meant it. Josh pushed his sleeves up and looked at the undersides of his wrists. Could he do it?

He thought about the reasons not to: Hallie, Ram, Nancy. Nancy and Ram would get over it, Josh thought, but Hallie might not. And then there was the question of Josh's life being over. If he was right, and there was no afterlife, then that would be it; he'd just be gone. If he was wrong, and his parents were in heaven, he wouldn't join them there if he killed himself. He'd go to either purgatory or hell. Killing himself, then, seemed to be pretty much a lose/lose.

Josh wondered about Hallie's mother, how she'd made up her mind to do it, chosen her method and planned it out. What would make someone with a daughter in the sixth grade actually kill herself? Josh was pretty sure *he* couldn't go through with it. He just wished there was a way to take a break from his life and have it continue with him absent, and then maybe return to his body just before graduation. He kind of wanted to do graduation. And he wanted to write a book when he was older. There were lots of things Josh was sure he couldn't do, but he was equally certain that he *could* write a book. He wanted to live for that. He just didn't know how he'd get through this year.

Still, he couldn't get the thought of cutting his wrists entirely out of his mind. Maybe he could just make little cuts without really hurting himself, the dark voice in his head suggested, but the second he thought of it Josh knew he couldn't become just another teenage cliché, a cutter.

He was crying again, and searched around the car for something to blow his nose on. He opened the glove compartment and pulled out a stack of napkins. They were from Dunkin' Donuts, and Josh knew how they'd gotten there. The Sunday before the accident, he and his mom had stopped after church. Mom had just ordered coffee; Josh had his usual, a jelly-filled and a chocolate-frosted.

"I wish I could eat like you," his mom had said. Her words made Josh self-conscious; he had been hungry and was tearing into the donuts, barely breathing as he swallowed. He slowed his chewing and looked at her.

"Why don't you?" he asked.

"Oh, Josh, you know. I put weight on so easily."

His mother would say things like that to him sometimes. He never knew how to respond.

"You're not fat," he said, hoping it was the right thing.

Mom smiled a little. "Thank you, dear. But I'm not exactly thin, either."

"You look okay," he said. He wasn't sure if this was true, by objective standards—she was his mother!—but he was pretty sure it was what he should say.

Mom had rolled her eyes. "I think I've hit a new low, fishing for compliments from my teenage son."

That was it, really—they pretty much left after that. Now, looking at the napkins, it killed Josh that his mom didn't have a donut. She was going to die in less than a week. She should have had five donuts! Or ten. Why hadn't he encouraged her to have one, or given her part of his? Why hadn't he told her how great she was, how much he loved her?

Josh felt nauseous again, and didn't want to throw up in the car, or the parking lot. Maybe Hallie *would* get over it, if he died. He cried harder and blew his nose into one of the napkins, and then he thought of Emma. What would happen to Emma if he died? Would Hallie keep her? Would

Cal Stutts take her back?

Josh got out of the car and slammed the door, then kicked it. Fuck! He could leave everyone else, but he couldn't leave Emma.

He felt like he was spinning, his stomach heaving. He pulled out his phone and hesitated over Ram's number; Ram was in Boston for the weekend, visiting with his parents and sister. Josh couldn't imagine having such an intense talk with him over the phone, while he was away. He looked at the other numbers: Nancy's, Hallie's and Missy's—she'd given him her number when she invited him to the party. And Nicki Kepler's cell was there, too. She'd grabbed his phone at lunch one day and called herself.

Josh selected Nicki's number and hit the call button before he even thought about what he would say. He wasn't sure why he was calling her.

She picked up on the fourth ring. "Josh?" Nicki asked. "Could this really be Josh Corson?" She was somewhere loud; he could hear people talking and dishes clanking.

"Yeah," he said.

"What's up?"

I'm sitting in my dead mom's car in the Cumberland Mall parking lot. I was thinking about buying razor blades at the CVS. I have nowhere to go.

"I just…felt like doing something," he said. "I know it's kind of late, but I thought you might want to, I don't know, do something." He sounded like an idiot.

"And you just assumed that I'd have nothing to do at 10:30 on a Saturday night?" She didn't sound mad, exactly, but what she said made him feel terrible.

"I'm sorry!" he said. "I didn't even think. I just wanted to talk, really."

She told him to hold on a second, and was gone long enough that he considered hanging up.

"I wanted to go outside where it wasn't so loud," she finally said. "What's going on?"

"Where are you?" Josh asked.

"At a café with my friends."

"A café?"

"Oh, in New York—sorry. This is my weekend with my dad."

She wasn't even home. There was really nobody he could talk to.

"I'm sorry I bothered you, Nicki. I'll just talk to you in school Monday."

"Don't hang up."

"But you're with your friends." Josh had never thought about it before—that she had friends she'd left in New York, that maybe in high school in Brooklyn she'd been popular, even.

"That's okay. I'm out with my best friend, her boyfriend and his brother. But the brother's kind of stupid."

"You're on a date?"

"If you want to call it that." Nicki was quiet for a moment. "I'm glad you called."

"You are?"

"Yeah."

"Why?"

"Just because. Tell me what's going on."

Josh took a deep breath. "I went to Missy Dalton's Halloween party."

Nicki snorted. "You were invited to a party at the Lake? Well, how very."

Josh thought for a moment about the phrase. "That's from *Heathers*."

He heard someone talking to Nicki in the background, and Nicki saying, "I'll be back in a few minutes." To Josh, she said, "So, the party wasn't good?"

"Put it this way," Josh said. "I'm sitting in my car in the parking lot of the Cumberland Mall feeling really sorry for myself."

"Oh, Josh," she said, and laughed a little. "I'm glad I'm not the only one who does that—driving around and feeling sorry for myself."

"You're not. I've joined the ranks of the self-pitying drivers."

"We should form a club. The Pathetic Teenage Driving Club."

"Teen Angst Behind the Wheel."

Nicki laughed. "Oh my God! That would be a great name for a band."

"It would."

Josh sat in the car and talked to Nicki for over an hour. At one point, she said she was walking down the street with her friend and their dates; she had Josh hold on while they all said goodbye. Then she said she was going on the subway and would call him right back. She did. By the time they ended the conversation, she was home, in her dad's home, in

Brooklyn. They'd talked about nothing, really. Josh never told her what happened at the party, and Nicki didn't ask. They'd just talked about music and books and movies, and Josh had confided about watching *Buffy the Vampire Slayer*.

"I love Buffy," Nicki said. "She's really empowering."

They finally hung up around midnight, with Nicki insisting that they go to a movie the following weekend, when she'd be back in Floyd. Josh thought they would. He didn't like Nicki the way she maybe liked him—if that was even true—but he thought he could be friends with her.

Josh turned on the light inside the car and looked at himself in the rearview mirror. He didn't look upset anymore. He could face Hallie. He dialed the home number and she picked up on the second ring.

"Hey!" she said. "Having fun?"

"I'm just leaving the party now," Josh said.

"Was it good?"

"Yeah, it was okay. I'll be home in about a half hour."

"I'll be up. I want to hear all about it."

Josh was grateful for the drive ahead of him, to think of what story he would tell his sister. He could tell her almost anything; she'd never know. He thought of all the teen movies he'd seen, the John Hughes ones and *Say Anything* and *American Pie* and *Mean Girls*. Even in movies, the parties never went so well for everyone. To make it believable, he'd have to tell Hallie a little of the truth, as much as he thought she could handle.

CHAPTER 12

Hallie groped at the coffee table and grabbed her cell phone, shutting off its alarm. Her neck was stiff from sleeping on the couch. She couldn't bear to sleep in her old bedroom or in her parents' room, still untouched in the six weeks since the accident. The two spare bedrooms were even more depressing, filled with Brenda's old junk from before she married Hallie's father.

Emma barked, and a few seconds later there was a knock at the front door. At 6:30 a.m.?

She opened the door to a middle-aged man in a black overcoat. "Hallie Corson?" he asked, and she nodded. She knew she looked a mess, in an old pair of flannel pajamas, her hair askew from sleep.

"Have a nice day," he said, and thrust an envelope into her hand. A summons. It was official now: the family of Kayla Janssen, the young woman who died in the pile-up caused by the Corsons' truck, was suing Donald Corson's estate.

"Who was that?" Josh asked as he headed down the stairs, already dressed.

Hallie handed him the summons as she shuffled into the kitchen. She couldn't think about it before coffee. Josh followed her, Emma at his heels. He sat and read the summons while Hallie started the coffee maker.

"But the autopsy said it wasn't Dad's fault," Josh finally said, looking up at her. "He had a stroke."

"I know." Hallie put a glass of orange juice in front of Josh.

"Are the other people in the accident suing?"

"The insurance company thinks they'll settle." Hallie leaned against the kitchen counter and stared at the coffee maker as it sputtered to life.

"So why don't these people settle?"

Hallie sighed. "Their daughter died, Josh. The other people lived."

Josh sipped his juice. "She wasn't much older than me. The girl who died, I mean."

"I know."

Emma started whimpering, and Josh looked down at her. "Sorry girl," he said, as Hallie handed him the leash.

While Josh and Emma were outside, Hallie poured two bowls of cereal and put them on the table. She felt a chill—the heat was turned down as low as they could tolerate—and she went into the family room, plucked her robe from the bottom of the couch, put it on. *The Awakening* fell to the floor, the overdue phone bill she'd been using as a bookmark fluttering out. She picked them both up as Josh and Emma came back inside.

"Could you drop me at school on your way in to work?" Josh asked.

"Sure." As Hallie poured a cup of coffee, there was another knock at the front door. Emma looked up and woofed.

"Who is it now?" Josh asked as he headed to the door, Emma at his heels. He returned quickly, pulling the growling dog by her collar. "It's Cal," he whispered to Hallie. "I'm taking Emma out back."

Hallie went to the door and found Cal standing on the porch.

"I'm sorry Josh didn't invite you in," she said, motioning him inside. He followed her into the front hallway.

Hallie waited for him to speak, but he remained quiet, standing awkwardly in the hall. "What's up?" she finally asked. Hallie hadn't been to the farm since that day of the first Wellingford Farms pickup. She had chosen to believe that Cal could handle the farm because she didn't have the time or energy to deal with it herself.

"That coffee smells good," he said.

"Want some?" She felt certain he had more on his mind than coffee.

"Sure."

"You mind if I give it to you in a thermos?" she asked. "I have to get to work."

"Okay," he said. "I'll take it with me."

Hallie pulled her dad's thermos from a cabinet and filled it with coffee.

"Thanks," Cal said, taking it from her. Josh stood on the back porch with Emma, glaring through the window.

"Guess I'd best get to work," Cal added, heading for the front door. He tipped his hat to her as he left the house.

"It's okay, girl," Josh said to Emma as he walked her back inside. "He's gone." Josh stood next to the table for a moment, looking at Hallie. "Ram thinks Cal has a crush on you. He says you need to be careful with him."

Hallie felt a dull throb beginning in the back of her head. "I know," she said, sitting down at the table.

"You know he has a crush on you, or you know you need to be careful?"

"Both." She didn't want to think about Cal; he, and the farm, were two more problems that she couldn't handle.

HALLIE'S PHOTO SHOOT that morning—at the Rivertown Manor nursing home, a ninety-fifth birthday breakfast for the oldest woman in Floyd—took longer than she expected. When she got back to the newsroom at nine-thirty, the weekly staff meeting was already in progress. Hallie slipped into the empty seat next to Marcus. As always, he smelled good—soap and pheromones, she supposed. He flashed her a quick smile.

"The SPCA called to see if we'd run a pet of the week feature—the *Floyd Daily News* dropped it for advertising space," Ben, the college intern, was saying as Hallie settled into her chair. The reporters, Jane and Chuck, both looked at Orren attentively. Marcus scribbled notes on a pad. Cecile filed her nails.

Orren was quiet for a moment. "An animal without a home," he finally said. "That's not really good news."

"But it would be good news if it got adopted!" Cecile put down her emery board.

"What if we started doing a feature each week on a happily adopted pet?" Jane asked. "Then the shelter could still get a plug."

Cecile smiled and resumed filing her nails. Orren paced the length of the conference room as if he'd just been pitched the Watergate story. He looked at Marcus. "That might work," he said. "Ben, see if the shelter can find someone who'd let us interview them."

"Will do," Ben said.

"And Hallie, you take the photos for the SPCA feature," Orren said. "Try to find a family with a puppy. Everybody loves puppies."

Marcus cleared his throat. "You said you wanted better photos for the student-of-the-week feature," he reminded Orren. He managed not to sound like it was crushing his soul to bring this up, though Hallie suspected it was. She had finally heard Marcus's story over lunch last week: he was a bona fide journalist who'd once worked for the *L.A. Times*. He had moved back home to Bridgeton to take care of his ailing parents, and, calamitously, had ended up at *Good News*.

"Student of the week! Yes! Thank you, Mr. Washington," Orren said. He turned to Hallie. "Can you start taking those photos?"

"Sure." She tried to sound enthusiastic.

"Good work, everyone," Orren said, clapping his hands together. "We'll meet again next Monday morning."

As Orren left the room, Cecile shot a paper airplane at Hallie. It landed in her lap. *Open it,* Cecile mouthed at her from across the room, and Hallie smoothed the paper out. Cecile had sketched a quick caricature of Orren, a basset hound in a business suit. Everybody loves puppies, it said. Marcus looked at it, too, and shook his head at Cecile.

ON FRIDAYS AFTER work, the *Good News* staff—minus Orren—congregated at an Italian restaurant, and Hallie decided that particular Friday to go along, and to bring Josh. She swung over to the library to pick him up, and found him sitting on the front steps with Nicki.

"You sure you don't want to go?" Josh asked Nicki as he got into the car.

"I do, but my mom would freak. She has a thing about having dinner together." Nicki rolled her eyes at Hallie.

"Maybe another time," Hallie said to her. "Or you and your mom can come to our house for dinner sometime." Hallie had no idea how she'd pull off such a dinner, but she wanted Nicki to feel welcome. She and Josh had been hanging around together for the past couple of weeks, and Hallie was grateful that Josh had a friend his age.

"Am I going to feel weird?" Josh asked as they pulled away.

"Weird?" Hallie asked.

"I don't know any of these people you work with."

"Oh, you'll like them," Hallie said. "Ben isn't much older than you. And Cecile—well, she's twenty-two going on thirteen."

"Huh." Josh opened the glove compartment, pulled a stack of paper napkins out, held them for a minute and then put them back and shut the door. His features creased into sadness.

They rode in silence for a few minutes, and then Josh cleared his throat. "Is that publisher going to be there?"

"Orren?" Hallie asked. "God, no. The whole point is to talk about him over drinks."

"Good."

"Why? Did I scare you with my stories?" Hallie slowed the car as the light turned red ahead of her.

"I just don't want to meet him," Josh said.

Hallie stopped at the light and looked at her brother. He tried to look away, aloof and distant, but she held her gaze, and his expression crumpled.

"His son dates Missy, okay?"

"I didn't know that," Hallie said. "I'm sorry."

"What are you sorry for?"

Hallie sighed. Mostly she could talk to Josh, but every now and then they'd get into one of these exchanges where everything she said seemed to be wrong. "I said I was sorry because you seemed upset."

"It's not *your* fault," he said, as if her apology were the lamest thing in the world.

The light changed and they drove the rest of the way in silence. Inside the restaurant, Marcus, Cecile and Ben were at a table in the back. Hallie introduced Josh around and nabbed the seat next to Marcus; Josh sat across from her, next to Cecile.

"What school do you go to?" Cecile asked Josh.

"Floyd High School," Josh said.

"High school?" Cecile grinned. "I thought you were in college."

"Next year," Josh said. He smiled back at Cecile.

A waitress came and distributed menus, took drink orders.

"Do you know where you want to go?" Cecile asked Josh after she'd ordered a rum and coke.

Josh shrugged. "I have applications for Stockton and Rowan." Hallie knew they'd been pressed upon him by his guidance counselor.

"I go to Rowan," Ben said.

"Do you like it?" Josh asked.

"Yeah, it's cool."

"We might look at some other schools, too," Hallie said. They'd discussed the possibility of taking a trip up north before Christmas, looking at colleges in New York or New England. She wanted Josh to see that there was a world outside of South Jersey.

"Where did you go to school?" Josh asked Cecile.

"University of the Arts," she said. "In Philly."

"You're an artist?" he asked. His eyes were warm, his face open. Oh no, Hallie thought. The only thing worse for Josh than his crush on Missy would be if he developed a crush on Cecile.

"I used to be," she said, "before I took this crazy job." She blinked at Josh.

Marcus's cell phone rang and he excused himself to take the call.

"It *is* pretty crazy," Ben said. "I didn't know when I took this internship that it wouldn't be, like, a regular paper." He stroked his patchy goatee.

Hallie glanced toward the corner of the restaurant where Marcus was leaning against a wall, smiling as he spoke. It certainly wasn't one of his parents he was talking to.

Cecile pulled out a pen and started drawing something on her paper placemat, Josh watching her with keen interest. Marcus returned to the table, smiling broadly.

"You look happy," Hallie said.

"Oh? Yeah, well." He opened the menu in front of him. "My girlfriend's coming next weekend."

"Your girlfriend," Hallie said, working to keep the disappointment out of her voice. Of course he had a girlfriend. A guy like Marcus would always have a girlfriend. "From L.A.?"

"Yeah," Marcus said. "When I moved here last summer, I wasn't sure if she'd hang in. I mean, I still have no idea when I'll be able to go back. But she's been great."

"How often do you see each other?" Cecile asked. She looked not at

Marcus, but at Hallie, then back at her placemat drawing. Her pen never stopped moving.

"She flies in when she can," he said.

Hallie wished she had someone waiting for her in New York. But her last relationship—which was not a real relationship, just a guy she'd slept with some Saturday nights—ended three years ago, and she hadn't gotten beyond a second date since then. The Friday night before the accident, Hallie had been stood up for dinner by another photographer, a younger one, a guy she'd met at the Bubble Lounge. She'd sat in the Indian restaurant for 40 minutes, going through glass after glass of water, until she'd finally called Lawrence and Kenneth to come eat with her.

And why hadn't Lawrence visited since the funeral? He kept telling her to come to New York for a weekend, but claimed to be too "antsy," with his *New Yorker* piece hitting the newsstands soon, to travel. She *could* go to New York for a weekend, of course, but Hallie suspected that revisiting her old life would just remind her of everything she'd lost.

"Hallie, I almost forgot to tell you," Josh said, his eyes still on Cecile's drawing, on Cecile as she drew. "Ram invited us to go to his sister's house with him for Thanksgiving. She lives near Boston."

"Really?" Hallie asked.

"Yeah. His parents will still be visiting from India. I think he doesn't want to deal with his family again alone." Josh looked at Hallie. "It's no big deal if you don't want to go."

Thanksgiving was only two weeks away. Taking Ram up on his invitation would be an easy solution.

"Maybe," Hallie said. "Let's talk about it later."

"Ta da!" Cecile cried, and held the placemat up. She'd drawn Hallie, a credible likeness.

"Wow, that's good," Marcus said.

Hallie took the paper and studied the drawing. It was not unflattering, though there was a tiredness around her eyes that made her look older than she hoped she really appeared. She tried to push back the thought that maybe this was what she looked like now, that everything she'd been through had aged her.

"You don't like it," Cecile said.

Hallie shot her a smile she hoped looked genuine, or at least polite.

"No, it's really good," she said. "I'm just always a little unnerved by my own image." It was true; she could never do the kind of work Joy did, photographing herself. She was only comfortable behind the camera, not in front of it.

"What made you want to be a photographer?" Marcus asked, and suddenly all eyes were upon her. She hated this question.

"Well, my mother was a painter," Hallie said, "and I was always drawn to art. I didn't have her talent, but I still loved it, so I majored in art history in college. I thought at first that I'd work in art conservation."

"I didn't know that," Josh said.

"Yeah. But I had taken a photography class in high school, and I kept taking photography in college, and somewhere along the way I just fell in love with it. It was like—" she paused, wondering if she should tell them what she'd told Lawrence when they'd first met—"like the camera was an extension of me. I loved everything about it: the weight and feel of it, the sound of the shutter, the smell of film. Having a camera with me, I felt less alone, especially as a teenager."

"That's how I feel with my books," Josh said. "I always like to have one with me."

The appetizers came and the conversation slowed as they began to eat. But then someone fired an opening salvo about Orren, and soon they had Marcus doing a dead-on imitation. Cecile did a quick unflattering sketch of Orren on Josh's placemat so he could see the man they were discussing. As they were finishing up and looking at the check, Cecile stared forlornly into her wallet.

"I'm sorry," she said. "I only have two bucks. Can you all spot me until payday?"

"Sure," Marcus said, but he exchanged a glance with Hallie. Cecile had done this the last three times they all went out, and she never paid up.

"I only have enough for my share," Ben said, an edge of irritation in his voice.

"How about I get this check," Marcus said. "We'll call it a business meeting and make Orren pay."

"You're the best!" Cecile said to Marcus, grabbing her bag and hopping to her feet. "I have to run. I'll see you all Monday." On her way past Josh, she bent down and whispered something to him.

Hallie studied Josh's face. She knew better than to ask him in front of everyone what Cecile had said, but she was already alarmed by the intimacy of it, Cecile's pouty lips in Josh's hair.

"What did she say to you?" Marcus asked Josh, a just-us-guys tone to his voice.

"Nothing," Josh said. "Just that she'd see me around."

Hallie wondered if there was more to it than that. On their way out of the restaurant, Marcus pulled her aside.

"You've got to watch that girl around your brother," he said. "She has no sense at all."

WHEN HALLIE AND Josh pulled up in front of their house that night, the sedan with the township logo was parked in the driveway. Todd Schwegel. Hallie got out of her car and found Todd and Ram sitting on the porch.

Todd stood up. "I don't want to alarm you," he said, "but Ram and I were headed out for a drink, and we saw Cal Stutts hanging around here."

That can't be good, Hallie thought. "He's working on the farm. He probably just needed something."

"He was drunk," Ram said.

"Can I talk to you a minute?" Todd asked, taking Hallie by the arm and walking her away from Ram and Josh. They stopped when they'd reached the back of the garage.

"Look," Todd said, "I understand why your father always gave Cal a break, and why you are. Ram never really knew Cal like we did, in grade school."

"I felt so sorry for him when we were little," Hallie said. Cal had often gone to school with inexplicable bruises; once, a black eye.

"Everybody did," Todd said. "He never really had a chance."

"He's not that bad," Hallie said. "I mean, I know he treated that dog terribly, but—"

"Well, that's the thing," Todd interrupted her. "He *is* that bad, now."

Hallie looked at him, tried to read his expression, but it was too dark to see clearly.

"He beat his ex-wife up pretty bad, before she left him," Todd said. "Broke two of her ribs."

Hallie tried to take this in. Could the Cal who seemed almost shy around Hallie, who'd been knocking himself out to help her at the farm, actually break a woman's ribs?

"He walked five miles to go to my mother's funeral," she said.

Todd put his hand on her arm. "He's not that kid anymore."

Hallie stared at the back of the garage as she mulled it over, watching a spider crawl along the windowpane. She could see a faint outline of the shelving her father had built inside, against that window, after he stopped using the building as a garage.

"I think Cal wants to ask me out," she said softly. "I don't know what to do."

"What's your arrangement with him?" Todd asked.

"I told him we'd split the profits for whatever he could sell."

Todd took off his Phillies cap, scratched his head. His blond hair was still thick.

"I doubt he's going to get much of a new crop going."

"I know. I really need to sell the place. But there's been so much to deal with, and now my father's estate is being sued."

Todd shook his head in sympathy. "What's Cal trying to grow now? Herbs?"

"Yes, and hothouse tomatoes," Hallie said, but she was embarrassed that she really had no idea what he was doing. She'd been using the job at *Good News* as an excuse to avoid the farm.

"He's probably not going to make much, so you can use that as your out. But I'd start floating the idea with him that you're selling the place."

Hallie could only nod. What potential disaster had she created here?

"And call me if you have any problems. Even if you just think you might have one."

"Thanks," Hallie said. She had never really understood the appeal of men in uniform for some women, but now she could see it—a strong guy to protect you, one with the authority to ensure your safety. "So he was drunk tonight?"

"Wasted," Todd said. "Could barely stand. He said he was waiting for you."

Hallie took a breath.

"I drove him home and tried to talk to him a little. Told him you had a lot to deal with and he should get any crazy ideas out of his head."

"You think it worked?"

Todd shrugged. "He does listen to me a little," he said. "More than anyone else." Todd glanced around the garage, back towards the porch. "He hates Ram. And Nancy."

"And Josh?"

Todd was quiet for a moment. "Not so much, I think. You both have a lot of clout with Cal because of your dad. He was the only person around here who would hire Cal. I don't think he'd deliberately do anything to hurt you or Josh." He leaned against the side of the garage. "But that doesn't mean he might not try something stupid."

Hallie nodded, shivering in the late fall air. She walked with Todd back to the porch, where Ram was still sitting. Josh had Emma on her leash and was a few yards away, walking her along the road.

"I think I'm just going to call it a night, Ram," Todd said.

"I'll walk," Ram said.

Todd nodded to them both and headed back to his car.

Ram looked at her. "I'm sorry if it seems like I'm interfering," he said, "but Josh keeps asking me to. He's been worried."

Hallie unlocked the front door, motioned him inside. "Well, I did feel that way," she said, "but I guess everyone else was right."

Ram looked her in the eyes. "You were trying to help someone. You just didn't know what you were getting into."

Hallie sat down at the kitchen table. The summons still sat there, underneath a pile of mail, and she hadn't yet called the insurance company. "This is a mess," she said, her hands in her hair. "I've made a huge mess of everything."

"Nothing that can't be fixed." He pulled out a chair and slid into it.

"Not just Cal," she said. "Josh, everything. And we're being sued. Every time I turn around, something worse happens."

Ram was quiet for a moment. "I don't know about the rest of it, but Josh is glad you're here."

"Yeah?"

He narrowed his eyes a little, studying her. "He's always looked up to you. If you hadn't decided to stay, he'd be in really bad shape."

"You think?"

"I know."

She smiled as best she could. "Thanks," she said. She looked at Ram, really looked at him, for the first time since she'd returned to Oyster Shell. All this time she'd been thinking of him, on some level, as the boy she'd known in high school: a kid who'd sometimes inserted himself into her social clique. But he didn't even look like that kid anymore, and he certainly wasn't the same person, any more than she was. Maybe they could be friends, she thought. She could use a friend.

CHAPTER 13

Josh woke up to music he didn't recognize, the slight static of a radio. For a second, he didn't know where he was; for a second, he thought he was home, and his alarm had awakened him, and soon Mom would come in and hurry him along. But his hoodie was curled up under his cheek, and he felt the road rushing beneath him, and then he remembered: he was in the backseat of the roomy car they'd borrowed from Nancy, Ram and Hallie were in front, and they were driving to Massachusetts to spend Thanksgiving with Ram's family. Josh had come to hate his first seconds of wakefulness, even from a nap; fogged by sleep, he would have to remember all over again that his parents were dead.

Josh scooched to a half-sitting position and looked out the window, caught sight of the rusted-out industrial expanses along what had to be the northernmost part of the New Jersey Turnpike. Or were they in New York already? Josh could see a bridge up ahead, as well as a clot of traffic.

"I shouldn't have taken the George Washington Bridge," Josh heard Ram mumble.

"It's okay," Hallie said. "We're not in a hurry, are we?"

"No," Ram said. "Not at all."

Their voices were low, as if they thought Josh was still asleep. He slid down in his seat.

"Maybe it won't be so bad," Hallie said.

"Sure. My family's great. They just have no respect for my work." Ram had long ago catalogued for Josh the ways in wish he'd disappointed his parents: unmarried, no children, living off grants in one room above his own office.

"I know how you feel, " Hallie said. "Art and photography were the only ways I had to make sense of the world, but my dad never took it seriously." She dropped her voice a little. "He called at the beginning of my sophomore year of college and told me he wasn't going to help pay for my school anymore because I was 'just fooling around studying art.' His words."

"He really did that?" Ram asked.

"He told me to come home and go to community college," she whispered. Josh only knew this story from Dad's perspective: that he'd nearly bankrupt the farm for Hallie to study something useless like art in a school meant for rich kids.

"From NYU. Wow." It was quiet for a moment. "I'm not defending him, but maybe he was just really broke?"

Whatever Hallie said then, Josh couldn't make out.

"Was that when you changed your name?" Ram asked.

"I started going by Hallie my junior year, but I couldn't get the money together to legally change it until I was two years out of college."

"I never understood the whole changing your name thing before," Ram said, "but I get it now."

"I felt like I didn't have a family anymore," Hallie said. "Lawrence was all I had. For years, I went home with him to Indiana at Christmas. His parents used to send me money sometimes, even though they didn't have so much themselves, and I was so broke I had no choice but to accept it. It's awful, to have people pity you."

This was the same thing that had been bothering Josh since his parents had died. She did it sometimes, to him—he could feel it when she pitied him—but she also understood how awful it was, to be pitied.

"Okay, you win," Ram said. "I have nothing to complain about."

Hallie laughed a little. "I didn't think it was a contest."

"No, but you made me realize it could be a lot worse. They torture me, but my parents never abandoned me." He was quiet for a moment. "Though there are times I wish they *would* abandon me."

No, Josh thought. *You don't wish that at all.*

AFTER THEY MADE their first stop, Josh took over the wheel. No one even suggested that Hallie drive, and she didn't volunteer.

"Are you sure your sister doesn't mind all of us staying with her?" Hallie, now in the backseat, asked Ram. "It seems like a pretty big imposition."

"Honestly, I think she's relieved," he said. "With you two there, she figures everyone will be on their best behavior. Our parents, me. Besides, she and her husband are dying to talk to Josh about colleges. Winslow fancies himself a molder of young minds."

A molder of young minds? Josh felt slightly sick.

"How so?" Hallie asked.

"He's from one of those old moneyed New England families. They all sit on various boards. Win's thing is teenagers. Charter schools, scholarships, that sort of thing."

Josh stole a panicked glance at Ram, who smiled.

"Don't worry," he said. "He'll just give you a little advice. You don't really even have to listen. Just smile and nod and he'll be happy."

Josh stared out at the road. It was bad enough that the guidance counselor had told Hallie about his big SAT score, the exact number and how it was the highest in the school; now Hallie, too, was after him to go away for college. He knew that was part of the reason she had agreed to go to Boston with Ram—so they could look at universities.

"Didn't your sister go to Harvard?" Hallie asked.

"She and Win both. It's where they met."

"I hope they don't want to show me Harvard," Josh said. "I could never get in."

"If they want to," Hallie said, "we'll just go look at it. It doesn't hurt to look, right?"

"I guess not," Josh said.

It was quiet for a while after that, and then Ram pulled a sleeve of CDs out of his backpack. He put one in. The music was sort of folksy but also kind of edgy.

"Who is this?" Hallie asked when the first song was almost over.

"This Philly band I used to follow when I was in college. Cloud Cuckoo Land."

"I like them," Hallie said. "You used to go see them in Philly?"

"All the time," Ram said. "I had a crush on the singer. Miri. Every guy who saw them did."

"I always wanted to be that girl," Hallie said. "The one all the boys had crushes on."

"I thought you were," Ram said. It was quiet again, and then he turned the music up.

A FEW HOURS later, having switched drivers when they first reached the Massachusetts Turnpike, Ram turned onto a road full of the biggest houses Josh had ever seen, bigger and nicer than the houses at the Lake, even. McMansions, Ram called them. They all looked new, had big lawns and small trees, the fallen leaves swept into tidy piles. Ram pulled into a circular driveway in front of a huge brick house. He sat behind the wheel, not moving.

"I have an urge to turn around and go back," Ram said.

The front door opened, and a woman who looked like she had to be Ram's sister stepped out and waved. She was pretty, with shiny, long dark hair, a fluffy-looking white turtleneck and tan dress pants. An older Indian couple walked outside past her; to Josh they looked small and gray-haired and kind of nice, but he thought of the word Ram had used when talking about them earlier: torture.

JOSH HAD NEVER spent the night anywhere other than his own bedroom; his father used to say that farmers don't take vacations, and even the two times they went to visit Hallie in New York, they'd only gone for the day. He didn't expect to sleep well in a strange bed, but he did. And something about not being in his own bedroom caused him to remember right away when he woke up that his parents were dead, which was less awful than a split second of thinking they were alive and then realizing they were not. There was a bookcase in the room where he slept—there were lots of bookcases at Tara and Win's house—and Josh spent an hour when he first woke up flipping through the books and writing down the titles of the interesting-looking ones. A lot of them were by Indian writers he had never heard of: Arundhati Roy, Bharati Mukherjee, Vikram Seth. Josh had a slightly panicked feeling: he wasn't as well-read as he thought. He'd mostly read American and British novels, and a few translated from French or German. There were entire *continents* full of writers he'd never read.

Josh gave Nancy a quick call, to say Happy Thanksgiving and to check on Emma, and then he got dressed and ready to head downstairs. He felt nervous about the day, about having to say "No thank you" to the turkey. Ram didn't care what people thought of his being vegan—he looked for opportunities to tell them—but explaining himself was the part Josh hated most about being a vegetarian.

"It's just a phase, Don," he'd overheard his mom saying to his dad, at the beginning of his sophomore year of high school, when he'd first stopped eating meat.

"First, he won't do his schoolwork. Now he won't eat meat. Where does it end?" Dad had said, his voice low and angry as it sometimes got.

"He does his schoolwork. He only refused to dissect the frog. And he got an A on the paper he did instead." Josh had worked hard on that paper; he'd wanted to prove to his teacher that he could learn something without killing an animal.

"He needs to stop worrying about frogs and start thinking about his future."

"He's got time to think about his future. And like I said, kids go through phases. Next year he'll probably go hunting with you."

"*That* boy will never go hunting," his dad had muttered.

It was the only time Josh could remember that his dad had seemed to understand him better than his mom did; he knew Josh was serious, about not eating meat, not dissecting, all of it. How could she actually have thought Josh would ever go hunting?

To Josh's great relief, Tara and her mother had made an Indian feast, all vegetarian. When they sat down to eat, Ram's younger niece, Molly, tried to take the empty seat next to Josh—Hallie was on his other side—but Kat, her older sister, beat her to it. The two girls started trying to wrestle each other off the chair.

"I'm sitting here!" Kat cried.

"My chair!" whined Molly.

"Girls, stop it!" Winslow said, but Tara and her mother were still in the kitchen, bringing out the last of the food, and the girls ignored Winslow.

Hallie got up and lifted Molly away from her sister. She put her on the chair where she'd been sitting.

"Josh has two sides," Hallie said. "You can both sit next to him." She walked around the table and took the seat beside Ram.

Tara emerged with a big platter in her hand. "What happened?" she asked, doing one of those psychic women things.

It was her father who answered. "This one here," he said, motioning to Josh, "is quite the ladies' man." He winked at Josh.

LATER, AFTER THEY'D stuffed themselves, after Josh and Ram had done the dishes and Molly had put *Shrek* in the DVD player, Winslow took Josh aside.

"Come into my study a minute," he said, "so we can talk."

Winslow's study was sleek and modern, with a bookcase that took up an entire wall. Josh walked over and scanned the titles; Winslow was big on the Russians. Josh picked up a copy of Nabokov's *Pale Fire* and looked at the back cover.

"You can borrow that, if you like," Winslow said.

"I don't know if I'll be able to finish it before I leave."

"Keep it. It's just a paperback." Winslow sat in the chair behind his desk.

"I haven't read Nabokov yet." Josh hoped he had pronounced the name correctly.

"That's a good one. The structure is unusual, but once you get that figured out, it's really funny."

Josh nodded, uncertain of what to say next. Winslow motioned him to sit, and Josh did, the book still in his hands.

"Ram tells me you're looking at colleges," Winslow said.

Josh nodded again and ran his fingers over the cover of *Pale Fire*. He didn't know what Winslow expected of him.

"Any idea where you want to go?"

Josh cleared his throat. Maybe if he just told the truth, Winslow would leave him alone, and he could go watch *Shrek* with Molly. Or better yet, start reading the book.

"At first I just wanted to go to community college," he said, "but my guidance counselor thinks I should apply to Stockton and Rowan, and maybe Rutgers, so I guess I will."

Winslow nodded, and was quiet for a moment. "Do you mind if I ask why you wanted to go to community college?"

Josh had to think about the question. For all the times people had tried to talk him out of it, no one had actually asked him why he wanted to go there.

"I don't want to go far away from home," Josh said. "I know that sounds weird."

Winslow shook his head. "Not to me. I went to college in the same city where I grew up."

"I like where I live," Josh said. But as he said it, a new thought occurred to him: he'd always imagined commuting to school and living at home with Mom and Dad. Hallie wasn't going to stay in Oyster Shell all through his college years. Did he really want to live in that house by himself?

"You can always go away to college and move back after you graduate," Winslow said. "I mean, that's sort of what Ram did."

"I guess, too, I just thought there wouldn't be much money." Josh hadn't meant to blurt this, but there it was.

"There are scholarships."

"I know," Josh said, but the talk of money made him think about his father's anger at Hallie for going away. Josh had gotten his message loud and clear: that he shouldn't go to a pricey college unless there was something practical he could study, lucrative, like business or engineering. But Josh had always known his talents were more like his sister's, talents that a tomato farmer would consider impractical. He'd never thought of it like this before, but was that the real reason he'd never wanted to go away—that he didn't want Dad mad at him, the way he was always mad at Hallie?

"I mean," Josh added, "the only thing I could possibly major in is English, and I don't know what kind of, like, job I could get. My guidance counselor says English majors end up working as waiters." This was the main reason he hated the guidance counselor, though he'd never doubted that what she'd said was true.

"I was an English major," Winslow said.

"You were?"

He nodded. "I minored in economics, and got an MBA after."

Josh sighed. "Yeah, but see, I don't think I could do *anything* but English."

"How are your grades?"

"Like a B+ average in English and French," Josh said. "Lower in everything else."

"How low?"

Josh thought about it. "Like a C, I guess."

"But a high B average in the humanities," Winslow said.

"Yeah, basically."

"SATs?"

Josh felt like he was being interviewed, though he didn't mind so much. Winslow actually seemed to be interested in Josh's life. "Okay, well, here's the thing. In Critical Reading I got the highest score in my high school. A 790."

Winslow whistled, soft and low.

"It threw everyone into a frenzy. I guess no one thought I was that smart." Josh felt like he'd been gulping air, and he swallowed. "But my math score was only in the 500s."

Winslow nodded, and tapped a pen on his desk. He seemed to be thinking it all over.

"What do you want to do, after college?" he asked. "I mean, if you could do anything you wanted, not worrying about money, what would you do?"

Josh stared at the book in his hands. He didn't know whether he should tell Winslow, or even if he *could* tell him. He'd always been afraid of being laughed at. Lately he'd been thinking that not only *could* he write a book, he *had* to do it. Since the night of the Halloween party he'd started keeping a journal, and sometimes he would reread his entries with a highlighter in hand, marking the thoughts that seemed especially true or well-said. He knew this wasn't the book he wanted to write, but it was a start. Josh felt a weird urge to tell Winslow, but what would he think? People who grew up like Winslow were expected to write books. Kids from Oyster Shell were not.

Josh waved the book at Winslow. He swallowed hard. "This," was all he could say, meaning the book.

Winslow looked puzzled for a second; then he smiled. "You want to write."

Josh nodded.

"What do you want to write?"

"I'm not sure," Josh whispered. He couldn't get his voice above a croak. "Maybe something like my beliefs or philosophy. Maybe a novel." He wondered if he sounded like an idiot.

"If you want to write," Winslow said, "you should get the best liberal arts education you can."

Josh had no idea what that meant.

"Look for schools with strong English departments, with writers you admire on the faculty. I'll make up a list, before you go." Winslow paused. "If you want, you can e-mail me your application essay after you write it. I'll help you shape it up."

"Really?" Josh asked. It occurred to him to wonder why Winslow was being so nice. Was it just more pity, the poor kid whose parents were dead?

"Sure. I read a lot of them, so I have a pretty good idea what these schools are looking for." Winslow smiled. "In return I'll want a signed copy of your first book."

Josh laughed, louder than he'd intended to, but Winslow looked serious. "I mean, it's just a dream," Josh said. "I don't know if I can promise you that."

Winslow leaned across the table and looked Josh right in the eyes. "You have to promise me," he said, "that you *will* write your book. It might take you five years after college, or ten, or longer, but you will write it." He straightened back up, cocked his head to the side. "Otherwise I can't help you."

Josh couldn't even imagine what his parents would have made of this. Winslow would help him if he promised he'd write a book; a promise he couldn't really be held to. Yet Josh didn't make promises he couldn't keep. If he said yes, he would have to write his book. He was certain he'd never forget this moment—the ticking of the clock, the leather of the sleek black chair (normally it would bother him, that the chair was leather, but not just then), and Winslow's face, looking so honest and true.

"I'll promise," Josh said, "but I don't want anyone else to know. About my book, I mean." He didn't think he could bear to reveal this part of himself to anyone other than Winslow—not even Ram.

"It's between us," he said, and he handed Josh a card. "E-mail me anytime."

There was a knock on the door, and Tara stuck her head in. "Dessert?" she asked, and then, looking directly at Josh: "He cornered you already, did he? Win, you should have given him a chance to recover from dinner."

"I was just saving him from watching *Shrek*," Winslow said, and winked at Josh.

"And he lent me a book," Josh said, holding up the Nabokov.

"*Pale Fire*," Tara said, shaking her head. "There's some nice light reading for your Thanksgiving break."

Josh knew that Tara was trying to be nice, but she was treating him like just some teenager, some kid who wanted to do nothing but sit around and play Xbox. Win seemed to get that Josh was not that person.

"What's for dessert?" Josh asked, smiling at Tara like he supposed an ordinary kid, the kid she thought he was, would smile.

CHAPTER 14

Hallie rose early on Saturday, the morning they were leaving Boston for New York. Downstairs, Ram's sister had him cornered in the kitchen; he nodded impatiently as she spoke. Hallie said a quick good morning, accepted the coffee Tara handed her, and joined the others in the family room. She watched as Molly gave Josh a drawing she'd made for him. Kat, not to be outdone, swiped a book from Winslow's study.

"This is your dad's," Josh said to Kat as she handed him a copy of *War and Peace*.

"Have you read it?" Winslow asked.

Josh shook his head no.

"Keep it," he said. "You finished *Pale Fire*."

Hallie looked at Josh. "Did you read an entire book in the three days we were here?"

"And discussed it with me," Winslow said. He winked at Josh.

Winslow clearly had affection for her brother, and Hallie was pleased to see it. Until now, their father and Ram had been Josh's only male role models. Dad, Hallie was sure, had done nothing but try to hold Josh back, as he'd always tried with her. And Ram—not that he wasn't a good person, or a good influence, but she didn't want Josh to end up like that, alone with the righteousness of his own beliefs, living off grants in a small room in Oyster Shell and spending his days wading through Mollusk Creek.

Winslow went upstairs and returned with Hallie's bags, motioned her to follow him outside. He set the bags next to Nancy's car.

"I hope you don't mind," he said, "but I offered to keep in touch with Josh. I can help him with his college applications, as long as I'm not stepping on any toes."

"Not at all," Hallie said. "I've been pretty overwhelmed since the accident. I'm grateful for the help." But she appreciated that he asked, didn't just take matters into his own hands as Ram often did.

"He's a great kid," Winslow said, and Hallie smiled.

Josh walked outside with his duffel bag, flanked by Molly and Kat.

"He likes my book better than your drawing," Kat said to Molly, who appeared on the verge of tears.

Hallie walked back in the house to get her purse and came upon Ram and his mother, Mrs. Rao holding her son's face in her hands, speaking to him in Telugu. His expression could only be described as appalled. Hallie saw Tara standing in the next room; she motioned Hallie over to her, and they stood there quietly until Ram's mother released him and both mother and son slipped out the front door.

"What did she say to him?" Hallie asked. "If you don't mind my asking."

Tara's eyes sparkled. "She said, 'Do not be so extreme that no one but your mother can love you.'"

"Wow," Hallie said.

Tara gave her an appraising look. "Would you mind if I asked you a question?"

"No."

"Is there anything between you and Ram?"

Hallie smiled. She knew she'd be fielding the same question from Lawrence later in the day. "What did Ram say?" she asked, surprised at her own coyness.

Tara rolled her eyes. "He said no, but he's very secretive. And you know how men can be when something's new. They hate to admit it."

"Well, you're not the first to speculate, but no, there's nothing between us yet." Yet? Had she really just said "yet"? It was a mere slip of the tongue, but it sent Hallie into a slight mental panic.

RAM WAS SILENT in the driver's seat until they reached the turnpike.

"You two have no idea what I went through yesterday, when you were off looking at colleges with Win," he finally said. Winslow had taken Hallie and Josh on a whirlwind tour of Emerson, Tufts and Harvard, while the Raos went to visit some distant family for the day.

"What happened?" Hallie asked.

Ram sighed, and pulled into the middle lane of the highway. "The trip to Ashland was a pretext to introduce me to some girl," he said. "Daughter of a friend of a cousin."

"They were trying to fix you up?" Josh asked.

"Yeah. But they'd lied about me. They'd told her I was a doctor, not that I had a doctorate in wildlife biology. My mom claimed it got lost in the translation."

Hallie laughed a little, and Ram shot her a quick look.

"Oh come on," she said. "It's funny."

Ram was quiet.

"When's the wedding?" Josh asked, so deadpan that Hallie couldn't help but laugh again.

"I fixed her up with you instead," Ram said to Josh. "She'll be arriving in Oyster Shell next week."

"Cool," Josh said. "When's *my* wedding?" It was nice, Hallie thought, to see Josh playful and upbeat.

Hallie looked at Ram. "Did you let her down easy?"

Ram shook his head. "It was more the other way around. She was not interested in frog deformities or a tour of the bay." He sighed. "My father wants me to quit the Mollusk Creek Trust and get a job teaching at a university."

"You're not going to do that, are you?" Josh's voice rose in alarm.

"Of course not."

Josh's cell phone rang just then. "Hi, Nicki," he said, and scooted back, as far away from Ram and Hallie as he could get, his voice dropping low. Ram glanced at Hallie and they both smiled.

"I have a question," Hallie said to Ram. "Suppose you find the cause of the frog deformities. Suppose you get the creek cleaned up. What will you do then?"

Ram was quiet for a minute. "I'll celebrate, then I'll look for a new challenge." He shifted slightly in his seat. "My parents think no one will ever marry me because I'm too wrapped up in this work, I'm too radical, I don't make enough money." He stared at the road for a moment. "They might be right."

"Do you want to get married?" Hallie asked. "I mean, some people prefer not to."

Ram shrugged. "Hypothetically, at some future time, if I met someone I was really compatible with, I think I'd like to."

Hallie was quiet for a moment. "Me too. With all the same caveats."

"You ever come close?" he asked. "To getting married, I mean."

Hallie looked out at the highway. There were more cars than she would have expected this early on a Saturday. "I thought so, once. But it wasn't as serious for him." She would have said more, if Josh weren't in the car. She couldn't mention Damien without seeing the hero worship in her brother's eyes.

IT WAS JUST after one in the afternoon when Ram pulled up in front of Hallie's building on Grove Street.

"Thanks so much for driving us all the way in," she said.

"I remember this building now," Josh said. "I came here with Mom and Dad a really long time ago."

"This is the West Village, right?" Ram asked.

Hallie nodded. "Are you sure you don't want to stay with us here tonight? Lawrence and Kenneth have a guest room."

"Thanks, but I really need to get back."

"Hot date?" Hallie asked. She'd meant it as a joke, but Ram's face reddened. "You actually *do* have a hot date?"

Ram rolled his eyes. "I don't know if it's 'hot,' but it is a date."

Josh leaned forward. "You have a girlfriend? How come you never told me?"

Ram sighed. "It's nothing serious. That's why I didn't tell you."

"Who is it?" Josh asked.

Ram glanced at the two of them sideways. "You don't know her. Her name's Brittany."

"Brittany? How old is she? Twelve?" Hallie had intended it as a joke, but the words sounded sharp, landing like little daggers. Ram winced.

Josh scrambled out of the car.

"I'm sorry," Hallie said. "That was supposed to be funny." But she felt annoyed in a way she couldn't quite pin down. Where had Ram even met a girl named Brittany? He seemed to spend all of his time in Mollusk Creek.

Ram shook his head. "She's twenty-four," he said. "It's not serious." Hallie was surprised at the relief she felt.

LAWRENCE HAD LEFT a note on Hallie's kitchen counter, next to a vase of white tulips: he and Kenneth were out shopping for a dinner party to celebrate the *New Yorker* article. Hallie and Josh should come up around seven.

"Well, it looks like we have the afternoon to ourselves," she said to Josh. "What do you want to do?"

"I want to go see the birds," Josh said, and Hallie thought: *Of course he does.*

"*MES CHÉRIES!*" JOY exclaimed at the door. She was wearing an old Rolling Stones tour shirt and jeans, Albert on her shoulder.

Josh said something to her in French and Joy blinked at him.

"Sorry, dear, but I don't speak that much French," Joy said. "I just picked up a few phrases from my ex. I like the way they sound."

She showed them in, offered them some pomegranate juice, which Josh accepted and Hallie refused, then took them to the aviary. Years ago, Joy had had the room's original wooden door replaced with a glass one. Hallie saw Josh's eyes widen when they reached the door. It really was something: a complex series of perches and artificial tree branches snaked throughout the room, which was alive with the brightly colored birds. Maya flitted up to the glass; Albert, still on Joy's shoulder, whistled.

"Can I go in?" Josh asked.

"Sure," Joy said, and she and Hallie watched as Josh entered the aviary. Maya hovered by his head at first, then lit on the finger he offered her.

"How's he doing?" Joy asked quietly.

Hallie shrugged. "Good days and bad. He was doing really badly for a while, but seems better lately. This trip has helped, I think."

They both watched for a moment as Josh moved lithely through the aviary, Maya walking the length of his arm. Teddy the toucan flew to a perch right in front of Josh, and regarded him first from one eye, then the other.

"And how are *you* doing?" Joy asked Hallie.

"Okay, I guess. It's surreal. I wake up and expect to be in my apartment here."

Joy nodded. "I miss you, you know." She was quiet for a moment. "And not just because I've been through two office managers since you left, and they were both *terrible*." She pronounced "terrible" the French way.

Hallie smiled and looked at Joy. She never would have guessed she'd feel this way, but she did. "I miss you, too."

"Maybe after the holidays you could come up for a few days and we could blitz through some work," Joy said. "There are all these back orders for prints that I can't get out. I'll pay you a *ton*."

She could certainly use the money. "I'll try to get away."

"Are you taking any photos now?" Joy asked.

"Sure. I recently shot a ninety-five-year-old woman, a student of the week and a happy puppy." When Joy stared at her blankly, Hallie added, "I got a job on a weekly newspaper. It's pretty awful."

"I meant your own work," Joy said.

Hallie wondered if Joy knew that she hadn't pursued her own work in years. She doubted she was about to experience a creative renaissance, given the circumstances. But looking at Josh, how his lanky body blended in with the trees, Hallie felt a strong urge to shoot him, and she hadn't had that kind of creative desire in some time.

"I want to shoot Josh with the birds," she said to Joy, gesturing to the living room where she'd left her Nikon.

Inside the aviary, Hallie put her finger to her lips when Josh looked at her. The first few clicks of the shutter startled him more than the birds, who were, by now, used to the sound of cameras. But soon he relaxed and went back to what he'd been doing, communing with the birds. Halfway through the roll of film, Joy opened the door and put Albert inside. The parrot immediately took Josh's right shoulder, the one Maya hadn't claimed. Hallie got a few decent shots. Oddly, she thought of Brenda: it would have made a nice Christmas present for her, a photo of her son. But none of this would have happened if Brenda were alive.

Hallie continued to shoot, Albert mimicking her camera's sounds so she had the odd impression a second camera was in the room. She finished the roll and pulled a new one from her pocket, quickly reloading. Josh had completely lost his self-consciousness by the second roll; *these* would be the shots. She wished she had gone home last summer— she almost had, Brenda had been pressing her—and taken photos of her dad and Brenda. The one Josh took that they'd displayed at the funeral wasn't bad, but it was posed, and Hallie knew she could have done more; she could have really caught them, when they weren't prepared, when they'd dropped their masks. Maybe, if she'd gone down there for her father's birthday in August, she could have captured him in her lens. Captured his soul, as some cultures believed. She'd never found any other way to capture it.

She looked at Josh, his nose shiny with oil from raging hormones, his shaggy hair hanging over both cheeks as he peered down at one of the sulfur-crested cockatoos. Two months ago, he went to school one day and came home to an entirely different life. The sadness that welled within her just then, a sudden desperation and longing too intense to be articulated, came from seeing the last two months through Josh's eyes, not her own. She had closed off her own feelings for her dad long ago. But she knew what it felt like to be Josh. She knew how it had felt when her mother died.

She was barely conscious of the shots she was still taking, barely conscious of the bird shit that hit her shoulder. She didn't realize anything was wrong until she saw Josh looking at her with concern, and even then, she didn't realize the extent of it. It wasn't until her legs collapsed that she realized she was not okay. Josh scrambled to her side; she wanted to say something to reassure him, but she felt so far away. He sat down next to her and took her hand, holding on more tightly than she would have expected, and they sat like that until Hallie was beyond the possibility of tears, safe to come back into herself.

IT WAS A small dinner party by Lawrence and Kenneth's standards: Alison and her current beau; a gay couple Hallie didn't know, friends of Kenneth's; and Carole Bloom, Jonathan's sister, escorted by her teenage son, Nathan. Carole and Lawrence had remained close in the years since Jonathan's death. The memoir, Hallie knew, had been her idea.

Nathan approached Josh before Hallie could introduce them; they started talking and appeared to hit it off. For a kid who seemed so introverted, Josh was handling it well, all these new people and situations into which he was being thrown.

"He seems to be doing better," Kenneth said to Hallie as he refilled her champagne flute. "He looks happier."

"He does, doesn't he?" She watched Josh as he chatted with Nathan. His hands were in his pockets, but his face was animated. "He had a good time in Boston." She smiled at Kenneth a little. "And he has a date later."

"A date?" Kenneth asked.

"Well, not really a date. He has a friend at school whose father lives in Brooklyn. She's here for the weekend. They're going to a movie later."

"I'm glad he has a friend." Kenneth poured himself more champagne. "Before I forget, I went over all that material you sent us—the figures on the farm, and the lawsuit information. We should talk tomorrow."

Hallie gulped the rest of her champagne. "What's the bottom line?"

"You're going to have to sell that farm. It's a money pit."

Hallie sighed. "I figured that."

After they ate dinner, Carole suggested a toast to Lawrence. She held his issue of the *New Yorker* up for everyone to see, announced that he had already been contacted by two agents wanting to see his book. Though she was full of her own worries, Hallie raised her glass and smiled, acting like the person she'd been before. When Lawrence sidled over and asked her what she was thinking about, she told him what she knew he wanted to hear.

"Your book," she said.

CHAPTER 15

Josh elbowed his way down the hall, crowded as it always was between classes. His school seemed busier with Christmas less than two weeks away and finals coming up; the other kids were buzzing with an excitement Josh could feel, though he didn't share it. The decorations on the walls—snowflakes and candy canes and sprigs of holly, carefully chosen to appear non-denominational—filled him with nothing but dread.

Josh's mother had loved everything about Christmas: the religious part of it—the celebration of Jesus's birth, and especially Midnight Mass on Christmas Eve—as well as the corny stuff. She'd had special towels and tablecloths and even sweaters that were Christmasey, and while Josh used to tease her about them, he missed seeing that stuff around the house. He had hidden all of it in the back of his closet. If he told Hallie about the decorations, she'd try to pretend she liked them, but she'd make a face, and it was the face that Josh couldn't bear to see. He knew that some of the things his mom had liked were dorky, but that was exactly what he missed: the floppy, bunny-ear slippers that Josh had laughed at when she'd first worn them last year ("What are you, Mom, like *ten years old?*" Josh had said, and she'd just smiled and shrugged); the way she would always, no matter how careful she was, get tomato sauce on her top when she was eating spaghetti, and how she'd laugh about it; the silly Polish songs she would sometimes sing, songs her grandmother had taught her.

Josh knew he needed to stop thinking about all this or he'd get really upset, so he focused his eyes straight ahead as he headed down the hall to Nicki's history class. Two of the jocks thundered by, laughing, one of them trying to grab something out of the other's notebook; the one with the notebook, Matt Harding, said hi to Josh in passing. A few of the popular kids had been saying hi to Josh ever since Missy Dalton's party, ever since a rumor went around the school that Josh had gotten drunk and thrown up.

Josh reached the door of Nicki's class. She was talking with her teacher, Mr. Flynn, gesturing wildly with her hands, the way she did when she was really into what she was saying. She and Mr. Flynn both laughed. Josh had never had Mr. Flynn; he was one of the younger teachers, Miss Piper's age, maybe. He seemed to like Nicki and it made Josh feel weird in a way he couldn't quite identify. Josh was about to knock on the door and motion through the window at Nicki when he felt a tap on his shoulder. He turned around and was face-to-face with Missy.

"Hi Josh," she said, smiling her big bright smile at him. She smelled the way she always did, clean and special, but it didn't make him dizzy the way it used to.

"Hey, Missy," Josh said.

"Where are you headed now? Lunch?"

"Yeah." Josh glanced into the classroom, but Nicki was still talking.

"I have study hall," Missy said, "but Mrs. Chartoff is pretty lax if we're late. I'll walk with you to the cafeteria, if you want."

Three months ago Josh's heart would have pounded and his stomach bottomed out at such a suggestion. Now, it wasn't such a big deal.

"I'm waiting for Nicki," Josh said, and gestured toward the door.

Missy glanced through the window. "Oh."

Josh shifted from foot to foot, unsure of what to say next. Finally he thought of something: "I really liked that disc you made me. I don't know if I ever told you."

Missy smiled. "Thanks," she said. "I hope they tour this spring."

Josh nodded.

"I wanted to give you this." She pulled a flyer from her notebook. It was for her Christmas party.

"Thanks."

"Do you think you'll come?"

"Maybe," Josh said, though he doubted he'd go. He glanced into the classroom; Nicki was moving closer to the door, but still talking to Mr. Flynn. Maybe he could handle going to the party if Nicki went with him. "Could I bring someone?"

Missy's eyes widened. "Who?"

"Nicki," he said. Right after he said it, he knew it was a bad idea. Nicki would never want to go to a party at Missy's house. And the look on Missy's face made Josh wish he'd just taken the flyer and walked away. It was the kind of face Hallie made when she didn't approve of something, the look he'd been avoiding by hiding his mom's Christmas stash. Missy was quiet for a minute.

"Are you going out with her?" she finally asked. "I see you guys together all the time now."

Josh shook his head. "We're just friends."

The look of disapproval melted away, and Missy smiled. "I'm glad."

It was a weird thing to say. A small place inside him that would always want Missy to like him stirred.

"I'm sure she's nice and all," Missy went on, "but I think you could do better."

Better? "What do you mean?"

Missy lowered her voice. "She's so…*controversial.* All those political flyers and everything. I mean, she crammed five pages about the Canadian seal hunt into my locker this morning. I didn't need to start my day with pictures of baby seals being clubbed to death, you know?"

Josh stared at Missy. So many times, Nicki had suggested that Missy was as shallow as the rest of the popular kids, and so many times Josh had defended her. "So you'd rather just not know what's going on in the world?"

Missy tilted her head and frowned. Josh thought it might have been the first time in her life someone had suggested she might be anything other than 100 percent smart.

"Of course not," she said. "I know about the seal hunt. I know about Darfur. I know about all the stuff in Nicki's flyers. I don't need her to come in from New York and tell me, like I'm some hick who never read a newspaper."

"She doesn't mean it like that," Josh said. "You'd like her if you got to know her."

Missy looked at him for a moment. "I'm sure I would," she said, but it didn't sound convincing. "She's not the kind of girl you'd want to go out with, though."

"Why not?" Josh asked. His voice came out louder than he'd expected. Missy shifted her books and squirmed a little.

"You sound mad," she said.

"I'm just not sure what you mean." But she was right—he did sound mad, though mostly he was mad at himself, for wasting so much of his life liking Missy. She had no idea what he had gone through that night, after he left her party. It was Nicki who was willing to really listen to him, Nicki who stayed on the phone with him that night until he felt better. Josh had always been so nervous around Missy, but around Nicki he could be himself.

"Well, you could get Monika. She still likes you. She understands that you're going through stuff, with your family and all, but she'd love to see you at the party."

Josh wasn't sure this was even true. Monika used to talk to him a lot in school, but she'd stopped not long after the Halloween party.

"Isn't she going back to Germany soon?" he asked, and Missy shrugged.

Nicki came through the door. She looked from Josh to Missy and back. "What's going on?" she asked. Her accent sounded more harsh than usual.

Josh felt his face flush as he looked at Missy. He *was* mad. It was awful, the way she had put Nicki down. Missy was like one of those terrible characters in an Edith Wharton novel who meddled with everyone else's business for their own selfish ends.

"Nothing," Josh said to Nicki, looking straight at Missy. "Let's go to lunch." He put his hand on Nicki's elbow and steered her away.

"What was that about?" Nicki asked once they were down the hall.

"Nothing," Josh said.

Nicki looked at him. "You're mad."

"I'm not mad." But he was, he was seething.

"You're *really* mad," Nicki said, but she looked pleased, like she'd waited a long time for this moment. "I've never seen you mad before."

Josh shrugged.

"What did she say?"

"Nothing."

They reached the entrance to the cafeteria. Nicki put her hand out to stop Josh.

"Was it about me?" she asked. She looked small, and a little afraid, and it got to Josh when she looked like that.

"It doesn't matter," he said, "what Missy thinks."

"I want to know."

Josh sighed. He knew she wouldn't give it a rest until he told her something.

"It's just that Monika likes me," he said. "Missy keeps trying to fix me up." He had told Nicki about the Halloween party, of course, and about Monika, though he hadn't told her how much he'd liked Missy back then, or how upset he was about Cole.

Nicki shrugged. "So? You can go out with Monika if you want."

"I don't want to go out with Monika," he said. "Give me your books and I'll grab our table."

Nicki smiled at him and got in the lunch line. Her smile suggested that he had said the right thing.

THAT AFTERNOON NICKI rode the bus home with Josh. There was a Mollusk Creek Trust meeting that night, and they planned to hang out and have pizza at his house first.

Normally Josh studied or slept on the bus and everyone ignored him, but being there with Nicki, he felt the other kids looking at him. Malik Turner and Ray Watson, Josh's friends from grammar school, tramped onto the bus and took the seats behind Josh and Nicki. Josh hadn't really talked to the boys since the wake. Malik tapped him on the shoulder.

"Homes," Malik said, "how you doin'?"

Josh had known the two boys since kindergarten. There was a time when the three of them were inseparable, playing at each other's houses nearly every day. But something had shifted around fifth grade. Malik and Ray got into sports, and Josh got into reading, and by sixth grade Josh was listening to Pearl Jam and the Foo Fighters and they were listening to Snoop Dog and Eminem, and after a while all they did was say hi to each other in school.

"Not bad," Josh said. "Do you guys know Nicki?"

"Sure," Malik said. "We got health class together." Malik smiled at Nicki. "You really gave it to Mrs. W. last week."

Nicki shrugged. "She told us her husband bought a Hummer," she said to Josh.

It was quiet for a moment, and then Ray leaned in toward Josh. "You know," he said, "I never told you…"

"Not now, man," Malik said, poking Ray in the ribs.

"It's cool," Josh said. Ray grabbed Josh's head and sort of awkwardly hugged it, then quickly leaned back in his seat.

"So what you doing riding out to No Man's Land, girl?" Malik asked. It was his nickname for Oyster Shell, the last stop on the long bus ride from Floyd.

"She's hanging out at my house, and then we're going to a Mollusk Creek Trust meeting," Josh said.

"That Indian dude still ain't fixed the frogs yet?" Ray asked, and Malik cracked up.

"That dude is in-tense," Malik said. "He freaked my Pops the hell out a few years ago when he showed him some of them eighteen-legged frogs. Pops won't let us anywhere near that creek."

"*Eighteen*-legged frogs?" Nicki asked Josh.

"I think six was the most he found," Josh said.

Nicki's phone rang—a System of a Down song, her favorite—and when she turned away from the boys to answer it, Ray grinned and made a sexual gesture to Josh with the thumb and forefinger of one hand and the index finger of the other. After that Josh was kind of relieved when Malik and Ray's stop came up and they all said goodbye.

Nicki got off the phone just before the bus rolled past Corson's Farm. Josh pointed it out to Nicki.

"Can I see it?" she asked.

"It's not that interesting," Josh said, "especially in winter. The greenhouses are the only thing going." Josh thought about the two-mile stretch between the farm and his house. "And it's a long walk home from there."

Nicki shrugged. "Let's look anyway."

Josh hadn't been to the farm in weeks. The last time he and Hallie had toured the greenhouses, what they'd seen hadn't been promising: pots of scraggly seedlings, some yellowed and blighted-looking, only about half green and lush the way they were supposed to be. The herbs had looked better than the tomatoes.

"Okay," he said, and they got off at the stop closest to the farm. Cal's truck was nowhere in sight, so Josh led the way to the first greenhouse.

He was shocked by what he saw. Where at least some of the plants had looked like they were making it a month ago, all of them were now half or totally dead. There were pots upended and broken, shards on the greenhouse floor along with cigarette butts, paper coffee cups, sandwich wrappers.

"This looks bad," Nicki said.

"Yeah."

"Is your sister going to fire that guy?" Nicki asked, rubbing a yellowed leaf from one of the basil plants between her fingers. "I mean, she should."

"She wants to," Josh said, "but it's tricky."

In a corner, a pile of dead tomato plants lay brown and withered. Nicki walked over and looked at them. "Maybe you should call her."

"I'll talk to her later," Josh said. "Let's go. Emma needs her walk."

When they got to the house, Josh checked the mailbox. There was a letter from the insurance company, and one from a law firm whose partners had scary-sounding last names. Josh knew it was all about the accident. He couldn't believe it, that you could sue someone who was already dead, when what it really meant was that you were suing the people who'd been left behind. He moved those letters to the bottom of the stack. Maybe he would wait to tell Hallie about the farm.

FEWER PEOPLE CAME to the Mollusk Creek Trust meetings in winter, especially in December before the holidays; but there were six people who went to almost every meeting, and that night Nancy and Josh were the only two of that core group there. After waiting almost a half hour to see if anyone else would show up, Ram finally pulled four chairs into a circle.

"It's silly for me to stand at the podium," he said. "We might as well just talk."

"I still want the full presentation," Nicki said. "I don't care if no one else is here."

Ram's face brightened then, and he handed out the fact sheets he'd printed with the preliminary results from last year's creek survey. There were slightly fewer deformities than the previous year, but not a huge difference. There was a page where Ram broke the figures down by the type of deformity.

"Eye stalks?" Nicki asked. "What does that mean?"

Ram motioned her to a display he had in the office, a frog he'd had preserved after it died. Josh had seen it many times, but it still made him feel queasy and sad.

"The poor thing's blind," Nicki said, running her fingers over the eyeless face.

"Look inside the mouth," Ram said.

"It's gross," Josh said. "I'm just warning you."

Nicki glanced at Josh, then opened the frog's mouth. She turned away quickly, but Josh knew what she had seen: the two stalks hanging down from the roof of the mouth, eyes dangling from their ends. Nicki's face looked pale.

"Are you alright?" Nancy asked.

"Yeah," Nicki said. She stared at the frog for a moment, then peered into its mouth again. This time she looked at it carefully. "That can't be real."

"I wish it weren't," Ram said. "I find a dozen or so frogs each year like this. It's not as prevalent as the extra or missing legs."

Nicki looked at Ram. "This is terrible!"

"That's why I'm here," Ram said, "living in one room and horrifying my parents."

They all laughed. "But horrifying your parents is kind of a bonus, isn't it?" Nicki said, and then Ram smiled.

"So what do we need to do here?" Nicki added. "Fundraising? Getting the word out?" Josh knew she'd be stuffing people's lockers with flyers about the frogs.

THE NEXT DAY after school Josh and Nicki walked over to the *Good News* office, which wasn't far from the high school, to see if Hallie would give them a ride to the mall. Josh had made enough visits to the newsroom by then to recognize everyone he saw: Marcus, Jane, Ben, and Cecile, all working on their computers.

"Hey," Marcus said, flashing Josh a quick grin as he continued to pound at the keyboard. "You looking for Hallie?"

"Yeah," Josh said.

"She's out on assignment," he said. "Orren has her taking photos of the Christmas decorations around town. She was *real* happy about it."

Josh smiled. If there was anybody who was hating the Christmas decorations as much as he was this year, it was Hallie.

Cecile walked over to Marcus's desk. "Hi, Josh," she said, in that voice she had that kind of killed him. Her hair was pale pink now; she'd cut it very short, and had sparkly gel in it. She was dressed in a pale yellow skirt, a long pink scarf, and a tight sky blue sweater that matched her eyes. She stood with one hip stretched out toward Josh. He imagined running his hand along her hipbone.

"Hi," he said to Cecile.

Nicki cleared her throat.

"Sorry," Josh said. "This is my friend, Nicki."

Nicki shook hands with Marcus, but not with Cecile.

"You two must have exams coming up," Marcus said. "I always hated those finals before Christmas."

Josh shrugged. "It's not too bad."

Cecile smiled at Josh with her eyes. They were the kind of eyes you could lose yourself in. "I like your hair," she said to Nicki, who had recently touched up the blue streaks.

"Thanks," Nicki muttered.

"So what are you guys up to?" Cecile asked.

"We need a ride to the mall," Josh said.

"I can take you," Cecile said. "I'm going to be here for hours tonight anyway. I need a break."

"That's really nice of you," Josh said. Nicki was flipping through a copy of *Good News*.

"My pleasure." Cecile touched Josh's elbow and ran her hand to his wrist, where it lingered for a split second and then vanished. No one else saw this, as far as Josh could tell, and it happened so fast that he wondered if he'd imagined it; but his arm still tingled from her touch.

Nicki put the newspaper back on Marcus's desk. "I can't believe it, but everything in there really *is* good news," she said.

"Watch out," Marcus said, "or we'll make you student of the week."

"Isn't it a riot?" Cecile said. "Most of the time I can't even believe I work here."

•

JOSH EXPECTED CECILE to drop them at the mall, but she went in with them. "I need a few things for my apartment, now that I have one," she said.

"Where do you live?" Nicki asked as they went through the mall's main entrance.

"For the past week, Mulberry Street, here in Floyd. I moved in December first. Before that, I was commuting from Philly. Except for the week I lived in my car."

"You lived in your car? You should have told Hallie you needed a place to stay," Josh said. "We have all these empty rooms at home."

Cecile looked at Josh. "You are *so* sweet," she said. "I didn't even think of that. I just had to get away."

"Why?" Nicki asked.

Cecile pushed her left sleeve up and held her arm out for them to inspect. There was a huge, dark purple bruise on her upper arm. It looked like a hand, with finger marks.

"Who did that to you?" Josh asked. He had an urge to defend Cecile, to find the guy and—do what? Beat him up?

"My ex," she said. "I pretty much left in the middle of the night, with what I could carry. The turkey I'd planned to cook for Thanksgiving may still be in the fridge."

Nicki stared at Cecile's arm. "That happened two weeks ago?"

Cecile followed her gaze. "Yeah," she said. "Wow, it's still really dark, huh?"

"You should have told somebody," Josh said. It was awful, the thought of some guy hurting Cecile, and then keeping most of her belongings. "Maybe you could get Marcus or someone to go with you to get the rest of your stuff."

Cecile smiled. "Don't worry about me. I have a plan." She looked at her watch. "And I'd better go down to Penney's and buy some sheets and get back to work." She squeezed Josh's arm. He saw Nicki notice it. "Bye. Have fun."

"Thanks for the ride," Josh said as she left. He and Nicki walked to Starbucks and ordered hot chocolates.

"There's something off about her," Nicki said. "Cecile, I mean."

"Off?" Josh asked.

"Yeah, off. Not quite right. Like, she didn't get that bruise two weeks ago. More like two days ago."

Josh shrugged. He didn't think it was important *when* she'd gotten the bruise. What was awful was that it had happened at all.

Their drinks came and they carried them to a small table.

"I guess it doesn't matter," Nicki said.

Josh shrugged. "You can say what you're thinking."

Nicki was quiet for a minute. "She reminds me of one of my dad's ex-girlfriends. Everything about her was all exaggerated and melodramatic. She turned out to be a compulsive liar."

"You're saying Cecile is a compulsive liar just because her bruise looked newer than she said it was?"

Nicki looked at him, a weird half-smile on her face. "Just because you're so honest and upfront, you think everyone else is. But they're not." She took a sip of her hot chocolate. "That's all I'm saying."

"What makes you think I'm so honest?" It wasn't that Josh minded the characterization, but he didn't think it was so true. There was a lot he didn't tell people.

Nicki gave him one of her you've-got-to-be-kidding-me looks. "Because you *are*."

"I'm not," he said. "You just think I am."

Nicki shook her head.

"There's a lot I don't tell you."

Nicki rolled her eyes. "Like what?"

Like that I was seriously considering killing myself on Halloween night, he thought, but he wasn't going to say that. He didn't want anyone to know.

Nicki put her hand on his arm. "I'm sorry," she said. "You're right. I'm sure there's a lot of stuff I don't know."

She had that look on her face that Hallie got sometimes, like whatever had happened to him was her fault.

"It's okay," he said, and pulled his arm away.

She looked at him like she didn't believe him. "I forget sometimes," she said.

"Forget?"

"What happened to you. Sometimes I forget."

He felt strangely relieved. "I'm glad."

They both sipped their hot chocolates until Nicki checked the time on her phone. "I'd better get going. My shift starts soon." She put on her Mario's cap and pulled out her name tag, pinned it to her t-shirt. "I loathe this name tag."

Josh smiled. "Are you working over Christmas?"

"I'll be at my dad's," she said. "Christmas Day to New Year's." She sounded happy about it; Josh realized he would miss her. "You should come up for New Year's," she added.

"New Year's?"

"Yeah. Remember that guy Nathan who went to the movie with us Thanksgiving weekend? He invited me to a party."

"He invited you to a party?" Nathan had seemed okay to Josh when he first met him, but he'd annoyed Josh as the evening wore on, reminding him of Cole Huxley.

"Yeah, he's having a big New Year's party. I'm sure you can come."

"So you guys are friends now?" It seemed weird to Josh that she'd never mentioned Nathan.

"Not really. He just invited me to his party. I'm not even sure if I'm going."

"You should go, if you want," he said. "I think I'm just going to stay home, though."

"How come?"

Josh tried to think of how to explain it. "Christmas is going to be weird," he said, "without my parents." He hadn't expected to say it like that; it just slipped out.

She looked in his eyes. "I know."

Josh's cell phone beeped just then; it was Hallie, answering his text about picking him up at the mall. Be there at 6:30, Penney's, it said. Hallie didn't abbreviate anything on text messages, but wrote all the words out. Nicki said that was how you could tell if someone was over thirty.

"I have to get down to Mario's," Nicki said, flicking her cap.

"I think I'm just going to sit here and read." Josh patted his backpack. "Hallie's not getting here for a while."

Nicki nodded and turned away, then turned back and looked at him. She leaned in and pecked him on the cheek, quickly, then wheeled back around.

"See you tomorrow," she called over her shoulder, moving fast down the mall. Josh wondered about it—why had she kissed him? She'd never done that before. He took a sip of his hot chocolate, pulled out the collection of Chekhov stories that Win had sent him, cracked open the cover, and began reading.

CHAPTER 16

A few nights before Christmas, Hallie lay in bed in her new room, unable to sleep despite the two Tylenol PMs she'd gulped with half a glass of wine. She stared at the pale green walls, a color Cecile had helped her pick out at Floyd Hardware. A week ago they'd had a painting party, Cecile, Ram, Josh, and Nicki all helping to transform one of the spare bedrooms. Hallie hadn't wanted to sleep in her old room, but she also couldn't bear to dismantle it; that bedroom was a 1980s time capsule, like Molly Ringwald's in *Sixteen Candles*.

Hallie took another sip of wine and focused on the lone piece of art opposite her bed: her favorite painting of her mother's, a winter seascape in subdued beiges and grays that she'd brought back from her apartment in New York. Hallie now had drawers for her clothes, a closet in which to hang them, and one painting. It could all be packed up quickly at the end of August, when Josh would go off to college, and reassembled in New York. But who would live here after that? Would she sell the house? She hated the idea—it had been in her family for generations—but she'd need money for Josh's college.

Hallie picked up the copy of *The Awakening* that she couldn't seem to finish; she'd stalled out about halfway through. Why had her mother held onto *this* particular book, cherished it enough to keep it in a drawer with her daughter's report cards and drawings, the photographic foundations of her own artwork?

For years after her mother's death, Hallie had tried not to think of her at all. From the moment her father told her, Hallie went to work burying everything about her mother deep within her, so that, by her teens, it was as if she'd never had a mom. In college, when she started trying to remember her mother again, all Hallie had left were fragments: a sheath of long golden hair tickling her cheek as her mom tucked her in and kissed her good night; a crooked smile at the kitchen table; the two of them cross-legged on the floor with a bowl of popcorn, watching *Fantasy Island*. Her father used to imitate Tattoo—"The plane, the plane"—and Hallie and her mother would laugh.

The only person she'd ever discussed her mom with at length was Damien. He was in her life at a time when Hallie was trying to make sense of her past.

"I'd love to know why she ran away from home so young," Hallie had said to him. "I wonder if there was a reason." She and Damien were sitting in the diner across the street from their Queens apartment.

"I'm sure there was," Damien said.

"Maybe not. It was the sixties. Wasn't rebellion kind of gratuitous then?"

Damien took a sip of his coffee. "For some. But with everything else you've told me—how she stopped taking you to visit her parents, stopped talking to them." He looked at her, a piercing look. "There's a reason."

"I guess." Hallie looked out the window. The newsstand on the opposite corner displayed an assortment of magazines and newspapers, at least half of them featuring Kurt Cobain's sad, cockeyed smile. He'd killed himself that week. "Did I ever tell you how she died?"

Damien shook his head, his straight black hair—dyed from a less-dramatic brown—swaying with the motion. His hazel eyes looked green in the morning light. He was so beautiful that sometimes she couldn't believe he was hers.

"Carbon monoxide poisoning," she said. "An accident."

"An accident?"

"It was January. She was warming the car up in the garage, and the door got stuck. She was trapped there." She always pictured it the way she'd pictured it at eleven: her beautiful Mommy, stuck in that awful garage, screaming for help with no one to hear.

Damien lifted an eyebrow while she spoke, then was quiet for a minute. "Why didn't she just go back in the house?"

Hallie shook her head. "No, it's a detached garage. The old-fashioned kind."

Damien was quiet for a moment. He smiled and nodded to the waitress as she offered to warm up his coffee.

"It's always kind of haunted me," Hallie said. "The thought of her trapped in there."

He looked out the window, then back at her again. His fingers tapped on the table.

"What?" she asked.

"Nothing." He pulled a discarded copy of the *Village Voice* from the booth, began flipping through it. "Are we going out tonight? We should see who's playing."

He wasn't generally in the habit of shifting gears so abruptly. "Damien," she said, snatching the newspaper shut. "Don't do that. Don't change the subject."

But she realized, looking at his face, that his discomfort wasn't his own.

"You really want to know what I'm thinking?" he asked, and she nodded.

"She opens the door to this garage," he said, his words slow and deliberate. "She walks in. She closes the door behind her *before* she turns the car on and backs out?"

Hallie pictured it, Mom in her winter jacket and snow boots, her blond hair in a long ponytail. "Dad said the door slammed shut and jammed. She couldn't get it open."

Damien nodded, sipped more coffee, was quiet for a moment.

"She's in the garage. The door is open. She gets in the car and turns it on, and then the door slams shut," he said.

"Exactly," Hallie said.

"Wouldn't she turn the car off then?"

It had startled her momentarily, that she'd never asked her father this; it was an obvious question. "She was overcome by the fumes before she could get the door open," Hallie said, but she knew she was just reciting what her dad had told her.

Damien's look was not unkind then. It was the kind of look he might have given a child. The kind of look he might have given her when she was still Holly.

"I'm not saying I know what happened," he finally said. "But think about it. That story doesn't add up."

Hallie had known what he wasn't saying, the word he was carefully avoiding. She'd looked out the window again, at the newsstand full of Kurt Cobain. No, she thought. My mom didn't do *that*. And she'd pulled the newspaper away from Damien and started furiously scanning the listings, and they'd never spoken of it again.

The idea had floated at the back of her consciousness after that, though she'd never fully allowed herself to revisit it. But being thrust back into this house had stirred those unwelcome questions to the surface. She pulled her iPod from the nightstand and cranked Nirvana, hoping the feedback would blast the thoughts away. Just as she began to fall asleep, an image flitted across her mind: a spider walking across a windowpane. But before she could put it in any context, she tumbled headlong into a fitful sleep.

THE NEXT MORNING, Hallie woke before dawn to the sound of a car idling outside. She looked out her bedroom window and saw Cal Stutts's truck. Shit, she thought. What does he want? He'd told her he planned to make some deliveries, that he was selling the tomatoes and herbs he'd grown, though Josh claimed there wasn't much in the greenhouses to sell.

She opened the door. "Hi Cal," she said, trying to keep the annoyance out of her voice.

"Hey, Holly," he said. "Just wanted to let you know I have everything ready to go."

"That's great." The flatbed of his pickup was half full of cartons and baskets.

"Yep, I'm heading to Floyd, and then Vineland and Mullica Hill and up to Bellmawr. Places your dad sold to."

Hallie looked at him. "Do you need anything?"

He cast his eyes downward. "Could use a little coffee, if you got some."

"Sure," she sighed. "I'll make some."

"Oh, don't make it on my account," Cal said, but he followed her into the kitchen.

"So where are you headed, exactly?" she asked as she waited for the coffee to brew. "Restaurants, or markets or what?"

"Both," he said.

"Are they expecting you?"

"Expecting me?"

Hallie could see what a mess this would be. Cal had no idea of how to go about any of this, and she felt it was her fault. She should have put a stop to it a month ago.

"I thought maybe you'd called these places and set something up," she said.

"Nah, I figured I'd just stop on by."

"You know, I've been meaning to talk to you about the farm," Hallie said. It felt like as good a time as any to float the idea to Cal that their partnership would come to an end. "I don't think I can afford to keep it running next year."

Cal was quiet for a moment. "Let's just see how much money I can make for you today," he said, and smiled a little, his lips tight.

"Sure," she said. "I really appreciate all the hard work you're putting in. I just wanted you to know I have some tough decisions ahead of me."

"You just leave all the worrying to me," Cal said.

She got up and pulled the thermos from below the sink. "You mind if I give you your coffee to go? I have to get Josh off to school."

"Sure."

She poured the coffee, screwed the lid on the thermos and handed it to him.

After Cal drove away, Josh came downstairs with Emma. "Did you tell him you're selling the farm?"

Hallie shrugged. "Sort of. I floated the idea."

Josh sighed. "When are you going to really tell him?"

Hallie poured a glass of juice for Josh, coffee for herself. She handed Josh the juice, and rubbed at the throbbing spot on her right temple. "After the holidays," she said.

HALLIE GOT UP early Christmas Eve morning and poured a cup of coffee while the machine was still spitting out short bursts of liquid. She sat at the kitchen table and confronted the mountain of unopened mail. For the past three weeks—she hoped no longer, but it was possible—Hallie had simply been tossing the mail on the table, barely looking at return addresses. She'd taken special pains to bury letters from law firms or the insurance company. The only exceptions were the college brochures that Josh extracted from the pile on a nightly basis.

Hallie took a long sip of coffee and started sorting with a sigh. After making several neat piles of bills—her own mail, letters addressed to Dad and Brenda, and catalogues and magazines—she made it to the bottom of the pile, to the letters about the lawsuit. She would save them for Lawrence and Kenneth, who were coming down for Christmas; she couldn't face opening them alone. Hallie put her head down on the table and closed her eyes, but sat back up as she heard Josh and Emma stirring.

As Josh let Emma out and then poured himself a glass of juice, Hallie studied the living room. Ram had put up a tree that Hallie and Nancy had trimmed, and she'd draped some pine sprigs and gold ribbon atop the mantel. But it looked bare without the tchotchkes Brenda used to have everywhere: poinsettia hand towels, Santa potholders, Rudolf tissue dispensers with red noses that lit up.

"Do you know where the rest of the decorations are?"

"Christmas decorations?" Josh sat at the table.

"Yes."

He was quiet for a minute. "I don't want you to put them out."

"Why not?"

Josh shrugged, fingered his juice glass without taking a sip.

"I really wanted to make the house look the way you're used to it looking at Christmas," she said softly.

"Just leave it alone."

"But if you just—"

"I don't want the house to look the way it used to look," he said, his voice loud enough that Emma barked outside. "It's not the same kind of Christmas. It's not the same kind of house." He pushed his chair out loudly and let Emma in, then trudged back up the stairs.

LAWRENCE AND KENNETH arrived that night, with bags full of gifts, in high spirits. Lawrence had just sent his memoir off to an interested agent, and he'd found a six-month subletter for Hallie's apartment. He reported gleefully that the new tenant would be paying enough in those six months to cover Hallie's rent for the whole year.

"He's a shark," Kenneth said, patting Lawrence on the cheek.

It bothered Hallie, the idea of a stranger living among her things, not to mention that if she went to New York between now and June, she'd have to stay with Lawrence. But she was in no position to protest. She hadn't paid Lawrence her rent since the accident.

They'd brought takeout from Hallie's favorite Indian restaurant in New York, and everyone sat at the kitchen table to eat. Josh, who had spent most of the day sulking, glumly pushed his vegetable biryani around on his plate. But when Lawrence mentioned that he'd brought a copy of his manuscript for Hallie, Josh seemed to perk up a little.

"Could I read it, too?" he asked, spearing a piece of cauliflower on his fork.

"Sure," Lawrence said. "You'll learn all about Hallie." He winked at her across the table; Hallie's neck prickled with panic.

"I'm not really in it that much, am I?" she asked.

"Well, it's the story of my life," Lawrence said. "You're a big part of that life."

"I thought it was the story of you and Jonathan," she said. Kenneth looked away, and she wondered if the talk of Jonathan made him uncomfortable. It had to be hard, competing with a ghost.

"I was living with you when most of that was going on," Lawrence said. "And then you and Damien."

"The *three* of you lived together?" Josh asked. "You two and Damien Dark?"

"Back then," Hallie said, "he was just another musician trying to make it."

"He was a bit more than that," Lawrence said.

"What do you mean?" Josh asked.

"Oh, he had that magnetism," Lawrence said. "Even then. Even when he wore terrible clothes and was sleeping in a warehouse."

"He slept in a warehouse?" Josh asked.

"That was how he wound up moving in with us," Hallie said.

"May I?" Lawrence looked at Hallie. "Let me give you a preview of how I described it in the book."

"Am I up for this?" Hallie asked, and Kenneth looked at her and shook his head slightly. "I don't think you have a choice," he said, and poured himself a hefty glass of wine. Hallie held her near-empty glass out to him, and he filled it.

"Once upon a time in the early 1990s," Lawrence said, and Hallie groaned.

"All night," Kenneth said, smiling at her. "This will take all night."

But Josh looked more engaged than she'd seen him look in a while.

"There were these two friends from college, Lawrence and Hallie. What little money they had they spent going to clubs. They sometimes had to choose between dancing and eating, and they always chose dancing. They became very thin and very happy."

Josh smiled and glanced at Hallie.

"There was this club we liked called the Sphinx. It had no cover charge, and the drinks were reasonable by New York standards. They had live music every night. Some of it awful, some not so bad."

"Tattered Halo played there, right?" Josh asked. "Damien's first band. I remember reading about it."

Lawrence exchanged a look with Hallie. "They did. And the first time we saw them play, there was this gorgeous guy on stage, and I said to Hallie, one of us has to take him home." He took a sip of wine. "So we hung around and talked to him after the show, but neither one of us got anywhere with him that night. He had a girlfriend clutching at him."

"The Claw," Hallie said. It had been their nickname for her.

"But we kept going back to the Sphinx. After a couple of months, the Claw disappeared. And then one night, Damien told us that he'd been sleeping in an abandoned warehouse since breaking up with his girlfriend, some horrible squat a bunch of musicians were using. He hadn't found another place to live."

"And you invited him to stay with you?" Josh asked, looking at Hallie.

"Lawrence beat me to it," Hallie said, laughing.

"I told him we had a very uncomfortable couch, or that he had his pick of two much more comfortable beds," Lawrence said.

Josh laughed, and flashed Hallie a "did that really happen?" look. She nodded.

"What did he say?" Josh asked.

Lawrence paused for dramatic effect. "He said, 'I think I'd rather share your roommate's bed.'" He folded his hands. "The rest is history."

Josh looked at Hallie. "And how long did he…live with you?"

"Three years," she said.

"Do you ever talk to him now?"

She shook her head. "A few years after he left me, I heard from his manager about using some of my photos on the first Some Dark Angel album. But nothing from him."

"Some of those pictures are yours?"

"The back cover, and the liner notes."

"And she took far too little money for them," Lawrence added.

Josh's eyes were wide. "How did I not know any of this?"

"I wish I'd realized you liked the band," Hallie said. She felt a familiar guilt that she hadn't made it her business to know Josh better, before.

"Hallie's greatest fault has always been her modesty," Lawrence said, walking to the kitchen counter and opening another bottle of wine.

"When I was really into Some Dark Angel a couple of years ago," Josh said, "there was this internet message board I started posting on. Supposedly Damien posts there."

"Really?" Lawrence asked, carrying the wine back to the table.

"I don't know if it's really him, but everyone on the board thinks it is."

Hallie felt a strange flutter. Why should she care, after all these years, about the possibility of getting back in touch with Damien? But she did. "Do you still post there?"

"Yeah. There's a group of us who still do even though most of us aren't all that into the band anymore." He took a sip of water. "The last album was kind of bad."

"I think we should post something," Lawrence said. "I'll get my laptop."

"No way," Hallie said. "We're half drunk."

"I'm fully drunk," Lawrence said. He disappeared up the stairs.

Hallie looked at Josh and Kenneth. "I don't know," she said. Her face felt flushed.

Lawrence returned and set his laptop on the table. Once it booted up he turned it over to Josh, who quickly navigated his way to the board.

"Hey," Josh said, "Damien posted."

Hallie and Lawrence stood on either side of Josh, reading the message. The subject header was "Me." He said he'd spent most of December in the studio, working on a new album, and was now headed to Vermont to spend time with his family. A tour of small theaters was planned for the spring. Hallie knew that Damien was from Vermont, of course, but anyone who'd ever read *Rolling Stone* would know it as well.

"Me," Lawrence said. "That's an interesting title."

"He always uses that for the subject header," Josh said.

"Well, he's narcissistic enough to be Damien," Lawrence said.

"There's nothing in here that tells me it's really him," Hallie said. "It could be anyone."

"So post a message to him," Lawrence said. "I dare you."

"I double dare you," Josh said. "You can use my screen name."

Hallie took a long sip of wine and started and erased several messages before settling on one.

My copy of Black Market Clash has been missing ever since you moved out of 3625 11ᵗʰ St., Apartment F. Any idea what happened to it?—an old friend.

Lawrence laughed. "I forgot, he took a couple of your albums with him, didn't he?"

"I don't think it was on purpose," she said. "Our stuff was all mixed up together."

"Send it," Josh said. And she did.

CHAPTER 17

When Josh was little and still believed in Santa Claus, he used to wake up early on Christmas morning—sometimes before sunrise. He would run to his parents' room, where his dad would say, "Go back to bed until it's light out." And Josh would open the blinds in his room and lie in bed, staring out the front window until he saw the first hint of brightness in the dark sky.

When Josh was older and fell into his habit of staying up and reading until 3 or 4 a.m., he would sleep in on Christmas morning, as would his dad—the one morning a year Dad slept past 5 a.m. They'd both wake up around ten to the smell of his mom's French toast, would go downstairs and have breakfast and then open their presents.

Josh hadn't expected anything to be the same this Christmas, but he woke to a smell so familiar that, in those few seconds between waking and full wakefulness, he was sure it was French toast. He would put on his bathrobe and head down the stairs and his mom would be there, in the kitchen, standing over the stove. She'd kiss him good morning and he'd get himself a glass of juice, lean against the counter and tease her about her bunny slippers while she finished making breakfast.

But when he sat up, he saw Emma's form by his feet, and remembered what had happened, that his mom couldn't be downstairs. He wondered when it would stop, at what point his brain would finally get over what it had been used to for seventeen years. It was Christmas, and Hallie was there, Lawrence and Kenneth were there, but his parents were not. Emma's tail began to thump against the bed. He reached over and patted her back.

"Merry Christmas, Emma," he said, and the dog flopped on her side, her tail thumping harder.

•

AFTER TAKING EMMA for a walk, Josh found Kenneth in the kitchen, but he was making omelets, not French toast. He had all sorts of vegetables chopped: onions, peppers, spinach, mushrooms.

"Good morning," Kenneth said, teasing at the edge of an omelet with a spatula. "I hope you don't mind that I took over your kitchen."

"No," Josh said, looking over the selection of fillings. There was also a bowl of shredded cheese, and one of diced ham.

"You eat eggs, don't you? And cheese?"

"Yep," Josh said, spooning dog food into a bowl.

"Good," Kenneth said. "Pick your veggies and I'll make yours when I'm done with this one."

"Everything except the ham," Josh said, his stomach rumbling. He was suddenly starving. He set the dog food down in front of Emma.

"Would you bring me a plate?" Kenneth asked. Josh did, and Kenneth slid the omelet onto it and put it aside, then started to make Josh's.

"Yours will get cold," Josh said.

"Oh, that's okay. They don't take long. I'll nibble at it while I make yours."

By the time Hallie came downstairs, Josh had eaten two omelets and Kenneth was making him a third.

"You should see this boy pack it away," Kenneth said to Hallie, motioning to the omelet fixings. "Let me know what you like. I'll make yours next."

"Pack it away?" Hallie asked, pouring herself a cup of coffee. "I've never seen Josh pack food away."

It wasn't so much that he liked Kenneth's omelets as he liked real cooking, not food from restaurants. His parents had rarely eaten out, and while Josh knew it was mostly due to money, it was also because his mother was a great cook.

Kenneth put a giant omelet on Josh's plate. "I defy you to be hungry after that."

Josh looked at Hallie. "Split it with me?"

She took a bite. "I guess I should learn how to cook," she said. "It's just so easy in New York to live on takeout."

And not as easy in Oyster Shell, or even Floyd, Josh thought. But he kept that to himself.

•

AFTER BREAKFAST THEY opened all their gifts. Josh felt embarrassed that there was so much stuff for him; he had bought Hallie a couple of things that Nicki helped him pick out at the mall, but he got so much more: a laptop from Hallie to replace his ancient computer that was always crashing, an iPod from Lawrence and Kenneth, plus some clothes and the concise Oxford English Dictionary that he'd coveted since he was about fourteen. Lawrence and Kenneth had even brought Emma a new collar and leash, made out of something purple that Josh hoped wasn't leather, and a box of dog biscuits that looked like cookies from a bakery.

"The best dog biscuits in Manhattan," Lawrence said as he fed Emma one.

After they had all taken showers and gotten dressed, after the adults had all started drinking wine, Nancy and Ram arrived, and they, too, had armfuls of presents. Nancy had also brought tons of food, including the macaroni and cheese that Josh loved. While Hallie was setting it all up, Josh heard a car outside, music blaring: the Yeah Yeah Yeahs. At first Josh couldn't imagine who it might be, playing the Yeah Yeah Yeahs in Oyster Shell. Then he looked out the window and saw it, the pink car with the leopard roof. Cecile. She was standing in his driveway.

Her hair was still short and pale pink, but the rest of her was dressed like a candy cane: red and white-striped top, a red mini-skirt with white tights and bright red boots that looked molded to her calves. She had nice legs, legs like Miss Piper's. Josh went outside.

"Hi!" Cecile said. "Merry Christmas!" She put her arms around his neck and kissed his cheek. She even smelled a little like peppermint.

"Help me with these?" she asked, pulling three big gift boxes from her car. As she handed them to Josh, her top rode up, and he saw that she had a pierced belly button. He wished he could put his hands on either side of that belly button, on the strip of skin that was exposed, just for a second. Cecile looked down and adjusted her top and he realized he'd been staring.

•

BY THE TIME they ate, Josh could tell everyone was drunk but him and Nancy. Hallie had poured him half a glass of wine, but he stopped after two sips; he hadn't liked the sharp taste, and he didn't think it would be a good idea to get drunk on the first Christmas after his parents died. It was a lot of work just to hold himself together, and a part of him wanted to go to his room and cry. But there was also the part that was enjoying the proximity of Cecile, next to him at the dining room table.

"So why didn't you bring Brittany?" Hallie asked, passing Ram one of the stuffed acorn squashes Nancy had made.

Ram shook his head. "She's history."

"You broke up?" Hallie asked, and Ram nodded.

Josh saw Lawrence and Kenneth exchange a look.

"Who's Brittany?" Cecile asked.

"Ram's former love muffin," Hallie said.

"Oh, you're a riot," Ram said.

"I need a love muffin," Cecile said.

"Everybody needs a love muffin," Lawrence said, and Josh laughed.

"That includes you, young man," Lawrence added. "By the way, where is *your* love muffin?"

Josh felt Cecile's eyes on him. "I don't have one."

"Oh, I beg to differ. There's a young lady with blue streaks in her hair who's got it bad for you."

"Nicki?" Cecile asked. "I liked her."

"We're just friends," Josh said quickly to Cecile. Then he repeated it to everyone else: "We're just *friends*."

"Sometimes the best relationships start as just friends," Cecile said. She poked him in the side with her finger, under the tablecloth where no one could see.

Ram whispered something to Hallie and she laughed a little and touched his arm. The whole day was getting deeply weird.

"So Ram," Josh said, "did you finish compiling the frog data for this year?"

"Almost," Ram said. "I have a grant deadline coming up, so I have to finish in the next few days. I'll present it at the next meeting."

"Any changes from the preliminary report?" Nancy asked.

"Well," Ram said, cutting at the acorn squash with his fork, "I ran a new study this year, and the early results are pretty interesting."

"Really?" Nancy asked. She put her fork down and looked at Ram.

"What frog data?" Cecile asked. "I'm kind of lost."

"Yes, what exactly is it you're studying?" Lawrence asked.

Ram looked around the table. "You all really want to hear about this?" Josh saw everyone nod.

"There's something in my truck," he said, "that will explain it better."

"I don't know if he should show those photos while we're eating," Nancy said after he'd left the room. "Some of them are disturbing."

Ram returned with the book he and Josh had dubbed The Frog Bible, and Hallie, Kenneth, Lawrence and Cecile all huddled together to look through it. Ram explained how he'd first discovered the frogs following Nancy's call to the Environmental Affairs Department. How, after that first summer, he couldn't get anyone in the state agency interested in studying the frogs further, despite the nightmarish deformities he was cataloguing.

"That's horrible," Lawrence said, and Kenneth and Hallie both winced, and Josh was sure he knew what photo it was.

"How can the state not care about this?" Hallie asked.

"Besides funding, which is a big issue," Ram said, "there are competing theories about the cause. One camp thinks the mutations are caused by UV radiation; another thinks it's a parasite. The other theory is that it's environmental, some sort of contaminant in the creek."

"If it's naturally occurring, that lets anyone who polluted the creek off the hook," Lawrence said.

"Exactly," Ram said. "I believe it's at least partially caused by a contaminant, but it's hard to pinpoint specifically."

"How so?" Lawrence asked.

"A variety of chemicals were dumped into the Maurice River in the fifties and sixties. And dozens of herbicides, insecticides and fungicides are used by farms along the river. Mollusk Creek is full of chemicals. It's hard to say which is the problem."

"So what's the new study?" Lawrence asked.

"I looked at the runoff from farms along the lower river, near Mollusk Creek," Ram said. "I'm trying to correlate high levels of nitrogen and phosphorus—found in fertilizers—with the number of deformities."

Lawrence looked at Hallie, then back at Ram. "Has anyone written about this?" he asked. "A newspaper, I mean."

"The *Floyd Daily News* has run a few articles," Ram said, "and the *Philadelphia Inquirer* picked up one of them and buried it deep in the paper. That's pretty much it."

Lawrence pulled Hallie out of the dining room, into the kitchen. Kenneth and Cecile continued to look through the Frog Bible. Josh finished the last of his macaroni and cheese as Lawrence and Hallie returned.

"If Hallie takes some really dramatic photos of the frogs," Lawrence said, "I'll send them around with a story pitch."

"Where would you send them?" Ram asked.

"Well, I'll mention it to my editor at the *New Yorker*, but they don't always run photos, and this kind of story needs photos. Maybe *The Atlantic* or *Harper's*."

"That would be amazing," Ram said. "I don't know what to say."

"I can't guarantee that I'll place it," Lawrence said. "But I think it's a big story. We just need the right angle."

As they made plans to start after the frogs spawned again in the spring, Nancy passed around slices of pecan pie. Before Josh could take a bite, there was a knock on the door, and Hallie got up to answer it. Emma growled softly from under the table; Josh was pretty sure what that meant. He followed his sister.

Cal was standing in the doorway with a bunch of wilted daisies. He handed them to Hallie.

"That was really sweet of you, Cal," she said. But Josh could hear the alarm in his sister's voice, and he wondered if Cal heard it, too.

"Well, it's Christmas," Cal said. "I have something else for you." He handed her some folded up money. Hallie looked at the bills.

"I made eighty-four dollars from them crops I sold, so this is your half," he said. "Forty-two bucks." He said it like it was a lot of money. Maybe it was, to him.

"Thanks," Hallie said. She stood in the doorway, not inviting him in; Josh could see that she wasn't sure what to do.

"Yep, we made out pretty good," Cal said.

"I really appreciate it," Hallie said. She turned a little and looked into the dining room. "Do you want to…come in?"

With that, Josh went back into the dining room to get Emma out of there. "Cal is here," he whispered to Ram.

"Shit," Ram said.

"I'm going to take Emma for a walk," Josh said. "Ram—"

Before he could finish, they all looked up and saw Cal in the doorway of the dining room, in his dirt-streaked jeans and raggedy shirt. Ram nodded to Josh like he understood that he was supposed to make sure nothing bad happened. Josh peeked under the tablecloth and coaxed Emma into the kitchen. She was still growling as Hallie handed him his jacket and Emma's leash. He led the dog outside.

WHEN JOSH RETURNED, Cal was gone. Everybody seemed to have an opinion on the best way for Hallie to let Cal know their partnership was over.

"I should be here when you do it," Ram said. "And Todd."

"That'll upset him more," Hallie said. "You all worry too much." But Hallie looked worried herself.

They all had coffee, and then Cecile left; Ram and Nancy were next. After they were gone and it was just Hallie, Lawrence and Kenneth again, Josh slipped upstairs to set up his new laptop. He was kind of excited about it. His old computer had been so slow he couldn't do much on it besides write papers and send e-mail.

Once he had the internet running, he checked his inbox. There were three messages: one from Win, saying Merry Christmas; one from Cecile, with a PDF attached for a birthday party at her house; and one from an e-mail address he didn't recognize. He figured it was spam and was about to delete it when he noticed the subject. *Hallie?* it said. He looked at the address again: dm1105@gmail.com. DM…could it be Damien? Josh opened the e-mail.

I'm guessing that message was from you, since only a handful of people could know that address in Queens, and you're the only one of that handful with intimate knowledge of my old vinyl collection. Assuming I'm right, how are you? Sorry about that Clash album—thought it was mine. Actually, I still DO think it's mine. Wouldn't mind hearing what you're up to. D.

CHAPTER 18

Hallie woke up at 9 a.m., the latest she'd slept on a Sunday since the accident. She pulled on sweats and an old work shirt of her father's, and went down the hall to Josh's room; he'd had a bad cold for the past few days, since New Year's, and she was surprised by how much she found herself worrying about him. She woke up worrying, went to bed worrying, and part of her worried throughout the day. What if it was something more serious than a cold? She opened his door a crack and looked in on him. He was still asleep, with Emma stretched out by his side, and something about the way he looked sleeping—his closed eyes, those lids rimmed with thick lashes any woman would envy, a wavy lock of his hair falling over his cheek and hiding, she knew, a small constellation of pimples—coursed through her in waves. It's just a cold, she told herself. He'll be fine. Emma sat up and cocked her head at Hallie, then scrambled quietly off the bed and followed Hallie down the stairs.

Hallie opened the back door and retrieved the lead from the snow-dusted ground. She clipped it to the dog's collar and went in to make coffee, but stopped short when she reached the kitchen sink. It was nearly filled with murky water, a recurrent problem since before Thanksgiving. Ram had given her some sort of environmentally-friendly drain opener which didn't work at all; she dug in the cabinet under the sink and found an old bottle of Drano. Hallie poured it in and hid the empty bottle in the back of the cabinet, hoping it would do the trick. She couldn't afford a plumber.

Before he and Kenneth left, Lawrence had slipped Hallie a check for $5,000. She'd put up a weak protest, telling him it was too much; in truth, she needed more. As she started a pot of coffee she glanced at the latest pile of mail, dominated by bills marked "urgent" and "second notice." After she'd let Emma back in and fed her, Hallie began sorting through the stack. Halfway through, a letter caught her eye.

It was from Pomodoro, the restaurant in Bellmawr her father used to supply with tomatoes; he had taken Hallie to dinner there on her fifteenth and sixteenth birthdays. The letter was from Ron Caruso, the restaurant's owner. He expressed his condolences about Don and Brenda's deaths, and went on to mention a visit he'd received from a man who claimed he now ran Corson's Farm. The man had tried to sell Caruso "the worst-looking tomatoes" he'd ever seen, and reacted angrily when turned away.

Don Corson was my restaurant's main supplier for the past twenty-five years, the note read. *He was a good man. I thought you should know there's someone shady using his name.*

AFTER SHE'D WRITTEN out checks for the bills, Hallie poured a glass of orange juice and walked upstairs with it. Josh was propped up in bed, reading Michael Cunningham's *The Hours*.

"Hey, thanks," Josh said, taking the glass from her. His voice sounded deeper from the cold. He took a gulp of juice.

"How are you feeling?" she asked.

"Better today," Josh said, but then he coughed violently for half a minute.

"I'm taking you to the doctor tomorrow if you're not *a lot* better."

Josh shrugged and took another sip of juice. Hallie sat on a corner of the bed and looked at the book on Josh's lap.

"Win said I should read *Mrs. Dalloway* first, but they didn't have it at the library," Josh said.

Hallie smiled. "You're e-mailing with Win a lot, huh?"

"Yeah." Josh sat up straighter and blew his nose. "He's really cool. Even though he made me rewrite my admissions essay, like, four times."

Josh looked like he was about to say more, but another coughing fit overcame him. He drank the rest of the juice and the coughing subsided.

"Are you hungry?" Hallie asked. "I can make you an omelet. Or I can try."

"I don't think I could eat one," Josh said. "Maybe just toast."

"That I can definitely make," she said. "I'll bring some up." She rose and headed toward the door, but remembered the letter from Ron Caruso and turned back around.

"By the way, I'm going to list the farm for sale tomorrow, and I'll sit Cal down and talk to him this week."

Josh nodded. "Wait 'til I'm better."

"Why?"

"Just in case he gets pissed off."

Hallie looked at Josh. "I don't think he'd do anything we'd have to worry about," she said, but the words didn't sound convincing, even to her.

AFTER SHE'D BROUGHT Josh some toast and more juice, Hallie went to her room, opened her laptop and checked her e-mail. Finally, what she'd been hoping to see for the past three days: an e-mail from Damien. She'd written him back a brief note after he first contacted her, and he'd written her at slightly more length; after that, she composed a long letter about what had happened to her dad and Brenda and how she was in Oyster Shell taking care of Josh. Perhaps because she'd once loved Damien, perhaps because he was no longer in her life, she'd told him things she hadn't told anyone. The guilt she felt that being back in Oyster Shell had made her miss her mom, who'd died so long ago, more than she missed her dad. Her regrets that she hadn't gotten to know Josh better, earlier.

She opened the e-mail.

Guilt? Damien wrote. *From what you said, you have nothing to feel guilty about. If I were you I would have taken Lawrence up on his offer to pay for boarding school. (And by the way—I had no idea Jonathan left him all that money. Lawrence must LOVE being rich. He kind of always seemed like he should have been rich.) Anyway, you've done a good thing, and maybe you should just be glad that you're getting to know Josh now.*

There were several paragraphs about what he was doing lately: living in Southern California, recording his next album. A lawsuit he was involved in against his ex-manager, who'd stolen money from him. (Millions, Hallie had read in a *Rolling Stone* article.) But then, at the end of the e-mail, there was this:

Since I get the feeling we're going to keep writing to each other, I want to get this out of the way. I was an asshole to leave with no explanation the way I did. I just didn't feel ready for where I thought we were headed. But it was shitty of me to do it the way I did, and I'm sorry.

Hallie read and reread the paragraph. It told her nothing; it was like the generic explanations Lawrence and Jonathan (poor Jonathan! Dying, and listening to Hallie sob about her boyfriend's leaving) had come up with at the time. "I didn't feel ready for where I thought we were headed." What did that mean, exactly? What she really wanted to know was if he'd fallen out of love with her. Especially since she had never really stopped loving him.

A FEW MORNINGS later, Hallie heard a car pull up outside as she and Josh were getting ready for work and school. She peeked out the window and saw Cal's rusted-out old truck; he was most likely there to mooch some coffee. She wasn't quite ready to talk to him yet. Cal had not made much in their deal to split the profits, and Hallie wanted to estimate how many hours he'd put in at the farm and give him some additional compensation, once she sold the place. She'd wanted to have a dollar figure to promise him. But he was there, and she had to get it over with.

"Hey, Holly." Cal stood with his hands in his pockets, a shy posture that reminded her of Cal the boy, the one who'd gone to her mother's funeral.

"Want some coffee?"

"Sure, if you can spare it." He followed her into the kitchen.

She poured him a cup, and he furrowed his brow. "No thermos?" he asked.

"Why don't you sit down a minute, Cal."

She refreshed her cup and sat across from him. She was quiet for long enough that his gaze went steely. "What's on your mind?" he asked.

"I don't really know how to say this, Cal. You've worked so hard at the farm, and I appreciate all the time you put in. But it's losing money by the day, and I'm going to have to sell it."

Cal took a long sip of coffee and looked at her. "You just need to buy some more seeds and things," he said. "Next crop'll be better."

Hallie shifted in her seat, straightened her back. She had hoped that Cal knew he was in over his head and would welcome a way out, but she could see that was not to be.

"I'm sorry, but I can't afford to keep it running. Josh and I are barely getting by on my photography, and I can't lose any more money on the farm."

Cal nodded, eyes cast downward. He ran two fingers along the rim of his coffee cup.

"I want to pay you something extra for the time you put in," she said. "I know you worked a lot of hours, and there wasn't much profit to split. Once I sell the place, we can sit down and figure out what I owe you. How does that sound?"

He looked at her full on now, and it was a look she'd never seen in his eyes before. They were narrowed, cold and hard; even their color seemed to change, from a warm brown to something darker, murkier. She understood, for the first time, why so many people were afraid of him.

"You don't owe me nothing." He spat the words out.

"I do," she said quickly. "You tried to help me out of a jam. I know how hard you worked. I want to pay you for it, when I can."

Cal continued to look at her through those new, scary eyes, a hint of a grimace in the set of his jaw. Hallie felt her heart race and she sat paralyzed for a second, watching him watch her.

Finally, Cal rose. He attempted a weak smile, but his eyes were still narrowed and cold. "Hey," he said. "You gotta do what you gotta do."

Hallie exhaled and relaxed a little. She'd been right about Cal; she knew him better, deep down, than anyone else in town did. She stood up, too.

"Thanks so much for understanding," she said.

Cal lifted the mug and finished his coffee in one long gulp. "No problem," he said. "I'll just take my dog and be on my way."

Hallie stared at him for a moment, thinking she hadn't heard him correctly. "Your dog?"

"That one your brother has upstairs. You know it's my dog. Time to bring it on home."

Hallie wondered if Josh was listening, if he'd heard all this. She looked at the phone, in its cradle on the other side of the kitchen. Her cell was nowhere in sight.

"I thought we'd settled that," she said, standing straight, trying her best to look unafraid.

"I thought we had a deal on the farm, too," Cal said. "Guess we was both wrong." He stood tall and threw his chest out and Hallie could imagine, suddenly, Cal beating his ex-wife badly enough to break her ribs. She could imagine him doing almost anything.

She took a step away from him. "Don't."

He smiled again and the smile reminded her, somehow, of a snake. Could snakes even smile?

"I do what I want," he said, and took a step toward her. Before she could say anything else, step back or scream or make a dive for the phone, Josh was there. He grabbed Cal by the arm and yanked him away from Hallie.

"You think you can take me, boy?" Cal looked at Josh and laughed. But while Cal was far more muscular than Josh, he was also several inches shorter, and Josh used his height to his advantage, drawing himself up and looking down on Cal. Hallie made a grab for the phone, but Cal whirled around and ripped the cord from the wall. Josh scrambled past him and positioned himself between Cal and Hallie.

"You're not taking Emma, and you're not going near my sister," Josh said. "You're gonna leave. Now." Hallie was stunned by the way he sounded; it was a man speaking, not a boy.

"You think you can stop me?" Cal asked.

"I think," Josh said, "that you remember our father. He treated you better than anyone else did."

Cal said nothing, but Hallie saw something shift in his demeanor. One shoulder started to droop, and his eyes widened slightly.

"He's watching you," Josh said. "He can see everything you do."

Hallie understood where Josh was going, and it was brilliant. He'd seen Cal at the funeral, seen the reverent way he'd prayed, and was counting on his having some real belief in an afterlife. Yet Hallie couldn't help but wonder if maybe their father *was* there, if he was giving Josh the strength he needed to stand up to Cal.

"And my mom," Josh added. "She always gave you sandwiches to take home. She used to make extra biscuits for you the mornings you worked. You remember that?"

Cal nodded. He took a small step backward.

"Get out now," Josh said. "The dog is staying here. And you're not going to bother Hallie again. Or Nancy." Josh's voice had grown confident and bold, and he took a step toward Cal. "If you do anything to any of us, I'll kill you." He took another step toward Cal. "I'll kill you and I won't even feel bad about it."

Josh's body started to tremble slightly. Hallie reached forward and steadied him, hoping Cal wouldn't see him shaking.

Cal stood still for a second, looking at Josh, looking past him at Hallie. She saw him shift back into the other Cal.

"You all take care," he said, as if nothing had happened, and he walked toward the front door, Hallie trailing him. Emma was at the top of the stairs, her fur raised high, her teeth exposed. Hallie was sure Cal saw her, too. He slipped out the door quietly and Hallie closed and bolted it behind him. Back in the kitchen, Josh was slumped in a chair.

"Wow," Hallie said, taking the seat next to his.

He looked at her but his eyes were far away. His whole body was shaking, and she reached her hands out and put them on his knees.

"That was amazing," she said. "If you hadn't been here—"

"I meant it," Josh whispered.

"What?"

"That I would kill him. I really meant it."

Hallie shook her head. "I don't think so. You just meant that you'd stop him."

"No," Josh said, his voice more forceful. "I never thought I could kill anyone—I mean, I don't think animals should be killed, let alone people. But I could have killed Cal right then. I knew it. I felt it. I *wanted* to."

Hallie got up and poured two glasses of water, brought him one. They both drank in silence for a moment. "I think we're all capable of violence," she said.

Josh shook his head. "I didn't think I was."

"Well, there are people who'll kill you for the fifty bucks in your wallet. That's pretty different from what just happened."

"Have you ever felt like you could kill?" he asked.

Had she? She'd felt a violent rage when her father had told her he was marrying Brenda, but it was more that she'd wanted to hit him, not kill him. She *had* hit him, actually, the night she ran away and he found her at the bus stop. She'd screamed and cried and pummeled his chest with her hands, because she'd felt certain of what would happen: she would lose him to Brenda. But she hadn't imagined what would really happen. She hadn't imagined losing her father to another child.

Hallie remembered sitting on the single bed in her dorm room, the phone in her hand, her father telling her that Brenda was having a baby and Hallie needed to come home and go to community college. Shortly after the call, Lawrence popped his head in to see if she was ready for dinner. She was still sitting in the same position on the edge of the springy bed, her backpack at her feet where she'd thrown it when she'd burst in to answer the phone.

"You're not leaving NYU," Lawrence had said, "to go to some crappy community college."

"If he can't afford the kid he has, why is he having another?" Hallie asked. And then, a thought she didn't voice: *Why didn't Brenda get rid of it, when she found out she was pregnant?*

That dark thought had stayed with Hallie. After she and Lawrence had talked to financial aid officers, after Hallie had taken another job in addition to the work study she already had, she'd written her father and explained that she wasn't coming home. She was nineteen, and hurt, and she'd put angry thoughts down on paper. If you can't afford the child you have, you shouldn't be having another, she'd said. Her dad had never answered the letter; the next communication she got was five months later, a birth announcement with a picture of baby Josh. After that, Brenda had started calling her once a month; when Hallie sent her graduation announcement two years later, Brenda attended with Nancy, but Hallie's father stayed home.

It occurred to Hallie that Brenda must have read that letter, too; but somehow she had been able to see it for what it really was, a hurt young girl's stupid wish to preserve what little family she had left. Why had Brenda been able to forgive her when her own father, her flesh and blood, could not?

Hallie looked at Josh and realized that he was the kid her father had gotten right; that if only one of them could survive, it should be him, not her. *I would kill for you*, she thought, looking in those sweet eyes of his, eyes that looked slightly less innocent than they had the day before. But she didn't know how to tell him this; how to tell him that she had never loved him before, but she loved him now.

"You should go get your backpack," she finally said. "I'll drive you to school."

CHAPTER 19

For the first few minutes of Cecile's birthday party, things looked promising to Josh. Cecile greeted him with a kiss on the lips—the lips!—and then winked at him when she handed him a Coke. He took a sip and knew immediately there was some kind of alcohol mixed in. It felt warm and fizzy down his throat.

But after that, Cecile disappeared for a long time, and Hallie was talking about photography with some guy named Caleb who had the right haircut and the right ironically silk-screened t-shirt and the right amount of five o'clock shadow, and Josh looked around and realized he was the youngest and least cool guy at the party. He would be lucky, in this crowd, if any girl would even talk to him. And what he really needed was not just for a girl to talk to him; he needed a girlfriend.

Josh had felt desperate since Christmas, consumed with thoughts of his parents and, since the confrontation with Cal, the fear that something worse might happen. A few nights ago Josh and Hallie had both been awakened by Emma's ferocious barking; when they went downstairs, they could see that someone had tried to pry the back door open. Everyone suspected Cal. Todd and Ram came over the next day and put better locks on the doors, but even so, Josh worried.

"Digital is great for a quick shot," Hallie was saying, "but I still prefer working with film," and Caleb was going on about how you can use Photoshop to get any effect you could get with film, and Josh knew there was no way he could get into that conversation. He overheard a snippet of talk about *Buffy the Vampire Slayer* between a guy in a Spiderman t-shirt and a girl who wore a paint-splattered hoodie and jeans. But the person Josh really wanted to talk to was Cecile.

Finally he heard her voice, coming from the next room. Josh followed the sound and saw two girls leading Cecile into her bedroom.

It was a small room—just a futon and a battered-looking chest of drawers—but it was beautiful: candles everywhere and gauzy lavender curtains, beaded artwork on the walls. It was a very girly room, a room of shiny things. He longed to be invited in. The only other girl's bedroom he'd ever seen—besides Hallie's old room—was Nicki's, and it wasn't warm like this. Her curtains were heavy, a dark burgundy color, and posters papered her walls: suffragettes, Dorothy Parker, System of a Down, Conor Oberst. Josh hung just beyond the bedroom doorway. The girls walked Cecile over to the futon and helped her sprawl on it. Cecile wasn't asleep, but she didn't look exactly conscious, either.

"What's she on?" one of them asked.

"X, I think."

"She drank margaritas, too. Roll her over in case she pukes." The girl walked to a corner of the room and picked up a wastebasket. When she turned back, she noticed Josh.

"She'll be okay," the girl said. She smiled a little but her eyes looked worried.

"Can I help?" Josh asked.

The girl put the wastebasket next to the bed, near Cecile's head. "Get my boyfriend Bret for me? The guy in the Spiderman shirt?"

Josh nodded and went to look for Bret. He finally found him sitting on the back steps of the house with a bunch of other people, including the Caleb guy. They were passing around a cigarette that definitely wasn't a cigarette. Before Josh could say anything to Bret, Hallie walked outside.

"Want some?" Caleb asked, holding the cigarette out to her.

Hallie shook her head. "Josh, I think we should go now," she said.

Josh looked at Bret. "Your girlfriend wants you," he said. "She's in Cecile's bedroom." Josh turned to Hallie. "Cecile's sick."

Bret headed to the bedroom, and Josh and Hallie followed him. Cecile looked better now. She was sitting up, talking to a girl in a skimpy dress.

"Is she okay?" Hallie asked, and the girl nodded.

"Hannah and I are staying over," Bret added. "She'll be fine."

"We should go," Hallie said to Josh, as Cecile looked up at them. Josh saw streaks of puke in the wastebasket.

"Happy birthday, Cecile," Josh said, not knowing what else to say, and she smiled sleepily at him and waved goodbye, and Josh was amazed at how beautiful a girl who had just puked could look.

THE NEXT MORNING Josh e-mailed Cecile to make sure she felt okay. She answered that night, said she was fine, and asked Josh if he'd had fun at the party. He wrote her back and said her friends were nice, she wrote him back and said she'd heard he was a *Buffy the Vampire Slayer* scholar, and within a week they were e-mailing each other every day. Mostly they just talked about music and films and books, but Josh spent a lot of time on his e-mails to Cecile, and he wondered if she did too.

After two weeks Josh told Nicki about the e-mails. They were hanging out in his room one night, their French books open in front of them but neither of them doing their homework. Nicki was talking about Nathan, the way she'd been ever since they started dating over Christmas break. Josh finally blurted it out: "I like Cecile," he said.

Nicki looked up from the doodling she was doing in the margin of her French book. "How old is she?"

"Twenty-three."

"Wow." Nicki was quiet for a minute. "Do you think she likes you?"

"I don't know," Josh said. "She e-mails me a lot."

"What does she write?"

Josh pulled his laptop onto the bed and brought up Cecile's last e-mail. Nicki read it with a look of intense concentration on her face.

"She's totally flirting with you," Nicki said.

"You think?"

She peered at him over the laptop screen. "You're kidding, right?"

"No. I wasn't sure if she was just being nice."

Nicki shook her head at Josh. She cleared her throat and read from Cecile's e-mail in an exaggerated sexy voice: "I just framed some of my new drawings, the ones I've done since moving to Floyd. You'll have to come over and see them sometime."

"You think she's flirting?"

"Oh my *God*. You're so dense." She was quiet for a moment. "It explains a lot, your density."

"What do you mean?"

Nicki had a weird look on her face. "I really liked you in the fall, and you never got it." Josh saw a flicker of panic in her eyes. "Don't worry, I don't feel that way any more. I mean, we're best friends now, and I have a boyfriend, so it all worked out. But I *really* liked you, and you totally didn't get it."

Josh didn't know what to say. He liked spending time with Nicki, maybe even had once liked the attention. He kind of missed her liking him, now that she was with Nathan.

"I hope I didn't just freak you out by telling you that," Nicki said.

Josh looked at her. It would hurt her to know that he had been not so much dense as disinterested. "I'm not freaked out," he said. "I just didn't know."

"Yep." Nicki glanced at the computer screen for a second. "I think it's better this way, though, being friends. Don't you?"

"Sure," Josh said quickly. He'd told at least one lie to Nicki tonight, but he wasn't exactly sure what it was.

"As for Cecile," Nicki said, "I don't know. I can see why you like her, but I still think there's something weird about her. Plus, she's an adult. That's weird, too. Like, why isn't she flirting with a guy her own age?"

Josh thought of the guys he'd met at Cecile's party. Probably any one of them would be with Cecile if she wanted. But Josh had thought most of them were kind of posy and pretentious, and maybe Cecile saw something in Josh that she didn't see in those other guys. He felt he had more substance than they did, and he wanted to believe that Cecile could see past his bad skin and his hair that still hadn't grown out to a cool length and the fact that he was seventeen.

"But you don't think it's crazy of me to think she likes me?" he asked.

"She likes you," Nicki said. "But I think the idea of it is crazy. She's already out of college."

"I know," Josh said, but in that moment he felt something close to happiness, that it might not all be a crazy fantasy existing only in his head.

BY FEBRUARY, HE'D only seen Cecile two more times, both too brief and with too many other people around, at *Good News*. But the e-mails were an everyday thing, and took enough time to read and compose that Josh stopped writing in his journal. He felt like he really knew Cecile now, and she'd had such an interesting life: living in Paris until her parents split up when she was ten, then moving to San Francisco with her American father and shuttling back and forth between California and France on school holidays. Josh even tried writing one of his e-mails to her entirely in French; but she didn't answer that one, and he was afraid he'd offended her by getting the grammar wrong, so he went back to English and neither of them said anything about it.

Josh decided to make a bold move and give her something for Valentine's Day. He thought about flowers or candy, but they both seemed so clichéd. Finally he decided to make a mix disc of all the most romantic songs he knew—there was a song by Some Dark Angel in particular that had always made him think, *I wish someone felt that way about me*—and he would make the cover of the disc look like a Valentine's card.

AFTER SCHOOL ON Valentine's Day, Josh walked over to the *Good News* building. On the way, he ducked into a drugstore and bought a small box of candy. Maybe it was corny, but he was afraid that the disc wasn't enough.

Neither Hallie nor Cecile were at their desks. Marcus was on the phone; he waved to Josh, and Josh waved back. Josh didn't want Marcus to see him leaving anything on Cecile's desk.

But Marcus seemed very involved with his phone call, and Jane and Chuck were talking in a corner, not paying any attention. No one else was in the newsroom. Josh's backpack was heavy, and he walked over to Hallie's desk, put his stuff down on the floor. He pulled out the candy and was about to retrieve the disc and walk both of them over to Cecile's desk when he heard Hallie's voice behind him.

"Josh! I didn't know you were stopping by here today."

"Um, I didn't either."

"You brought me candy?" she said. "That was so sweet."

Josh looked at the heart-shaped box in his hands. Now he felt like an idiot. He used to give his mother a Valentine's card, and he'd never even thought to get one for Hallie.

"Well, yeah, Happy Valentine's Day," Josh said, handing it to her.

"I really needed some chocolate today, too." She was smiling, and looked so happy that Josh felt terrible.

As Hallie unwrapped the cellophane, Cecile walked into the newsroom. Josh hadn't seen her in two weeks. Her hair was platinum blonde, and long enough now that she wore it in two short pigtails. Her red dress had a short skirt and very long sleeves. She looked amazing.

"Josh just brought me some candy!" Hallie said to Cecile, holding out the box toward her. "Wasn't that sweet?"

"Totally sweet," Cecile said, smiling at Josh. He wondered if there was a way he could tell her with his eyes that the candy was supposed to be for her.

Hallie offered Cecile a piece and she took one, biting into it slowly. Josh wanted to be alone with her so badly he could barely stand it. As Cecile licked a little chocolate from her lower lip, Josh started getting hard. He had to get the disc to her and get out of the newsroom.

"I have that disc I borrowed from you," he said to Cecile, hoping she'd know enough to play along. "I'm just going to leave it on your desk."

"Okay," she said, not missing a beat. Cecile was clearly very good at this sort of thing.

Josh retrieved the disc from his backpack and walked over to her desk. He turned it over so the front wasn't showing. But Cecile's desk was messy, and he feared it would get lost in the chaos of marking pens and newspapers and empty cans of Red Bull, so he grabbed a Post-it and wrote his cell phone number on it. He put the post-it on the back of the disc.

Josh returned to Hallie's desk.

"How's it goin'?" Marcus asked Josh.

"Not too bad," he said. "You?"

"Can't complain."

"I can," Hallie said. "I just shot an anniversary party at the Rivertown Manor, for a couple that got married on Valentine's Day sixty years ago."

"That's sweet, though," Cecile said. She walked over to her desk, and Josh watched as she moved a newspaper over the disc, then turned it over. A few seconds later she looked up at Josh and smiled.

"Well, I'm heading over to Nicki's," Josh said, which was true, though he wouldn't tell Nicki what he'd done. "Happy Valentine's Day and all."

"Thanks, Josh," Hallie said. "I'll be here until about six. Should I pick you up from Nicki's then?"

"Sure," Josh said. He left the newsroom quickly, walked past the main building of the Huxley Glass Works, and was heading down Second Street toward Nicki's house when he heard his cell phone beep. He pulled it out of his pocket and looked at it; he had a text.

Tnx for the V-tine, Josh. Call u tonite.—C

CHAPTER 20

O n the first warm Saturday in March, Hallie packed her work camera—the digital—and left the house early. From her back door down to Bivalve she walked along the bay, Laughing Gulls scattering ahead of her, the sun glinting off the water. She had a mission for *Good News*, to take photos of the A. J. Meerwald, a restored Delaware Bay schooner now used for educational programs. But as she walked, an idea formed in the back of her mind: a photo essay of the bay. She scanned ahead, struggling to see it clearly, without bias, as she changed position. So far she wasn't seeing the bay in any way other than what she'd seen growing up, the vision her mother had reflected in her paintings: an expanse of silty sand leading to brackish water, an occasional weather-beaten house perched on precarious wooden stilts.

She remembered taking walks like this with both her parents, her mom occasionally photographing something she would later paint, her dad pointing out natural wonders that varied with the seasons: the red knots feeding on horseshoe crab eggs in the spring, monarch butterflies and purple martins in the summer. Her father had been animated back then, happy even. But once her mother died, those walks along the bay stopped, and her dad's expression creased into the perpetual wince that came to define him. Hallie had almost forgotten that other father once existed, though she could picture him just then, smiling at her, pointing out a dinner-plate-sized turtle hiding in a patch of marsh grass. It had felt like a gift, that turtle, an enormous Easter egg planted there for her to find. In her memory even the light of the bay looked different, brighter somehow, the turtle and plants and water shimmering with a sort of magic. Was that what Oyster Shell had looked like back then, before her mother died? Would it still look that way to an unbiased eye? Josh and Ram both saw great beauty in the bay, the river. Hallie took a few shots of the shoreline, wishing she had brought her other camera, hoping this one could sort it out for her; but she couldn't erase from her mind that image of a younger, happier Dad. She shot everything in sight, water and gulls and grass as she tried to forget.

By the time Hallie reached the A. J. Meerwald she'd photographed almost everything along the way: not just the bay and the river but some dilapidated shacks tucked inland, separated by lots overgrown with weeds, scattered with discarded toys and auto parts. She stood on the dock and shot the schooner from a variety of angles, its three great sails flapping slightly in the wind. When she was certain she had enough frames she stopped in the ship's office, where she spotted a stack of pamphlets about the Meerwald next to a pile of flyers for the Mollusk Creek Trust. She picked up one of each, walked out and sat on the dock. The sun was now bright and she gazed at the water, the small boats moored not far from the tall ship. *It really* is *beautiful here*, Hallie realized with a start. Why had she so completely bought into her mother's way of seeing it—the melancholic grays, the diffuse light?

One of the pamphlets about the Meerwald included a history of the oyster industry, and she began to read it, hoping for a mention of her great-great-grandfather. She couldn't help but wonder what it might have been like if the oysters had never died, if she'd grown up rich and been left a thriving family business. But her father would never have married her mother, a teenage runaway, if his family had remained wealthy. He never would have married Brenda. Neither Hallie nor Josh would exist if the oysters hadn't died.

Hallie looked up and saw Todd jogging toward the dock, slowing as he approached her. His sweatpants and plain white t-shirt were damp with sweat.

"Hey," she said. "Chasing bad guys?"

Todd smiled. "Just out for a run." He leaned against a flagpole at the edge of the water, stretching his hamstrings. "By the way, I've been meaning to call you. You shouldn't have any more trouble from Cal, at least for a while."

"How come?'

"He's in the county jail. Outstanding warrants."

Everyone felt certain it was Cal who'd tried to break into the house in January. But she'd had no trouble since then.

"What kind of warrants?" she asked.

"He always has a few. Speeding tickets, drunk and disorderly. He missed a court appearance a week ago, and got picked up."

"How long will he be in?"

Todd shrugged. "Jail's not the worst place for Cal. Three squares a day and he dries his liver out a bit. He's been in jail before. He can handle it."

Hallie nodded. "Thanks for telling me," she said, and Todd was off and running back down the street. But she sat rooted in her spot, staring out at the water, unable to shake the feeling that she was the cause of Cal's jail stint.

Marcus was the only one in the newsroom when Hallie got there Monday morning.

"How was your weekend?" he asked, peering at her over his computer terminal.

Hallie shrugged. "I looked after Josh, worried about money, took photos for a story I'll bet *Good News* runs every spring." She stashed her bag in her desk drawer. "You?"

"I looked after my folks, worried about money, and now I'm editing a story we do every week." Marcus rolled his eyes.

Before uploading the photos of the schooner, Hallie checked for an e-mail from Damien. But there was nothing from him, just a forward from Lawrence: another agent had turned down his book. Before she could craft an encouraging reply, Marcus cleared his throat loudly; Orren had just walked in. Hallie quickly exited the internet and clicked on Photoshop, but Orren wasn't looking in her direction. He had stopped by Cecile's desk.

"I know everyone else is out on assignment," Orren said, "but do you two have any idea where Miss O'Neill is?"

Hallie shook her head, as did Marcus. Cecile seemed to be coming to work later and later, and, when she was there, spending most of her time texting.

Orren walked over to Hallie's desk. "How did the A. J. Meerwald photos turn out?"

"I got some great shots," Hallie said. "I'll show you after I get them uploaded."

Orren nodded. "I'll be in my office." Once he was gone, Hallie clicked back on the internet and went to the website of *Farm and Dairy*, checking her mailbox for the "Farm for Sale" ad she'd posted. It was empty. The ad had been up for six weeks, and she'd only received four responses, none of them serious offers. She let out a sigh, loud enough that Marcus glanced over at her.

"What's the matter?" he asked.

"No one who reads *Farm and Dairy* wants to buy my dad's property."

Marcus leaned back in his chair. "Maybe you should try running ads more locally. Our paper, the *Floyd Daily News*, maybe the *Press* and the *Inquirer*."

"That's not a bad idea." She tapped a pen against her keyboard. "The realtor isn't having any luck, either."

He smiled sympathetically, and Hallie couldn't help but think about what a great boyfriend he'd make.

"How are things going with your girlfriend, anyway?" she asked as nonchalantly as she could.

Marcus turned toward her. "I forgot to tell you. She's moving here."

"Here?" Hallie slumped in her chair.

"I think we're going to live in Philly. We're both applying for jobs there. I'm setting up some care for my folks, but this way I'll be close enough to check in."

Hallie smiled, but her face must have betrayed something, for he added, "Hey, you're gonna be out of here pretty soon, too. You'll be back in New York by the end of the summer."

"Sure I will," she said, turning back to her computer. But her own happy ending felt light years away.

As Hallie uploaded the photos she'd taken Saturday morning, something at the edge of two of the frames caught her eye. It was a rusted-out old car of a make she couldn't identify, its size and boxy shape suggesting origins in the 1980s. The tires were sunken halfway down in the mud; the hood was missing, and weeds sprouted through the remnants of the engine. She had an impulse to ride back out to Shellpile, shoot some frames of it. But she'd have to put it off for another day. Today she needed to work on the photography that paid.

AFTER LUNCH, HALLIE spent most of the afternoon writing and placing ads for the farm in *Good News* and the other papers Marcus had suggested, while checking her e-mail every fifteen minutes. By the time she was done, it was after four, and she knew she'd have to stay late to finish the layouts. She called Josh and asked him if he'd mind being on his own for dinner.

"That's cool," he said. "I'm hanging out with Nicki. How late will you be?"

Hallie looked at the three windows of photos open on her computer screen. "I think I can finish by seven," she said. "Should I pick you up at Nicki's?"

"Umm, pick me up at the library. Nicki goes to work at five, so I'll do my homework then."

"I'm sorry to make you wait around so long."

"It's cool. I totally don't mind." He almost sounded happy about it.

"Okay. I'll call Nancy and ask her to go over and let Emma out."

"Sure," Josh said. He sounded distracted. "See you later."

Hallie ended the call, left a message for Nancy, and turned back to the photos on her screen. Twenty minutes into tackling the first layout, she decided she needed better graphics, and walked over to Cecile's desk. Cecile was texting when Hallie approached her; she looked up and smiled, sliding her phone under a newspaper.

"You only have to do that when Orren's around, you know," Hallie said quietly. "I don't care if you're texting."

"Thanks," she said, "but I was done anyway. What's up?"

"Could you do some artwork for the A. J. Meerwald page?"

Cecile called the layout onto her screen. "Sure. Mind if I do it later? I'm having an early dinner with a friend and was planning to come back."

"No problem," Hallie said. "Is this the mystery man?"

"The mystery man?" Cecile sat up straight in her seat.

"You get a lot of texts lately. New boyfriend?"

"Nah," Cecile said, too quickly, Hallie thought. "Just various friends."

•

HOURS LATER, AFTER she and Josh were back at home, after she'd sorted through the bills and put on her pajamas and had a glass of wine, Hallie checked her email to find a message from Damien. She felt her heart speed up a little as she opened it.

It was mostly about the mixing of his new album, with a paragraph full of the kinds of technical details that had bored her when they were together. She skimmed it, and then came to this:

I'm doing a limited tour of small theaters this spring before the album drops at the end of the summer. Philly's on the list—early May, I think. I'll send you the exact date when my manager gets it confirmed. Do you and Josh want to come?

Early May gave her seven weeks to lose enough weight to get back into her skinny jeans. Could she lose fifteen pounds in seven weeks? If she starved herself, definitely.

Hallie knocked on Josh's door. He was sprawled on his bed reading Lawrence's manuscript, Emma by his side.

"Listen to this: I got an e-mail from Damien that he's doing a tour before his album comes out, and he'll be in Philly at the beginning of May," she said. "He invited us to go."

Josh stuck an index card in the manuscript to mark his place. "Both of us? Really?"

"Yeah. I think we'll get backstage passes and all."

"Cool." Josh was quiet for a moment. "Will it be weird for you, though? I mean, he was your boyfriend."

Hallie waved her hand in the air. "Oh, that was a long time ago."

Josh gave her a very penetrating teenage stare.

"Okay, I *am* curious about seeing him again. We've been e-mailing a lot and I'm not sure what it all means."

"You look happy," Josh said.

"Do I? Yeah, I guess I do want to see him."

Hallie returned to her room and considered answering Damien immediately, but she didn't want to appear too eager. Instead she climbed into bed and pulled the envelope of photos—her mother's last photos, the meditations on death—from her dresser drawer. The possum photos were the most overtly disturbing, but Hallie felt herself returning, each time she looked at them, to the bowl of rotting fruit. The moldy, blackened bananas and pears were in an earthenware bowl, on the kitchen table Hallie recognized from her childhood. Was the rotting fruit an assault on domesticity? Was it meant to convey a disdain for housework, for motherhood itself? Hallie stared at the photo until it became pointillistic, just dots of color. Then she tucked the photos back in her drawer, turned out the light and went to sleep.

AROUND THREE THAT morning, Hallie woke abruptly. The house seemed quiet, but she felt that something had startled her out of a dream. Diane Arbus had been there, in a room Hallie didn't recognize, not taking photos but regarding Hallie with an expression that was almost maternal. Just above her head was a small window, a black spider walking across the glass. Hallie tried to clear the weird tableau from her mind as she heard Emma bark. She went downstairs and found Josh sitting with the dog on the back porch, holding his cell phone to his ear. She could see he'd been crying.

"I have to go," he said. "I woke Hallie up." There was a pause. "I'm okay. Sorry I kept you up so late. Talk to you tomorrow." Josh turned off the phone. He rubbed his eyes, then hugged his knees, the phone still clutched in one hand.

"Are you okay?" she asked.

He nodded, then glanced at his phone's display. "Oh my God, it's after three. I'm sorry I woke you up."

"Who were you talking to? Nicki?"

She saw Josh's expression shift. "Umm, it was Cecile."

"Cecile?"

"Yeah, I couldn't sleep and I got online, and then I saw her on IM. I was kind of upset so we switched to the phone."

Hallie had a gnawing feeling in her gut. Why was Cecile talking to her little brother at three a.m.? "What upset you?" she asked. "I mean, was there something specific?"

Josh was quiet for a moment. "Tomorrow is Mom's birthday," he said. "I mean, today. It's already here."

Hallie ached for Josh. "I should have known that."

"You weren't close to her or anything. I didn't expect you to remember." His voice wavered a bit; he was still on the edge of tears.

"No, I really should have known. I'm sorry." She stepped back inside, retrieved a box of tissues from the family room, brought them out to Josh.

"Thanks," he said, and blew his nose loudly enough that Emma sat up straight and gazed at him.

"He's okay, girl," Hallie said to the dog, and the thought that she now had to comfort the dog, too, made her laugh a little. Josh gave her an odd look.

"Just ignore me," she said. "I'm demented from lack of sleep."

"I feel bad about waking you."

"No, I wasn't sleeping well anyway. I had this weird dream about Diane Arbus."

"Who's Diane Arbus?"

"A famous photographer."

They went back inside. Josh poured himself a glass of water from the pitcher in the fridge, then downed it. "I'm going to bed."

"You sure? We can stay up and talk for a while."

He shook his head. "I'm okay now," he said, and disappeared up the stairs.

But Hallie couldn't fall back asleep. As she lay in bed cataloguing her failings as a surrogate parent, she recalled an image from the dream. She'd seen that spider before, she knew. She'd seen that window.

She stared up at the ceiling in her darkened room as she pictured it. The garage. That window was on the back wall of the garage. She hadn't been inside it since she was eleven, though she'd been drawn to the building in the months after her mother's death, only working up enough courage to peek through the glass a few times. Hallie's mind drifted to the shacks she'd photographed in Shellpile, the rusted-out car in the overgrown lot, and she almost started to fall asleep when it hit her, so suddenly and with such force that she sat up in her bed and turned on the light. *There's a window in the garage.* A window her mother could have opened or broken to let out the exhaust fumes.

Hallie got up and walked to her bedroom window. From this side of the house she could see the front of the garage, but not the back. And she'd known that before she parted the curtains. She didn't want to look at the back of the garage, or inside it. Damien had been right, of course.

The story her father had told her didn't add up. And she'd known it, on some level, long before.

Hallie went downstairs, quickly downed a glass of wine, went back up and lay in bed, wishing for sleep. She finally began to doze just after the sun came up. And while she didn't have any other dreams, as she awakened for the second time that morning she clearly recalled the image of Diane Arbus, leaning against the garage wall with an enigmatic smile on her face. Diane Arbus, who had killed herself in the 1970s. Hallie only allowed the thought to linger for a second before she built a wall around it, banished it.

CHAPTER 21

Halfway through the Franklin and Marshall tour, his third campus of the day, Josh became convinced that visiting colleges was a boring waste of time. He couldn't concentrate on anything the guides said, for his brain was consumed with Cecile. Cecile, Cecile, Cecile. Sometimes when Hallie asked him a question, the only response that came to his mind was "Cecile." Sometimes he looked at Emma and thought "Cecile." And now, as Kendra the tour guide talked about the library, Hallie and Ram weirdly playing the same role as the other kids' parents, Josh was thinking about Cecile's perfect, pouty lips.

Kendra the tour guide was pretty and smart and very much not a teenager—she had to be twenty, or even twenty-one. Josh found her a little intimidating, not easy to talk to like Cecile. He hadn't been on an actual date with Cecile yet, though they talked and e-mailed all the time, and she sometimes snuck away from work in the afternoons to hang out with him after school. But he loved her in a way he'd never loved anyone before—so much deeper than his feelings for Missy Dalton had ever been—and he had an odd sort of confidence about her. His birthday was less than two months away and, once he turned eighteen, Cecile had said they wouldn't have to sneak around. He could finally take her out. He thought about having sex with Cecile so often and in such detail that he sometimes felt like it had already happened.

Ram and Hallie and the other kids and their parents smiled and nodded at whatever Kendra was saying, but Josh had stopped listening. The tour was really just a commercial for the school. The guides weren't going to show you kids freaking out over finals, or begging the financial aid office for more money. They weren't going to show you those dark moments in the middle of the night when a kid misses his dead parents so much he can't fall asleep, can't bear to be awake. Josh sometimes had trouble imagining how he could possibly deal with four whole years of college. He wished there was a way he could just live in a room somewhere and read books for four years, without being tested or graded, and then maybe he could start his own writing at the end of those years. Doing nothing but read and write was sort of his idea of heaven, though he didn't really believe in heaven.

"What did you think?" Hallie asked him.

Cecile. Josh looked around and realized that the tour was over. "It seems cool," he said. After reading the disappointment on Hallie's face, he added, "I think I'm kinda toured out."

"Me too," she said, glancing at Ram. "Let's go."

THEY WERE ALL quiet on the ride home from Lancaster, until Hallie started motioning toward an exit.

"Hey, turn down that road," she called out.

"Here?" Ram asked, pulling into the right lane, and she nodded.

"What's down there?" Josh asked, but as they took the turn, he saw it: a huge wooded lot full of abandoned cars and trucks in various states of decomposition.

"Do you guys mind if I just take a few photos?" she asked. "I've had this idea cooking for a little while." She was already loading film into her Nikon.

"What's the idea?" Ram asked.

"I've started taking some shots of junked cars," she said. "I just want to see what I can get here."

Nobody said anything as Hallie began snapping photos: a car from the 1950s that was missing both doors; the bed of a rusted-out pickup, sans tires and most of the cab; two sides of an old yellow school bus, propped one atop the other. There were also smaller bits of vehicles—engine blocks, windshields, disembodied steering wheels—but Hallie was mostly taking photos of the bigger remnants. Josh could see why; they were the most dramatic, some with weeds or even bushes growing through the places where doors or windows once had been.

Hallie shot a roll of film while Ram wandered off to another part of the yard. After she reloaded the camera, she looked at Josh. "What do you feel when you look at this?" she asked.

Josh focused on the pieces of trucks and cars and really thought about it. There was something both sad and beautiful about the cars that had become huge planters, but the smaller automotive bits were somehow deeply disturbing. He thought about the phrase "auto body"—that's what they were like, these disembodied steering wheels and batteries and drive shafts. Internal organs. Body parts.

"It's like a morgue, or a mad scientist's lab," Josh said. He wasn't sure if what he'd just said would make any sense to Hallie, but she smiled and nodded.

"I'm really drawn to the ones with the plants growing through them," she said. "They remind me a little of a series of Jonathan Bloom's paintings. The Renewal series. Lawrence has a few hanging at his place."

"The ones with the bright green line and the dark background?" Josh asked. He had noticed them; they were at once hopeful and very sad, and Josh had wondered at the fact that something so abstract—just a line of color, really—could make him feel that way.

Hallie nodded. "They're supposed to be about life emerging from death."

Josh looked at the shell of a big old Cadillac, the front and back ends both missing, just two sides and a roof and a front seat and a steering wheel with weeds and bushes intertwined throughout what remained. And he thought about what it would be like when his father's farm was sold, and how upset he might be if it didn't remain a farm, but became something else entirely. Still, wasn't it better for an abandoned thing to change, to become home to something or someone else, than to just remain abandoned?

"I can't wait to see these photos," Josh said, and Hallie surprised him with a quick hug. She finished off two more rolls of film.

The following Friday night, Josh and Hallie were in the car, on the New Jersey Turnpike, headed to New York for the weekend.

"So how much work are you going to have to do?" Josh asked. It was weird how he never used to go anywhere and now, with Hallie, he'd been to New York enough that he actually had a favorite rest stop on the turnpike—the one named for James Fenimore Cooper. It had both a Cinnabon and a Carvel.

"A lot. Joy fired her last office manager three weeks ago. But it'll be worth it. She'll pay me a ton and I'll be able to use her darkroom. She has the greatest darkroom."

"Are you sure you'll have time for the NYU tour?" This was one college tour Josh really did want to take, after reading Lawrence's manuscript.

"I'll make time. Lawrence wants to come, too. And Nicki's dad is taking the two of you to see Hunter College, right?"

"Yeah." Lately Josh and Nicki had been talking a lot about going to college in New York together. There were big plusses, like the fact that he could maybe live with Hallie and Emma—Hallie had promised to take Emma to New York with her when she moved back—and not have to live in a dorm. Josh didn't want some roommate he didn't know. But it all depended on where he got accepted.

"Any other plans?" Hallie asked.

"I think I'm going to a Yankees game with Nicki and her dad. They have an extra ticket."

"Have you ever been to a game before?"

"No. But Dad used to watch them on TV all the time." It was so easy to picture his dad leaning back in his recliner, a glass of Scotch in his hand, watching a ball game. The times he watched baseball were the only times he had seemed to actually relax.

"Is Nathan going?" Hallie asked.

"No. That's why they have the extra ticket." Josh thought about it for a moment. "I think they're, like, having problems. Nicki and Nathan, I mean." Josh kept hearing stories about Nathan canceling plans at the last minute, or meeting her hours late. He'd told Nicki to break up with him, but she said she loved him.

"You know," Hallie said, "I've always thought Nathan was kind of a prick."

Josh laughed. "Really? I thought you and Lawrence liked him."

"We love his mom. Carole is great. But her ex-husband was a jerk, and Nathan reminds me of him."

"I didn't like him when I met him, either."

"You didn't? I thought you kind of hit it off."

"No. I just thought you guys wanted me to like him."

Hallie glanced over at him. "Oh Josh," she said. "You don't have to pretend to like people I introduce you to. I think Lawrence just told Carole to bring him so you wouldn't be the only teenager there."

"I know. That's why I pretended." But Josh knew it really had more to do with the fact that months ago, when he met Nathan, he didn't feel certain that Hallie would stay. He was still trying to be the perfect stoic orphan Josh. Now he was more himself, most of the time. The only thing he really couldn't talk to Hallie about was Cecile.

JOSH HAD TO get up earlier than he would have liked the next morning to fit everything in: first the NYU tour, and a late breakfast afterward in some diner where Lawrence and Hallie said they used to spend hours talking and drinking coffee; then Hunter College with Nicki and her dad; and then the Yankees game. Josh had more fun at the game than he expected to. He gorged himself on French fries and drank so much Coke that he had an urge to run around the bases. Mr. Kepler was always nice, and so different from any dad Josh had ever met in South Jersey; only a few years older than Hallie, Mr. Kepler wore a ponytail and an earring, an actual hoop earring. He had his own website design business, and Josh guessed that when you had your own business you could look however you wanted. Josh had tried pulling his own hair into a ponytail after the last time he saw Mr. Kepler, but it hadn't looked so good. His hair still wasn't quite long enough yet.

"My dad liked to watch baseball," Josh said to Mr. Kepler while Nicki was texting Nathan, "but he never went to, like, actual games."

"What was his favorite team?" Mr. Kepler asked.

"The Phillies."

Mr. Kepler nodded. "I come from generations of Yankees fans. My dad and my grandfather starting taking me to games as soon as I could walk."

Josh wished he had memories like that, some sort of family tradition, but most of what he remembered about his father involved work: at the farm, around the house. Maybe hard work was their tradition.

When one of the Devil Rays caught the third out and the Yankees were no longer at bat, Nicki left to go to the bathroom, and Mr. Kepler turned to Josh. "What do you think of Nicki's boyfriend?" he asked, with an urgency that suggested he'd been waiting for Nicki to leave.

"I don't really know him," Josh said, which was the truth.

"But what's your impression? Do you like him?"

Josh shrugged.

Mr. Kepler looked at him. "I won't repeat it to Nicki, whatever you tell me." He let out a long breath. "I don't think he's treating her right."

"How so?"

"Between you and me?" Mr. Kepler asked, and Josh nodded. "I think he has another girlfriend."

Josh was kind of stunned. It seemed to him that it was hard enough to get one girlfriend, let alone two. But guys like Nathan probably did stuff like that all the time.

"I didn't like him when I first met him," Josh said. "My sister knows his parents. She says his mom's really nice but his dad's a jerk, and she thinks Nathan is more like his dad."

Mr. Kepler nodded and then looked off in the distance, watching the game. "Do you have a girlfriend, Josh?" It was a weird, unexpected question.

"Not really," Josh said, and he was immediately sorry he hadn't just said no, because Mr. Kepler smiled at him a little.

"But sort of?"

Josh mulled it over. Nicki knew all about Cecile; sometimes she covered for Josh when he and Cecile got together. But he couldn't tell Mr. Kepler anything that would make him feel like he had to tell Hallie.

"There's someone I like," Josh said.

"Does she like you?"

"I think so."

Mr. Kepler took a sip of his beer. "So what are you waiting for?"

There was no way Josh could explain that he was waiting to turn eighteen because the girl he liked was twenty-three. It was too bad, because Mr. Kepler seemed to Josh like the kind of person who could give him good advice about girls. Mr. Kepler almost always had a girlfriend; Nicki never liked any of them.

"I'm going to ask her out soon," Josh said.

Mr. Kepler nodded. He looked like he was about to say more, but then Nicki came back with a big pretzel covered in mustard, and she and Josh shared it and they all went back to watching the game. The Yankees won, and Josh had to admit, it *was* fun, being there in person.

THE NEXT DAY, Josh and Nicki spent hours at the Strand Bookstore, and then they walked to Joy's studio to see the photos Hallie was developing. Josh had hoped Cecile would call or text him while he was away, but he hadn't heard from her since Friday. He mentioned it to Nicki as they walked to the studio.

"Maybe she went away for the weekend," Nicki said.

"Yeah, but she could still call, or text," Josh said.

"Maybe she found a boyfriend her own age." She punched him lightly in the arm.

"Don't kid about that." Josh couldn't even begin to think about Cecile with another guy.

"Sorry. I wouldn't kid about it if I really thought it was true."

At the studio, Hallie showed Josh and Nicki around, though they couldn't see the aviary because Joy wasn't home. Framed photos of Joy's lined the studio walls, and a lot of them were really cool: shots of fashion models that looked very seventies, and photos of the Rolling Stones and Aerosmith. And then there were some weird shots of Joy, naked, covered with feathers and bird shit. Josh was both creeped out and turned on, looking at Joy's naked body.

"These are really interesting," Nicki said.

Josh couldn't pull himself away from one photo. Joy's hair was almost, but not quite, covering her nipples. Albert was perched on her shoulder, and a lovebird was hovering above her, shitting down her breast. He knew he shouldn't be attracted to Joy—she was really old!—but he couldn't stop looking at her breasts. They looked different than the ones in his father's magazines—more real, he guessed, and Joy was a lot older than those girls. The way Joy was sitting in the picture, he could only see a tuft of pubic hair between her legs, or else he'd have been staring there, too.

"Josh," Nicki said, "stop staring at the photographer's tits."

He saw Hallie smile a little, and felt totally embarrassed. "I wasn't."

"Uh huh," Nicki said.

As Hallie picked up a stack of 8 x 10 prints, Josh's phone rang: Cecile. There was no way he could answer.

"The last batch are still wet," Hallie said, "but these are the rest."

Nicki started on the pile first, handing Josh each one when she was done. Nicki said "Wow" and "These are cool" a few times, but then she stopped at one, and held onto it for so long that Josh had to look over her shoulder. It was the car that had most captured Josh's attention when they were at the auto graveyard, the Cadillac. The way Hallie had framed it, it was like you were in the car, looking through the absent windshield to a lush green landscape outside. Josh took the rest of the stack from Nicki; there were several others of this car, but the one Nicki was holding was the best.

"This is amazing," Nicki said to Hallie.

"Thanks," Hallie said.

"I'd totally hang this in my room," Josh said. "I could look at it all the time." His phone beeped; Cecile had texted him. He didn't dare read it in front of Hallie.

"Me too," Nicki said. "I could look at all of these for a long time."

Hallie smiled. "I'm going to make a few extra prints and leave them for Joy, to see what she thinks." She flipped through a few of the shots. "I haven't done this in so long, but I might start submitting to galleries again."

"You totally should," Nicki said.

Josh's phone beeped again; another text.

"Who's trying to get a hold of you?" Hallie asked.

When Cecile called Josh a lot at home, he led Hallie to believe, when she asked, that it was Nicki. Usually he didn't have to directly lie; Hallie would say, "Who's that, Nicki?" and Josh would murmur something noncommittal. But Nicki was standing right there, now. Who could he say it was? Josh looked at Nicki, but she kept flipping through the photos. She wasn't going to help him.

"Josh?" Hallie asked.

"It's Cecile," Josh said. "You know we talk sometimes."

Hallie looked at the phone. "Why the urgency?"

"I don't know," Josh said. "I should probably check the messages." He walked a bit away from Hallie and Nicki and quickly texted Cecile— *Stop! Hallie!*— knowing that she'd understand the rest.

"It's nothing," Josh said, walking back over. "She was just saying hi."

"With one call and two texts," Hallie said.

Josh looked at Nicki, hoping she would step in and say something; but she just shrugged slightly, as if to say, you're busted.

"Well, you know Cecile," Josh said. "She's friendly."

It was probably a stupid enough thing to have said without Nicki then bursting out laughing. Hallie glared at Josh; Josh glared at Nicki.

"Cecile's a little whacked," Nicki said. "I'm not surprised she'd call a bunch of times. She's the kind of person who will just call and call until you answer her."

Hallie's eyes were narrowed and her lips were kind of puckered. It was the exact facial expression his dad had always made when Josh pissed him off. She was quiet for what felt like a long time, just looking at Josh with Dad's mad face.

"You should go back to Lawrence's and get your stuff together," Hallie finally said.

"I'm all packed," Josh said. "I'll go with you to pick up your stuff, Nick."

Hallie looked at Josh for another long moment.

"Okay," she said, but before he could leave she fixed him with a look that very clearly told him they weren't finished discussing Cecile.

CHAPTER 22

Almost a week went by before Hallie was able to confront Cecile about whatever it was she was doing with Josh; during that time Cecile called in sick for several days, ignoring Hallie's phone messages and e-mails. On the morning Cecile finally returned to work, Hallie followed her into the bathroom and waited by the sinks until Cecile emerged from a stall.

"Oh, hi," Cecile said, brushing past Hallie to wash her hands.

"We need to talk." Hallie's heart was pounding.

Cecile soaped her hands and ran them under the water. "Sure," she said brightly, but her posture was defensive. Her hair was now razor cut in a chin-length shag, platinum blonde, bangs brushing her mascaraed eyelashes.

Hallie leaned against the wall, arms folded. "I know you've been seeing Josh and lying about it."

Cecile turned off the faucet and started the dryer, running her hands under it for a good thirty seconds before she answered. Hallie grew angrier with each passing second. Even as she imagined strangling Cecile, she wondered why she felt such complete rage. She didn't believe anything had actually happened, did she? Josh had sworn that they were just friends, and Hallie wanted to believe him.

"Look," Cecile said when the dryer stopped. "It's completely innocent. Really. I know he's seventeen."

"That's not the point."

"You're mad that we snuck around," Cecile said. "I get that. I just didn't think you'd understand. We really like hanging out, but we were both afraid people would make it into something other than what it was."

"For you it may just be hanging out," Hallie said. "I think it's a lot more for Josh."

"I wouldn't do anything to hurt him. He's a sweet guy."

Somehow, Cecile made it sound so wholesome. But what had she been up to, exactly? "What's in this for you?" Hallie asked.

"What do you mean?"

"I mean, I get why Josh would want to hang out with a cool, attractive woman who's a few years older than him. What's in it for you, spending all this time with a teenager?"

Cecile regarded Hallie with a funny half-smile. "Well, he's a great *person*," she said. "Don't you know that?" She sashayed out of the bathroom.

There had always been something sketchy about Cecile; she'd told conflicting stories about her childhood, though they always involved Paris and a wealthy American father. But if Cecile was so wealthy, so Parisian, why did she go to art school in Philly? Why was she living in a run-down apartment in Floyd and working for *Good News?*

Hallie returned to her desk in time to see Orren escorting Cecile back to his office. "You don't *look* like you've had the flu all week, Miss O'Neill," Orren said.

"Busted," Ben whispered.

Hallie looked at Marcus. "Do you think she's getting fired?"

"He's giving her a warning," Marcus said. "If she screws up even a little again, she's outta here."

LATER THAT AFTERNOON, Orren summoned Hallie to his office. "Ooh, somebody's in trouble," Marcus mouthed to her.

Orren had a copy of *Good News* on his desk, open to the classifieds. Hallie's ad for the farm was circled.

"I thought employees here could run ads for free," she said. "If I need to pay—"

Orren shook his head. "It's fine," he said, cutting her off. "I'm interested in the property."

"Really?" She sank into the chair opposite him.

"My kids have wanted horses for a while now. Where we live, at the lake, it's not zoned for a stable." Orren cleared his throat. "I've been thinking about buying some land out towards the bay and putting up a barn. I only want a couple of acres, so the size of your farm seems perfect.

Could I come out and take a look at it? Perhaps tomorrow afternoon?"

"Sure," Hallie said. She wondered how difficult it might be to negotiate a price with her boss, but considering how badly she needed to sell the property, and the fact that the land would remain some sort of farm, she was pretty sure she'd take whatever he offered.

THE NEXT MORNING, Hallie pulled out Emma's leash, clipped it to the dog's collar, and soon the two of them were headed down the road at a moderate trot. She was starving, but had allowed herself just half a banana for breakfast. She needed to step it up if she wanted to fit into her skinny jeans by the night of Damien's concert.

As they approached Nancy's house, Hallie decided to stop and see her. But before they reached her yard, Cal passed by in his truck, and pulled into his driveway. Hallie hadn't known he was out of jail.

Emma snarled and snapped as Cal got out of the truck. He looked at Hallie but didn't say anything. His eyes were steely.

"Hey, Cal," Hallie said, and waved. She thought it best to be friendly.

Cal didn't wave back. He stood by his truck and glared at her for a long moment. Then he went into his trailer, slamming the door behind him. Hallie dragged Emma away, toward Nancy's house.

EMMA GREETED NANCY by lunging at her as if she hadn't seen her in a year. Nancy's black cat sat on the kitchen table, her eyes narrowed to slits as she stared down the dog.

"Is Isis okay with Emma?" Hallie asked, but Nancy shook her head.

"Never mind Isis. What just happened with Cal? I saw you wave to him."

"Nothing happened. When did he get out of jail?"

"This is the first I've seen of him," Nancy said. "I'm surprised Todd didn't say anything."

"Maybe he just got out this morning." Hallie sat down at the table. "Do you think he blames me?"

"Cal?" Nancy put water on for tea.

Hallie nodded.

"Why would he?"

"It sounded like Todd had something to do with Cal's getting picked up."

Nancy shook her head. "Cal's always in and out of jail." She put tea bags in two cups and sat across from Hallie. Isis meowed loudly and walked across the table to Nancy, then turned and fixed her large yellow eyes on Hallie.

"Your cat is suspicious of me," Hallie said.

Nancy picked the cat up and set her on the floor. "Oh, Isis is suspicious of everyone."

"Not Josh." The last time they'd been there, the cat had curled up on his lap.

Nancy smiled. "I've never seen an animal that didn't love Josh. When he was little, stray cats and dogs were always following him home. It drove your father crazy."

"I bet."

Nancy looked at the wall, at the painting of her horse, and Hallie followed her gaze. She had been only four or five when her mother painted Zeus; she remembered playing with her dolls just outside the pasture, her mom seated on a folding chair in front of an easel.

"You know who else was like that with animals?" Nancy asked. "Your mother."

Hallie felt her whole body snap to attention.

"Especially with the horses. When she walked up to the pasture fence, they'd gallop over. She didn't have to buy their love the way I did, with sugar cubes and carrots."

"She wanted me to have a horse, didn't she?" Hallie had a vague memory of riding Nancy's horses with her mom, a promise that she'd have her own one day.

Nancy nodded. "She was hoping for your birthday..." Her voice trailed off, and Hallie realized she must have meant the year her mom died. Hallie's mind shifted to that cold January, the garage, the window, and the question that had been submerged for as long as she could remember. She struggled to wall it off, to push it back down.

"Hallie?" Nancy's eyes were soft and open.

The garage, the window. Mom in her snow boots on a January day.

Hallie could smell the exhaust fumes as if she'd been there.

"Dad always said the garage door slammed shut and Mom was overcome by the fumes." She saw Nancy's eyes widen. "But there's a window in the garage."

Nancy's shoulders arched back. "There's a window?"

"Yeah."

The teakettle whistled, and Nancy got up, poured the water. She was quiet as she brought the cups to the table, quiet in a way that felt ominous. What had made her bring this up with Nancy? Today was not the day to find this out. Maybe next week, or next year, but not today.

"Hallie," Nancy finally said, but Hallie cut her off.

"I had no idea it was getting so late," she said. "I should go."

"You just got here."

Hallie shook her head. She slipped Emma's leash around her wrist as she got up and put her untouched tea cup in the kitchen sink, Emma trailing her. "Orren Huxley is coming over later. He might buy the farm."

Nancy put her hand on Hallie's arm. "Holly," she said, and Hallie wondered whether it had been a slip, or deliberate. For a moment, Nancy didn't look fragile and white-haired. Instead Hallie saw the woman she'd known when she was a child: trim, sturdy, with a face framed by brown curls. Hallie had an eerie sense of time slowing to a full stop, the same sense she'd had when her father had picked her up from sixth grade and told her that her mother was dead. It had taken her years—well into her college years—to experience the passing of minutes and hours at a speed others took for granted.

"I really have to go," Hallie said, wrenching her arm away with more force than was necessary. She and Emma were out the door before Nancy could say anything more.

"Come on Emma," Hallie said, "Let's run," and Hallie moved as fast as her legs would allow, the dog trotting by her side.

ORREN WAS AT the farm for only fifteen minutes before he made her an offer—a reasonable one. Hallie knew she should haggle but didn't have the energy; she agreed to it and sent Orren on his way. When she checked her voicemail, there was more good news, from the lawyer: the teenage girl who'd been killed in the accident sent a text message seconds before the collision. The lawsuit would, most likely, be settled.

Hallie spent the rest of the afternoon driving around the most rural South Jersey roadways she could find, stopping when she spotted an abandoned or rusted-out car or truck. Around four she spotted what she was looking for in Franklinville: a lot full of ancient junks and wrecks. She got out and inspected the old sedans, station wagons, and pickups, then was drawn to a stack of fenders and bumpers, wild vines growing behind them. As Hallie approached, a small brown bird flew out, cawing and flapping its wings. There were three eggs in a nest inside the bumper. Hallie backed off as quietly as she could, put a long-range lens on her camera and shot the nest while the mother bird circled overhead.

Hallie stood nearly immobile for a long time, hoping the mother bird would relax. The bird darted back and forth, close to the nest, but remained aloft; she had to be afraid, yet she would not abandon her eggs.

Just as the sun was starting to set, the mother returned to the nest, and Hallie got a few shots off before the bird flew at her once again. They were the shots she'd been waiting for. When she got back to the car, she was stunned to see the time on her cell phone: 6:05.

"I'm sorry I didn't call sooner," Hallie said when Josh answered. "I was shooting some photos and completely lost track of time."

"That's okay."

"I'm in Franklinville, but I'll swing by Nicki's and pick you up." She climbed into the driver's seat and closed the car door. "Maybe we can go out for dinner."

Josh didn't say anything for a moment. "Actually, Nicki's mom invited me for dinner," he finally said. "We're just about to eat. Is it okay if I stay?"

"Sure," Hallie said, but it tugged at her: she hadn't been there, so he'd found another mother—a real mother—to make him dinner. "I'm really sorry I didn't call sooner."

"Oh, it's okay. I only just noticed the time myself." She heard a brief rustling sound. "Nicki will drop me off at home around ten, if that's cool."

"Sure," Hallie said. "I'll see you later."

Hallie closed her cell, packed up her camera and lenses and rolls of film, and stared out at the stack of fenders, harder to see in the waning light. Did Nicki's mother mind, having Josh for dinner like this? She located the girl's home number in her address book.

"Hi, Nicki, it's Hallie," she said. "Can I talk to your mom for a minute?"

"My mom?"

"Yeah, I just wanted to ask her something."

"Umm, she's making dinner." Something in Nicki's tone of voice made Hallie immediately suspicious.

"Let me talk to Josh, then," Hallie said.

There was too long of a pause before Nicki said, "He's in the bathroom. I can have him call you right back."

Clearly Nicki was covering for Josh.

"Nicki, put your mother on the phone *now*," Hallie said.

Nicki was quiet for a moment. "Josh isn't here," she finally said. "He asked me to say he was." She cleared her throat a little. "If you still want to talk to my mom, I'll put her on."

Hallie considered it. There was no reason to get Nicki in trouble. "If you tell me where he is, we can keep your mom out of it."

"I don't know where he is, exactly. He's with Cecile." There was silence for a moment. "I don't like her," Nicki added.

"Do you have any idea where they might be?"

"Usually they just drive around."

"Nicki," Hallie said. "I'm not upset with you for covering for Josh, but I need you to be honest. I'm worried about him. What's going on with him and Cecile?"

Nicki was quiet for a few seconds. "He likes her a ton."

"Are they…" Hallie didn't know how to phrase it.

"They're not, like, doing it," Nicki said. "To be honest, I think Cecile is stringing him along. She tells Josh she's waiting until he turns eighteen. But I think she just likes the attention." Hallie heard Nicki's mom in the background, asking who was on the phone. "I'll be right off," Nicki called out, and then to Hallie: "The girl is, like, a compulsive liar."

Hallie started the car up and turned back onto the highway, in the direction of Floyd.

•

SHE DROVE FAST enough that Brenda's little Geo rattled and groaned. She didn't care if the car flew apart; her anger would fuel the rest of the trip. She had asked Josh to stop spending so much time with Cecile, and to be truthful with her about it. Instead he was seeing her more, and lying. She hit the speed dial for his cell several times, but hung up before putting the call through. She didn't want to tip him off. She wanted to catch them together.

Hallie started at Cecile's apartment; she rang the bell several times, but there was no answer.

Next she went to the newsroom, hoping to get a fix on how long ago Cecile had left. She discovered she wasn't the only one looking for her. Marcus and Orren were in the newsroom, hunkered over Marcus's computer. They both looked up as Hallie walked in.

"Call me if she comes in to clean out her desk tonight," Hallie heard Orren say to Marcus. Marcus nodded.

"Good night, Hallie," Orren said as he left the building, briefcase in hand. "My attorney will be in touch soon."

"Good night," Hallie said. After Orren had left, she turned to Marcus. "What was that about?"

Marcus sighed. "Cecile took off again this afternoon," he said. "It was Orren's last straw. He called her and left a message that she's fired."

"When's the last time you saw her?"

"Around 3:30."

"Well, I'm looking for her too. She's been with Josh all afternoon."

"Whoa." Marcus looked at her. "What are you going to do?"

"I'm not sure," Hallie said. She knew Josh was all right, unharmed physically, at least. "Strangle Cecile, maybe."

"That sounds about right," Marcus said, and laughed a little. "Look, don't do anything crazy. You don't want to go off and make a bigger mess of it."

But Hallie couldn't imagine how her life could be any more of a mess. Sure, the farm was sold and the lawsuit might be settled. But Cal was out of jail, and Josh was sneaking around with a twenty-three year-old. She pulled out her phone and looked at the time. It was almost 8 p.m. She called Josh's cell.

"Tell me where you and Cecile are and I'll come pick you up now," she said when he answered. "We have some talking to do."

Josh was quiet for a moment. "We're at the mall. I'll meet you in front of Penney's."

At the mall, Hallie thought, like any innocent teenage couple strolling around on a weeknight. But they weren't both teenagers, and there was nothing innocent about Cecile. Hallie closed the phone and looked at Marcus.

"Good luck," he said. She walked on unsteady legs to the car and hoped she'd figure out what to say to Josh in the ten-minute drive from the newsroom to the mall.

Chapter 23

They were halfway back to Oyster Shell, and Hallie hadn't said a word. She was moody like their father, and Josh had come to recognize, as he had with his dad, when her head was somewhere else.

"Am I grounded?" Josh finally asked.

Hallie didn't answer him. She just looked out at the road, her hands rigid on the steering wheel. She was starting to freak him out.

"Hallie?"

She glanced at him, then back at the road. "I don't know. I have to think about it."

"I know you're really mad," Josh said. Mostly he just wanted to get her talking. He wanted things to feel normal.

"I'm not sure what I feel." She stopped at a red light. "This is serious, Josh."

"I'm sorry I lied to you," he said. He really was sorry; he hadn't wanted to lie. But he also wasn't going to give up the girl he loved. He would lie again, if he had to.

The light changed, and Hallie drove in silence for long enough that Josh started desperately trying to think up something else to say. But then she spoke. "The lying hurt my feelings, but more than that, I'm worried. You're in love with a girl who's way too old for you, and I'm afraid she's going to break your heart."

"Is that really what bothers you about it?"

They came to another red light at the beginning of Shellpile Drive. "I'm not some sort of strict moralist on age differences. If Cecile were a different kind of person, I might not be as concerned." She cleared her throat. "Of course, I'd rather you didn't have sex until college, but maybe that's unrealistic."

Josh wasn't used to talking about sex with anyone in his family. His mom had never seemed to get over thinking of Josh as a little boy, and Dad had only talked to him about sex once, when Josh was in the seventh grade, after Ray Watson's fourteen-year-old sister got pregnant.

"You know how babies are made, right?" his dad had asked, standing awkwardly in Josh's bedroom doorway.

Josh was lying in bed, reading *Fahrenheit 451*. The question struck him funny. He nodded, trying not to laugh. But he didn't really know *exactly* how babies were made; he just had a basic idea from things he'd read and seen in movies.

Dad closed the door and pulled something from his pocket. He sat on the edge of the bed and showed it to Josh. A condom. Because Josh was only twelve, it made him giggle when Dad opened the packet and put two fingers inside the condom, stretching it out.

"You put this on yourself before you put yourself inside the girl," Dad said. "*Every time*. It don't matter if she says she's on the pill. It'll ruin your life, getting a girl pregnant before you're ready."

Josh had been sort of awed that his dad was talking to him like that, so he'd simply nodded and promised that he'd do what he said. But Josh had the feeling that Hallie's concerns were different.

"Why do you think I should wait until college?" Josh asked.

"Because it's better when you're more emotionally mature," Hallie said. They had sat through one complete change of the light, and Hallie didn't look like she was about to drive on yet. It didn't matter; there were no other cars around.

"How old were you?" Josh blurted. He looked at Hallie, wondering if he'd gone too far.

Hallie sighed. She looked up and seemed to notice the light, finally. She pulled the car over to the side of the road and put the flashers on.

"Actually, I was out of college," she said. "I was twenty-three."

Josh thought about it for a moment. "Damien?"

"Yeah."

Josh wasn't sure what blew his mind more: his sister talking to him about sex, or that she'd lost her virginity to Damien Dark.

"You look a million miles away," Hallie said.

"Yeah, I'm just...wow."

"Think about it, Josh—I was twenty-three and I was still immature.

You're *seventeen*. That's all I'm trying to say. I don't want you to get into something you're not emotionally equipped to handle."

I wasn't emotionally equipped for my parents to die, he wanted to say, *but I'm handling that*. He could have tried to explain to Hallie that loving Cecile had made him feel better about being alive, like maybe there was a future for him that he was supposed to live and that was why he hadn't died with his parents. But any of that would upset Hallie, and she was being pretty cool, overall, about all the lying he'd done.

"I'll think about it," he said.

"Okay." She pulled back onto the road and drove toward their house. "But I can't let you see Cecile anymore."

"Yeah, I figured that." He'd have to be more careful, see Cecile less for a while, maybe.

Hallie slowed the car as they passed the farm. "Orren Huxley made me an offer today," she said, motioning towards the greenhouses. "He wants to build a horse stable."

Josh tried to imagine it, the greenhouses dismantled, horses grazing where tomatoes used to grow. It felt weird. "That's good, I guess."

"It'll help with your college, having that money. And at least it will still be a farm."

Josh dreaded the thought of running into Cole Huxley. He'd probably have the most perfect looking horse imaginable—Josh pictured an Arabian—and a brand new English saddle and ridiculous riding pants. Everyone who rode horses in Pearl Township rode Western, but rich kids from other parts of the county always rode English. Josh remembered this from 4-H fairs when he was little. His dad used to dismiss English riders as "fancy pants."

Hallie cleared her throat like she was going to say something, but then she was quiet. She glanced over at him.

"What?" Josh asked as Hallie pulled into their driveway.

"It's about Cecile. Orren fired her today."

"Fired her? For what?"

"For coming to work late every day, leaving early, and spending most of her time there not working."

Josh knew the leaving early was his fault, that she had been spending her afternoons with him, but he had no idea why she went in late. As he got out of the car, Josh felt a pang of jealousy. Cecile wasn't staying out late with some other guy, was she?

THAT NIGHT, JOSH waited until one in the morning, when he was sure Hallie would be asleep, to call Cecile. She sounded very upset, though she didn't want to talk about what was going on at work. But she asked Josh to meet her first thing in the morning, and the next day, he did. He got off the bus in front of his high school, snuck away through the parking lot, and walked to Cecile's house. He'd never ditched school before, and would have to fake a note from Hallie the next day. But as he walked to Cecile's, he was more worried about her than he was about his excuse. He'd never heard her sound as upset as she had the previous night.

Cecile opened the door in bare feet, clothed only in a silky, sky blue bathrobe. Josh briefly allowed himself to imagine untying the tiny piece of material that kept the robe in place. "Can you believe they fired me *by phone*?" she asked, leading Josh up the stairs.

"That's terrible," Josh said. He didn't know what else to say.

They entered her apartment and Cecile motioned him to the kitchen table. "Coffee?" she asked.

Josh shook his head no. Cecile poured herself a cup and sat opposite him.

"Maybe you should go talk to Orren," Josh said. "Tell him you're sorry?"

Cecile shifted in her seat, and Josh saw a hint of the curve of her left breast. He tried not to stare. She cocked an eyebrow at him. "Why would I do that? I hated that job."

"I thought you were upset about being fired."

"I am. But that doesn't mean I want the job back."

Josh didn't know how to respond, so he got up and helped himself to a glass of water from the tap. He drank a few sips at the sink, then stood there and looked at her. The sunlight was streaming in the window behind her. He could see hints of sparkles in her pale blonde hair. The way the blue blue robe draped over her shoulders beneath her sparkly hair was maybe the most beautiful thing Josh had ever seen.

They were both quiet for a minute. Then Cecile's eyes filled up with tears.

"Oh, Josh." She rose from her chair and walked over to him. "Maybe you're right. Maybe I should go talk to Orren." She moved closer to him. "I've been fired from my first job! I've ruined everything." She batted her lashes; the redness from her tears made her eyes look even bluer.

"It's not that bad," Josh said. He couldn't stand to see her cry. "I mean, you hated the job anyway, right?"

"Would you give me a hug?" She bit her lower lip, her face inches from his.

He set his water glass down on the counter. Josh put his arms around Cecile and she pressed her body into him. He could feel her shoulder blades, and her breasts against his chest. Her head was just below his chin; her hair smelled like peaches. He hoped that she couldn't hear how hard his heart was pounding, and he wondered if she could feel his hard-on through his jeans. They stood like that for what Josh guessed was a few minutes, and then he took a chance and kissed the top of her head, very lightly. She responded by tilting her head up to him and kissing him full-on, her tongue darting around his mouth. Josh was afraid he might come in his underwear just from the kiss. He'd never been kissed like that before. He'd never been kissed at all before, by a girl, a beautiful girl. But he managed to control himself, and they kissed for a few minutes, and then Cecile pulled away and took his hand.

"Come on," she said. She was leading him to the bedroom.

"I thought you said we had to wait until I was eighteen," Josh blurted, and then immediately wished he could take it back. Cecile, the beautiful Cecile, was taking him *to her bedroom!* Only a complete idiot would remind her that he was underage.

But Cecile didn't seem to care. She pulled him into her room and untied the belt on her robe. It was off her in a second and she was standing there, naked. There were no words for how beautiful her body was, how perfectly imperfect, how much better it looked than the pictures in his dad's magazines.

"It doesn't matter," she said, her hands undoing his jeans. "I'll be leaving town soon, anyway." She pulled his jeans down to his ankles and pressed herself against his boxers, his hard-on now very obvious. She kissed him again, and for a moment all he wanted was to pull off his underwear and be inside her. He put his hands on her breasts as he felt her fingers working through his hair. Her breasts were not as perfectly round as he'd expected, but they seemed better this way. Her nipples were hard and pink. It would be magic to be inside her, he thought. It would be the most perfect feeling. There was a tiny corner of his brain that wondered what she meant about leaving town, but he pushed it away.

"Fuck me," she said, her hands moving down Josh's back, inside his underwear, and squeezing his ass. It wasn't the word "fuck" itself so much as the way she said it—hard and emotionless and hungry, like a soulless hooker in some bad movie—that pulled Josh out of the moment. Her words felt like a slap, their harshness ruining everything. It wasn't just fucking, for him. Was that all it would be for her? Suddenly the things Hallie had said last night no longer seemed like a desperate adult's attempt to keep him from growing up.

From the pocket of the crumpled jeans on the floor between them, Josh's phone rang. It was the ring tone that meant it was Hallie: Pearl Jam's "Daughter." Josh took his hands off Cecile and moved away a little.

"Don't answer it," Cecile said, but Josh reached down for his jeans anyway. He did it partly because he was a little mad at Cecile for ruining their beautiful moment, and partly because he was afraid he was in trouble. How could Hallie know that he'd ditched school? It wasn't even 9 a.m. yet.

"Yeah," Josh said into the phone.

"Where are you?" Hallie asked. She sounded very, very mad.

"What do you mean?" Cecile had been right; he shouldn't have answered the phone.

"It's a simple question, Josh. Where *are* you?"

Obviously she knew he wasn't at school. While he stood there in his underwear, trying to figure out what to say, Cecile let out an exaggerated sigh and put her robe back on.

"I'm at Cecile's," he said. "I'll walk over to your work right now."

"If you're not here in fifteen minutes, I'm coming over there to pick you up," she said. He imagined her pinching her eyes together the way she did when she was upset.

"I'll be there. I promise." Josh looked at Cecile. "I have to go."

"Fine," Cecile said, in a way that suggested it wasn't fine at all. She walked out of the bedroom, her hips swaying. Josh dressed quickly and found her sitting on the living room floor. Her tattered old couch—Cecile had told him that she and her friend Hannah found it on the street in Philly one garbage day—was piled with drawings and collages in various states of completion.

"I'm sorry," he said. "I just feel really bad, lying to Hallie."

"I thought you cared about me, Josh." Her eyes looked watery again.

"I do care!" He looked at her and wondered if he should say it. The reservations he'd had a few minutes ago were gone, replaced again by what he'd been feeling for months. He sat down next to her. "I love you, Cecile."

She smiled. "You do?"

"Yeah." He reached for her hand, and she let him take it in his.

"I thought you were—I felt so *rejected*," she said.

"No. It was just—I don't know, I guess it wasn't how I'd always pictured it."

"How did you picture it?" She moved closer to him so their hips were touching.

"I always thought that the night after my birthday, I'd take you out on a real date, like to a fancy restaurant down the shore or somewhere. And then I thought it might happen after that. Like, at night, when I wasn't ditching school and on the verge of getting in trouble." In his imagination, they'd been the only two people in the restaurant, a small, warm place illuminated only by candles and tiny white lights.

"Will you still do that, Josh? Take me out like that?"

"I will," Josh said. "But I think I'm going to be grounded for a while." Cecile nodded. "You'd better go."

Josh checked the time on his cell phone. "Yeah," he said. He kissed her on the lips, and she kissed him back, but not like before. "I'll call you later, if I can."

"Find a way," she called out as he left her apartment.

NOBODY AT *GOOD NEWS* was acting the way they usually did. Everybody seemed freaked and stressed. At first Josh thought they all knew he'd been with Cecile, that Hallie had told everyone; but he quickly realized that it had nothing to do with him. Marcus's fingers were flying over his keyboard. Hallie wasn't at her desk, so Josh sat in her chair.

"She's in Orren's office," Marcus said, without looking up from his computer screen. "She said you should wait here."

"Okay," Josh said. He wondered if Marcus or anyone else in the newsroom could tell that he'd almost had sex. Josh glanced over at Cecile's desk, piled high with her stuff. How would she collect it all? He texted Hallie's cell so she'd know he was there, and pulled *Le Petit Prince* out of his backpack. They were reading it for French class, and Josh had gotten a little behind with everything else going on, the trips to New York and hanging out with Nicki and then Cecile, Cecile, Cecile. It occurred to Josh that he hadn't talked to Ram in a while, and a sinking feeling gnawed at his gut as he pulled his phone back out and checked the date. He'd missed a Mollusk Creek Trust meeting two nights ago. Shit! He'd never missed a meeting before. He wished he could talk to Nicki, but she was in school, where he was supposed to be. She was probably mad, too, because he'd had her lie to Hallie for him. He wrote her an apology so long that it broke into four separate texts, and sent it, hoping she would check her messages between classes.

Josh pulled out his French dictionary and tried to read the book, but all he could think about was everyone he'd let down. He couldn't help it; he was in love. Didn't people in love act impetuously? They did in novels. He glanced over at Cecile's desk again, pictured the way she'd looked standing naked in front of him, and then he realized: when he told her he loved her, she didn't say it back. While he was trying to figure out what that meant, he heard Hallie's voice behind him.

"Let's go," she said, and he stuffed his books into his backpack and followed her out to the car.

HALLIE PUT THE keys in the ignition but didn't turn the engine on; she just sat in the driver's seat, looking out the windshield. He shifted his legs in the cramped passenger's seat.

"Are you taking me to school?" Josh asked.

"I don't know where to take you," she said. "What am I supposed to do with you? I told you last night you couldn't see Cecile any more, and then you pull this shit the very next day."

Josh had no good defense for it—she was right, it was awful, the way he'd directly defied her. "I didn't mean to," he said. "When we talked in the car, I really thought I wouldn't see Cecile for a while. But after you told me what was going on at work, I called her, and she was really upset and wanted me to come over this morning, so I did."

Hallie sighed and turned to him. She had dark circles under her eyes. "Would you have done this if Dad and your mom were still alive? Snuck around and lied like this?"

At first, he seriously pondered the question. It was hard to know the answer, since he'd never been in love when his parents were alive. He thought that maybe he would have done everything up through last night, but he would not have ditched school today and seen Cecile after promising his mom not to see her anymore. It was hard to imagine, having the conversation with his mom that he'd had with Hallie. It would have been an entirely different conversation. As he tried to imagine it, his stomach started churning, and he felt tears springing to his eyes. It hadn't happened in a while, a month maybe, and he was amazed by how suddenly the feeling could take hold of him. He opened the passenger's door and threw up in the parking lot. It looked mostly like water; he hadn't eaten anything that morning.

Hallie reached over and opened the glove compartment, pulled out the stack of napkins from Dunkin' Donuts. The napkins Josh's mom had put there before she died. Hallie tried to hand them to Josh, but he pushed her hand away.

"Put them back!" he said. "Mom put those in there." He could hear it in his own voice, the quiver, the edge of completely losing it.

Hallie put them back, neatening the stack before she closed the glove compartment. She pulled a pack of tissues from her bag and got out of the car, walking around to his side. Josh took a couple of the tissues she offered him and wiped his mouth. He hated Hallie for making him feel this way.

"Josh," she started, but he cut her off, jumping to his feet, his face inches from hers.

"I can't believe you brought them up! You had no right to bring them up. Fuck you. Fuck *you*, for doing that." He was stunned by what he'd just said, but something made him repeat the last two words again, more softly: "Fuck you."

Hallie tried to put her arm around him, but he shuddered away from her. "Don't touch me! Leave me alone!"

He had to get away from Hallie. He'd been walking on eggshells since she came to Oyster Shell, afraid of saying or doing something that would send her away. *Fuck that*, he thought. *Go back to New York if you want. I don't need you.* He looked around to figure out how he could get away for a while. When he whipped his head to the left he saw the car keys in the ignition, and he sprinted around to the driver's side and hopped in, started the engine, pulled away with the passenger's door still open. Standing there in the parking lot, Hallie looked small and afraid, her mouth a tiny "o."

JOSH STARTED CRYING as soon as he left the parking lot. His first thought was to drive to Cecile's, but he didn't want her to see him like this. He was acting like a kid, a crybaby, and he had to get a grip on himself. He pulled over and shut the passenger's door, and then he drove from Floyd through Millville, circled part of Vineland and headed back to Floyd, listening as his cell phone played its snippet of "Daughter" repeatedly. Now he'd stolen the car and left Hallie stranded at work, on top of everything else. It was almost funny if he could step outside himself and look at it. He'd never done anything even remotely this bad before; it was like he'd stored up a lifetime's worth of defiance and unleashed it all in a twenty-four-hour period. He came to the Dunkin' Donuts where he and Mom used to go, where the napkins came from, and something compelled him to park the car there, to go in.

It was 10 a.m., and the only people sitting in the donut shop were old, probably retired. Josh wondered if he could eat a donut. He was afraid he would throw it up, so he ordered a hot chocolate instead, and sat in the farthest corner he could find, sipping it.

His phone beeped with a text. It was Nicki, answering the message he'd sent her. She was probably between classes now—it was that time between second and third period.

He texted her back. "Can u leave school?"

"Why?" she wrote back.

He hesitated over his response. "I need u," he wrote. It was embarrassing, but Nicki was the one person he never really felt embarrassed with.

A few seconds later, his phone rang with Nicki's song—Joan Jett's "Bad Reputation." He flipped the phone open.

"I just ducked into the bathroom," she whispered. They weren't supposed to use cell phones in school. "What's going on?"

"I'm in so, so much trouble." He heard the quiver in his voice again. "Hallie's looking for me, but I don't want to see her."

"Where are you?"

"I'm at that Dunkin' Donuts near the mall."

"What are you doing there?"

"Getting, like, more depressed and fucked up by the minute."

She was quiet for a moment. "I have to figure out how to get over there. It would take me forever to walk."

"I'll come pick you up."

"Does anyone here know you ditched school today?" Nicki asked.

"Maybe." He still had no idea how Hallie had found out.

"Then you shouldn't come here. I'll figure something out. I'll borrow a car."

"From who?"

"I have an idea. Just sit there, okay? It might take me a little while. Promise me you'll stay there."

"I promise."

Hallie called twice more while Josh sat there waiting for Nicki to show up; he turned the phone off after the second call. He couldn't talk to his sister and he couldn't listen to the voicemails she was leaving. He just kept thinking about his mom and dad, how he would never see them again, how they wouldn't be at his high school graduation, wouldn't be there when he went away to college, how he'd never watch a stupid movie with his mom again, and he didn't realize he was crying or how much time had passed until he saw Nicki thunder through the door. He looked out the window; Missy Dalton's red Miata was parked outside.

"You borrowed Missy's car?" Josh asked, as Nicki took the seat opposite him.

"I told her it was for you. She doesn't need it back until four." Nicki looked right in his eyes. "What's going on, Joshie?" She called him that sometimes; no one else did. The softness of her voice made him start crying really hard. She leaned across the table and held both his hands in hers while he cried. When he was finally able to stop, he blew his nose in several napkins, then looked at her.

"I don't even know where to begin," he said. "I could write, like, a novel about the last twenty-four hours."

"Then let me get a donut first," Nicki said. "You want one?"

He was suddenly very hungry. "Yeah. Chocolate frosted." After she got in line, he held two fingers up to her, and she brought him back the two donuts, and a jelly for herself.

As they ate, Josh told Nicki everything, even how he and Cecile almost had sex that morning. He and Nicki had never really talked about sex before, though he was pretty sure she'd slept with Nathan. When he got to what happened in the parking lot, what Hallie had said and how it made him feel, Nicki got a funny look on her face, but Josh kept talking until he reached the donut shop, the end of the story.

"You should text her and just let her know you're okay," Nicki said, meaning Hallie.

"I can't talk to her right now."

Nicki sighed. "I bet she's really worried."

"I don't care," Josh said, though he did care.

"Okay." Nicki shrugged. "So what are we going to do this afternoon?"

Josh glanced at his phone and saw that it was almost 1 p.m. It had taken him more than two hours to tell the story.

"Maybe you should get Missy's car back to school," Josh said. "I don't want to get you in any more trouble."

"I'm already in trouble. I haven't shown up in a class since second period. I say we hang at the mall for a while and bring the car back for Missy at four. We might as well have a little fun before we're grounded."

Soon they were slurping down smoothies and trying on sunglasses and making fun of the cheap necklaces at the little jewelry kiosk. He almost forgot, for two hours, how upset he had been, and how much trouble he would soon be in.

They went back to the high school at three-thirty, Josh following Nicki so he could give her a ride. At first, he didn't understand the gestures

Nicki was making to him in her rearview mirror; but then he looked ahead and saw Missy and Mr. Cicirello sitting on the steps at the edge of the parking lot. Nicki was trying to tell him to drive away, but he wouldn't. Nicki and Missy shouldn't get in trouble over him.

He parked his car next to Missy's. "Didn't you see me waving?" Nicki asked as they both got out.

"Yeah, I did."

Mr. Cicirello was on his cell phone when they walked up. Missy looked upset.

"I'm so sorry," Josh said to her, and then he looked at Nicki and said it again. "I'm really sorry."

"How did you get busted?" Nicki asked Missy, handing her the keys.

"The cheerleading coach saw you drive away in my car," Missy said. "She thought someone had stolen it."

"Shit," Nicki said.

Mr. Cicirello snapped his phone shut. "That was your sister," he said to Josh. "She's on her way over." He gave Josh a very sharp look. "She's been out looking for you *all day.*"

Josh nodded. Could he get expelled for this? He followed his principal and the girls into the school, into Mr. Cicirello's office; Miss Piper was already gone. Josh hadn't been in that office since the day Nancy told him his parents were dead, but he tried not to think about that. He could see Mr. Cicirello was about to talk, and he felt like he had to do something to get Nicki and Missy out of trouble before the principal made up his mind.

"This is all my fault," Josh said. "They only got mixed up in it because of me. Nicki never would have skipped school if I hadn't called her, and Missy wouldn't have had to lend her the car. It wouldn't be fair to punish them."

"I think it's up to me to decide what's fair and what's not," Mr. Cicirello said.

Josh nodded.

Mr. Cicirello straightened a stack of papers on his desk. He sighed. "Missy, Nicki, go wait in Miss Piper's office. I want to talk to Josh alone."

After the girls left, Josh waited for Mr. Cicirello to start yelling. But he just looked at Josh, and his voice was very calm. "What's going on with you?" he asked. And the look on Mr. Cicirello's face was so soft and kind that Josh completely lost it. He had prepared himself to be yelled at, but he wasn't prepared for this. He started crying again, and the more mortified he became that he was crying in front of his high school principal, the harder it was to stop. After a few minutes Mr. Cicirello handed him a box of tissues, and Josh blew his nose.

"I'm so totally embarrassed," Josh choked out.

Mr. Cicirello smiled a little. "You don't actually think you're the first student to cry in this office, do you?"

"Probably the first *guy*," Josh said. He could imagine girls crying in the office, but not guys. His father had told him, a boy who wants to grow up to be a man doesn't cry.

Mr. Cicirello shook his head. "*Lots* of guys have cried in this office."

"Maybe freshmen," Josh said.

"Plenty of seniors."

"Really?"

"Yeah. It's a stressful time, graduating and getting ready for jobs or college. And I'd say you've had more stress than most this year."

And then it occurred to Josh that Mr. Cicirello felt so sorry for him over his parents being dead that he might actually give him a pass on skipping school.

"I was really, really upset, and Nicki cut school because I called her and asked her to. She borrowed Missy's car to meet me. Please don't get them in trouble. It's really all, totally, my fault."

Mr. Cicirello nodded. "I'll think about that," he said. He was quiet for a minute. "Was there something specific that upset you today? What made you cut school?"

There was no way he could tell his principal about Cecile. "Just stuff," he said.

"The bus driver saw you leave the school grounds," Mr. Cicirello said. "Most kids who cut enter the school first and then duck out the side exit."

Josh smiled without meaning to, and Mr. Cicirello smiled a little too. Josh could see they were both thinking the same thing: that he was clearly a rank amateur at being bad.

"I won't do it again," Josh said, and he meant it. "It's, like, way too stressful."

Just then they heard a knock on the door, and Hallie was there. Mr. Cicirello motioned her inside. "Why don't you two talk while I go settle things with Nicki and Missy? I'll be back in a few minutes."

Hallie slumped in the chair next to his. She looked very tired.

"I'm totally sorry," Josh said. "I did everything wrong today."

Hallie didn't say anything. He wouldn't be able to stand it if she did that silent treatment thing again.

"I need you to yell or scream or something," he said to her.

"I don't feel like yelling or screaming."

"What do you feel like?"

"Part of me is really sympathetic to you, and part of me is sick of your teenage narcissism. You scared me today. Taking off like that—I was so afraid you'd get in an accident."

"I didn't mean to scare you," he said. "I just had to get away."

She nodded. "I know that feeling." Her phone beeped with a text message, and she pulled it out and looked at it.

"Who's it from?" Josh asked.

"Lawrence," she said. "Moral support."

"You told Lawrence about all this?"

She leaned forward and looked right in his eyes. "Josh, you were missing *all day*," she said. "I didn't know where you'd gone. I called everyone I could think of, including Lawrence, in case you decided to go to New York."

It would never in a million years have occurred to Josh to go to New York. "The farthest I got was Vineland," he said, hoping she would find it a little funny, but her serious expression didn't change.

"Do you have any idea what it does to you, when your kid is missing and you don't know where he is?"

The words floated in Josh's head, *your kid*. Was that how she thought of him, now?

"I'm sorry," he said again, not knowing what else to say, and just then Mr. Cicirello knocked on the door and walked in.

"I just sent the girls home," he said. "They'll have two nights' detention. Josh, you'll have four nights."

"Okay," Josh said, thinking he'd gotten off light.

Mr. Cicirello clapped Josh on the back as he left his office. "My door's always open," he said. Josh couldn't think of anything worse than talking to his high school principal about his problems again, but he nodded and tried to look grateful.

NOT LONG INTO the ride home, Hallie said to Josh, "You're grounded for a month, and I'm taking your cell phone. You'll get it back at the end of the month. But until then, you'll come home every day, call me from the land line in the house so I'll know you're really there, and you'll go nowhere else except Nancy's or Ram's."

He couldn't really argue; it was probably less punishment than Dad would have given him. "Okay," he said, and he handed her his phone, just to show that he wasn't going to give her a hard time.

Back at the house, there were three envelopes waiting for Josh from colleges: thin envelopes from NYU and Tufts, and a fat one from Hunter College.

Hallie smiled a little when she saw the acceptance letter. "That's great, Josh," she said as she unlocked the front door, Emma scrambling to meet them. "Too bad you're grounded. We'll have to celebrate in a month."

CHAPTER 24

The day before the Some Dark Angel concert, Hallie stood in a dressing room at Victoria's Secret, examining a racy pair of red lace panties from all angles. She could see that she'd lost the weight she'd hoped to. Hallie liked the way the panties fit, the way her hip bones jutted out. She tried on the matching push-up bra: sold, she thought. If she could get Damien to the point of seeing her in this—if she could get any guy to the point of seeing her in this—she was pretty sure she wouldn't have to work very hard after that.

While Hallie stood in line to buy the lingerie, her phone rang. It was Josh, calling to let her know he was home.

"Convict 001, reporting to the cell block," Josh said, as he'd been saying every day since he'd been grounded. He said it in a good-natured way, like it was a private joke between them. As always, Hallie was reminded of how different Josh was from her. She would have sulked and pouted and rolled her eyes through the entire period of grounding.

"Warden 001, reporting from shopping," Hallie said, and Josh laughed. "I'm at the mall. Do you need anything?" Hallie handed the cashier her credit card.

Josh was quiet for a minute. "What do you think I should wear to the concert? Just, like, a t-shirt and jeans?"

Hallie knew she was undercutting Josh's punishment by taking him to the concert. His grounding period technically wasn't over for four more days. But as far as she could tell he'd behaved himself perfectly over the past few weeks, coming home on time, without complaint. And not taking Josh to the concert would punish Hallie; she felt she needed him there, an excuse, a buffer. "Any t-shirt except a Some Dark Angel t-shirt." She signed the receipt the cashier pushed toward her.

"Yeah, I figured that."

Hallie knew what she would wear: her high-heeled boots, her skinny jeans, and an old Pixies t-shirt that hugged her breasts just right. "So which college is it today?" she asked. Josh had been accepted at Rowan and Franklin and Marshall as well as Hunter.

"It's Hunter today."

Hallie smiled. "It's been Hunter for three days now. I think you're coming to a decision."

"Yeah, maybe."

She took her bag from the cashier. "I'd better go, Josh. I need to stop back into work before I come home."

"Okay, see you later," he said.

She wandered into Aéropostale to look for something for Josh—if not for the concert, for his birthday, which was coming up in a couple of weeks. Hallie felt completely out of place in the teen-oriented store, like she was someone's mom, but anything was better than being at work. Since Cecile was fired, Hallie had taken over the paper's graphics as well as the photography; while she wasn't as adept as Cecile with the programs, her work seemed to please Orren, and the extra money didn't hurt.

Hallie's phone rang again; she pulled it out, saw that it was Nancy, switched it to silent.

DAMIEN HAD INVITED Hallie and Josh for soundcheck, and they met his tour manager at the back door of the Tower Theatre. He ushered them to the seating area in front of the stage.

"You can watch from here," he said. "I'll be right back with your laminates."

Hallie and Josh stood in the empty theater, watching as guitars and drums and amps were carried out and set up on the stage.

"Wow," Josh said. "I've never seen anything like this."

The tour manager returned with their passes. "Damien will be out in a few minutes," he called over his shoulder as he hurried backstage.

"This is so cool," Josh said, slipping the string over his head.

Hallie hung hers around her neck, worrying that it broke the line the push-up bra and tight t-shirt formed. A couple of the guitar techs had set up and begun the soundcheck, but Damien was still nowhere in sight.

He'd come a long way from those shows at the Sphinx, she thought, when she and Lawrence had often been the ones carrying the amps, lugging them to the van when the show was over.

Hallie fidgeted with the pass, wondering if she should knot the string shorter, until Josh poked her in the side; she looked up and saw Damien squatting at the edge of the stage, smiling. He looked good. Really good. A little older, and he had that kind of careful haircut favored by men starting to go bald—light bangs, brushed forward—but his body was great, and he still had those hazel eyes. Her stomach fluttered.

"Hey," he said.

"Hey yourself." They looked at each other for a moment; it was impossible to hug from where he was on the stage. "This is Josh," she said.

"Hiya," he said to Josh. "Let me just get through this soundcheck, and then you two can join me for dinner, if you want."

"Sure," Hallie said, hoping her elation wasn't obvious.

Damien and the band played five Some Dark Angel songs in their entirety—three new ones and two Hallie recognized. Because there was no one else in the audience besides a few scattered roadies and people who worked at the club, it felt intimate, like a private concert just for them. Hallie felt Damien's eyes on her the whole time, taking her in. But was he really looking at her, or was it Damien the rock star, making eye contact like he would with any fan?

After four songs, Josh whispered in her ear, "This is the most amazing thing I've ever seen."

When the band was finished with the soundcheck, Damien motioned them to come around backstage. There, he finally gave her a hug, with a squeeze that she couldn't quite read—was it an old friends kind of squeeze, or an intimate squeeze?—and then he shook Josh's hand. He stood and looked at Hallie for a moment after that, long enough that she started to feel self-conscious.

"You look *great*," he said. Was there a hint of surprise in his inflection, like he hadn't expected her to look great? Or was she overanalyzing?

ALL THROUGH THE dinner in Damien's dressing room, Hallie couldn't shake the feeling that it wasn't what she'd hoped for. The food was good enough, but the setting was more squalid than intimate. Damien mostly talked about his band, his career. Halfway through the meal, Hallie began longing for it to end so that she could finally get him alone.

After they finished eating, Damien posed for the pictures Hallie knew Josh wanted, and then Josh went to watch the stage set-up. Finally, she and Damien were alone.

He smiled at her. "You've always been hard to read."

She had to laugh. "I could say the same about you."

He poured a little more wine into her glass. "To past relationships," he said. They were sitting close, but not touching. He smelled good, familiar, and Hallie wondered if it would be too obvious if she moved closer. She couldn't shake the feeling that she needed some release, some physical contact. It had been so long since she'd been touched, really touched.

"Are you in one now?" she asked, in a tone she hoped was both flirtatious and uninvested.

"In one?"

"A relationship."

"Oh." He shifted ever so slightly away. "As a matter of fact, I am."

"Is it serious?" she asked.

"It's still kind of new." He took a sip of wine.

She decided to take "kind of new" as a green light. He'd just started seeing someone. Whoever she was, she meant nothing to him. "To new relationships, then," she said, clinking her glass with his and looking deeply into his eyes.

He pulled his cell phone from his pocket, glanced at the time, slipped it back. Was he bored? Worried about the show?

"I loved the new songs," she said.

He smiled. "Yeah?"

"Yeah. That last one in particular."

"That's my favorite too. I had to rearrange it to play it live. In the studio…" He blathered on about programmable drum beats and overdubs. Damien had the most beautiful lips she'd ever seen. It was so easy to imagine kissing them. And when they stopped moving, when he'd stopped talking, she did just that. She leaned over and kissed him. For a second he kissed her back, but then he pulled away.

"This isn't a good idea," he said.

She put her hand on his thigh. "Why not?"

He brushed her hand away. "I told you. I'm seeing someone."

"That never stopped you before."

His eyes flashed, and for a moment, she thought he might yell at her, or storm away, as he used to when she would find the phone numbers in his pockets, or when she got the hang-up calls. But then he appeared to soften. "I'm not the same person I was back then," he said.

She wanted to say that she wasn't the same, either, that she was no longer the timid girl scurrying about to please him, but was now a woman who knew what she wanted and how to go after it. Yet even as she thought it, she knew it was a lie. She *was* the same person she'd been fifteen years ago.

"Hallie?" Damien had a strange look on his face.

She felt the walls inside her cracking, years oozing through the loosened mortar. It was 1994, and they were in that diner in Queens, and Hallie was looking out the window at the newsstand full of Kurt Cobain, his sweet, sad smile so much like her mother's.

"You always thought my mother killed herself, didn't you?"

Damien visibly flinched. "What?"

She needed to erase the awkwardness, to take back what she'd just uttered, and Hallie could think of only one thing to do. She leaned over and tried to kiss him again. This time he pushed her away and stood up. He looked down at her for what felt like a long time.

"I don't know what's going on with you, Hallie," he finally said. There was something about the way he said her name, Hallie, that she had never liked. A tic of pronunciation, the "a" flatter than it should be. The first time they'd had sex, she remembered hearing him say it, "Hallie," and being so disappointed. It was like he was having sex with someone else, someone who wasn't her. But it hadn't been so long, then, since she'd been Holly.

"I think you should go to your seat now," he added. "I have to get ready for the show." She felt she could cry at any moment if she allowed herself to; more than that, if she really let go, she could drown in tears.

"Go," he said, pulling her to her feet and ushering her to the door. "Just go."

Hallie couldn't look at his face as she walked out the door.

She found Josh and they filed into their seats in the third row. As they sat through the opening band, then through the intermission, Hallie felt herself slipping away. As a child, she'd pictured her beautiful Mommy screaming and clawing at that garage door, desperate to live. Hallie had never allowed her later doubts to linger long enough to take form, but now, she could see it all clearly: her mom in the driver's seat, the garage door closed, the car door open. What kind of car had it been? Hallie couldn't remember. But she could see her mother as she pulled her long blond hair into a ponytail, calmly—impatiently?—waiting for the fumes to fill the small building.

Hallie saw Damien take the stage, in his trademark white makeup and leather pants, but she registered little else. She was aware that there was music; aware that occasionally Josh would lean over and say, "Isn't this great?"; aware that her brother was softly singing some of the lyrics. But she wasn't there, not really. She was in the garage. Had her mother thought about what her death would do to her daughter? Had she thought about Hallie—Holly—at all?

Josh nudged Hallie and she looked at him, suddenly aware that the music had stopped, that people were leaving the theater. "It's over," Josh said. "Where *were* you?"

She looked around at the crowd exiting the aisles. She felt frightened and small and longed to be home. "I'm sorry," she said.

Josh seemed to be studying her. "Are we supposed to go backstage again? To say goodbye?"

"I don't think so."

He was quiet for a moment. "Did something happen?"

Hallie shook her head. "I think Damien has to leave soon."

They walked through the lobby and out of the theater. "Are you okay?" Josh asked.

"Yeah, fine. I'm just tired."

THE DRIVE FROM Philly to South Jersey seemed an impossible task. She made a wrong turn before finding the signs for 76, the Schuylkill Expressway, and they briefly drove through a seedy Upper Darby neighborhood. When they finally made it onto the highway, Hallie drove slowly in the right lane, but she had trouble staying between the lines. Several cars honked as they passed. Had her mother thought about it, thought about killing herself, every time she made this ride? Had she ever considered driving off the bridge?

"Hallie, I think you're kind of, like, swerving," Josh said.

"Sorry," she said, and tried to hold the car steady, but her hands were shaking.

"Are you okay?" Josh asked.

She looked at him. If her father had only had enough love for one child, perhaps he'd been right to invest it all in Josh.

"Hallie, look at the road!" Josh sounded alarmed now.

She looked back and realized that she was straddling two lanes. She needed to pull over. But she was already on the bridge.

"Sorry, Josh," she said, trying to snap herself out of it. "I don't feel so well."

She saw Josh turn and watch the cars behind them; then he straightened and looked forward. His eyes kept darting to her.

Once they were over the bridge, Josh said, "Why don't you let me drive home?"

"As soon as I see a good place to pull over," Hallie said. She felt the car swerve a little, and worked to correct it. A car to her left flashed its lights. She drove for a few minutes, thinking she'd gotten herself under control, but then a second car honked and flashed its lights at her.

Josh leaned forward and pointed. "Put on the flashers. Up there. Pull over now!" He was yelling at her, and it was such a rare thing for Josh to yell that she could think of nothing to do but obey.

After she put the car in park, the flashers on, Josh turned to her.

"What is wrong with you?" he asked. "Do you see where we are?"

It was only then that Hallie looked out at the highway and saw the exit sign for Bellmawr not far in the distance.

"Oh my God, Josh. I'm so sorry."

"You're scaring me! What's wrong with you?" Josh looked almost as close to crying as Hallie felt. She tried to summon some sort of inner strength, to pull herself together, but she couldn't stop the tears leaking from her eyes.

"I should have asked you to drive," she choked out. "I'm sorry." She looked at the Bellmawr sign, and imagined how Josh must have felt, her driving erratically so close to the place where his parents had died.

He took the keys out of the ignition, as if afraid she might try to start the car again. "Did something happen with Damien?" he asked.

She pulled her purse from the floor of the seat behind her and fished out a tissue, then wiped her eyes. "Yeah," she said. She couldn't tell him the rest of it. He had his own grief to deal with.

"What happened?"

"I don't want to talk about it right now," she said. "Drive us home, okay?" She got out of the car and walked around to his side. Before he got out, he looked at her for a few seconds, like he was trying to figure out whether to ask her more; but then he slipped past her, took over the driver's seat, and they were both silent for the rest of the drive.

JOSH SLOWED THE car as they passed the farm; Hallie could see that the stable was completely built now, where the greenhouses had once stood. A fence around the front of the property was nearly finished. Orren had told her he planned to move the horses in next weekend. After they passed Nancy's place, Hallie noticed flashing blue lights down the road.

"What's going on?" Josh asked, as he pulled up in front of their house, next to the police cruiser. Todd's car was parked in their driveway.

The front door of the house opened, and a uniformed officer walked a handcuffed Cal out of the house. Josh looked at Hallie. "Emma!" he cried. He hopped out of the car and ran past Cal and the officer, into the house.

Hallie sat in the passenger's seat and watched as Josh disappeared into the house, watched as Cal's head was pushed down into the police car, the door slammed after him. Hallie had considered leaving the dog at Nancy's that night, since they would be out so late, but she hadn't been able to bring herself to talk to Nancy, to set it up. She pictured the dog's sweet face, and Cal's angry look the last time she'd seen him. Why hadn't she put it together, that Emma wasn't safe?

She'd failed the dog, as she'd failed Josh. As she'd failed her mom. She'd been aware that her mom wasn't happy, and she'd done everything she could to cheer her up. It wasn't enough. Hallie tried to get out of the car, but she couldn't make her legs work. She sat there with the door ajar, still seated, as Nancy's car pulled up behind her. Nancy got out and walked over to Hallie, pulled the car door open.

"I saw the lights," Nancy said.

"Emma," Hallie said, motioning to Cal in the back of the cruiser. But just then, Josh burst through the front door.

"Emma's okay," he said. "She was hiding under my bed." He motioned toward the house. "It's a mess in there, though."

Todd walked up and stood with Josh and Nancy, peered into the car at Hallie. "I think we got him before he made off with anything," Todd said, "but I need the two of you to go through the house to make sure."

Hallie used the car door to pull herself up, but she found, once she got her legs working, that she wasn't heading to the house. She was walking, instead, to the garage.

"Where's she going?" she heard Todd say behind her.

She reached the garage, opened the side door that her father had installed after it became the "tool shed," after he'd claimed that the overhead door wasn't safe. She groped for the light switch, turned it on, and walked to the back of the garage, to the metal shelving unit, full of tools, that her dad had installed—when? Sometime in that year after her mother died. The window was partially visible behind the shelves.

Hallie heard footsteps walking up the driveway, and she turned to see who it was. Nancy. She motioned her in.

"Just tell me what you know," Hallie said. "About my mom."

Nancy was quiet for a moment. "I adored her, you know. Your mother had a sweet soul." She leaned against a workbench. "But she was moody. And since she'd always been moody, as long as I knew her, it never occurred to me that she was seriously depressed. I thought she was a little down. I figured she'd snap out of it." Nancy shook her head. "You have to remember, those were different times. Your mind didn't automatically go *there*."

Hallie nodded, more to keep Nancy talking than out of any real agreement. Nancy went on to tell Hallie how innocuous it had seemed, at first, when Jenny called her at the *Floyd Daily News* that January morning and asked her to pick Holly up from school. She had to go see her parents in Red Bank, Jenny said. She didn't want Holly to take the bus—the roads were icy. She asked Nancy to take Holly home with her, said she or Don would collect her later.

Nancy had been writing a story on deadline that morning Jenny called, and hadn't had much time to think it all over until lunch. Once she did, a few things didn't add up. There was a rift between Jenny and her parents, Nancy knew, so why was she going to see them now? And why wouldn't she have Don pick Holly up from school? Nancy called Don at the farm. At that point, she wasn't concerned so much as puzzled. When she told Don how Jenny had specified that Nancy take Holly home with her, he hung up abruptly.

"So he suspected she might...hurt herself?" Hallie croaked the sentence out.

Nancy nodded, her face grim. "Later, when we were driving to the hospital, he told me she had tried once before. When she was fourteen."

Hallie knew her mother had run away from home when she was fifteen. She'd told her it was a grand adventure during the Summer of Love, that she'd wanted to see the West Coast—carefully adding that it was no longer safe for a girl to hitchhike across the country. But Hallie had always known that it couldn't have been safe even in the 60s. As Damien once said, something happened to drive her mother from the Bartons' house.

"Did you...*see* her that day?" Hallie asked.

Nancy nodded. She said she'd pulled up in front of the Corsons' house and found Jenny stretched out at the top of the icy driveway, Don trying to resuscitate her. The garage door was open. Nancy could smell the fumes from Jenny's Pinto.

The Pinto! Hallie gasped softly. Her father had sold it in the weeks after her mother's death; one day, she came home from school and the car was gone. It led to the first of many fights as her father attempted to erase her mother from the house.

"Should I stop?" Nancy asked, but Hallie shook her head no. She needed, finally, to hear it all.

As they waited for the rescue squad to arrive, Nancy said, Don continued breathing into Jenny's mouth. Hallie knew that it had snowed that day—she remembered sitting in the cab of her father's truck, watching the snow fall as he told her that her mother had died—and she filled in the picture Nancy was painting, saw her father crouched over her mother, attempting CPR, snowflakes falling in his then-dark hair.

When the siren became audible, Nancy said, Don started crying harder than she had ever seen a man cry in her life.

"Dad…he cried?" Hallie asked. She had never seen him cry, not even at the funeral.

"He wailed," Nancy said. "On the drive to the hospital he punched my dashboard."

Hallie looked up and saw that Josh was standing in the doorway. She had no idea how long he'd been there. How much had he heard? But when she made eye contact with him, he left the garage, quietly shutting the door behind him.

"So when did you both decide…to lie to me?"

Nancy winced. "It wasn't my idea. We were in my car, following the ambulance to the hospital, but we both knew Jenny was gone. About halfway there, your dad said, 'Holly can never know this.'"

"And you just went along with it?" Hallie was surprised by the anger she felt toward Nancy just then; surprised, too, by how much less angry she felt at her father. He'd been robbed of reason by shock and grief. But shouldn't Nancy have known better?

Nancy sighed. "Not at first. But he kept insisting, reminding me that you were only eleven." She put a hand on the shelving unit, steadying herself. "We were both out of our minds that day. Once we came to our senses, months later, we were trapped in this lie." She looked Hallie in the eyes. "I am *so* sorry."

Hallie looked at Nancy, saw how frail she looked in the bright light of a naked bulb. She knew she would need to forgive her. But not just yet.

"I have to get out of here," Hallie said. "I need to be alone."

Nancy was quiet for a minute. "That doesn't sound like a good idea to me."

"Take Josh and Emma to your house. Tell him I'll call him in the morning."

Nancy shook her head.

Hallie narrowed her eyes. "I think we've established that your judgment isn't always the best."

Nancy grimaced as if she'd been slapped.

"Do this *one* thing for me, Nancy."

She expected further argument, but Nancy got up and walked out of the garage, her gait stiff, her hand on her back. It felt like forever until Hallie heard the dog bark, car doors slamming shut, engines starting. When she was certain everyone was gone, Hallie walked to the house and locked the front door without glancing inside. She would deal with that tomorrow, or the next day. She had enough to deal with tonight.

Hallie got in her car and drove with no idea of where she was going. She turned down Shellpile Drive, heading out of Pearl Township, toward Floyd; but where would she go? The idea of being alone suddenly seemed intolerable. She pulled the car over and dug her phone out of her bag. She knew she could call Lawrence, and that once he made some coffee and shook off the sleep he'd be sympathetic. But she didn't want to hash this out on the phone. She couldn't.

Hallie continued scrolling through her address book until she got to R: Ram Rao. It was now close to 3 a.m., yet she drove to the Mollusk Creek Trust office. Both floors were dark inside.

She rang the bell; a light went on upstairs, and then an outdoor floodlight caught her in its glare.

Ram stuck his head out a window. "Hallie?"

She looked up at him. "Can you let me in?" She wondered, for a moment, if Ram would send her away, and she wondered, too, what would happen after that, if she ended up alone, thinking about how her mother had died.

But Ram's face disappeared from the window, and a few seconds later she heard him pounding down the stairs. He opened the door for her and something in his expression, the bittersweet upturn of his mouth, the way he put his arm around her and ushered her inside, told her that this was one man who would not turn her away.

PART III

CHAPTER 25

Josh had never seen the Mollusk Creek Trust office as crowded as it was the night of the May meeting. In addition to the core members of the Trust, at least thirty more people had filed in, people Josh didn't know. Ram had mailed flyers about the annual report everywhere he and Josh could think of, from Oyster Shell to Philly and back, and Josh had left them in libraries and waiting rooms and at the East Point Lighthouse; Nicki had stuffed them in lockers at school. Still, the turnout was a happy surprise.

Hallie walked through the back door with her arms full of folding chairs, and Josh hurried over to help her. She'd become much more involved with the Trust these past two weeks, now that she and Lawrence had started work on the frog story. Nancy and Hallie were on opposite sides of the office, avoiding each other.

As Josh and Nicki set up the last of the chairs, the front door opened, and Missy Dalton walked in with Cole Huxley.

"Oh my God," Nicki said.

Josh had known they might come; Missy had mentioned it to him. "We should say hi. They must have come because of your flyer." But before they could make a move, the door opened wider, and Lawrence burst through.

"I broke twenty laws to get here on time!" Lawrence announced. Josh and Nicki looked at each other and cracked up; the guy always made a dramatic entrance. As Ram called the meeting to order, Josh motioned his friends to some empty chairs in the back.

WHEN THE MEETING was over, Josh stretched his legs out into the aisle and looked at Nicki; she was huddled over a text. Nathan, he imagined.

Josh caught Missy's eye farther down the row, and she smiled at him.

"What did you think?" he asked Missy, leaning behind Nicki to talk to her.

"It's awful," she said, pushing her chair back a little. "Do you think it's pollution? Or those parasites?"

Josh shrugged. "Ram thinks pollution is the biggest problem."

"My father says the state exaggerates environmental concerns so they can make money through fines," Cole said.

Nicki looked up from her cell phone, giving him a sharp glance; Josh and Missy looked at him too.

"Hey, I'm not saying he's right! I'm just saying that's the mentality anyone involved in this is up against. People who don't see the whole presentation aren't going to get how bad it is."

Cole had a point. "You're right," Josh said. "And the pictures Ram showed tonight aren't even as bad as seeing the actual frogs." He'd never forget that first summer he saw them. It was the last time he'd ever gone swimming in Mollusk Creek.

Cole whispered something to Missy, and the two of them moved together for a moment. It didn't bother Josh the way it used to.

"Hey, do you guys want to take a ride over to Cole's farm with us?" Missy asked. "They just brought the horses in this week."

In Josh's mind it would always be his dad's tomato farm. And it wasn't really Cole's farm anyway; it was *his* dad's. Josh couldn't believe how quickly it all had happened, the equipment sale and the barn being built and now, the horses were there. Josh glanced at Nicki, and she shrugged.

"Maybe," he said. "I'm not sure if Nicki has to go home."

Nicki shook her head. "I can go to the farm."

Josh made his way over to where Hallie was sitting.

"Here's our future lit major," Lawrence said.

Josh smiled and motioned to Lawrence's tape recorder and notebook. "Did you get what you needed?"

Lawrence nodded. "It's a start. I'm going to interview Ram a little more tonight, and then I'll come back down when the frogs begin hatching."

Josh looked at Hallie. "I wanted to ask you if I could go for a ride with those guys," he said, motioning to where Nicki, Missy, and Cole were standing.

Hallie glanced at the three kids. "Just with them, right?"

She was still suspicious about Cecile. But he hadn't talked to Cecile since that day he skipped school, and the truth was, he missed talking to her less than he'd thought he would.

"Just them," Josh said to Hallie.

He still fantasized about Cecile—often, though not as often as he used to—and he definitely missed the almost-sex they'd had. Josh had e-mailed her once since his grounding was over, but she hadn't answered. He figured she was back in Philly by now.

"Okay," Hallie said. "But it's a school night. Be home by eleven."

"Thanks," Josh said, and he gave Nicki, Missy, and Cole the thumbs up sign as they all headed for the door.

WHEN THEY PULLED away from the Trust office in Cole's convertible, Missy pointed to a small "Mollusk Creek" sign.

"Is the creek right down there?" she asked.

"Yeah," Josh said, "About a five-minute drive."

Cole backed his car up to take the turn. "Let's check it out," he said, driving faster than Josh thought he should.

"We're not going to see anything at night," Josh said, but Cole kept going until the road ended, and they were near the water. Josh could hear the different calls of the tree frogs and the Southern Lion frogs, with crickets chirping in counterpoint. The moon reflected off the water. It was a nice night, warm, but not too warm. Spring was Josh's favorite time of year; he liked it even better than summer. He used to like fall a lot, too, but he was pretty sure he'd never feel the same way about fall again.

"They're in there," Nicki said, pointing toward the water. "Frogs with six legs and three heads."

Missy laughed. "We should make a horror movie. We could call it—Creek." She said "Creek" in a very dramatic voice, and Josh then remembered all the school plays she'd been in. "Four unsuspecting teenagers were sitting by the side of a creek –"

"Smoking dope," Cole added, and it was then Josh saw that he had a bag full of what had to be pot and was rolling it into a cigarette.

"Smoking dope," Missy said, "when suddenly, the frogs attacked."

Josh looked at Nicki and they both cracked up. He knew he should be nervous about the pot, but he wasn't.

Cole lit the joint and took a drag, then passed it to Missy. She shook her head.

"I have too many tests next week," she said. "I need a clear head to study."

"What do you care?" Cole asked. He turned around and passed the joint to Josh. "You've already gotten in to Cornell."

"AP exams," Missy said.

"And you want to be valedictorian," Cole said.

Josh looked at the joint, the end burning in his hand. He wasn't sure whether to try it or not. He kind of wanted to, but he was scared. "You want to be valedictorian?" he asked Missy.

"Well, I'm in the running. It's not that big a deal, but if I have a chance, why shouldn't I try for it?"

"Have you ever smoked pot?" Nicki whispered to Josh. She said it very quietly, but Missy heard her.

"Oh, don't do it if you don't want to," she said. "Cole doesn't mind smoking alone."

"I don't know," Josh said. "If I do something really crazy, will you all laugh at me?"

"We'll applaud you," Cole said.

"You probably won't get high the first time you smoke, anyway," Nicki said, and Missy nodded.

"Well, somebody smoke it or hand it back to me," Cole said. Josh quickly inhaled, then passed it to Nicki, choking violently.

"It's hard to get used to if you've never smoked cigarettes," Missy said. "I choked a lot at first too."

Josh didn't think he felt high, but there was something very nice about the texture of the night: the earthy smell of the creek, the sound of the frogs and crickets, the Postal Service disc, playing very softly, that Missy had popped into the CD player, and sitting there with two girls he liked. He didn't even mind that Cole was there.

As they passed the joint around they talked more about colleges—Cole was going to Tufts, news that annoyed Josh a bit since he'd been rejected. Nicki talked excitedly about how she and Josh were both going to Hunter, and how much fun it would be.

And after some time had passed—Josh wasn't sure how long, but there was a point where things started feeling fuzzy and warm and he started thinking that despite what Nicki had said, he really *was* high— Cole said they should go to the horse farm so Josh could have a look before they all had to get home. It occurred to Josh that he should be worried about Cole driving stoned, but he wasn't.

They parked outside the barn and Cole unlocked the door, fumbling a little with his key. Inside, Josh saw three horses. They were beautiful, sleek-looking Quarterhorses, not the Arabians Josh had imagined. One of them stuck its head out as Josh walked by the stall, and he patted the animal's nose. The horse vibrated its lips and half-closed its eyes.

"God, you have such a thing with animals," Nicki said. She looked at Missy and Cole. "You should see his dog. She, like, has a crush on him."

Josh laughed. "I don't think my dog has an actual crush." But he knew that she did.

"Oh my God. She moons around after him." Nicki made a face that did, in fact, resemble the way Emma sometimes looked at him.

"What kind of dog do you have?" Missy asked.

"A mutt," Josh said. "I think she's part beagle, but she's smaller. I stole her from this guy who used to starve her."

"Good for you," Cole said. It surprised Josh that he would care.

Cole lit another joint and began to pass it around, but Josh declined this time. He had to act normal if Hallie was still up. Nicki and Cole shared the joint.

"I'm never going to be able to drive home," Nicki said.

"You can stay over my house," Josh said.

Nicki was quiet for a minute. "Yeah, I'll call my mom." She looked at Josh. "Hallie won't mind?"

He shook his head. "Lawrence will be there, but we have lots of space."

Nicki took another hit. "We'd better give Hallie and Ram time to finish up, before we go back there," she said, and then started laughing.

"What do you mean?" Josh asked.

"Come on." Nicki gave him a look she sometimes gave him, one that suggested he was very dense. "Don't play dumb."

"I'm not playing dumb. I actually am dumb."

"Your sister is totally doing Ram!" Nicki said.

"What?" Josh remembered Lawrence had teased Hallie about it, months ago, but it had never occurred to him that something might actually be happening.

"He kept touching her, but only when he thought no one was looking. And the way she looked at him…"

"Yeah, I noticed that too," Missy added. "I kind of wondered."

"How was she looking at him?" Josh asked.

"The way Emma looks at you," Nicki said, and she made that face again. "Like she's in loooooooove."

"I totally didn't see that," Josh said. He wondered if they were just imagining things, because they were high.

"Guys never notice things like that," Missy said. "I'll bet Cole didn't, either."

"No, but I was stoned before we even got there," Cole said with a smile. He sat on one of the brand-new, black-and-red tack boxes, and it was only then that Josh noticed the name painted on the boxes: "Fifty-First State Farm."

"Why is your dad calling it Fifty-First State Farm?" Josh asked, as much to get the conversation off Hallie and Ram as because he wanted the answer.

Cole looked at Missy and they both started laughing. "My dad is obsessed with South Jersey becoming the fifty-first state."

"No way," Nicki said.

"Way. Back in, like, the 70s or 80s, there was some kind of South Jersey secession movement my dad was part of. He never really got over it."

"My dad was part of that too," Josh said. "He always complained about how they make all the decisions in North Jersey."

"Your dad should totally meet my dad, then," Cole said, and Josh saw Missy nudge him in the ankle.

"Josh's dad passed away, Cole," she said quietly.

"Oh man, I forgot. Sorry."

"It's okay," Josh said. The truth was, he kind of missed talking about his parents. He and Hallie talked about them, and sometimes Nancy would mention one of them, but everyone else, even Ram, seemed afraid to bring them up. "Sometimes I like talking about them." He wondered if it was a weird thing to say.

"What were they like?" Cole asked.

"My mom and I got along really well," Josh said. "She used to read the books for my English class so we could discuss them."

"Really?" Nicki asked.

"Yeah. She dropped out of school when she was sixteen, so she never really got to read, like, classics. So when I was reading *The Scarlet Letter*, and then *Pride and Prejudice*, she started reading them with me. She loved Jane Austen."

"*Emma*," Nicki said quietly, and Josh nodded.

"That's so cool," Missy said. She was quiet for a minute. "Your mom was so nice, Josh. Remember when you were in Drama Club freshman year and she helped out with the costumes for *The Wizard of Oz*?"

He smiled. Of course he remembered it. He had joined after Missy landed the role of Glinda the Good Witch, just to be close to her. He'd ended up working on set design, and had drafted his mom for the costumes. But it didn't get him anywhere with Missy, and he had no real interest in the plays, so he never did it again after that year.

Missy hopped up on the tack box opposite Cole. Her hair looked very shiny and dark against the pale yellow of her fleece jacket. "That play was right before finals freshman year, and I got all stressed out studying and gained some weight. Like, a week before the play I couldn't fit into the costume. I completely freaked out."

"I didn't know that," Josh said.

"Just Mr. Howard and your mom were there. Mr. Howard got kind of aggravated with me, but your mom was *so* nice. She calmed me down and said she could let the dress out and no one would know."

Now Josh remembered it, his mom at her sewing machine with that dress, night after night just before the play.

"She never told me," Josh said.

"That's what I mean. She promised me no one would know, and no one did."

"I wish I had met her," Nicki said.

Josh looked at Nicki. "She was totally great, but she was also kind of goofy. Like, she wore ridiculous slippers. I made fun of them all the time."

"She didn't mind," Nicki said.

"No, she didn't." An orange tomcat that had been skulking along the wall sidled up to Josh and began rubbing on his ankles. It was one of the semi-feral colony his dad used to leave food and water for.

"So your dad grew tomatoes here?" Cole asked.

"Yeah, and herbs."

"How long had he been doing that?"

Josh thought back. "Since long before I was born. He started the farm after his family business was, like, ruined."

"What was the family business?"

"Oysters," Josh said. "There was a disease that wiped them all out. When my dad was a teenager." Josh thought it over, the bits of the story he'd gleaned. "I think his family was really rich, before the oysters died. Once I saw a picture of my dad standing next to a brand new-looking Thunderbird. Like out of an old movie. He was our age then. He said his parents gave it to him when he turned seventeen."

Cole and Missy exchanged a look. "Do you still have the car?" Cole asked.

Josh shook his head. "My dad sold it when his parents were losing their business."

"Wow," Cole said. "I can't imagine what my dad would do if he lost the glass business. I don't think he'd start a farm. I think he'd just curl up in a ball and die."

"I think that's kind of what my grandfather did," Josh said.

Cole had a very strange look on his face, like he was really thinking it over, and it occurred to Josh then how easily their places could have been reversed. If the oysters had never died, Josh might have been the one going to the prep school, driving the convertible.

"We should go soon," Missy said. "It's getting late."

Josh looked at his cell. "Yeah. I was supposed to be home, like, twenty minutes ago."

Missy hopped off the tack box and put her hand out to Cole; he sighed dramatically and pulled his keys out, handed them to her. They were quiet for the short ride back to Josh's house. When they pulled up, Josh saw that Lawrence's rental car was in the driveway, but his mom's

Geo was nowhere in sight.

"I guess Hallie's not back yet," Josh wondered aloud.

"I told you!" Nicki said. "She's totally doing Ram." They waved goodbye to Cole and Missy, and headed inside.

THE FOLLOWING SATURDAY, Josh slept in. He kept waking briefly, then dozing again; he was pretty sure Hallie put Emma out at some point, then returned her to his room. When he finally came fully awake, it was twelve thirty, and Emma was snoring at the foot of his bed. Hallie had left early that morning to go back to New York with Lawrence and work on her photography for a few days. She'd left the Geo in Oyster Shell for Josh. He was supposed to go to Nancy's for dinner.

Josh got out of bed and turned on his computer. He opened the file for this thing he'd started, this long story—he didn't dare call it a novel—and checked to see how many pages it was up to now. Thirty-four. He'd begun writing it a few days into his grounding, just a series of observations about what his life was like now versus what it used to be like. And then he'd imagined places where the story could be more interesting. And pretty soon he'd created a character named Quentin—Josh's middle name—who grew up in rural Pennsylvania, and whose father owned an auto junkyard, and whose mother was the nicest person who had ever lived. There was also a female character who was kind of a cross between Miss Piper and Cecile, but she looked more like what he thought Missy might look like in a few years.

Josh didn't feel awake enough to write, so he closed the file and checked his e-mail. There were three new messages: one from Win, a Greenpeace forward from Nicki, and an e-mail from Cecile. Finally, an e-mail from Cecile.

I'm leaving town in two days. I'd like to see you before I leave. I miss you, Josh.—C

Calling Cecile less than three weeks after his grounding was over could not be a good idea. But she was leaving town, and he needed to say goodbye. And Hallie was away for the weekend.

Nicki was also in New York—Nathan was taking her to his prom that night. The Floyd prom was in two more weeks, but Josh had no plans to go. The only girls he could ever consider taking, Missy or Nicki, already had dates, and he couldn't exactly take Cecile. Josh pressed the speed dial for Nicki's cell.

"What's up, Joshie?" Nicki asked.

"Are you busy glamorizing yourself?"

"Oh, sure. I have the makeup artist from *America's Next Top Model* here." It was a show they'd made fun of. "You know," she added, "I haven't heard from Nathan yet today. Should I be worried?"

"When was the last time you talked?"

"A few nights ago. He was supposed to call last night. I texted him and left a voice mail but haven't heard anything back."

Josh felt a gnawing in his stomach, especially after what Nicki's dad had said about Nathan. "But you have definite plans for the prom, right?"

"Oh, yeah. He said he'd pick me up at six tonight."

"He'll call you soon, I bet."

"I hope so." In the background, Josh could identify Billy Bragg's voice, but not the song. Nicki liked to play her dad's albums.

"So I have a question," Josh said. "Cecile is leaving town on Monday and wants to see me. Should I?"

He heard Nicki sigh. "You'll be in an assload of trouble if Hallie finds out."

"Yeah, I know. And I feel bad to lie to her again." He thought about Hallie's mother, what Hallie had found out about her, and how it seemed to him like she wasn't dealing with it. He didn't want to be the cause of her finally, completely losing it.

"Then don't. Tell Cecile you can't see her."

"But Hallie's in New York. I can't imagine how she'd find out." And she was lying to him about seeing Ram, so how bad should he really feel?

"You said Cecile wants to see you," Nicki said. "Do you want to see her?"

Josh had to think it over for a minute. "Not like before, but I want to say goodbye. That whole thing was this whirlwind, but I would feel bad if she went away and I never saw her again."

"Closure," Nicki said.

"I guess." The thing was, even though Cecile was older, she was still a girl, and they'd done things together that almost qualified as sex. He thought it would be deeply wrong of him to not at least say goodbye. "I think I have to."

Before Nicki could say anything else, his phone beeped: Cecile.

"She's calling me now," he said to Nicki. "I have to go."

"Make sure you erase your phone log!"

"Yeah. Bye," he said, and then switched over to Cecile's call. "I was just going to call you," he said. He wasn't sure if it was the truth.

"Josh," Cecile said. "My long lost Josh." He had forgotten about the way her voice sounded, about how she actually purred—not like barn cats, but some sleek, exotic cat.

"It's good to hear your voice," he said, and that, he knew, was true.

"You're allowed to talk to me now?"

"I don't think so. But I'm not grounded anymore."

"Oh."

Josh imagined her in her apartment, in that silky blue bathrobe, and he remembered how he'd felt not so long ago, how desperately he'd wanted her, and he remembered why.

"Hallie's away this weekend," he said.

Cecile let out a laugh that was part contented growl. "Then I want my date."

"Your date?"

"You promised me a nice date, Josh. I'm leaving for California Monday morning. I want you to take me out."

Could he pull this off? He had the car. He had the hundred dollars Hallie had given him, and about two hundred more that he'd saved. Would that be enough? Where would he take her? What excuse would he give Nancy for not having dinner with her? Would he and Cecile have sex after he took her out, and would Cecile get in trouble if anyone found out? He wouldn't turn eighteen for ten more days.

"Sure," he said.

"Really?"

"Yeah. I'll have to figure some stuff out, but, yeah. Let's go out."

"Yay!" This was the side of Cecile that Josh liked best, when she was sweet and kind of childlike. "Pick me up at seven."

•

AFTER ENLISTING THE help of both Nicki and Missy—Nicki for the sneaking-around logistics, Missy for the name of a nice restaurant at the shore—Josh found himself showered, dressed, and alibied by six-thirty. A half-hour later, he stopped at the CVS in Floyd to buy a small box of condoms; he was nervous going in, but the clerk didn't bat an eye as he rang up the purchase. As Josh left the store, his phone rang. Nicki. He figured she was just wishing him good luck, so he let it go to voicemail.

When he pulled up in front of Cecile's apartment five minutes later, his phone beeped with a text. Also from Nicki.

Need 2 talk 2 u, it said.

He turned off the engine and pressed Nicki's speed dial number. She answered but didn't say anything. Josh wished she would get right to whatever it was; he was already five minutes late.

"What's up, Nick?" he asked, getting out of the car.

She let out a choking sob that gave way to full-on crying.

"Nicki, you're freaking me out," he said. "What happened?"

"He broke up with me," she managed between sobs.

"Nathan? What happened?"

He heard her cry a little more, then blow her nose before she started talking. "He texted me around five and said he couldn't take me to the prom. I tried calling him, and then I went to his house." The next thing she said Josh couldn't make out, she was crying so hard.

From where he stood, leaning against the car, Josh saw Cecile part her living room curtains. He waved at her.

"Nicki, I didn't understand what you just said. What happened after you went to his house?"

"He..." She was struggling to get it together. He had never seen or heard Nicki like this. "He was dressed for the prom."

"What?"

She was quiet for a moment. "He has another girlfriend. She's older than us, in college. She went abroad for the semester, and he thought she wouldn't be back until June."

"Oh my God," Josh said.

"He said she came back early, to surprise him, so he had to take her to his prom." She whimpered a little.

"So...they were still together all this time?"

Nicki let out a noise that sounded like a cross between a laugh and a wail. "Yes, Josh! I was just like some kind of side dish."

"Oh, Nick." The front door of Cecile's building opened, and she emerged, looking amazing as always in a very short, very sheer blue dress. He smiled at her and tried to indicate with his eyes that the call was an emergency. She walked toward him.

"I feel like I can't breathe," Nicki said.

"You're not alone, are you?"

"Yeah. Dad went out with his latest girlfriend."

"You didn't tell him?"

"No. I just let him think everything was still on for tonight, and that I was meeting Nathan at his house. I told him Nathan's mom would take pictures."

"Call your dad."

"I don't want to."

"Nicki, you can't stay there by yourself." Josh looked at Cecile, who was now standing just inches from him, and whose beautiful blue eyes were starting to narrow into hard, mean slits.

"I called my friend Adriana, but she's away for the weekend. And we're not that close anymore anyway." She started crying again. "He was the first guy I ever slept with," she whispered, in a tone that kind of broke Josh's heart.

"I know," he said.

"Why wasn't it you?"

"What?"

"It should have been you." She said it so quietly that Josh wasn't even sure, at first, if he'd heard her correctly.

"I'm sorry," was all he could think of to say.

Josh felt Cecile's gaze upon him, and he tried to give her a little smile, but it didn't change anything in her expression. She pulled the phone from his hand and switched it off. Before he could react, she kissed him, on the lips, the kind of kiss that made him feel like she was going to devour him. The kind of kiss that held the promise of so much more.

"Let's go," she said, motioning to the car, but Josh shook his head. "I have to call Nicki back."

Cecile folded her arms and glared at him.

"Her boyfriend just dumped her, like, an hour before they were supposed to go to the prom," he added.

"Proms are bourgeois. She's better off."

"She's really, really upset."

"What do you want me to do about it, Josh?"

"Maybe we could…both go up to New York?" He knew it was a dumb idea the second it came out of his mouth.

"On our *date*?" She slipped her foot out of her sandal and rubbed it on his ankle. "That's not what I had in mind."

Part of Josh wanted desperately to just go along with Cecile, whatever she wanted. But he thought of that Halloween night he'd called Nicki, and her skipping school and getting in trouble for him last month, just because he'd needed her.

"It's not what I had in mind either. I want to go out with you tonight more than anything. But this is an emergency."

Cecile shook her head at him. "It's always something with you. Your sister doesn't approve, or your little school friend is upset. I don't ever come first."

It wasn't true. She'd come first with him for an entire month earlier that spring, and it had gotten him in all kinds of trouble.

"My best friend is really upset," he said. "She's always been there for me."

"Then I guess you need to go to her. Have a nice life, Josh." She handed him back his phone and began walking toward her front door.

"Don't be like that," he said, following her. She turned on her heel, sort of a ballerina's pirouette, and looked at him.

"I'm flying out to California Monday morning," she said. "This is it."

He shifted his weight from foot to foot. "I don't know what to do," he said. But he did know. He was going to New York. As much as he wanted to be with Cecile, to please her, it wasn't even that hard a decision.

"I just wanted to have our date," Cecile said.

"I did, too. I really did. I'm totally sorry." He thought for a minute. "What if I come back tomorrow? Could we go out tomorrow night?"

She shook her head. "I'll be packing," she said.

"I'll help you pack."

She put her hand on his arm. "No," she said. She looked off into the distance. Her dress clung to her body, and her eyes looked sparkly and beautiful again, not hard and angry like before. "Maybe it's better this way."

"Will you keep in touch with me? Maybe I can come visit you in California," Josh said. He meant it. He would love to go to California. He would love to go anywhere.

"Maybe," she said, slipping quietly back into her building, shutting the door behind her.

Josh stood rooted in that spot for a few seconds, his heart pounding with what he'd just done. Parts of his body were very disappointed. But then he thought of Nicki. He hit her speed dial as he walked back toward the car.

"I'm sorry it took me so long to call you back," he said when she picked up. "I'm coming to New York." He got in the car, put his seatbelt on, turned the key.

"Tonight?' Nicki asked, her voice ragged from crying. "What about your date?"

Josh glanced back at Cecile's house before he drove off. "It doesn't matter," he said. "I'm on my way."

CHAPTER 26

Hallie slipped away from Marcus's farewell party at *Good News* and drove back to Oyster Shell, to the Trust office. She and Ram would have about an hour before Josh got home from school.

Hallie didn't know how to define it, this thing with Ram. At first, they'd agreed it was a one-time only experience. But having crossed that line once, it was easier to cross again, and soon, they'd decided to call it a fling, its duration limited by the move Hallie would make at the end of the summer. They both thought it best not to tell Josh.

There was something about the secrecy that made it all the more thrilling. Speeding down Route 47, the brilliant late May sun made Hallie feel youthful and reckless. She slipped her favorite disc from high school into the car stereo—Duran Duran—and sang along with "Hungry Like the Wolf."

After she reached the Trust office, she saw that she'd missed a call while the music was blaring: Todd. Cal's court case was scheduled for the end of July. "He can't make bail," Todd's voicemail said, "so he'll be in jail until then."

Hallie's feelings about Cal were complicated; she'd considered visiting him in jail, though Ram had convinced her not to. It wasn't pity as much as a feeling that she'd set the events in motion leading to Cal's break-in. He'd put in all that time at the farm, and she'd promised him some payment, but never delivered. Perhaps he felt she owed him whatever he could take from the house. Perhaps he had a point.

Hallie glanced at herself in the rearview mirror, applied lipstick, fluffed her hair. Her phone rang again: Lawrence. She blotted her lips and answered.

"I can only talk for a minute," she said. "I'm at Ram's."

"Delicious! I'm sorry to interrupt your Afternoon Delight. But I have some news."

"What?"

"I have an agent for the Jonathan book."

"Lawrence! That's great!" She headed up the wooden stairs in the back, which led to Ram's apartment; he met her at the door. "I'm so happy for you."

"Tell your sex machine that she's also interested in shopping the frog article around."

"I will," she said, accepting the glass of wine Ram offered her.

"Oh, and that I'll be down to look at the frogs next month, the weekend of Josh's graduation."

She handed the phone to Ram and sipped her wine while they briefly chatted.

"He has such a sexy voice," Lawrence said, after Ram had returned her phone. "I'm jealous, you know."

She laughed, and then Ram's hands went around her back and unfastened her bra. There was so much she still needed to talk to Lawrence about: she would need a larger place in New York this fall so Josh could have his own room during school breaks and holidays, and she still hadn't figured out how she could afford a bigger apartment and the upkeep on the house in Oyster Shell. But right now, Ram was moving over her, kissing her neck, and that was all she wanted to think about.

"I have to go now," she said to Lawrence. "Call you tomorrow." She tossed the phone down, where it skidded across the hardwood floor and plunked against the far wall with a slight thud.

HALLIE TOOK THE Friday before Josh's birthday party off from work, and she sat at the kitchen table that morning, running down the list she'd made. The party wasn't a surprise—she'd wanted Josh to be able to invite whoever he wanted, without his sister making some gross blunder—and it wouldn't be huge: just Nicki, Missy and Cole, Hallie, Ram and Nancy. But she wanted it to be special, something he'd look back on fondly. She wanted it to be nothing like her eighteenth birthday.

With no idea there was a party at home planned for her—there had been no birthday parties since her mother died, though Nancy had always brought over a cake—Holly had made plans with her closest friends that summer night. Christie, Suzanne, and Lara would celebrate Holly's birthday, and then the four of them would go to Ocean City, to a house rented for the week by five of the boys they'd graduated with. They planned to crash there, with Holly and Christie pretending they were sleeping over at each other's houses. But when Holly called home on the afternoon of her birthday—she'd slept at Christie's the night before as well—her stepmother had seemed upset that Holly wouldn't be home that night. A few minutes later, Holly's father called her from the farm.

"Brenda planned a surprise party for you. You have to come home tonight."

Holly put her hand over the phone and looked at Christie. "Did my parents invite you to a surprise party?" she asked, and Christie shook her head no.

"Dad, I'm at my best friend's house and she has no idea there's a party."

Her father was quiet for a moment. "Who's your best friend?"

Holly sighed loudly. "Christie," she said, rolling her eyes.

"I don't know them kids from Floyd you run around with."

"So who's invited to this party?" she asked, trying to contain her anger.

"Nancy, and your friends from around here. Kimmy Butler, Wanda Beers, and the Fallon girls."

Holly hadn't talked to any of them since her eighth grade graduation from Pearl Township Elementary School. "I'm not friends with those girls anymore."

"Well, maybe you should be. All this running around in Floyd. It's no good."

Holly had been furious, but still, she'd acted surprised for Brenda's sake when she and Christie walked through the door, and she'd spoken politely with Kimmy Butler, the only one of the Pearl Township kids who'd shown. Kimmy looked to be about seven months pregnant, and while Holly had felt bad for her, she also exchanged a sharp look with her father, who'd winced when he saw Kimmy's swollen belly. Just when Holly had thought the party couldn't get any more awkward, Brenda brought out the birthday cake she'd made: a huge strawberry shortcake.

"Holly's allergic to strawberries," Nancy blurted.

Brenda threw a sharp, horrified glance at Holly's father. "Why didn't you tell me?"

"I thought you knew," he said.

Holly and Christie had laughed about it when they drove back to Floyd that night, had laughed when they cut into the chocolate cake that Holly's other friends brought over to Christie's. They'd laughed about it on the way to Ocean City, and up until the third beer Holly had from the keg at the boys' party. After that, she could only remember briefly making out with a guy she barely knew, crying, and then throwing up off the side of a deck.

Hallie knew exactly how she'd felt that night. Her mom, her wonderful mom, hadn't been there, not for her graduation, not for her eighteenth birthday. And worse than the absence of her mother was Brenda's presence, frumpy in her K-Mart clothes and home perms, her cheap tchochkes taking up the uncluttered spaces Hallie's mother had favored.

But twenty years later, all Hallie could think of was how Brenda must have felt. How beautiful that strawberry shortcake had been—even Christie had said so. How hard Brenda had tried, and how nothing she'd ever done could please this uppity girl, this social climber who had no idea of how to escape Oyster Shell without looking down upon it.

Brenda had tried to love her when her own mother had chosen to leave her.

Hallie was startled by the sound that came from her just then; it had more in common with a groan than a sob. Emma scrambled over and cocked her head.

"It's okay, girl," she said to the dog, but it wasn't. She got up and went into the family room, flopped on the couch and buried her head in the cushions. Perhaps it wouldn't be so bad, to let herself cry, just a little. She felt Emma jump up and snuggle by her side, and Hallie flung one arm around the dog as her eyes leaked tears into the couch.

BY ONE THAT afternoon Hallie had vacuumed the house, framed and matted Josh's favorite of her wrecked auto photos, and wrapped it along with the biggest gift she had for him: a passbook to a bank account she'd opened in New York. She planned to deposit a little money each month so that Josh could spend a college semester abroad. She'd longed to do that, when she was in school.

Hallie checked her e-mail, hoping for a response from Damien to the apology she'd sent; there was nothing from him, though she was pleased to see a copy of a message Joy had sent to a gallery owner, suggesting he consider Hallie's photos for a show in the fall. Hallie quickly shot Joy her thanks, and then resigned herself to the task she'd been dreading: stopping by Nancy's.

Through two glasses of iced tea Hallie and Nancy nervously chattered about Josh's party. They hadn't talked in depth since that night in the garage, almost a month ago. But after fifteen minutes, they ran out of things to say.

Finally Nancy cleared her throat. "So did you come over to talk about the party? Or is something else on your mind?"

Hallie sighed. "I don't want things to be weird between us at Josh's party."

"I don't want things to be weird, period. Are you still mad at me? I could understand, if you were."

What Hallie felt towards Nancy was a complicated knot of emotions. Anger might be in there. "I'm not sure."

"What do you feel, then?"

For Hallie, emotions were slippery things, places within her that she could only access unpredictably, sometimes without warning. But she wasn't about to explain this to Nancy.

"I guess I am pissed off. Not so much because you lied to me, but because I have to deal with it now."

Nancy nodded. "It's okay to be mad at me for lying. I would be, if I were you."

"I get the feeling you want me to be mad at you."

"I just want you to react," Nancy said. "Even that night, when I was telling you the story, you seemed so disconnected. At times I wasn't sure if you were hearing me."

"I reacted later." But Hallie hadn't realized she'd appeared calm that night in the garage. She hadn't felt calm.

Nancy didn't respond. She looked intensely at Hallie, her face soft with concern. Finally Hallie added, "Don't worry so much, Nancy. I'm handling it."

"I don't want you to just handle it. I want you to move beyond it."

The black cat brushed against Hallie's ankles just then, and it was only when she reached down and rubbed the cat's head, saw its yellow eyes become blurry, that she realized she had teared up. *Why didn't Mom love me enough to stay alive?* she wanted to ask Nancy, but it wasn't a question that could be answered. She blinked away the tears.

"Did Brenda know?" Hallie asked.

"Know?"

"About my mom."

Nancy shifted uncomfortably in her seat. "Eventually, yes. Your father told her after the two of you had your...falling out."

"What did she think?"

Nancy drained the last sip of iced tea from her glass. "She understood why your father lied about it, but she thought it was wrong. She tried to talk him into telling you."

"Really?"

"Yeah. They had a terrible fight about it, around the time she was pregnant with Josh. But she didn't think it was her place to tell you, and she couldn't sway Don."

Hallie tried to imagine it, Brenda about to become a mother herself and then faced with her husband's poor decisions, his stubbornness and inability to admit he'd been wrong. Had it worried her, the thought of having a child with this man? Had it worried Hallie's mother? She wanted to hate her father for this lie, but it was the lie itself that complicated everything. He wouldn't have lied to her if he hadn't loved her. Hallie looked at Nancy, who sat there with her open, kind face, waiting for Hallie to go on. But she couldn't talk about this anymore.

"Ram and I are seeing each other," she blurted. It was all she could come up with to change the subject.

Nancy smiled. "I wondered."

"You did?"

"Yeah, I felt like something had shifted, but I wasn't sure."

"Don't say anything to Josh. We haven't told him."

"Why not?"

Hallie took a sip of her iced tea. "I don't want him to have any expectations. It's just a fling."

"A fling?"

"Yeah." She studied Nancy's half-smile. "I'm moving back to New York at the end of the summer. It can't go anywhere."

"Sure."

Hallie sighed. "I mean, I suppose we could try to keep it going long-distance, but that rarely works out." She had caught herself fantasizing about it—a tryst every other weekend, alternating between the city and Oyster Shell; another Thanksgiving with Ram's family, now as his girlfriend—but she wasn't about to admit any of that to Nancy.

"New York's not that far away," Nancy said.

"I suppose not." She finished her tea and carried the glass to the sink. "Anyway, I should be going. I still have some shopping to do for the party."

THE NEXT NIGHT, when Josh's cell phone rang as he was cutting his birthday cake, no one except Hallie seemed to notice. She was happy that Josh appeared to be having a good time, happier still at how he'd hugged her when she'd explained the passbook, the trip abroad. But it had nagged at the back of her mind, the question of who was calling Josh when all of his friends were at the party, and so, after he and Cole and the girls left for a midnight movie, when just the adults were there cleaning up and Hallie noticed that Josh had forgotten his phone, she snuck a look at who had called. Cecile. Hallie put the phone down and sighed. Josh was now eighteen. There wasn't much she could do about it.

CHAPTER 27

Josh and Nicki were huddled over her digital camera as they headed to the cafeteria on their third-to-last day of high school ever. Nicki was flipping through their prom photos, and even though Josh had already seen them he didn't really mind looking again. They'd ended up going together to the Floyd prom; Josh had always thought school dances were lame, but this had been way more fun than he'd expected. Josh danced with Missy for one song, and Cole with Nicki, and the four of them hung out together pretty much the whole night. Nicki told Josh she'd overheard Missy's popular friends gossiping about it in the bathroom.

"I look like a dork," Josh said, pointing to a shot where his long hair was hanging in his face.

"No, you look good," Nicki said. "The longer hair is working for you, Corson." He'd been thinking about cutting it really, really short once he moved to New York, as a way of marking the next part of his life.

Just before Josh and Nicki entered the cafeteria, Mr. Cicirello walked up to them.

"Come to my office for a second, Josh," Mr. Cicirello said, smiling in a way that made his eyes crinkle. "I have some good news."

Josh looked at Nicki, and she shrugged in return. "I'll meet you in the caf."

He followed Mr. Cicirello to the office, where Miss Piper grinned at him as he walked by. A man in a business suit was sitting across from Mr. Cicirello's desk, and stood up when Josh walked in.

"Josh," Mr. Cicirello said, "this is Daniel Piedmont."

Josh reached forward to shake the man's outstretched hand, unsure of what to say, and Mr. Cicirello added, "Annie Piedmont was his daughter."

The Piedmont Scholarship. Everybody in Floyd knew the sad story, that some time in the eighties there was a girl named Annie Piedmont who lost a leg to some sort of cancer but got better, only to be hit and killed by a drunk driver the summer after she graduated. There was a picture of her in a display case in the main hall: a pretty girl with huge eighties hair.

As Mr. Cicirello started talking about "triumphing over adversity" and "exemplary behavior," Josh thought about how everyone in school called it the Pity Scholarship. Two years ago, they'd given it to a boy who'd had leukemia; last year, to a girl who'd moved to Floyd from Cambodia and started her freshman year barely speaking English, then graduated tenth in the class. Josh could see where someone who went through months of chemotherapy or whose grandparents were killed by the Khmer Rouge might deserve a special scholarship, but he didn't think he did.

"I didn't even apply for this," was all Josh could think to say.

Mr. Cicirello and Mr. Piedmont exchanged glances. "There's no application process," Mr. Cicirello said. "We ask the teachers to nominate students."

"And I was really impressed with what I heard about you, Josh," Mr. Piedmont said.

"Like what?" He hadn't meant to blurt the question out like that, but he couldn't see what about him would make someone want to give him a special scholarship.

"Josh is very humble," Mr. Cicirello said.

And then Josh realized what should have been obvious: it was because his parents had died. Just like he'd received way too much stuff both last Christmas and for his birthday, now someone wanted to give him college money because his parents were dead. It was embarrassing. But he could use the money, however much it was. Mr. Piedmont was looking at him like he expected Josh to say or do something that made him worthy of this gift.

"I'm just, like, surprised," Josh said, his mind racing in a panic. "I mean, thanks."

Mr. Piedmont smiled at him. "I hear you're going to college in New York this fall."

"Yeah. Hunter College. I'm going to live with my sister." It wasn't decided yet; Hallie kept saying that he should have the "dorm experience," but Josh didn't want to share a small room with a stranger. He had gotten used to living with Hallie, and he didn't want to have to get used to living with anyone else.

"Well, five thousand dollars should help with that," Mr. Piedmont said.

"Wow," Josh said. He had no idea the Piedmont Scholarship was for so much money.

"I understand you're a tremendous writer," Mr. Piedmont said.

Had Mrs. Wyckoff or one of his previous English teachers been the one to nominate him?

"I'm writing a novel," he blurted. He hadn't told anybody else. He still had trouble allowing himself to think of it as a novel, exactly.

"I didn't know that," Mr. Cicirello said.

"Well, I mean, I just started it, and I don't know if it's any good. But yeah, I've been working on it for about two months."

"How much have you written?" Mr. Piedmont asked.

Now Josh felt panicked that they would ask to read it. He wasn't ready for anybody to read it. "Just, like, thirty pages." He really had double that number, but he thought that if he were forced to show it to them, he could maybe come up with thirty not-terrible pages out of the sixty or so he'd written.

"That's a good start," Mr. Piedmont said. He smiled at Josh in a way that suggested he had passed some sort of test.

NICKI WAS WAITING just outside the office door.

"So what was that all about?" she asked.

Josh filled her in about the scholarship as they walked. "I guess it wasn't a very tragic year for the rest of Floyd High."

Nicki rolled her eyes at him. "How much is it for?"

"Kind of a lot. Five thousand dollars." Josh looked at Nicki. "It's embarrassing. They say stuff about you before they give it to you at graduation."

Nicki shrugged. "It's five thousand bucks for college."

But Josh was worried about what they might say: that his parents had died in an accident, burned to death and left him to be raised by a sister he hadn't even seen in a couple of years. What else could they say?

Josh thought there maybe were things about him that were sort of special, but they weren't things he expected anyone else to see or appreciate, and he hoped—he felt a slight burst of panic at the thought—they wouldn't mention, on stage, in front of all his classmates, that he was writing a novel. Why had he told them that?

Mr. Cicirello and the teachers knew the sad part of his story, but they didn't know the rest of it. They didn't know that some of the changes in his life since last September—maybe even a lot of the changes—had been for the better. They didn't know that he had gone from living his life through books to actually living. They didn't know he was constantly aware that if his parents hadn't died, he wouldn't be going to college in New York. It wasn't that he wouldn't trade it all for having his parents back; he would. But since he couldn't, it seemed to him that he shouldn't enjoy the good things that had happened in the past year.

As Josh followed Nicki into the cafeteria line and grabbed a tray, he realized that he liked his life now a lot more than the life he had then, even with how much he missed his dad and, especially, his mom. And he wasn't sure he could ever forgive himself for liking this life more.

FOUR NIGHTS LATER, Josh filed onto the football field with the rest of the Class of 2007, taking his designated seat in the second row. As the administrators and mayor began their boring speeches, Josh squinted and tried to make out Hallie and Ram, Nancy and Lawrence and Kenneth in the bleachers, but he couldn't see them. He turned and looked for Nicki a few rows back, waved when he saw her; she stuck her tongue out at him and then smiled.

Josh listened during Missy's valedictory speech as she talked about the school, and how much they'd all grown over four years, and where they were headed. She made a point of mentioning how the Floyd kids had come together with the kids from the bay, from Pearl and Commercial and Maurice River townships.

When they called Josh up to the stage, he felt less nervous than he'd expected. And when, as Josh took the steps to the stage, Ray Watson called out at top volume, "Josh Fuckin' Corson, man!" and let out a whoop, Josh laughed with the rest of his class. And when Mr. Cicirello talked not about Josh's dead parents but his character, how active he'd been in his community—the church coat drives, the Mollusk Creek Trust—Josh thought for a second that his principal was talking about someone else. He'd never thought of himself as one of those kids, the kids like Missy who were involved in everything; but maybe he was, even if the things he was involved with were not school things. The only reference the principal made to Josh's dead parents was something about a hard year, and grief, and something about grace. It was over really fast, and all Josh had to say was "Thank you" when he took the envelope Mr. Piedmont handed him, and tons of flashes were going off and people were applauding and then Josh walked back to his seat to wait for the procession, to get his diploma.

He sat down and felt weirdly disconnected from his body. Josh squinted again into the bleachers, searching for Hallie. He couldn't find her, but his eyes landed on a slightly chubby woman in a yellow dress, just like the dress his mom had worn when they went out for Mother's Day last year. He looked at the man beside her, the stern set to his jaw, the angle at which he held a back whose aches were legendary. They were there, his mom and dad, in the crowd with everyone else's parents. His mom was smiling broadly; his dad had the funny half-smile that he got sometimes, the closest he could come to expressing joy. But they couldn't be there. His parents were dead. He blinked, and looked again, and couldn't find the two people he'd seen or imagined.

Josh stared at the envelope Mr. Piedmont had given him, hoping that the thoughts about his parents would go away. When they didn't, he got up, vaulted over four kids in his row, and ran in a crouch to where Nicki was sitting.

"What's up?" she whispered, smiling as he squatted next to her.

"Ghosts," he said.

"You have to stay in your seats until the processional," Mrs. Wyckoff whispered, and then Nicki moved halfway over, patted the empty half-seat. Josh sat next to her, his ass mostly off the chair.

"He's seated," Nicki said.

Mrs. Wyckoff smiled and shook her head. "Just get back to your spot when they call the first row," she said, and walked away.

Josh had his arm around Nicki's back to keep from falling off the chair. The wind blew a lock of her blue-streaked hair into his face. It smelled like coconut. "Good thinking," he said.

"Yeah. You okay?"

"I think so." He didn't feel upset about his parents anymore, now that he was sitting with Nicki. It was kind of nice, being near her like that. He didn't usually think of Nicki as a girl, not the way he thought of Cecile or Missy or Miss Piper; but there was something about how close their thighs were, the way her hair smelled, and her general Nicki-ness that was giving Josh a hard-on. He had never before gotten a hard-on from being with Nicki. Before he could panic about it, the first row was told to stand. Josh leapt up and ran back to his spot.

TWO HOURS LATER, they were all finishing dinner at the China Palace—Josh's group along with Nicki's mom and dad—when Josh's cell phone rang. It was Cecile. Josh excused himself to the men's room.

"Congratulations," Cecile said when Josh answered the call. "It was tonight, right?"

"Yeah. Thanks." He was glad she'd remembered.

"Got your diploma?"

"And they gave me a scholarship, too. It was kind of a big deal."

"That's great! So, where are you now?"

"At the China Palace."

"Ah, the China Palace. I can almost smell the eggrolls from here."

"Where are you?"

"Parked on Main Street."

Josh leaned against the bathroom sink. "In Floyd?"

"Yeah."

"I thought you were in California."

"I'm crashing in Philly these days. Should I drive over to the restaurant?"

"No!" Josh blurted, more harshly than he'd intended. "I mean, Hallie and a bunch of other people are here."

"Then come meet me, Josh."

He was quiet as he thought it over. "I don't know if I can." Josh wished he didn't want to go as much as he did.

"Try."

There had to be a way, Josh thought. He was eighteen, and he'd just graduated from high school, and he'd never really gotten to say a proper goodbye to Cecile. "It's going to take a little time."

"I'll be here, sitting in my car."

Josh went back to the table, opened his fortune cookie and tried to pretend nothing was up. *Life brings you great surprises*, the fortune read.

"Who was that?" Hallie asked.

He shot a glance at Nicki. "Cecile."

Hallie shook her head. "What did she want?"

"Just to say congratulations," Josh said, and Nicki started talking about college and then everyone at the table had opinions about majors and freshman course loads and dorm living, and by the time Josh and Nicki said goodbye and drove off in Josh's mom's car—they had permission to stay out all night, a Floyd High School tradition—Hallie seemed to have forgotten that Cecile had called.

Once they were in the car, Nicki said, "So what's up with Cecile?"

Josh was quiet for a moment. They were supposed to go to Missy's graduation party and then watch the sun rise over the lake, and he knew Nicki would be upset if he didn't do all that with her. "She's here. Parked on Main Street."

"Oh my *God*," Nicki said.

"I know."

She was quiet as Josh headed toward the lake, toward Missy's house. "What are you going to do?" she finally asked.

Josh sighed. "Would you be really mad if I just left the party for like an hour and went to see her?"

Nicki raised an eyebrow. "An hour?"

"Maybe two. Tops. I'll definitely come back and we'll do the whole watching-the-sunrise thing at the Sailing Club like we talked about."

Nicki looked out the car window. "It doesn't take two hours. It only took Nathan like fifteen minutes."

"Nicki."

"Fine. Whatever."

Josh pulled up in front of Missy's house. "Look. I totally blew Cecile off when you were upset last month. She and I never really got to talk after that."

Nicki glanced at him out of the corner of her eyes. "Yeah, I know." She got out of the car and started walking toward Missy's door. Josh quickly followed.

MISSY'S INVITATION HAD said to bring bathing suits if they wanted to swim, but so far, everyone was just standing around the pool in t-shirts and shorts or summery dresses, sipping the punch that Missy had said her dad intended to taste every half-hour. Josh took Cole aside.

"I have to cut out of here for a little while," Josh said.

"What's going on?"

Josh glanced at Missy and Nicki. "Remember I told you there was this girl I liked?"

"Yeah."

"She's parked on Main Street, waiting for me."

"Really," Cole said, in a tone of voice that suggested he approved.

"She's twenty-three," Josh blurted.

"Twenty-three?" Cole smiled at him. "Well, don't keep the lady waiting."

"I'm definitely coming back," Josh said. "Could you..." He didn't know quite how to ask it. "Make sure Nicki has a good time, until I get back? She doesn't know very many people here."

Cole looked over at the girls. "Yeah, man. Sure." He patted his pocket, which Josh figured held his stash of weed.

"Thanks." Josh started for the car, but Cole followed him.

"You have a rubber?" Cole asked after he'd caught up with him.

Josh hadn't dared think about it. The ones he'd bought last month were hidden at the bottom of his sock drawer. "Not with me."

Cole pulled a small packet out of his wallet. "Here."

Josh felt weird about it, realizing that Cole had intended to use the condom with Missy, but he took it anyway. "I hope I get to use it," Josh said, and Cole laughed. But as he drove away from the lake and back toward Main Street, Josh felt bad. Cecile wasn't just some dirty joke.

•

CECILE LOOKED SO beautiful sitting on the hood of her car in one of her short dresses, glitter on her eyelids and in her now-red hair, that after they'd said hi to each other he whipped out his cell phone and took a picture. He couldn't help himself. He tried to make a joke of it, and she laughed and struck goofy poses on the car.

"You drive," she said, climbing into the passenger's side of his Geo. She smiled at him. Her teeth looked perfect, white but not fake-white; the gloss on her lips had something in it that shimmered under the street lights. Josh's mind was sparkling and popping like that, too, going places he didn't dare hope for, couldn't help but hope for.

"Let's go to the lake," Cecile said. "I want to swim."

She pulled a disc from her purse and slid it into the player. Louis Armstrong's unmistakable voice rose from the speakers. Cecile had once told Josh that Louis Armstrong made her horny. Was this a message? He stopped at a red light and looked over at Cecile: reclined in her seat, eyes closed, listening to the music. Her face looked pale, her features tiny and delicate. He watched her enjoy the music until a car behind him beeped; the light had turned green. Cecile opened her eyes, blinked languidly, and closed them again, smiling.

Josh parked a short walk from the sailing club, next to two cars, two couples, each too involved to notice anyone else. He and Cecile walked in silence, side by side, to the lake. In the moonlight Josh could see how her dress clung to her body's curves, and he couldn't help but think how easy it would be to take that dress off her. His heart was starting to speed up, to miss beats altogether.

As they approached the dock, Cecile took Josh's hand. His palm started to sweat. The dock and the sailing club were both empty, the whole area abandoned by graduation night revelers, save for the two couples parked in the woods; Josh knew more kids would be there later, at dawn, including him and Nicki. The key to the clubhouse had been left under a mat by some Laker who was a sailing club member. Cecile led Josh by the hand to the end of the dock, where, in a motion so swift and so sure it felt to Josh organic, like taking a breath, or like a tide, she dropped his hand, lifted her dress over her head to reveal that she was wearing no bra, no panties; arched her back and dived into the lake, her body slicing through the water with minimal splash. Her head popped up.

"Come on in," she called. "Have you ever skinny dipped before?"

Josh shook his head. He had no idea what Cecile would think of his body; she'd only seen glimpses. The idea left him equally embarrassed and excited. He pulled his t-shirt over his head.

"Woo-hoo!" Cecile yelled. "Take it all off!"

He stood uncertainly on the edge of the dock for a few seconds, the t-shirt in his hands. Cecile swam closer to him.

"The water's really nice, Josh," she said, her voice softer than before. "Come on in." And then she swam off, her back to him, sparing him the embarrassment of turning away as he pulled off his shorts and boxers.

Josh entered the water feet-first, less gracefully than Cecile had. She turned toward him, splashed water in his direction. Josh splashed back. Soon it was an all-out splash fight, bursts of water shooting back and forth between them. Josh dunked Cecile under a little, not hard. He pulled her up almost immediately.

"I'm sorry," he said. "Was that okay?"

In response Cecile pushed down on his shoulders from behind and held him there, under the water, her forearms on his shoulders, her legs wrapped around his hips. Josh knew he was a lot stronger than Cecile and could come up any time he wanted, but oh, he didn't want to, not yet, he would hold his breath for as long as he possibly could with Cecile pressed against him.

Finally he pushed up hard, with such force that Cecile popped from the water with him. He turned and faced her as she moved slowly toward him, the water lapping all around, the stars looking brighter than the moonlight but still dim enough that Cecile appeared silvery, wispy, like a ghost, or a negative from one of Hallie's photos. He knew, all at once, that she wanted what he wanted and that in a few seconds they would be kissing, touching, and he would be inside her, and his certainty made him enjoy those last few seconds before she put her hands on his face and kissed him, made him enjoy them almost as much as the kiss. Josh was operating on some sort of delay: while she was kissing him, he was still enjoying the seconds it had taken for her to swim over; when he started to kiss her back, he was still enjoying the moment that she touched her lips to his, the way the tip of her tongue began to gently probe; and by the time he was really feeling the kiss, her mouth soft and warm and tasting, somehow, like a peach, she had already taken his penis in her hand and it felt better than he could ever have imagined. And just when he thought they were going to do it right there, in the water, a piece of something slimy floated by and clung to his leg. Technically the lake was considered okay to swim in, and most people didn't worry about it; but Josh knew the waters flowed into Mollusk Creek, maybe carrying whatever substance was hurting the frogs. He wished he hadn't thought of these things, but once he started he couldn't stop. He reached down and slapped the slimy thing away from his leg without looking at it.

"Let's go in the clubhouse," he whispered in Cecile's ear. "I know how to get in."

He climbed up on the dock and held his hand out to her, pulled her up. They gathered their clothes and ran to the clubhouse.

"Interesting," Cecile said, strutting around the deck chairs and beach loungers which Josh knew were scattered outside when the club was open. Cecile pulled a towel from a stack that looked clean, then stretched it out on a cushioned beach lounger in a corner of the room. She lay on top of it. Josh was about to join her when he remembered the condom in the pocket of his shorts, his father's advice, and so he located the packet, dropped his shorts on a chair, and went to her. He stood uncertainly for a moment, taking in how beautiful she was, until she reached up and pulled him down on top of her and they started kissing and moving together again. He dropped the condom on the floor.

At that point, Josh's brain stopped. Everything stopped. The clubhouse wasn't there; neither was the dock outside, the lake itself, the steamy-windowed cars parked at the edge of the woods, the road leading back into Floyd. There was no Floyd, no Oyster Shell, no larger world; there were no lost parents, there was no sister, no animals that cried out for him to save them. There was no Josh, no Cecile. There was just this world of sensation that stretched as infinitely as the universe. She picked up the condom from the floor and opened it herself, rolled it onto him.

But as he entered her, as he looked in her blue blue eyes, he found that instead of thinking of Cecile, her beauty and mystery and the wonder that they were finally, actually doing it, he was thinking of Nicki. *It should have been you, Josh.*

"Flip over," Cecile said to him, and he did, somewhat awkwardly, slipping out of her for a few seconds; she climbed on top of him, guided him back inside her, and began moving. She placed his hands on her breasts, and suddenly it all felt wrong; he didn't like the way she was orchestrating everything, and he didn't like the look on her face. He felt like she was looking through him. Still, his mind had little control over his body, and as she moved and he was closer and closer to coming he forgot about it all, he was purely sensation once more in a world without time, and he closed his eyes and moved with her, again, again.

And when it was over, when Cecile had stopped making little panting breaths in his ear and he realized that he had done it, he had come, he opened his eyes and looked at her and felt not the joy he'd felt seconds before, but a vague sadness. Who was Cecile, really? He didn't even know where she actually lived. He wrapped his arms around her, thinking that was what he should do, and they lay there quietly for a few minutes; but as he felt his penis slipping out of her, he thought that maybe Nicki had been right. It should have been her.

THEY DIDN'T TALK much afterward, not after they got up, not after they'd dried off with clean towels from the stack, dressed and walked back to Josh's car. He held her hand on the way to the car, but when she dropped his, he didn't mind.

"There's a party in Glassboro tonight," Cecile said. "I guess I'll go meet my friends there."

Josh noticed that she didn't invite him along, though he couldn't have gone even if he'd wanted to. "I have to get back to a graduation party."

They got in the car and drove in silence for a few minutes; Josh waited for Cecile to put a disc in the player, but she didn't. Finally Josh said, "So how did you end up in Philly?"

Cecile sighed. "You know the story. I got fired."

"I thought you moved to California."

"That didn't work out."

Josh couldn't stop himself from asking; he had to know. "Did you ever really move away?"

She reached down and dug through the debris on the floor beneath her, coming up with three of Josh's discs. She put one in the player, and soon, Josh heard Arcade Fire coming from the speakers. It was a favorite of his and Nicki's.

"Did you really live in France?' he asked as he turned onto Main Street.

Cecile smiled at him and closed her eyes, and he knew she would never answer him, just as he knew what the answer probably was. He'd never know how much of Cecile's life was real and how much was made-up, but it occurred to him, as he glanced at her in the passenger's seat, that it didn't really matter. He wasn't in love with her anymore.

Neither of them said another word as he pulled over behind Cecile's car. But before she got out, she turned to him, put her hands on his face and looked at him, really looked at him, and for a moment she wasn't the Cecile that Hallie and Nicki saw—a liar, a troublemaker. She was the old Cecile, the one he'd loved.

"You are a sweet, sweet guy," she said. "You have a blast in New York this fall." She brushed her lips against his, and was out of his car, had slipped behind her own wheel and was driving off before he could even think of anything to say.

BACK AT MISSY'S, the party was in full swing; lots of kids were in the pool, and others were wet, sitting on plastic chairs in the yard. Josh spotted Nicki, soaked in her cutoffs and t-shirt, sitting with a guy who looked about Cecile's age.

"You're back," Nicki said to Josh when he approached. "This is Missy's cousin, Jason. He lives in New York."

"Hey," Jason said. He reminded Josh of that Caleb guy from Cecile's party last winter, everything about him too perfectly disheveled.

"We're going to Hunter College in the fall," Josh said, moving closer to Nicki.

"So I heard," Jason said. "You guys will have to come hear my band."

There was something about the way he said "my band" that made Josh immediately dislike him.

"Sure," Josh said, but he thought: *I will never ever go see your band.*

Missy and two of her friends ran by, and Jason followed them, tossing Caitlin in the pool.

"How old is that guy?" Josh asked, taking Jason's seat. "He's, like, a pedophile."

Nicki rolled her eyes at him. "Oh *please*," she said. "This from someone who just spent an hour and fifteen minutes with Cecile."

Josh shrugged and kind of smiled. Nicki reached out and touched his hair.

"You're wet," she said. "Where were you?"

"At the lake," Josh said.

"Remind me never to swim in it."

"We didn't do it there."

Nicki was quiet for a minute. "So you did it."

He didn't know what to say to her then, how to explain that while he wasn't exactly sorry he'd done it, he also knew he shouldn't have. But maybe he'd needed to do it; maybe he'd needed to have sex with Cecile to know for sure that he didn't love her anymore.

"It wasn't what I expected," Josh said.

Nicki looked off in the distance, towards the pool. "It never is."

Josh looked at her, right in her eyes. "Maybe sometimes it is." He hoped that Nicki was a little bit psychic.

She ignored him for a second, looked away, glanced back. "Stop looking at me like that, Corson." She gave him a playful shove. Then she moved her chair closer to his.

JUST BEFORE DAWN, the twenty or so kids who remained at Missy's party piled into cars and headed for the lake. Dr. Dalton and his wife had spent the night inspecting everyone's drinks, so no one was actually drunk, but a lot of kids had smoked pot behind the bushes. Josh and Nicki took the front seats of his car while three girls he barely knew squeezed into the back. One of the girls was very wasted and kept screaming "Rock and roll!" out the window.

A lot of kids sat on the dock, and Josh and Nicki found a spot, not far from where he'd stood a few hours earlier, taken his clothes off, leapt into the lake. They dangled their feet in the water and talked about everything, college and politics and books and music and how they were both weirdly attracted to mystical things even though neither of them really believed in God. When Cole circulated a joint to them a few times, they both returned it without smoking. And when the sky started to change color, Josh understood for the first time what Ram meant when he said that he thought God was everywhere, in the sun and the trees and the rocks and the rain and, of course, in the frogs, in all the animals. It wasn't God, Josh thought, so much as the atoms and molecules everything on earth had in common, but he really felt it just then, his connection to the world. He was a part of the dock, the lake, the trees surrounding it. He was a part of Nicki. Without thinking about it Josh put his arm around her shoulders.

"You're such a *dog*," she said, but she didn't move away.

She was right, it was kind of gross to hit on her right after he'd had sex with Cecile, but he knew then that he wanted to. He would have kissed Nicki right there on the dock, in front of everybody, were it not for the fact that he thought the chances were only fifty-fifty she'd kiss him back or push him in the lake. Still, he felt closer to her than he'd ever felt to anyone, and as he sat there with his hand on her shoulder, the sky turning from black to sepia to a pink-streaked blue, it occurred to Josh that he was no longer sorry he was alive, that he no longer wished he'd died with his parents. There were reasons to live, he thought. *This moment is a reason to live.*

"Ow-woo," he said, imitating Emma's bark, and Nicki laughed and leaned a little bit into his shoulder.

CHAPTER 28

The morning after Josh's graduation Hallie sat in an empty house, sipping her third cup of coffee, waiting for her brother to get home. He'd texted her that he was having breakfast at Pete's—a school tradition—and that he'd be home soon. She wasn't sure what she would say to him. She and Ram had followed Josh after he left the China Palace; she knew he'd seen Cecile. How would Dad and Brenda have handled this?

She thought some fresh air might clear her head, so she took Emma for a walk along the bay. As she and the dog returned and approached the back door, Emma began whimpering, and a few seconds later Hallie heard the car pull up in the driveway. The dog straining at the leash, Hallie walked around to the front of the house, skirting the back of the garage before she could think better of it. She hated the way that window now seemed to wink at her, its truth revealed. She let the dog off the leash and Emma bounded through the bushes. When Hallie reached the driveway, Josh was standing there, the dog in his arms, licking his face.

"Oh my God, she just, like, threw herself at me," Josh said, laughing. He gently put Emma down.

"Let's go inside." Hallie led the way. In the kitchen she poured Josh a glass of juice. "Are you hungry?" she asked as they both sat down.

"I'm stuffed," Josh said. "I just ate a ton of pancakes."

Hallie studied his face. She'd expected him to appear hung over, but he didn't look that way. He didn't even look like he'd been up all night. He looked exhilarated. Happy.

"Did you have fun?" she asked.

Josh was quiet for a minute. He took another sip of juice and then looked at her. "I did," he said, "but there's something I have to tell you. I mean, I guess I don't have to, but I want to."

Hallie felt a knot in her stomach even though she knew, at least in part, what he would say. "Okay." She aimed for a neutral, non-judgmental tone.

Josh took a breath and let it out. "I spent most of the night with Nicki and the other kids, but I saw Cecile too."

Hallie hadn't planned to admit that she'd followed him, but something about his honesty made her want to come clean. "I know," she said, "because Ram and I followed you. But I'm glad you told me on your own."

"You...*followed* me?"

"Yeah. I was worried about that call from Cecile, and I talked Ram into following you. And he talked me into leaving it alone."

"Like that would ever happen," Josh said in his most irritated teenage voice.

"What do you mean?"

He leaned back in his chair and folded his arms. "You don't ever leave things alone. You just come back around at them another way." Josh's eyes flashed at her. "You're such a hypocrite."

"A hypocrite?"

"Yeah, a hypocrite. You pretend to be cool and hip about things, but then you're like the FBI when it comes to Cecile. And on top of it, you and Ram are, like, doing it, and I'm supposed to pretend I don't know." Josh's voice rose. "Why don't you just go to the library and see what books I've checked out? I hear you can do that now with the Patriot Act."

"Josh—" she started.

"Or read all my e-mails. I'll bring my laptop down so you don't have to get up. Why don't you read my novel, too? Or maybe you already have."

Hallie took a gulp of coffee. "You're writing a novel?"

He glared at her.

"I've never gone in your room like that. Ever." It was true; she knew she would have been horrified, at his age, by such a violation.

He looked at her for a moment, as if trying to decide whether to believe her; his expression softened. "So why have you and Ram been lying to me all this time?"

She floundered for an answer. Why *had* she felt the need to keep it secret? She knew she'd had some misguided idea about protecting Josh in case it didn't work out, but it occurred to her that he might not have been the one she was protecting. It wasn't casual anymore, this thing with Ram.

Her eyes felt teary; a trickle in the back of her throat made her choke, and a sob escaped. Soon, Hallie was crying, loud and wet, unable to stop, and the evolving expressions on Josh's face, from anger to puzzlement to sympathy just made her cry all the more.

"Hey," he said. "I didn't mean to upset you so much."

She shook her head. It was typical, she thought. Instead of being able to talk through things with Josh, something always brought it back to her, and she ended up dissolving. She felt that old desire to slip somewhere inside herself, but she didn't want to do that anymore; she couldn't. This was the only important thing she'd ever done in her life, this thing with Josh. She got up, went to the kitchen sink and splashed cold water on her face.

After she'd dried her face with a dishtowel, she turned back to Josh. He was out of his chair, standing near the table, watching her. "I'm sorry," she said. "I'm back."

"Okay." He shifted from one foot to another. Hallie walked into the family room and sat on an end of the couch. Josh followed her, sitting at the opposite end.

"I should have told you about Ram," she said. "I'm sorry about that."

Josh nodded. "But why didn't you guys want me to know?"

She took a breath. "I'm not very good with emotional stuff, Josh. I don't know if you've figured that out."

He smiled slightly. "Kind of."

"I'm a bit fucked up," she said, and Josh chuckled a little.

"Or maybe really fucked up," she went on. "In the past I always just kind of separated myself from my emotions. I didn't deal with them."

"Like Dad," Josh said.

Hallie was about to say, no, not like Dad, I'm nothing like Dad, I've always been just like my mom. But Josh was right. She *was* like their dad, a man so unable to deal with his wife's suicide that constructing an elaborate lie for his daughter had seemed a reasonable option.

"Wow," Hallie said.

Josh just looked at her.

"I mean, I never thought I was anything like Dad, but you're right.

I am." She picked at the stitching on the ancient couch. "That's pretty profound."

Josh was quiet for a moment. "My mom said that."

"She did?"

Josh turned toward her. "Do you remember when we talked on the phone, after 9/11?"

Hallie thought back to that day when the world had seemed about to end. She and Lawrence had both been home that morning, and they'd alternated between watching from the roof of their building with two other tenants, more as the day wore on, or watching on TV. Neither of them had tried to leave the city.

"Where would we go?" Lawrence had said. "Indiana? South Jersey? No thanks. If New York dies, I'll die with it."

It wasn't until two the next morning that a call came through on Hallie's cell phone. Twelve-year-old Josh. He and his mom and dad had been trying to reach her all day, he said, but his parents had finally gone to sleep. And Hallie had sat there on the rooftop, where Lawrence had set up a bar and most of the building had congregated, and talked to Josh for more than an hour, describing what she saw, what it was like, what she felt. She'd gone down to visit her family a few days later, on the weekend, but after forty-eight hours with her father she'd been reminded of why she kept her distance, and didn't return for three more years.

"I remember," Hallie said. "We talked for a really long time."

"Yeah. And it was, like, the first time we ever had a deep conversation. I thought it was so amazing. And then when you came down that weekend, I thought that was it. We were finally really going to be brother and sister."

Hallie felt a knot tighten in her stomach. "But it didn't happen."

"Nope. I kept trying to talk to you, but you seemed kind of checked out. And then you and Dad got into it, and I knew that was that." Emma hopped onto the couch between the two of them, and Josh patted her head as she snuggled close to him. "I was kind of upset about it."

"I'm sorry, Josh," Hallie whispered. She was doing everything in her power not to cry again.

"No, I'm not saying it to make you feel bad. It's just, like, true." Josh shifted slightly, and Emma rolled on her side, her belly to him. Josh rubbed it absently. "Anyway, Mom said then that she thought you were like Dad, that both of you just kind of mentally went away somewhere when you were upset about something. She said it took her a while to get used to that in Dad."

Hallie folded her legs in front of her and leaned against the arm of the couch so she was facing Josh head-on. "I wish I'd been nicer to your mom," she said. "I wish that more than anything."

"She didn't take it personally."

"No?" How could Brenda not have taken it personally, when seventeen-year-old Holly had thrown a K-Mart outfit back at her and said, in her most condescending voice, "I don't wear blue light specials." What a little bitch that girl was, Hallie thought. *What a bitch I was.*

"No. She thought you were upset by your mom's death, and that you felt like your dad had a new family. 'She'll come around one day,' she used to say."

"Well, she was right," Hallie said softly. "I've come around now."

Josh smiled a little. "Yeah."

Emma rolled over and presented her belly to Hallie, as if offering her a gift. Hallie reached down and rubbed the dog.

"So am I going to hear anything about last night?" Hallie asked. She doubted her ability to talk any more about her dad and Brenda without dissolving.

Josh leaned back. "What do you want to know?"

"Anything you'll tell me," she said. "I won't freak out. I'll pretend to be hip and cool."

He smiled. "It was the most amazing night of my life."

So he did have sex, Hallie thought. But his earnestness and obvious joy reminded her of some of those nights in her youth, the nights when the world seemed to expand and everything in it felt extraordinary. Josh needed to experience the world, the good and the bad. This entire year she had feared for him because he'd seemed to her less tough than she was, so much more open to being hurt; but the truth, she could see now, was that he was a lot stronger than she had ever been. She couldn't imagine how he could possibly get past losing both parents when she had never gotten over losing the one. But he was a different person, and would be okay in a way that she never was.

"I'm glad you had that kind of night," she said.

He eyed her suspiciously.

"I mean it," she said. "And I'm going to butt out about Cecile."

Josh looked off in the distance. "I think that's pretty much done."

"Really?"

"Yeah."

"And you're okay with that?"

"Yeah. I figured some stuff out." Josh yawned. "I think I'm finally, like, tired."

"You should go to bed," Hallie said. "We'll wake you up for dinner."

Josh got up and walked behind Hallie, on his way to the stairs; but she felt him hesitate, and then he surprised her with a quick hug, his arms squeezing her shoulders. Just as quickly, he was gone.

AN HOUR LATER Hallie drove down to Mollusk Creek. Lawrence and Ram were sitting at the water's edge, a tape recorder between them, Lawrence scribbling notes while Ram talked. Kenneth was perched on a tree stump a few yards away, talking on his cell.

"Hey," Ram called as she got out of the car. "How did it go with Josh?"

"Fine," she said. "I'll tell you later."

"I already caught a few young frogs with extra legs," Ram said. "They're in a tank in the bed of the truck."

Hallie retrieved her camera bag from her car, loaded film into her Nikon. She walked over to Ram's truck, looked at the frogs through the clear glass of the tank. Up close, the deformities were obvious: extra legs, a withered limb branching from a real leg, hanging limp as a noodle. She removed the tank's lid and shot a few photos from above, but she would have to wait for Ram's help to get better shots. She took some photos of the creek itself, getting the state's "No Fishing or Swimming" sign in the background. It was beautiful there despite the unseen menace, lush and green around the water, the air smelling fertile and grassy, but a sudden melancholy washed over her.

It came to her first as an image, her mother and father sitting next to a huge picnic basket, her mother's long hair wet from swimming in the creek. It was a very hot day. Had Hallie been four? Five? She remembered trying desperately to catch a frog, plunging her little hands into the water over and over and coming up empty, even the baby frogs too fast for her. Her mother was calling her name, Holly, come eat your sandwich, but she couldn't give up, she was so close to catching one, and she kept trying and trying until finally, she snatched her fist into the water and could feel it, a little frog inside her fingers. Her father waded into the creek, and as he reached her she opened her fist, holding her breath, afraid that the frog had escaped; but it was there, a tiny, perfect little frog, and it sat as if stunned on her palm for a magical moment before it realized it was free and leapt back into the water. She had looked at her father then; the smile on his face was huge. This was the father she should mourn, Hallie realized—the one who died with her mother. The one Josh never got to know.

Ram's hand on her shoulder startled her. "Sorry," he said as she flinched.

"It's okay."

Ram glanced over at Lawrence. "He's asking me a lot of personal questions. He said the story is going to be partly a profile of me. I feel weird about that."

"He knows what he's doing. Everything about the frogs will be in there."

"I hope so." Ram leaned against the truck. She saw his waders in the bed and realized she would have to get him to put them on and go back in the creek, to get a good photo of him working. "So what happened with Josh?" he asked.

"We actually had a really good talk. Everything's cool."

"Cecile?"

Hallie nodded and rolled her eyes. "Yep. But he said it's over now. He 'figured some stuff out.' I couldn't get anything more specific. He seemed really happy, though."

Ram smiled. "Well, of course he's happy. He got laid."

Hallie shook her head in disgust as Kenneth came up behind them. "Who got laid?" he asked.

"Josh," Ram said.

"Aw, our boy," Kenneth said, his voice filled with affection, and Hallie couldn't help but smile. She certainly hadn't done everything right, but at least she'd brought other people into Josh's life, people who'd grown to care about him, too.

"Did you see these frogs yet?" Ram asked Hallie, motioning to the tank.

"I need you to get them out of there," Hallie said, and she envisioned the shot she wanted as Ram plunged his hand into the tank.

THAT NIGHT THEY all had dinner at Nancy's. Hallie tried not to notice the beeps coming from Josh's cell phone, but after his third round of texting, he looked at her.

"It's Nicki," he said. "Can I take the car and go see her after dinner?"

"Is this a date?" Kenneth asked. Hallie suspected he'd simply meant to tease Josh, but the boy's face quickly reddened.

"Is it?" Ram asked.

Josh shrank back in his seat. "Maybe, kind of," he said. "I don't know." He looked around the table, and Hallie realized they were all staring at him. "You guys are freaking me out." He got up from the table. Hallie watched Nancy's cat slink away after him.

"Josh and Nicki," Nancy said after he'd left the room. "I wondered when the two of them would figure it out."

"He's quite the operator," Lawrence said.

"What?" Nancy asked.

"Cecile," Hallie whispered to her. "Last night."

"Oh my," Nancy said. She got up and put the graduation cake she'd made on the table.

"This cake is beautiful, Nancy," Hallie said, rising from her seat. She carried over the stack of small plates and forks Nancy had set on the counter.

Josh walked back in and looked at the table. "Aw, thanks," he said.

Nancy cut a slice and passed it to Ram. "I have some news," she said, cutting a second piece.

"News?" Ram asked, passing the slice down to Lawrence.

"Yes," Nancy said. "As we all know, my sometime stable help is going away to college this fall, and I haven't found anyone to take his place. So I'm going to board my horses at Orren's."

"Really?" Josh asked, taking his seat again.

"Yeah. It's close, it's not terribly expensive, and I can go over and see them any time I like." Nancy cut the last slices of cake and sat down.

"So when are the horses going there?" Josh asked. "At the end of the summer?"

"Sooner than that. July 1. You have the rest of the summer off barn duty, Josh."

"I really didn't mind doing it," he said.

Nancy smiled at him. "I know. But I figured you'd be busy this summer."

Josh shrugged. "It won't be that different from last summer. I'm working with Ram on the creek."

"Well, it will be a little different," Hallie said. "You'll be getting ready to go to college."

"What do you mean, getting ready?" Josh crinkled his brow at her.

"We'll need a little time to set you up at my place in New York, for one thing." Hallie looked at everyone else. "I couldn't convince him to live in the dorm."

Lawrence and Kenneth looked at each other, then grinned at her. "We have a surprise, too," Lawrence said. "Or we will, by the time you get back to New York."

"What?" Hallie asked.

"Let's just say that your address will be slightly different."

"Different?"

"You'll be on the third floor now, across from us."

"Where the Greens live?" The Greens' apartment, Hallie knew, was a two-bedroom.

Lawrence nodded. "She's pregnant. They're moving to Westchester at the end of the summer." Lawrence winked at Josh. "You'll have your own room."

"That's so great!" Josh said before Hallie could react.

Hallie saw Lawrence beam; he loved being the philanthropist. But it made her even more indebted to him.

"We'll have to talk about this," she said to Lawrence, but he waved his hand.

"Don't worry about the rent," he said. "You can pay what you paid before. I'll just jack up the rent on your old studio."

"I don't know what to say." Hallie hoped that she looked as happy and grateful as Josh did. It had been eleven years since Jonathan left Lawrence all that money, and she still wasn't comfortable with the way it had changed their friendship, or with how dependent on Lawrence's generosity she'd become. As she screwed on a big bright smile and turned it to Lawrence and Kenneth, she noticed a glum expression on Ram's face. But when she tried to catch his eye, he turned away from her.

"What are you going to do with the house?" Nancy asked. "I know the upkeep must be kind of rough."

Hallie sighed. "I'm not selling it yet, but I'll probably have to at some point."

Nancy nodded. "I heard Todd's lease was up, and he hates that little place he has in Port Norris. Maybe you could rent to him. It would be terrible if you had to sell the house. It's been in your family for…how many generations?"

"Five," Hallie said. It was a good idea, and as with Lawrence and Kenneth's plan for her apartment, she knew she should feel grateful. But she had hoped to have Christmas back in Oyster Shell this year, to use the house as an occasional retreat from the city. This was the place where her new work had taken root. And Ram was here. "I'll talk to Todd," she added, hearing the weariness in her own voice.

Nancy smiled at her. "That's so great about your apartment, too. I was fretting about you and Josh tripping over each other in a studio."

"Yeah," Hallie said. "It seems like everything is working out." But as she said it, she felt a flutter in her stomach. Could it really all fall into place so easily? She looked at Ram, wondering if he felt as conflicted about her leaving as she did, but he would not return her gaze.

CHAPTER 29

When Josh wrote about the summer his character Quentin was having, the summer before the first anniversary of the day his parents disappeared—in Josh's book, the parents just disappeared, nobody could find them, and Josh hadn't decided yet whether it was human foul play or vampires or a parallel universe science-fiction thing—he called it "the most awesomely awesome summer of Quentin's life." The phrase "awesomely awesome" always made him smile when he read it, because it was so ridiculously redundant. It was like calling something "really real." His writing was full of things like that, private jokes to himself, and he wondered if it would make sense to anyone else but right now he didn't care. Since graduation he had been working on his novel almost every night, late at night—whatever time he got home, midnight or one a.m. to three or four in the morning—and he'd never before felt anything quite like it, the joy of finding some order and meaning in the random thoughts and ideas that had always swirled around his brain. Lying on his bed in the middle of the night, Emma snoring by his side, crickets and tree frogs and an occasional owl providing background noise through the open window, Josh felt exhilarated as he typed away on his laptop. The best moments were the ones when he came up with a phrase or a description that felt so original and true he thought maybe he was a genius, that someday scholars would go back and read this first book of his and marvel at the fact that an eighteen-year-old could have written it in a bedroom in Oyster Shell, New Jersey with a dog dozing by his side. Sometimes the sentences that made him feel that way at three a.m. didn't seem so genius when he reread them later, but that was okay. Thinking for even five minutes that you were a genius was, Josh believed, the second best feeling anyone could have.

But on that late August night, his awesome summer coming to an end and his move to New York just a week away, Josh felt antsy. Missy was heading off to Cornell in two days, and Josh had promised her and Cole and Nicki he'd read them a little bit of his novel. What if they didn't like it? What if they didn't get that his opening sentence—"When Quentin Samsa awoke that morning, he felt himself transformed into a teenage boy"—was a riff on *The Metamorphosis*? What if they thought the passages from the dog's point of view were stupid rather than funny? Josh wished he hadn't told his friends about the book, but there was no getting out of it. As he printed the first ten pages he felt a burst of panic: what if Missy had some of her other friends over, the popular kids she used to hang with? There was no way Josh would read his novel in front of those kids.

Josh texted Nicki and asked her if she thought Missy's other friends would be there the next night. It was 2:30 a.m. but he thought she'd be up; neither of them slept much. She texted back, "I hope not." Then she texted, "Sleep tight," and he wrote, "U 2." Sometimes she wrote "luv u," and he wrote "luv u 2," though they never said things like that aloud to each other.

Josh still hadn't done anything about the Nicki situation. There had been that moment graduation night when Josh realized he liked Nicki— *liked her* liked her—and he'd thought that maybe she still liked him too. There had been moments all summer when she'd said or done something that had made him think he was being given an opening, that perhaps he should confess his feelings or put his arm around her or lean in and kiss her. But by the time Josh realized he was in one of those moments and could think of something to do about it, the moment was always gone. And then there was the fear of what might happen if he *did* seize one of those moments. Nicki was his best friend, and Josh sometimes thought he'd be better off finding some other girl to go out with. He couldn't imagine not having Nicki in his life. What if they went out for a while and then split up, like Hallie and Ram? They had broken up not long after Josh's graduation—after a big fight, he knew, though neither of them would tell him what they'd argued about—and barely talked to each other now.

He scrolled to the bottom of his novel—he'd written over a hundred pages!—and started to add something about Quentin's best friend, a girl named Dani. But he felt himself getting sleepy as he tried to think of something clever for Dani to say, so instead he closed his laptop and stretched out next to Emma, and soon, he drifted off.

PARKED AT THE edge of Mollusk Creek late the next afternoon, Josh sat on the tailgate of Ram's truck, laptop open, entering data as Ram called it out to him.

"Extra leg, left hind," Ram shouted from where he stood ankle-deep in the water, the mesh collecting bag slung on his shoulder, a frog in his hands. Josh marked the appropriate column on the spreadsheet.

"That's the last one," Ram said, releasing the frog back into the creek. He climbed up onto the flatbed as Josh saved the data on the laptop. As Ram removed his waders, Josh had the unsettling feeling that an era of his life was about to end. Would he ever work on the creek with Ram again? After he moved to New York City, how often would he even see Ram?

"So what are you doing tonight?" Ram asked as he lay the mesh bag out flat to dry.

"Nicki and I are hanging out with Missy and Cole."

Ram smiled at him. "How's it going with Nicki?"

"I don't know," Josh said. "Maybe things will change after we're in New York."

"Kiss her," Ram said. "That's all you have to do."

Josh shrugged and hopped off the bed. He heard a car coming down the creek access road, and he looked at Ram, saw his eyes widen. Josh knew they both feared the same thing: Cal.

"He's still in jail," Ram said just as Josh realized it himself. Cal had pled guilty to the break-in, and would be sentenced soon.

Nancy pulled in a few yards away from the truck and stepped out of her car, waving a copy of the *New York Times*' Sunday magazine. "Hallie asked me to drop these off at the Trust office, but I thought I'd just bring them right to you."

Ram was on the cover, standing at the edge of Mollusk Creek in his waders, staring fiercely into the camera and holding one of the deformed frogs in his hands. The frog's extra limb was clearly visible. The headline read "What's Wrong With This Picture?" And below it: "One man's mission to save the frogs (and maybe the rest of us)."

"Isn't it great?" Nancy asked. "Hallie got some really amazing shots. There are more inside."

Ram opened the magazine to the page where the article began. Josh looked on with him. There was a large photo Hallie had taken of one of the most severely deformed frogs; it looked very dramatic, the frog's withered extra legs dangling.

The first paragraph was a description of Mollusk Creek and where it was located, how people in Pearl Township had grown up swimming and fishing in it. There was a little bit, too, about how the decline of the oyster industry had left the area "impoverished." Josh had never really seen Pearl Township that way—he didn't think of himself as poor!—but then he thought of Cal, and of the people who lived in the shacks on Shellpile Drive, or the small trailers on Possum Run Road.

JOSH AND RAM returned to the Trust office to find its voice mail nearly full, and scores of e-mails in Ram's inbox. There were two from his parents—in India, they had read the article before he did!—and others from concerned citizens, a few from biologists studying frog deformities in other parts of the country. The one that excited both Josh and Ram the most was from a private foundation, asking to make an appointment to talk with him about funding his work.

"This is amazing," Ram said to Josh after he'd read a few of the e-mails aloud. "I don't know how I'm going to answer all of this."

"Maybe Hallie could come down to the office tomorrow and help you," Josh said. He thought that if they could just be in the same room together, maybe they'd start talking, and find a way to make up.

Ram narrowed his eyes at Josh. "Nice try," he said. Before Josh could ask him anything else, the phone rang. Ram picked it up, listened for a second, and launched into his pitch.

JOSH PICKED NICKI up from her job at the mall later that night, and they went over to Missy's. After they all had a giant splash fight in the pool, after they'd ducked behind the bushes out of sight of Missy's parents and smoked a little of Cole's pot, Josh pulled his pages out to read. The four of them were seated on the edge of the pool's shallow end, feet dangling in, citronella candles providing most of the light.

Josh pulled his feet out of the water and sat cross-legged by the pool, facing the three of them. Nobody had read a word of his novel except for him. What if they hated it? But they were all waiting, looking at him like they expected something, and there was no way he could wuss out. He took a breath, let it out, and then began.

WHEN HE WAS done, Josh felt his stomach flip over. His friends had laughed in almost all the right places, so they couldn't have hated it too much; in fact, Nicki had laughed loudly both times he uttered the phrase "awesomely awesome." But they were quiet for long enough that Josh started thinking he might throw up.

"It's okay if you don't like it," he said.

"I loved it," Nicki said. "I'm just processing."

"Me too," Missy said. "It's kind of surreal. I was expecting a straightforward story, and this is more like Faulkner or something."

Faulkner? He hoped he would remember to jot this down later. He wanted to always remember that a smart, pretty girl had compared his writing to Faulkner's.

"Am I really stoned, or did Quentin age six years in one night?" Cole asked.

"Yeah, he did," Josh said. "He was twelve when he went to bed that night, and when he woke up the next morning, he was eighteen and his parents had disappeared." Because Cole still looked slightly puzzled, Josh added, "the opening sentence is, like, a riff on *The Metamorphosis*."

"Oh, I liked that," Missy said. "And I thought maybe you called your character Quentin because of Faulkner—you know, Quentin Compson?"

"Yeah," Josh said, feeling slightly bad for the lie. He'd just used his own middle name.

"So what happened to the parents?" Nicki asked.

"I'm not completely sure yet," Josh said.

"Are they dead?" Cole asked.

Josh shook his head. "I definitely don't want them to be dead. They're just—gone." The way his three friends looked at him then made

Josh feel naked and exposed. He hadn't thought the parents in the book had anything to do with his real parents, but he could see, now, that his friends thought so. And that maybe they were right.

"My absolute favorite part was the dog," Nicki finally said, and Josh was so grateful for the change of subject that he wanted to kiss her. "I love that she's smarter than any of the people in the book."

"The dog was awesome," Cole said, "but the best thing was the description of Dani's legs."

"Oh God," Nicki groaned, and Missy rolled her eyes.

"It was like an ode to girls' legs," Cole added. "I think I got a woody just picturing them."

Josh laughed. When he pictured the legs in *his* mind, they were Miss Piper's legs. "Maybe I shouldn't talk about her legs for so long," he said.

"You should write *more* about the legs!" Cole said. "In fact, I think you should write porn. I bet you'd write really great porn—like, intellectual porn."

"That's an oxymoron," Missy said, and Nicki put her hand up and the girls high-fived.

"I'm going swimming," Nicki said, slipping back into the pool. "I think the conversation has devolved."

"Me too," Missy said. She got up and turned the boom box on—the new Death Cab for Cutie—and followed Nicki into the water.

But Josh was still thinking about what Cole had just said. "I *could* write really great porn," he whispered.

Cole smiled. "Oh, I know you could."

Josh looked at Missy and Nicki, now talking with each other as they treaded water in the deep end. "Do you think you and Missy will keep going out?"

"I hope so," Cole said, and something in his voice made Josh realize that Cole really loved Missy.

"How about you?" Cole added. "When are you finally going to *do* her?" He nodded his head toward Nicki.

"It's complicated," Josh said. "She's my best friend."

"Yeah." Cole was quiet for a moment. "Well, keep me posted. I mean, I have to find out if you two ever consummate."

Josh couldn't help but laugh a little. "Okay."

"You can come visit me at Tufts sometime," Cole said. "I mean, if you want."

"Sure," Josh said. All summer, Josh had been increasingly surprised by how friendly Cole had been towards him; now, he realized, Cole wanted to be actual friends. They were so different, but that made it kind of cool. "You should come to New York sometime, too," Josh added.

"Oh, I will," Cole said, as if he'd been expecting the invitation, and then he got up and dove into the pool. Josh considered following him, but instead he sat there for a moment, looking at the three of them in the water. His friends. A year ago, he'd barely known any of them. What would things be like between him and Nicki next summer, or the one after that? Would he even still be in touch with Missy and Cole? He hoped so, but it almost didn't matter. It was such a perfect moment, and even immersed within it he couldn't help but step outside himself a little, observe it. The smell of the chlorine and citronella candles, the plaintive voice coming from the boom box, the dim flickering light and occasional drops of water from the splashing going on in the pool. He would remember all of this, he knew. And if he ever had a night like that night back in October, the night of Missy's party, or a day like that one in April when he had his mortifying breakdown at Dunkin' Donuts, he would make himself remember moments like this one. Once you've had a few of them, Josh thought, you know you can have more, no matter how bad things might seem.

Nicki popped up out of the water, directly in front of him. "Earth to Josh," she said.

"Sorry."

She tilted her head to the side, almost like Emma. "You okay?"

"Better than okay," he said, and he slipped into the water beside her.

THREE DAYS LATER, Josh sat at the edge of Mollusk Creek with Ram, both of them eating their lunches. It was the last day Josh would work on the creek. He slapped away a greenhead as he chewed on a bite of his sandwich.

"You know, I miss Dad's tomatoes," Josh said, spitting out a rubbery bit of tomato skin and wadding it into his napkin. He used to laugh at his dad for how fussy he was about the seeds and growing conditions, but now he understood why. There were lots of good tomatoes in South Jersey, but his dad's had been great.

"I was thinking that the other day," Ram said. "I bought a bunch of tomatoes from a stand in Heislerville. They were good, but your dad's were really something special."

Josh would never taste one of his dad's tomatoes again—the sweetness of them, the redness, the way the juice used to run down his hand when he bit into a big ripe one. Even Lawrence had said he'd had no idea tomatoes could taste like that until he'd eaten one from Corson's Farm.

"What day are you leaving?" Ram asked, taking a swig of the lemonade he always brought for the two of them.

"Friday," Josh said. "School doesn't start until Tuesday, but Hallie thought we'd need some time to finish moving her stuff, and to get my new room fixed up. Plus Emma has to get used to being a city dog. We don't want to leave her alone too much the first few days."

Ram smiled. "Lawrence doesn't mind about Emma?"

"I don't think so. He bought her a winter coat. Leopard print." Josh had been concerned at first that it might be real, but Hallie assured him it was not.

Ram laughed. "You'll have to send me a picture, if you can actually get the coat on her." He took a bite of his sandwich, chewed and swallowed. "Will you stop by to see me before you go? I'll be mostly in the office the next few days, working on that presentation for the Pratt Foundation." It was for a huge grant, Josh knew—one that would allow Ram to hire year-round help, and to conduct studies he'd never had the time for on his own.

"Why don't you take a break and come by the house Friday morning? We can use some help packing the U-Haul."

Ram cocked an eyebrow at Josh. "You know why I can't."

"But we really need help." It wasn't entirely true, but Josh still held out hope that Ram and Hallie could patch things up if he could just get them talking.

"No you don't. Todd told me he's helping you guys pack before he moves in."

Josh took a sip of lemonade. "Oh yeah," he said. "I forgot."

"You're a terrible liar."

Josh stared out at the creek for a moment. An enormous bumble bee buzzed past. "I don't understand why you guys broke up."

"I don't completely understand it either."

"Did you love her?" Josh hadn't meant to blurt it out like that. The way Ram's eyebrows shot up and his face reddened slightly made Josh feel like he'd crossed some sort of line. Ram stood up, brushed crumbs from his jeans, sat back down again.

"I might have. But sometimes that's not enough."

"Not enough?"

"I mean, I just don't think we're compatible. You can love someone and not be compatible with them."

"That's the lamest thing I've ever heard." Josh knew it sounded harsh, but he couldn't help himself.

"Lame?"

"Yeah, lame." Josh took his last sip of lemonade. "I think you both could find a way to be compatible if you wanted to."

Ram seemed to consider this for a moment. "Maybe we would have worked it out if she were staying here. But there's no point now."

"You could still see each other," Josh said.

"Sure, some weekends, maybe an occasional vacation. But eventually one of us would have to move, and that would be the end."

It seemed ridiculous to Josh that Ram would stay broken up with Hallie simply because they might have to split up sometime in the future. If everyone thought this way, no one would ever go out with anyone. But then Josh's mind turned to Nicki. Were all the reasons he had for not saying or doing anything with her as lame as Ram's reasons for not getting back together with Hallie? Was he not as much afraid of ruining their friendship as just afraid?

"I'll call her, maybe," Ram said.

"What?" Josh's brain was buzzing with the idea that maybe he *should* just kiss Nicki and see what happened. His stomach fluttered. She planned to come over Friday morning and help Josh and Hallie finish packing. Should he wait until they were in New York? Should he just kiss her Friday morning? He tried to picture it, finding a quiet moment, getting Nicki alone outside somewhere as Hallie and Todd carried boxes to the U-Haul. But then he let his imagination go too far. His hands were in Nicki's hair, his lips moving down her neck. If he let himself keep thinking this way, he would get a hard-on. *Creek. Frogs. Greenheads.* None of those things could shut off the porn movie in his mind, starring Nicki. *The Strand bookstore. The Statue of Liberty. Rows and rows of tomato plants.* His dad's farm didn't look like that anymore, would never look like that again, but Josh would always carry a picture in his mind of the way it had been, once.

"After she's back in New York," Ram said. "I could call her."

"You want to wait to talk to her until she's already gone?"

Ram shrugged. "It might be easier that way." He shifted slightly, then reached down and gently removed a Daddy Longlegs that was crawling over his pants leg, placing it in a patch of grass to his left.

Josh had always admired this about Ram, the way his compassion encompassed all animals, even insects. He could remember a time when he'd wanted to grow up to be exactly like Ram. But although he would always look up to him, Josh knew, in that moment, that he did not want to be like Ram in every way. Not when it came to love.

"I still think you should stop by the house Friday morning," Josh said.

Ram was quiet for a minute. "Maybe," he said, but something in his voice told Josh not to expect him.

CHAPTER 30

Hallie wove through the maze of packed boxes in the front hall, a coil of rope in her hand, until she reached the front door and, beyond it, the U-Haul parked in the driveway. Todd and Josh were inside, trying to secure Josh's enormous bookshelf. She poked her head in, and held out the rope.

"I don't think we need that now," Todd said from behind Josh's dresser. "We shifted some stuff around."

She saw that they had moved the bookshelf onto its side, and had slid the mattress and boxspring in next to it. "That looks more stable," Hallie said.

"Is Nicki still inside?" Josh asked.

"She's with Nancy, up in my old room," Hallie said. Todd would take that room over when he moved in, and Hallie had been quietly dismantling it over the past few days.

"I think you're in pretty good shape here," Todd said, shimmying out of the packed truck. Josh slid out behind him and went back into the house.

"Yeah, that's almost everything," Hallie said.

"My dad's gonna help me move my furniture in this afternoon. You need anything before I go?"

Hallie looked around the packed truck. "I think we're set. We can handle the last-minute stuff."

Todd gave her a quick, awkward hug. "You take care," he said. "And I guess I'll see you at Thanksgiving? Nancy said you'd be down then."

"As long as you don't mind sharing the house for a few days." Hallie knew it was an odd arrangement, renting the house to Todd and expecting him to let her and Josh stay there, but he didn't seem to mind.

"Not at all," he said. "See you then." He headed for his car.

Hallie went back in the house, reaching her old bedroom in time to see Nicki and Josh carefully removing the Culture Club poster from the wall. Nancy was perched on the lone chair left in the room, sipping coffee.

"I can't believe you want to keep these old posters," Hallie said.

"They're cool," Josh said, peeling from the back of the poster the twenty-year-old, putty-like substance Hallie had once used to affix it to the wall.

"Really vintage," Nicki said.

"I find that disturbing," Hallie said as she handed Nicki a cardboard tube. "Because that means *I'm* vintage."

"You're not as vintage as I am," Nancy said.

Hallie laughed. She had made her peace with Nancy, or at least, she was working in that direction.

"I was just going down to get another donut," Josh said. "Anyone else want one?"

"More coffee would be great," Nancy said. "Thanks."

"Refill my cup, too?" Hallie asked. Josh took the empty cups and headed down the stairs, Nicki trailing him.

"I think you may now have two kids," Nancy said.

"I don't mind," Hallie said. "Nicki's great." She glanced out into the hallway. "She told me her father wants to ask me out, once I'm back in New York."

"Her father?"

"Yeah, you met him. At the graduation."

Nancy was quiet for a moment. "Guy with the ponytail," she said, and Hallie nodded. "I thought he was handsome."

"Yeah, he's not bad. He has his own website design firm."

"Is he your type?"

Hallie shrugged. "I don't even know what my type is anymore." She liked the idea of a date, but wasn't sure she was ready to be involved with David Kepler, or anyone. She wasn't really over Ram. "He seemed nice. We'll see. I sent him an invitation to my opening next month." She still couldn't believe the way Joy had come through for her, helping her get a show.

"It might be complicated, with Nicki and all."

"It might." Hallie wished she hadn't allowed herself to think about

Ram. She squatted down next to Nancy's chair. "I was hoping Ram would stop over before I left, but he hasn't."

Nancy shook her head. "I was sure he would have made up with you by now. I don't understand him."

Hallie had told Nancy about their fight. She'd broached the idea with Ram of their continuing to see each other after she moved; at first, he'd seemed to want this too, but then she'd made the mistake of suggesting that spending time in New York might be good for him, might give him more access to foundations and private donors to fund his work. Ram had somehow taken this to mean that she wanted him to give up the Mollusk Creek Trust. "You want me to be that guy my parents want me to be," he'd yelled, after the fight escalated. But he was wrong. She'd just wanted to continue being with him.

Nancy shifted her position on the chair. "He's painting himself into a corner," she added. "You'll be off in New York meeting all kinds of men. You've already got someone interested. But he's never going to have another opportunity to meet someone like you. Not if he stays in Oyster Shell."

Hallie sat down on the floor. "Thanks for saying that."

"It's true. I love both of you, but I think the bigger loss is his. You'll find someone, Hallie. I know you will."

Hallie turned her head away from Nancy as she felt her eyes get watery. It was embarrassing how easily she cried these days.

Josh, Nicki and Emma came pounding back up the stairs. Soon they were all drinking coffee—except Josh, with his orange juice—and then Nancy helped Hallie empty the contents of her childhood desk into a box and tuck it in the closet in the bedroom across the hall. Josh and Nicki moved the remaining pieces of furniture up to the attic so Hallie's old room would be empty, for Todd to move in.

"I can't believe it," Hallie said, surveying the room. "We're pretty much done, and it's only 11 a.m."

Hallie heard the sound of an engine outside; it stopped, and then there was a knock on the door. Ram?

Emma's bark became a series of agitated yips, punctuated by growls as the dog ran downstairs.

"What's she upset about?" Hallie asked, and then she looked out the window, saw not Ram's truck but Cal's. "Oh my God. Cal's here."

Nancy's eyes widened. "I meant to tell you that I saw him yesterday. It was the first I knew he'd gotten out of jail."

Hallie nodded. "He was sentenced last week. Time served, with a ton of probation. If he screws up at all again, he'll be in jail for years." What she didn't say was that this was at least partly her doing. Todd had suggested Hallie go to court and testify against Cal, explain why he should remain locked up; instead, Hallie had written the judge to tell him what Cal had been like as a boy, laying out the events that had led to the break-in. She had left it up to the judge to decide whether Cal should languish in jail, or if his behavior had been as much a result of Hallie's own mistakes as Cal's.

Josh and Nicki returned from the attic. "Where's Emma?" Josh asked.

Hallie heard the front door open downstairs. "Hey, Holly, you still here?" Cal called out.

Less than halfway down the stairs, Hallie only heard what happened next: a loud growl, three sharp barks, and then Cal's cry: "Son of a bitch!"

When Hallie got to the bottom of the stairs, she saw Josh pulling Emma away from Cal. The dog struggled at first, growling and snapping at Cal, but she soon yielded to Josh and let him spirit her out back.

"Did she bite you?" Hallie asked. She could see a tear in Cal's pants leg, near the ankle.

For an instant, anger flashed in Cal's eyes, but he composed himself. Something about him seemed different to Hallie. Less ragged.

"Not too bad," Cal said, wincing a bit.

"Here, come in the kitchen," Hallie said, and she gestured him to follow her. She saw Nancy and Nicki exchange glances as they walked into the kitchen as well. Cal sat down and rolled up his pants leg. There were two clear puncture wounds, bleeding slightly. Shit, Hallie thought. This was the last thing she needed today.

"She broke the skin," Hallie said. "Let me get some peroxide."

"No need for that," Cal said. "Ain't no more 'n a scratch."

Hallie shook her head at him and went out into the U-Haul, relieved to easily find the box of bathroom stuff. She pulled out a bottle of peroxide, Neosporin, a handful of cotton balls and band-aids, and carried it all back into the kitchen.

"You should go to the doctor," Hallie said as she cleaned and bandaged the bite. "She really sunk her teeth in."

Cal shrugged. "It's nothin'."

"No, really. Let me pay for the visit."

Cal shook his head. "You don't owe me nothin', Holly. I just came by to say so long." He dropped his voice a little. "And thanks—for that letter," he mumbled.

She could see Josh watching through the back window, keeping an eye on things. Nancy and Nicki were in the kitchen, staring at her and Cal as well. "Why don't you two go outside for a minute, so Cal and I can talk?" Hallie asked.

Nicki looked about to protest, but Nancy put her hand on the girl's back. "Let's go, Nicki," she said, steering her onto the back porch.

When they were alone, Hallie sat at the table across from Cal. "You're welcome," she said.

"Wouldn't a blamed you if you told the judge to lock me up."

Hallie shook her head. "I screwed up too. I didn't handle things right, with the work you did on the farm."

Cal was quiet for a moment. "I ain't been drinkin'."

"That's good."

"Yep." He coughed, then cleared his throat. "So you headin' back to the big city?"

"We are. Todd's going to live here." She may have forgiven Cal, but she knew enough not to trust him.

"The boy's goin' to college up there?"

The question took Hallie by surprise. "Yes."

"That'd make his Momma happy."

Hallie smiled. "You think so?"

"Yep."

"And his dad?"

Cal snorted. "Oh, Don woulda railed about it for a while. Then he woulda been proud his kid did good."

Hallie looked out the back window. Josh was right there, watching her, waiting for a cue to come back inside. She hoped it was true, that Brenda and her dad would have been proud of everything Josh had accomplished in the past year, of the man he was becoming. But she also felt that Cal might not have been talking about Josh just then. Had her father been proud of her? She wanted to believe it was true.

"Well, I should go," Cal said, pushing his chair out and standing. "You—take care."

"You too," Hallie said, following him to the door. He limped to his truck, and she watched as the vehicle sputtered down the driveway, out to the main road.

NANCY LEFT A few minutes after Cal did, and then Nicki announced she had to get home as well. Hallie said a quick farewell to the girl—she'd see her soon enough in New York—and went upstairs to make sure they hadn't forgotten anything. As she surveyed Josh's bedroom, bare except for the battered desk and chair they'd decided to leave behind, a shaft of light, thick with dust motes, caught Hallie's eye. When the room was an art studio, she used to play near her mother's feet as she painted, in the light that poured through the front window. Her mom had once told her that the bits of dust trapped in the light were fairy dust. If she looked hard enough, her mom had said, she might even see a fairy. Hallie could picture her young mother, smiling down from where she stood at the easel. She had not always been as unhappy as she was in those last years before she died. Something had shifted. Something that maybe no one—not even Jenny herself—had any control over.

Hallie walked to the front window, looked outside, and saw true magic: Josh and Nicki, kissing. She stared for a minute, looked away, wondered if she had really seen it and looked back again. They were still kissing, their bodies pressed together, Josh's hands in Nicki's hair, hers around his waist. Hallie watched for a few more seconds; when had *this* started? And then, when it began to feel too voyeuristic to watch any longer—when Hallie was filled to bursting with feelings she had not yet found a language to describe—she turned away, glanced once more around the room, and shut the door behind her as she left.

Acknowledgments

At the start of my high school years, my mother and I moved from the Central Jersey shore town where I'd spent most of my childhood to the city of Millville, about two hours' drive south in the same state. We left Springsteen country, its strip malls and decaying boardwalks and 7-Elevens, for the part of New Jersey that earns its "garden state" moniker: a place of back roads and pickup trucks, tomato farms and Wawas. *The Fifty-First State* is my love letter to my adopted home of South Jersey, whose culture and physical beauty have continued to provide such fertile ground for my imagination.

In addition to my gratitude for moving us to the region which would shape so much of my writing, I'd like to thank my mother, Ruth Borders, for her continued support, and my late father, Bert Borders, for instilling in me a love of the written word. I'm grateful to the rest of my family as well, especially my cousins, the Knipschers, and my niece, Uriel Stephens.

The following five writer friends deserve a special mention for reading an early, 730-page draft of this book, and offering wise advice on what could be cut: Ron MacLean, Peter Ruggiero, Stephanie Farrell, Susan Altman and Sandra Deden.

Victoria Barrett at Engine Books is one of the most gifted editors on the literary scene today. This novel is so much the richer for her insights and attention. I'm delighted to be part of the Engine Books family.

My agent, Esmond Harmsworth, is brilliant, dedicated, and patient, and I'm incredibly lucky to have him on my team.

Another stroke of great fortune was to have two gifted photographers, Pelle Cass and Jason Eskenazi, assist me with details pertaining to my character Hallie's work. Any inaccuracies in my depiction of the art of photography are mine, not theirs.

Bill Fenton, Dr. Jill Mortenson, John Dooley and Meghan Wren provided crucial assistance with South Jersey research. The book *A Plague of Frogs* by William Souder (University of Minnesota Press, 2002) was essential to my understanding of the kind of frog deformities detailed in this novel. Visi Tilak was instrumental in helping me to shape my character, Ram.

The Virginia Center for the Creative Arts, the Millay Colony for the Arts, the Blue Mountain Center and the Somerville Arts Council all provided support at critical times. Arcade Fire's brilliant album *Funeral* fueled much of my early work on the book, most of which was written at the Diesel Café.

Grub Street, and the community I've found there, means more to me than I can possibly articulate. I'd especially like to thank Eve Bridburg, Christopher Castellani, Sonya Larson and Whitney Scharer, colleagues whose friendships I hold dear. I'd also like to thank my students, past and present, who inspire me every day with their talent and dedication.

For providing additional feedback, encouragement, and/or support, I also wish to thank Nassim Assefi, Jenna Blum, Cathy Carroll and Thor Erickson, Rhonda Cutler, Catherine Elcik, Dr. Todd Farchione, Rebecca Newberger Goldstein, Becky Hemperly, Scott Heim, Michelle Hoover, Sheri Joseph, Daphne Kalotay, Svetlana Katz, Kathryn Kulpa, Teresa Leo, Yael Goldstein Love, Craig Rancourt, Kelly Robertson, Michelle Seaton, Sylvie, Judy Casulli Tan, Steven Tiberi, Kay and Rose Toscano and Anya Weber, as well as my colleagues at Harvard Vanguard Medical Associates.

Jeffrey Page entered my life late in this novel's genesis, but quickly became one of its—and my—biggest supporters. My gratitude, and my love, are immeasurable.

ABOUT THE AUTHOR

 Lisa Borders' first novel, *Cloud Cuckoo Land*, was chosen by Pat Conroy as the winner of River City Publishing's Fred Bonnie Award and was published in 2002. *Cloud Cuckoo Land* also received fiction honors in the 2003 Massachusetts Book Awards. Lisa's short stories have appeared in *Kalliope, Washington Square, Black Warrior Review, Painted Bride Quarterly, Newport Review,* and other journals. Her essay "Enchanted Night" was published in *Don't You Forget About Me: Contemporary Writers on the Films of John Hughes* (Simon & Schuster, 2007) and an essay on Kate Bush was published in *The First Time I Heard Kate Bush* (Rosecliff Press, 2012). She has received grants from the Massachusetts Cultural Council, the Somerville Arts Council and the Pennsylvania Council on the Arts, and fellowships at the Millay Colony, Virginia Center for the Creative Arts, Hedgebrook and the Blue Mountain Center. Lisa lives in Somerville, Massachusetts and teaches at Grub Street, Boston's independent writing center. She also works as a cytotechnologist.

Learn more about Lisa's work at lisaborders.com.

Author photo by Jeffrey Page